WORTH IT

"I've waited a long time to see that honey hair on that green pillow." Judd's husky voice vibrated with passion. "And to see that look in your eyes."

His mouth kissed the hollow of Valerie's throat as his skilled fingers unbuttoned her blouse. His hand wandered over the bareness of her waist and taut stomach. Its leisurely pace sent a languorous feeling floating through her limbs. His mouth trailed a fiery path to intimately explore the rounded softness of her breast. Her nails dug into the rippling muscles of his back and Judd brought his hard lips back to hers.

from "Bed of Grass"

CRAZY IN LOVE

JANET DAILEY

ZEBRA BOOKS
KENSINGTON PUBLISHING CORP.

http://www.kensingtonbooks.com

ZEBRA BOOKS are published by

Kensington Publishing Corp.
119 West 40th Street
New York, NY 10018

All Kensington titles, imprints and distributed lines are available at special quantity discounts for bulk purchases for sales
promotion, premiums, fund-raising, educational or institu-
tional use.

Special book excerpts or customized printings can also be
created to fit specific needs. For details, write or phone the
office of the Kensington Sales Manager. Attn.: Sales Department. Kensington Publishing Corp., 119 West 40th Street, New
York, NY 10018. Phone: 1-800-221-2647.

Zebra and the Z logo Reg. U.S. Pat. & TM Off.

First Mass-Market Paperback Printing: July 2008
ISBN-13: 978-1-4201-4085-9
ISBN-10: 1-4201-4085-X

10 9 8 7 6 5 4

Printed in the United States of America

Contents

BED OF GRASS

Chapter 1

With efficient, precise motions, Valerie Wentworth folded the lingerie and laid it in the suitcase. Tucking a strand of toffee-colored hair behind her ear, she walked back to the open drawer of the dresser for more. There was a determined line to the sensuous curve of her lips and a glint of purpose in her light brown eyes. Her complexion had a hint of shocked pallor under its light tan.

A woman stood in the room watching Valerie pack. Her expression was not altogether approving of what she saw. She was in her forties; her figure had the solid build of middle age and her brown hair had touches of gray. Her mouth was pinched into lines that discouraged smiles.

"I still think it's crazy to go tearing off to Maryland like this, Valerie."

Valerie felt a flash of irritation at the other woman's acerbic tone. It wasn't the first time she'd heard the comment, either.

"He was my grandfather," she replied quietly. Valerie didn't pause in her packing as she walked to the closet and began taking clothes off the hangers. "He didn't have any other family but me."

"Elias Wentworth didn't want you around when he was alive. What makes you think he'd want you at his funeral?" came the challenging retort.

"He isn't in a position to say what he wants, is he?" A trace of anger laced Valerie's voice, triggered by the reference to the estrangement between herself and her grandfather. "And nothing you can say is going to make me change my mind, Clara," she warned.

"That sanctimonious old man turned his back on you seven years ago, at a time when you needed him most," Clara Simons reminded her sternly. "Him and his self-righteous ways," she murmured under her breath with a sniff of contempt. "After all the letters you wrote him, you never got so much as a Christmas card back."

"Please—"

"After all this time. It's a shame."

"It doesn't matter now."

Clara would not give up. "He disowned you. Blood ties meant nothing to him. After the way he treated you, I wouldn't think they'd mean anything to you, either."

Too preoccupied to answer, Valerie chose her clothes. A tailored suit in dark blue was the best she could do for a mourning outfit; her limited budget couldn't stretch to cover a new dress. She was inwardly grateful that head-to-toe black was no longer mandatory at family funerals.

"Granddad took me in and raised me after my parents died," she replied to Clara's comment. "I owe him something for that."

"No, you don't!" the woman scoffed at her logic. "How can you feel obligated to that heartless, straight-laced coot? Anyone with an ounce of compassion would have supported you seven years ago. They might not have approved of what you'd done, but they wouldn't have turned a scared girl out in the cold to fend for herself with no money and no place to go."

"Don't be so melodramatic, Clara. You didn't know me back then," Valerie said. "I was way too wild. And irresponsible. As in looking for trouble, starting when I was thirteen. I couldn't even sneak a cigarette without it turning into a disaster."

"Come on. One cigarette is no big deal."

"One cigarette is enough to set a stable on fire—and I almost did. I heard granddad coming and threw away a burning cigarette in some hay, like an idiot. If he hadn't spotted it, the stable would have gone up in flames and the horses with it. Granddad had every right not to trust me. It scared me when I realized what I'd done, but being yelled at and grounded didn't straighten me out."

"Most teenagers experiment with cigarettes. Believe me, there's worse things."

Nice try, Valerie thought. But rationalizing her behavior wasn't going to change the past.

"In your case," Clara went on, "I wouldn't be surprised if you got into trouble just to get your grandfather's attention."

"You don't understand." Valerie sighed and turned to face the woman who had become her friend, her family and something like a mother over the last seven years. "It wasn't just the smoking. I hit the liquor cabinet whenever I could until he finally had to put a lock on it. I'd take one of his thoroughbred horses and go night-riding. I don't know how many times I led a lame horse home after a midnight gallop. They were valuable animals, his livelihood, and I treated them like toys."

"Okay, that was bad," Clara admitted. Her defense of Valerie didn't sound quite as vigorous as before, but she was still steadfast in her loyalty.

"There was more." Valerie felt driven to make a full confession, needing to deal with her guilt. "I used to steal money from him to hitchhike into Baltimore and go to movies or just buy things. Sometimes I'd be gone all weekend, but I never told him where I'd been. Can you imagine what I put him through?"

"I still think you're being too hard on yourself," was the stubborn reply. "I remember how frightened you seemed when I met you. And starved for love."

"Oh, yeah. Love," Valerie said thoughtfully. An ache that still hadn't receded after seven years flickered in her tawny eyes. "Maybe I was starved for it," she conceded, since it was the easiest explanation. "But I still can't forget the look on Granddad's face the day I told him I was pregnant."

"In this day and age that's not unforgivable."

"Well, it hurt him. A lot." She could still see the anguish in his eyes when her revelation had sunk in. "He was such a moral, upright man. He couldn't help it if he felt shamed and disgraced by what I'd done."

"I still say—"

"I'm just telling you how it happened. Not how it should have been."

Clara fell silent.

"When he demanded to know who the father was and I belligerently refused to tell him, it was the last straw that broke him."

Tears burned her eyes at the memory of that stormy scene. She hid them in a flurry of activity, hurriedly folding the blouse to her blue suit and laying it in the suitcase.

"But to throw you out!" Clara refused to consider her grandfather's actions as justified.

"For a long time I resented him for it, even hated him," Valerie admitted. "But I was eighteen. Turning me out was probably the best thing that ever happened to me, because it made me responsible for myself. And someone else."

Clara nodded.

"Now I know the heartache of worrying over a child, and I only regret that I never had the courage to go back and tell Granddad how sorry I was for the pain I caused him."

"And that's your reason for going to his funeral," Clara concluded, crossing her arms in front of her in a stance that suggested disapproval. "Forgive me for being so blunt, but it's an empty gesture, don't you think? And not worth getting docked for."

"Mr. Hanover gave me family leave and two paid days off." She tried to dodge the issue as she closed the suitcase and locked it with a decisive snap.

"What about the other three days you'll be away?" The pointed reminder pinned Valerie to the spot. "You won't be getting paid for them. And the price of gas is sky-high. You have to drive all the way to Maryland."

"I'll just have to cut back on a few things." She was determined not to let money issues—a polite way of saying she was close to broke, as usual—affect her decision to attend her grandfather's funeral. Somehow she'd get by.

"Humph!" Clara breathed out the sound. "You're barely making ends meet now."

"That's my problem." Valerie opened a second,

smaller suitcase and set it on the bed. "You can't talk me out of going, Clara. You're just wasting your breath."

Walking to the dressing table, she opened a different drawer and took out half a dozen sets of little-boy-sized underpants and socks. When they were in the second suitcase, she began adding pajamas and pants and shirts.

Clara watched in silence for several seconds, her expression growing more disgruntled. "Okay, I guess you're going. But it doesn't make sense to drag Tadd along with you."

"He'll think it's a vacation like all his school friends take in the summer," Valerie reasoned. She frowned. That wasn't much of an answer but it was the best she could come up with.

"Well, you won't think it's a vacation while you're driving there and back with him bouncing all over the car seats," her friend declared. "What will you do with him when you get there? A six-year-old boy isn't going to understand about funerals . . . or sit through one quietly."

"I don't have much choice." Valerie glanced at the second single bed in the room, a twin to her own, except for the worn teddy bear resting against the pillow. She was aware of the validity of Clara's argument.

"I'll look after him," Clara volunteered. There was a grudging quality to her voice, and impatience that she hadn't been able to persuade Valerie not to go.

Valerie glanced at her friend, her strained features softening as she looked at the stern-faced woman. For all her gruffness, Clara had become her rock. She had been the cook in a restaurant Valerie had stumbled into a week after leaving her grandfather's home. She had been frightened, broke and hungry, looking for any kind of job that would put food in her stomach. Clara had taken pity on her, paid for the meal Valerie couldn't afford, persuaded the owner to hire Valerie as a waitress, and taken her to her apartment to live until she could afford a place of her own, which wasn't until after Tadd was born.

"If school weren't over for the summer, Clara, I might accept your offer," Valerie replied, and shook her head in refusal, her brown wavy hair swinging loosely around her shoulders. "As it is, you've barely recovered from your bout with pneumonia. The doctor insisted you had to rest for a month before going back to work at the restaurant. Looking after Tadd twenty-four hours a day doesn't qualify as a rest."

"What about Tadd's father? Will you be seeing him when you go back?" Clara's shrewd blue eyes were watching her closely.

A chill of premonition made Valerie shiver. Her hands faltered slightly in the act of folding one of Tadd's shirts. The moment of hesitation passed as quickly as it had come and she was once again poised and sure of her decision.

"Probably," Valerie admitted with a show of indifference. "Meadow Farms adjoins Granddad's property, so somebody from the Prescott family is bound to put in an appearance at the funeral. I don't know whether it'll be Judd or not."

"Right."

Valerie could hear a warning in Clara's tone. It made her feel even more defensive. "He runs the farm now, you know. Maybe he won't think the funeral's worth his time, neighbor or not. He may ask someone else to represent the family."

"Do you still care about him, Valerie?" came the quiet but piercing question.

A wound that had never completely healed twisted Valerie's heart, squeezing out a bitter hatred that coated her reply. "I wouldn't have married Judd Prescott if he'd begged me—not that he's ever begged for anything in his life. He takes what he wants without ever giving a damn about anybody's feelings. He's ruthless, hard and arrogant."

"Valerie—"

"I can't believe I ever thought for one minute that I was anything more to him than a fast—" She stopped herself. "Anyway, that's why I never told Granddad who the father of my baby was. I knew he'd go over to Meadow Farms with a shotgun, ranting and raving about making Judd do the right thing."

"I suppose so. But—"

"No way. I got out of there as fast I could. Just thinking about Judd Prescott laughing about being forced to marry me—ugh!"

The suppressed violence in Valerie's denial and rejection of Tadd's father brought a troubled light to Clara's eyes. Her expression was uneasy, but Valerie was too caught up in her own turmoil to notice the reaction to her reply. She continued folding and packing her son's clothes into the suitcase.

"Hey, maybe there's a sensible solution to our problem," Clara said after a long pause.

"What problem?" Valerie glanced briefly at her friend. There was none as far as she was concerned.

"I'm going crazy sitting around my apartment doing nothing and you're going to have your hands full trying to cope with Tadd on this trip." It was more of a statement than an explanation. "A change of scenery would do me good, so I'll ride along with you to Maryland. And I'll pay my share of the expenses."

"I can't let you do that," Valerie protested. "I'd love to have you come with me—you know that. But you've done so much for me already that I couldn't take any money from you for the trip."

Clara shrugged, and looked Valerie up and down, as if making a silent comment on who would win the argument. "You aren't big enough to stop me." Turning toward the door, she added over her shoulder, "I'll go pack and fix some sandwiches to take along on the trip. I'll be ready in less than an hour."

Before Valerie could raise an objection, Clara was gone. A half smile tilted the corners of Valerie's mouth when she heard her apartment door closing. Arguing with Clara was useless: once she had made up her mind about something, not even dynamite could budge her.

Valerie didn't like to contemplate what her life might have been like if she hadn't met the other woman. It hadn't simply been food, a place to live or a job that Clara had given her. She had encouraged Valerie to take night courses in computer skills and business administration, so she could eventually get a better-paying job and do more than live paycheck to paycheck in order to support herself and Tadd.

Many times Valerie had thanked God for guiding her to this woman who was both friend and adviser, supporter and confidante. Clara's insistence on accompanying her made her doubly grateful. Although she'd refused to admit as much, she was apprehensive about going back for the funeral. There were a lot of people to be faced, including Judd Prescott.

Walking to the single bed in the corner, Valerie picked up the teddy bear to put in the suitcase. A combination of things made her hold the toy in her arms—the notification a few hours earlier of her grandfather's death, her hurried decision to attend his funeral, her discussion with Clara and the memories attached to her departure from Maryland seven years ago.

Those last were impossible to think about without Judd Prescott getting mixed up in it. She fell into a reverie, not unwillingly. . . .

Her interest in him had been sparked by a remark she'd overheard her grandfather make. He'd been condemning the oldest Prescott son for his bad-boy reputation. Before that Valerie hadn't been interested in the family who lived at Meadow Farms, dismissing them as stiff-necked snobs.

Meadow Farms was a renowned name in racehorse circles, famous for its thoroughbreds. The farm itself was a showcase, the gold standard, in fact, for other horse breeders. Few had ever matched its size or the quality of horses that were bred and raised there.

Her grandfather's low opinion of Judd Prescott had aroused her curiosity. She'd ridden onto Meadow Farms land with the express purpose of meeting him. One glimpse of the tall, hard-featured man with ebony hair and devil green eyes had fascinated her. A dangerous excitement seemed to pound through her veins when he looked at her.

In the beginning, Valerie pursued him boldly, almost brazenly, arranging chance encounters that had nothing to do with chance at all. The glint in his eyes seemed to tell her he was aware they weren't, too. It angered her then, the way he had silently mocked her initial attempts to flirt with him.

The first few times Judd kissed her, it was almost like he didn't care. Young as she was, it hadn't taken Valerie long to discover how to rev him up. Their kisses got hotter—and he was definitely into it.

Her previous experiences had been with boys her own age or a year or two older, never with anyone more than ten years her senior. She had kissed many boys, gone a little farther with a few . . . just far enough to know that the sensations Judd aroused in her weren't ordinary. And he had an advantage, to say the least. Talk about sensual skill. His mouth knew how to excite her and his hands how to caress her.

What had started out as a lark became something more, and Valerie fell in love with him. Aware that he was a man with experience, she realized that her kisses wouldn't hold his interest for long, and her fear of losing him outweighed her fear of the possible consequences.

As if teenagers ever thought about consequences.

One afternoon Valerie noticed him riding alone through a wooded pasture adjoining her grandfather's land. Saddling a horse, she swallowed her nervousness and her pride and rode out to meet him. They rode only a short distance together before pausing to dismount under the shade of a tree. An embrace followed naturally. When Valerie demanded that he make love to her, Judd's hesitation was brief, his affirmative response given in a burning kiss.

So much for her virginity.

Afterward he was oddly uncommunicative, an expressionless glitter in his green eyes whenever he looked at her. Valerie suspected it was because he was the first. Secretly she wanted him to be disturbed by the fact, to feel a little obligated, perhaps even guilty. Because she loved him so intensely, she could see now that she'd almost wanted to blackmail him emotionally, making him into the seducer and herself into a wide-eyed neophyte. When they parted he had said nothing, but Valerie was unconcerned.

Days went by without her seeing him before she finally realized that Judd was avoiding her. Hurt grew into indignation and finally a smoldering anger. Her injured pride demanded revenge. She began haunting the edges of the Meadow Farms stable yard, hoping to catch Judd alone.

At the sight of the luxury sports car that Judd usually drove coming slowly up the driveway to the stable, Valerie set her fleet-footed horse on a route that would intersect the car's path before it reached its destination. Jumping her mount over a paddock fence, she halted it in the middle of the road to block the way. He'd had to brake hard to bring it to a skidding stop before hitting her.

Judd got out, storming over to her, his features stone-cold with rage. "What the hell were you trying to do? Get yourself killed?" His icy gaze flicked to the lathered horse, dancing nervously under her tight rein. "And if you don't give a damn about yourself, you have no business abusing blooded animals that way. His mouth will be raw if you don't quit sawing on those reins."

"Don't tell me how to ride a horse! And what do you care what happens to me anyway!" Valerie had flamed. "At least I know what kind of man you are! You got what you wanted and then you dumped me!"

"I didn't want it." Judd made the denial through clenched teeth. "Too bad I didn't have the willpower to say no to you. I should have known better. I assumed you'd lost your, uh, innocence years ago."

Valerie went white with rage at his insulting

remark. She jabbed her heels into the sides of her hunter, sending it lunging toward him. He stepped to the side and she began striking at him with her riding crop. Catching hold of the end, Judd pulled her from the saddle. Her horse then bolted for home pastures.

After he had twisted the riding quirt out of her grip, he crushed her twisting, kicking body against him. "Good thing I have a thick hide!" His savagely muttered words made Valerie struggle all the more wildly, cursing and swearing at him, calling him every name she could think of. He only laughed. "Why are you so angry? You weren't the one who got hit!"

An animal scream of frustration sounded in her throat, but immediately his mouth covered her lips and kept her silent. The dominating quality of his kiss subdued the rest of her until the only twisting Valerie did was to get closer to his lean, muscled frame.

When his mouth ended its possession of hers, she whispered, "Make love to me again, Judd."

"Girl, you're way too tempting." His voice was husky with passion, the smoldering light in his green eyes heating up her trembling desire.

Valerie received the answer she wanted when he swept her off her feet into his arms and carried her to a secluded bed of grass that was to become their meeting place during the following months.

What Valerie lacked in experience, she made up for in willingness. Under the guidance of a master in the art of love, she learned rapidly. He brought the condoms—she wasn't that ignorant or that impulsive—and he promised to use them when they went that far.

Over the course of time it became clear to her that Judd desired her as much as she desired him. Secure in this knowledge, it never bothered her that he didn't take her out anywhere. Besides, there was her grandfather's wrath to be considered if he should find out about the two of them.

But everybody knew condoms weren't foolproof. Headstrong to a fault, she'd been willing to take that chance. He didn't argue. And even when she first suspected she was pregnant, she wasn't worried. No way was she going to go into the local drugstore and buy a pregnancy test. Later, when she got a ride to Baltimore to a medical clinic for confirmation of her condition, she wasn't all that apprehensive. She'd been stupidly sure that Judd would be as pleased as she was about a positive result and would be moved to propose.

She was saddling a horse to ride over to Meadow Farms when her grandfather walked up. "Where you going?" he demanded.

Valerie responded with a half-truth, patting the sleek neck of the bay horse. "I thought I'd take Sandal out for a canter, maybe over toward Meadow Farms." Just in case he would see her heading in that direction.

"The place will be hopping, what with the party and all," he commented in a disapproving way.

"What party?" It had been the first Valerie had heard about one.

"The Prescotts are hosting a great big whoop-de-do tonight. Guess you didn't know."

"Sounds like fun."

His eyes narrowed on her in accusing speculation. "Don't you be getting any ideas. No granddaughter of mine is going to crash parties she wasn't invited to."

"Yes, Granddad." Despite the feigned meekness of her tone, a vision had already begun to form of Judd possessively holding her hand while he introduced her to friends and family at the party.

Wrapped in her romantic imaginings, Valerie rode off to the secluded place in the wooded pasture where they always met, but Judd wasn't there. Even though the meeting hadn't been prearranged, she was positive he would appear. Within minutes after she had dismounted, he rode into the clearing.

There were so many things she wanted to tell him in that instant: how ruggedly handsome he was, how much she loved him, about the baby—their baby— and how ecstatically happy she was. But something made her keep all that inside. She even turned away when he dismounted and plucked a green leaf from a low-hanging branch.

"It's a beautiful day, isn't it?" she observed instead.

"Beautiful," came his husky agreement from directly behind her.

When his hands circled her waist to cup her breasts and draw her shoulders against his chest, Valerie breathed in sharply and exhaled in a sigh of pure pleasure. Her head lolled backward against his chest while his mouth moved against the windblown waves of her caramel hair.

"How do you always know when I come here?" she murmured, the wonder of it something she had never questioned before.

"I just do." His mouth moved against her hair as he spoke. "We're connected in a lot of ways I don't understand."

More than you know, she wanted to say. Valerie turned in his arms, in answer to the flames he had started within her. Hungrily he began devouring her lips and she felt herself begin to surrender to his appetite. But she wanted to talk. Finally she dragged her lips from the domination of his, letting his mouth wander over her cheek and ear and nibble sensuously at her throat.

"I thought you wouldn't come today," she said weakly.

"Why?" Judd sounded amused.

"Because of the party."

"That isn't until tonight." He dismissed its importance, but made no suggestion that she should attend.

Valerie did understand why no invitation had been given to her grandfather. He was not in the Prescotts' social or financial sphere. Besides, he was morally opposed to drinking and dancing. He would have considered it an offense to be invited, not a courtesy.

"I've never been to a party like that before." Valerie tried not to be too open about wangling an invitation. "Bet it's going to be fabulous. I suppose the women will be wearing diamonds and beautiful gowns."

"I guess. Not one will even come close to the way you look without any." Even as he spoke, his hands were unbuttoning her blouse.

Valerie attempted to gently forestall his efforts. "Why didn't you invite me?" Her question was light, not betraying how much she wanted to know.

"You wouldn't like it." His mouth worked its way to the hollow of her throat, tipping her head back to allow greater access.

"How do you know?" She strained slightly against his hold.

Judd lifted his head, ebony hair gleaming in the sunlight. There was impatience in his lazy regard. A firmness strengthened the line of his mouth.

"Because it isn't your kind of party," he replied in a tone that said the discussion was at an end.

At that moment fear began to gnaw at Valerie's

confidence. Proud defiance was present in the way she returned his look.

"Maybe you aren't inviting me because you'll be with somebody else," she challenged.

"It isn't any of your business." A cold smile touched his mouth as it began to descend toward hers.

Hurt by his attitude as much as his words, Valerie tried to draw out of his arms. Her blouse gaped open in the front and his gaze roamed downward to observe the creamy breasts nearly spilling free of her lacy bra. His hand moved to help them, but she managed to stop it.

"Please, I want to talk, Judd," she insisted.

"Why? I don't," he argued, and pressed her hips against his so she could feel his urgent need for her.

With a sickening rush of despair, she realized that they seldom talked when they met. They made love, rested and went their separate ways. Their past communications had always been physical, never verbal. It was beginning to dawn on Valerie what a fool she had been to think otherwise.

"Let me go!" She pushed angrily at his chest, her brown eyes flashing.

"What's this little display of outrage about?" Judd eyed her with cynical amusement, holding her but no longer forcing her close to him. "After as many times as we've made love together, it's kinda late to be playing hard to get."

Her temper flared, adrenaline surging through her muscles to give them strength. She broke out of his encircling arms.

"That's all I mean to you, huh?" she accused. "Am I just someone to roll around on the grass? Not good enough for you to be seen in public with?"

"What? You're the one who started all this," Judd reminded her with deadly calm.

A couple of long jerky strides carried Valerie to the place where her horse was tethered. She gathered up the reins and mounted before turning to face him.

"Go to hell, Judd Prescott." Her voice had begun to tremble. "I hope it's a long, hot trip!"

Putting her heels to her mount, she turned and galloped the horse toward her grandfather's farm. Tears drenched her cheeks with hot, salty moisture. All her rosy dreams were shattered that day when she realized Judd had never felt anything other than sexual desire for her.

An hour later she informed her grandfather that she was pregnant, steeling herself inwardly against his wrath when she refused to tell him it was Judd who'd fathered the life she carried. It was almost a relief when he ordered her out of the house. She put as much distance between herself and Maryland as possible. . . .

That was how she had ended up here in Cincinnati, Ohio, living in the same apartment complex as Clara, with a six-year-old son, and a job as an assistant to an industrial plant executive.

Thinking of all that happened was like traveling back in time. Right now she felt just as she had then. She lifted the hand that had been clutching the teddy bear and touched her fingers to her face. They came away wet with tears. The wound inside her was as raw and fresh as it had been seven years ago. She scrubbed her cheeks dry with the back of her hands and blinked her eyes to ease the stinging sensation.

"Mom!"

A three-foot-tall whirlwind came racing into the

bedroom. It stopped its motion long enough for her to gaze into a pair of hazel eyes predominantly shaded with olive green. Hair a darker shade of brown than her own fell across his forehead, crowding into his eyes.

"Clara told me to come into the house, but you said I could play outside until you called me," he declared in a breathless rush, already edging toward the door again. "Can I go back out? It's my turn after Tommy's to ride Mike's bike. Hey, what are you doing with Toby?" He saw the teddy bear in her arms.

"I was just packing him in your suitcase," she explained. "We're going on a trip, remember?"

Tadd momentarily forgot his turn on the bike. "Where's Maryland?"

"A long way from here. We'll have to drive all day." Valerie set the teddy bear on top of his suitcase. "We'll be ready to go soon, so you'd better wash your face and hands and change into those clean clothes." She pointed to the colored T-shirt and jeans lying on the bed.

Tadd made a face when she told him he had to wash. "Why are we going to Maryland?"

"Because your great-grandfather died and I want to go to his funeral," she answered patiently.

"Why?"

Valerie concealed a sigh. She was never certain whether his questions were asked out of genuine interest or as an excuse to postpone something he didn't want to do.

"When I was your age, I didn't have a mommy, so your great-grandfather took care of me. I cared about him the way you care about me. That's why I want to go to his funeral."

"Did I know him?" Tadd tilted his head to one side, his expression showing only innocent curiosity.

Valerie shook her head. "No."

Her teeth nibbled at the inside of her lower lip. She had written to her grandfather about Tadd's birth, but had never received any form of acknowledgement. None of the letters she had regularly sent had ever been answered.

"Do I have a grandfather?" He altered the subject slightly.

Valerie hesitated. The only relatives Tadd had that were still living were on the Prescott side. But for the time being it was better if he didn't know about them. The time would come soon enough for him to learn about his heritage.

"No." Not legally.

"If you died, there wouldn't be anybody to take care of me, would there? I'd be an orphan," he stated with a round-eyed look.

"Clara would look after you," Valerie reassured him, bending to kiss his forehead before he could dodge away. "Go and wash." She administered a playful spank to his backside as he scampered toward the bathroom. "You'd better hurry, too," she called the warning after him. "Clara's coming with us and you know how upset she gets if people aren't ready on time."

Chapter 2

Valerie had done most of the driving, with Clara spelling her for an hour every so often to give her a rest. They had traveled well into the night before stopping at an inexpensive motel along the highway for a few hours' sleep. The morning sun dazzled their eyes, its light shining on the countryside of Maryland.

"How long before we get there, Mom?" Tadd piped the question from the back seat and leaned over the middle armrest to hear her answer.

"To save the wear and tear on your vocal cords, Tadd, we should have made you a banner with that question on it." Behind the dry tone of Clara's voice was a hint of amused tolerance. "You must have asked it a thousand times."

"How long, Mom?" he repeated.

"Not long. We'll be seeing the lane to the farm any minute now." Valerie discovered her hands were gripping the steering wheel until her knuckles were white.

Seven years had brought some changes to the area where she had once lived, but they had just driven past the entrance gates to Meadow Farms. Charcoal black fences marked off its paddocks. Just over that far hill near that stand of trees was where she used to meet Judd. If only her memory would let her forget.

"That's a fancy-looking place," Clara observed, but her eyes were on her companion when Valerie shot her a startled look.

"Yes," she agreed nervously. "It belongs to the Prescotts." She knew she was confirming what Clara had already guessed.

"Look at all the horses!" Tadd breathed, pressing his face against a side window. "Did they ever let you ride them when you were a kid, Mom?"

"I didn't ride any of those, but your great-grandfather owned horses. He raised them," Valerie explained, shifting the subject away from the breeding farm they were passing. "I used to ride his."

"You can ride?" There was a squeak of disbelief in his voice. "Gee, I wish I had a horse."

"Where would you keep it?" Clara wanted to know. "It's too big for the apartment. Besides, you're not allowed to have pets."

"When I get big, I'm going to move out of there and get me a horse," Tadd stated, his tone bordering on a challenge.

"When you get big, you'll want a car," Clara retorted.

"No, I won't." After being stuck in the back seat for almost twelve hours with infrequent breaks, Tadd was beginning to get irritable. Usually he enjoyed arguing with Clara, but he was starting to sound mutinous.

"Here's granddad's place." Valerie distracted his attention as she turned the car onto a narrow dirt lane.

A sign hung from a post on the left-hand side. The

paint had faded, but enough of the letters were still clear enough to make out the name Worth Farms, shortened from Wentworth. Board fences flanked the lane. Once they had been painted white, but the sun had blistered the paint away, leaving the wood gray and weathered. Half a dozen mares with foals could be seen grazing in the green carpet of grass in the pasture.

"Look, Tadd." Valerie pointed to the opposite side of the car from where he was sitting. "There are horses here, too."

But not for long, she thought to herself. With her grandfather gone, they would be sold off, and the farm, too. It was difficult to accept that the place she had always regarded as home would soon belong to someone else. It was a sorrow, a resigned regret.

But Valerie had no hard feelings against her grandfather for disinheriting her. It was up to everyone to make their way in the world—a self-made man, he'd always said as much, had lived his life that way. After seven years on her own, she understood what it meant to earn what you had: bad things could happen, did happen, but no one could ever take the hard-won knowledge of how to survive away from you. She'd inherited some of his toughness, if nothing else.

"Can we stop and see the horses, Mom?" Tadd bounced anxiously in the back seat, not satisfied with the slowed pace of the car that gave him a long time to watch the sleek, glistening animals.

"Later," Valerie qualified her refusal.

"Promise?" he demanded.

"I promise," she agreed, and let her gaze slide to Clara, whose shrewd eyes were inspecting the property. "The house and barns are just ahead." The roofs and part of the structures were in view.

"Are you sure there'll be somebody there?" Clara asked skeptically.

"Mickey Flanners will be. I know he'll let us stay long enough to wash and clean up. We can find out from him the details about the funeral arrangements and all," she explained, and smiled briefly. "You'll like Mickey," she told her friend. "He's an ex-jockey. He's worked for Granddad for years, taking care of the horses and doing odd jobs around the place. He's probably looking after things now until all the legal matters are settled and the farm . . . is sold." Again she felt the twinge of regret that this was no longer her home, not when her grandfather was alive nor now. She covered the pause with a quick, "Mickey is a lovable character."

"Which means he's short and fat, I suppose." Clara's blunt statement was tinged with humor.

"Short and stocky," Valerie corrected with a twinkling look. "That sounds better."

As they entered the yard of the horse farm, the barns and stables were the first to catch her eye. Although they were in need of a coat of paint, they were in good repair. Valerie hadn't expected differently. Her grandfather had never allowed anything to become rundown. The two-story house was in the same shape, needing paint but well kept. The lawn was overgrown with weeds in dire need of mowing.

Her sweeping inspection of the premises ended as her gaze was caught by a luxury car parked in front of the house. A film of dust coated the sides, picked up from dirt roads. A tingling sensation danced over her nerve ends. Her mouth felt dry and she swallowed hard.

"Did you really live here, Mom?" Tadd's eager voice seemed to come from a great distance.

"Yes." Her answer was absent of emotion.

"I wish I did," was his wistful response.

Automatically Valerie parked beside the other car. It could belong to any number of people, she told herself, a lawyer, a banker, someone from the funeral home, just anyone. But somehow she knew better.

Their car's engine had barely stopped turning before Tadd was opening the back door and scrambling out. Valerie followed his lead, but in a somewhat dazed fashion. A small hand grabbed hold of hers and tugged to pull her away from the house.

"Let's go see the horses, Mom," Tadd demanded. "You promised we would."

"Later." But she was hardly conscious of answering him. An invisible magnet was pulling her toward the house, its compelling force stronger than her son's pleading.

"I want to go now!" His declaration fell on deaf ears.

The screen door onto the front porch opened and a man stepped onto the painted board floor. The top buttons of his white shirt were unfastened, exposing the bronze skin of his hair-roughened chest. Long sleeves had been rolled back, revealing the corded muscles of his forearms. The white of his shirt tapered to male hips, dark trousers stretching the length of his supple, muscled legs.

But it was the unblinking stare of green eyes that held Valerie in their thrall. Fine lines fanned out from the corners of them. Harsh grooves were etched on either side of his mouth, carved into sun-browned skin stretched leanly from cheekbone to jawline. His jet black hair was in casual disorder that was somehow sensuous.

Her heart had stopped beating at the sight of

Judd, only to start up again at racing speed. Blood pounded hotly through her veins. The seven years melted away until they were no longer ago than yesterday.

She tried to stay calm but couldn't squelch a wildly romantic reaction. Untold pleasures seemed no farther away than the short distance that separated them. That chiseled mouth had only to take possession of hers to transport her to the world of secret delights.

The compulsion was strong to take the last few steps to reach that hard male body. Valerie would have succumbed to it if the small hand holding hers hadn't tugged her arm to demand her attention. Reluctantly she dragged her gaze from Judd and glanced down to the boy at her side. Only a few seconds had passed instead of years.

"Who's that man?" Tadd frowned, eyeing Judd with a look that was both puzzled and wary.

Valerie couldn't help wondering what would happen if she told him Judd was his father. But of course she couldn't, and didn't. Tadd's question had succeeded in bringing her to her senses. Valerie realized the painful truth that the aching rawness of her desire for Judd hadn't diminished over the years of separation, but she was equally determined not to be consumed by that love as she had been seven years ago.

Her gaze swung back to Judd. "It's a neighbor, Judd Prescott." Her voice sounded remarkably calm.

A muttered sigh came from Clara, her words low, meant only for Valerie. "I didn't think it was your lovable Mickey." Her comment implied that she had guessed Judd's identity the minute he stepped out of the house.

Valerie didn't have time to acknowledge her friend's remark. Judd was walking down the porch steps to greet her. He extended a hand toward her.

"Welcome home, Valerie." His deep voice held little else than courtesy. "I'm sorry about the circumstances."

His words of sympathy were just that—words. They carried no sincerity. A bitter surge of resentment made her want to hurl them back in his face. One look at his hard features cast in bronze told her he was incapable of feelings. Except maybe the crudest kind.

Valerie swallowed the impulse and murmured a stiff, "I'm sorry, too."

Unconsciously she placed her hand in his. When she felt the strong grip of his fingers closing over her own, she was struck by the irony of the situation. She was politely and impersonally shaking hands with a man who knew her more intimately than anyone ever had, a man who was the father of her child. There wasn't any part of her that the hand she held hadn't explored many times and with devastating thoroughness. She felt the beginnings of a yearning desire and withdrew her hand from his before she betrayed it.

"I'm Tadd." Her son demanded his share of the attention.

Her hand drifted to his small shoulder. "This is my son," she told Judd, and watched his reaction.

He didn't seem surprised by her announcement, nor was there any suspicion in his expression that he was looking into the face of his child. Valerie supposed that she saw the faint resemblance between the two because she knew and was looking for it.

"Hello, Tadd." Judd bent slightly to shake hands

with the boy. It was a gesture minus the warmth of affection or friendliness, prompted only by good manners. He was a Southern man—those were bred in.

At first Tadd seemed slightly overwhelmed by the action. Then a smile of importance widened his mouth. "Hello," he replied.

Valerie realized it was the first time an adult had ever shaken hands with him; usually they rumpled his hair and tweaked his chin. No wonder he was looking so proud and important. She was almost angry with Judd for being the one to treat Tadd like that, because she knew he meant nothing by it. She suppressed the rush of antagonism and turned to introduce him to Clara.

"Clara, this is Judd Prescott. He owns the land that adjoins my grandfather's." The explanation was unnecessary, but Valerie made it to show Judd that she hadn't found him important enough to discuss with her friend prior to their arrival. "This is my friend Mrs. Clara Simons."

"I'm pleased to meet you, Mrs. Simons." Judd issued the polite phrase and shook Clara's hand.

"Same here." Clara was just as polite but the two of them eyed each other like a pair of opponents measuring one another's strengths and weaknesses. Tension seemed to crackle in the air.

"I didn't expect to see you here when we arrived, Judd." Valerie's brittle comment was a challenge to explain his presence on the farm. "I thought we'd find Mickey instead."

"Did you?" The gleam in his eyes seemed to taunt her, but Judd went on smoothly without waiting for a reply. "Mick is here. I just stopped by to check on things and see if there was any way I could help out."

"A neighborly call, hmm?" Clara's sharp voice seemed to question his motive.

But he remained unperturbed, his green gaze swinging to the stoutly built woman. "Something like that," he agreed. Turning to one side, he called toward the house, "Mick? Valerie has arrived."

"You don't say!" came the muffled exclamation in a lilting tenor voice that Valerie remembered well, and seconds later a short man came out of the house. Mickey looked older and wasn't as agile as she remembered. The wispy crop of hair on his head still reminded her of straw, but it was thinner. "As I live and breathe, it's Valerie!"

"Hello, Mickey." She smiled, unaware of the warmth and affection her expression held or the way Judd's eyes narrowed at the unconsciously alluring transformation.

With slightly bowed legs, Mickey Flanners was built so close to the ground that he appeared to tumble down the steps to greet her. A head shorter than she was, he clasped one of her hands in the powerful grip of both of his. She realized that his hands still had the strength to control the most fractious of horses.

"I got word yesterday afternoon that you was coming for the funeral, but I didn't know how soon you'd get here." His knowledge was of horses, not subjects like grammar, but his brand of reckless Irish charm made it easy to overlook.

"We drove practically straight through," Valerie explained. "We stopped here before going into town to rest and find out the details about the funeral arrangements. I thought you would know about them."

"Of course I do. You—" Mickey began, only to be interrupted by Tadd.

"You aren't even as tall as my mom. When are you going to grow up?" he wanted to know.

"Mind your manners, Tadd!" It was Clara who snapped out the reproval, but Valerie just smiled and Mickey laughed, never having been sensitive about his size, and Judd's green eyes simply observed.

"To tell you the truth, me lad—" Mick adopted a poor imitation of an Irish brogue and winked at Valerie. "I don't intend to ever grow up," he confided to Tadd in a loud whisper. "Wouldn't you like to stay little like me all your life?"

Without hesitation, Tadd made a negative shake of his head. "No, I want to grow tall like him." He pointed at Judd.

Valerie caught her breath at the amused twitch of Judd's mouth. But he didn't know it was his son who wanted to grow up like him. At the rate Tadd was growing out of his clothes, she guessed he probably would top the six-foot mark like Judd.

"Well, if that's the way you feel about it, there's nothing I can do." Mickey looked properly crestfallen, but laughter danced in his eyes as he turned toward Valerie. "Where's your luggage? I'll carry it in the house for you."

"We were planning to stay at a motel in town." Valerie's instinctive response was a protest.

"A motel?" Mickey stepped back. "Eli would have my hide if I let you and the boy stay at a motel! I mean—if he was alive," he corrected with a sobering look. "You're the only family he had. There's no sense in sleeping in a strange place when your old bedroom is empty."

"Our luggage is in the trunk of the car and the keys are in the ignition." Clara offered this information while Valerie was still absorbing Mickey's reply.

He had made it sound as if her grandfather would have wanted her back. And he had known about Tadd, and obviously hadn't kept it a secret or Mickey would not have taken his presence for granted. For that reason alone Valerie wasn't going to argue about staying, discounting the fact that she couldn't really afford the cost of the motel room.

Mickey's ebullient spirits could never be dampened for long. They surfaced again as he obtained the key from the ignition and walked to the rear of the car to unlock the trunk. He began unloading the suitcases, chattering continuously.

"When you left here, Valerie, old Eli seemed to lose heart. He didn't quit or anything like that—he'd never give up his horses—but he just didn't seem to have the enthusiasm anymore." Mickey paused to glance around the place. "For the last three years he'd been talking about painting everything, but he never got around to it. The truth is, I don't think he had the money to have it done and neither one of us was spry enough to paint it ourselves. And you know your grandfather: if he couldn't pay cash for what he wanted, he did without." He set the last suitcase on the ground. "Is this all of them?"

"Yes," Valerie nodded.

He glanced down. "Guess I'll have to make two trips."

"I'll help you carry them inside, Mick," Judd volunteered, as the ex-jockey had evidently expected him to do. Judd was aware of Mickey's limitations, but tactful.

"Thanks, Judd." Mickey picked out the heaviest suitcases and handed them to him.

That was when Valerie noticed that Tadd had tagged along after Judd. He tipped his dark head way back to look up at him, a determinedly adult look on his childish face.

"I can carry one," he insisted.

"Do you think so?" Judd's glance was indulgent and tolerant, but indifferent. He nodded toward Valerie's smallest duffel, the one that held her blowdryer and makeup. "That one looks about your size. Can you handle it?"

"Sure." Tadd picked it up with both hands. It bounced against his knees as he walked behind Judd toward the house.

"I'll tell you one thing, Valerie," Mickey was saying as he led the way up the porch steps and into the house. "Your granddad sure perked up when he found out he had a great-grandchild. Proud as a peacock, he was, passing out cigars to anybody that came within hailing distance."

A lump entered Valerie's throat. Her grandfather had been proud; he hadn't been ashamed when he learned of Tadd's birth. Why hadn't he let her know? She would have brought Tadd for him to see. Hadn't he realized that she had expected him to slam the door in her face?

"No coffee made," Mick added. "But I guess you could make a pot while we take the luggage to your rooms. Ain't nothing been changed since you left, so the fixings are where they always were. You know what old Eli always said, a place for everything and everything in its place."

She remembered how often her grandfather had recited that and smiled.

"A cup of coffee is just what I need," Clara stated briskly. "You go and fix some, Valerie, while I see to our luggage and hang our clothes up before they're permanently wrinkled."

Valerie was left downstairs to make her way to the kitchen while the rest of them climbed the steps to the second-floor bedrooms. She hadn't realized how tense she had been in Judd's presence until she was away from him. Her nerves seemed to almost shudder in relief when she stood alone in the simple farm kitchen. She had wanted that fiery attraction between them to be dead, but it wasn't—not for her.

She heard footsteps approaching the kitchen— footsteps made by more than one pair of feet—and began filling the coffeepot with water. She turned off the faucet as Judd entered the kitchen, followed closely by Tadd and Mickey.

"I saw the bedroom where you slept as a little kid, Mom," Tadd announced, bouncing over to the counter and standing on tiptoe to see what she was doing. "Mickey showed it to me. He said it was the same bed you used to sleep in. Can I sleep in it?"

"Sure, if you want to," she agreed, and turned to open the cupboard on her left.

Her gaze encountered Judd's. She had the disturbing sensation that she had just given permission to him instead of her son. The canister of coffee was where it had always been kept. Her shaking hands lifted it down to the counter top as she turned to avoid the glitter of his eyes.

"When can we go see the horses?" Tadd reverted to his previous theme.

"Later on, I told you that before," Valerie replied with a hint of impatience.

"But it is later," he reasoned. "And you promised."

"Tadd, I'm making coffee." She shot him a warning look that said *don't whine* and his lower lip jutted out in a pout.

"So it's horses you're wanting to see, is it, lad?"

Mickey's lilting voice brought the light of hope back into Tadd's hazel green eyes.

"Yes, would you take me?" he asked unashamedly.

"First I have to find out how bad you want to see them," Mick cautioned, and walked over to open a cupboard drawer. "You can either have a piece of candy"—he held up a chocolate bar—"or you can come with me to see the horses. Which will it be?"

Except to glance at the candy, Tadd didn't hesitate. "The horses."

Mickey tossed him the chocolate bar. "Spoken like a true horseman! Your great-granddaddy would have been proud to hear you say that."

Tadd stared at the candy. "Aren't you going to take me to see the horses?"

"Of course, lad." Mickey reassured him with a wink. "But you'll be needin' some energy for the walk, won't you?"

"You mean I can have both?" Tadd wanted to be sure before he tore off the paper wrapping around the bar.

"Isn't that what I just said?" Mick teased, and moved toward the back door. "Come along, lad. And don't you be worrying about him, Valerie. I'll watch over him the same as I watched over you."

Valerie had enjoyed the way Mickey worked his Irish charm on her son. It wasn't until the door shut that she realized she had been left alone in the kitchen with Judd. What was keeping Clara, she wondered desperately, but was determined not to lose her composure.

"Mickey's always had a way with children," she said into the silence, not risking a glance at Judd as she spooned the ground coffee into the swing-open basket of the coffee-maker.

"That's because there's a little bit of truth in the fact that he's never grown up." Judd had moved closer, Valerie was fully aware of his disconcerting gaze on her. He leaned against the counter a few feet from where she worked, in her line of vision. "I knew you were coming," he said with studied quietness.

She glanced up, the implication of his words jolting through her. Judd meant that he had known she was coming the same way he had always known when she would be at their meeting place.

She didn't want to be reminded of that.

Deliberately she pretended she was unaware of a hidden meaning in his comment. "Word gets around fast, doesn't it? I did tell the hospital when they called that I'd be coming as soon as I could. I suppose everyone in the area knows it by now." She finished setting up the coffeemaker and plugged the cord into a socket. Out the kitchen window she could see Tadd skipping alongside Mickey on their way to the barns. "I suppose you're finally married and have a family of your own now." She turned away, trying not to picture Judd in the arms of some beautiful debutante.

"No, to both of those." An aloofness had entered his chiseled features when she glanced at him. "You've grown up a lot. You're a beautiful woman, Valerie." It was a statement, flatly issued, yet with the power to stir her senses as only Judd could.

"Thank you." She tried to accept his words as merely a compliment, but she didn't know how successful she had been.

"I'm sorry your husband wasn't able to come with you. I would have liked to meet him," he said.

"My husband? Who told you I was married?"

Except for startled surprise, there was little expression in her face.

"Your grandfather, of course." He tilted his head to one side, black hair gleaming in a shaft of sunlight.

Oh no. But it made sense. Valerie realized that she should have guessed her grandfather would come up with a story like that in order to claim his great-grandson without feeling shame. "Silly question, I guess," she commented dryly.

Judd didn't make any comment to that. "I suppose your husband wasn't able to get time off from his job."

Valerie was toying with the idea of revealing her grandfather's lie and correcting Judd's impression that she was married. When she had decided, shortly after Tadd was born, to keep her baby rather than give him up for adoption, she'd also decided not to hide behind a phony wedding ring.

Before Valerie could tell Judd that she had no husband and never did, Clara walked into the kitchen. She glanced from Valerie to Judd and back to Valerie.

"Where's Tadd?" she asked.

"Mickey took him out to see the horses," Valerie explained.

"Is the coffee ready?" Clara sat down in one of the kitchen chairs, making it clear that she wasn't budging. "Are you having some, Mr. Prescott?" Behind the question was a challenge to explain the reason he was still here.

"No, I don't believe so." Amusement glinted in his green eyes at the protective attitude of the older woman. His attention returned to Valerie. "The funeral home will be open from six until eight this evening so your grandfather's friends can come to pay their respects. You're welcome to ride in with me if you wish."

"Thanks for the offer, but we'll find our own way." Valerie refused in the politest of tones.

He inclined his head in silent acceptance of her decision. Bidding them both an impersonal good-bye, Judd left. Neither woman spoke until they heard the roar of a powerful engine starting up at the front of the house.

"Well?" Clara prompted.

"Well, what?" Valerie was deliberately vague.

"What did he have to say?" Clara demanded, a little gruffly.

"Nothing, really, if you mean any reference to our former . . . relationship." Valerie removed two cups from the cabinet above the stove.

"Did he say anything to you about Tadd?"

"No. Judd thinks I'm married. Seems like my granddad cooked up a story."

"Did you straighten him out?" Clara wanted to know, an eyebrow lifting.

"I was thinking about doing that when you walked in." Valerie shrugged. "I suppose it's just as well I didn't. Whether I'm supposedly married or single doesn't change anything."

"Are you going to tell him that Tadd is his son?"

"If he asks me, I will. What difference does it make?" Valerie said diffidently. "He has no legal right to Tadd—at least I don't think so."

"So long as he doesn't suspect, and there's no DNA test involved . . ." Clara trailed off.

"Not going to happen. He just thinks Tadd's my kid. Which he is. No doubt about that."

"But Judd still gets to you, doesn't he?" Clara's voice was understanding and vaguely sad.

"Yes," Valerie sighed. "After all this time, I'm not immune to him. He's a player and I got played, but he would only have to hold me to make me forget that."

"Don't let him hurt you again, honey." It was almost a plea.

Shaking the honey-dark mane of her hair, Valerie curved her mouth into a weak smile. "I'm not going to give him the chance."

Chapter 3

At a quarter past six that evening Valerie slowed the car to park it in front of the funeral home of the small Maryland community. A few vehicles were already in the lot. Rugged SUVs, trucks—she felt a little out of place in her citified car.

"Is this where we're going?" Tadd was draped half in the front seat and half in the back.

"Yes." Valerie glanced at him briefly. His little bow tie was already askew and his shirt was coming loose from the waistband of his trousers. "Clara, would you mind tucking his shirt in and straightening his tie?"

"Hold still," Clara ordered when the boy tried to squirm away. "I don't know if it's a good idea to bring him along."

"He's old enough to understand what's going on," Valerie replied calmly.

"Are we going to a funeral?" Tadd asked.

"No, Granddad's funeral is tomorrow," she answered patiently.

"What's a funeral?"

At his question, Clara sniffed, a sound that

indicated Valerie was wrong to believe Tadd knew what was going on.

"When a person dies, all his friends and family come to say goodbye to him. Do you remember when your turtle died? We put him in a box, buried him in the ground and asked God to take care of him for you because you couldn't."

"Is that a funeral?" Tadd was plainly fascinated by the discovery.

"Yes." Valerie parked the car next to the curb. "Let's go inside. Remember, Tadd, you promised me you'd be good."

"I will." He tossed off the agreement as he eagerly climbed out of the car.

The hushed atmosphere inside temporarily impressed Tadd. He stood quietly at her side, holding her hand while Valerie spoke to the funeral director. Several of her grandfather's friends had already arrived. Some Valerie remembered; others she didn't.

Tadd didn't really understand the condolences the strangers offered. He was too busy looking around him in awed silence. He mutely nodded at Judd when the older man arrived and came over to speak to him and Valerie.

Valerie realized she was clenching her jaw in tension and tried to relax. "Granddad knew just about everybody in the area, didn't he?" she remarked.

"Everyone didn't agree with his strict code, but they respected him," Judd stated. "Have you had a chance to go up front?"

Valerie glanced toward the satin-lined casket. "No. Each time I started, someone stopped to offer their sympathies."

"Come on." His arm curved impersonally behind her to rest his hand on the small of her back.

The heat of his touch seemed to send a fire racing up her spine. She was powerless to resist his guidance. Her fingers curled tightly around Tadd's small hand, bringing him along with her.

At the open casket Judd stopped, and Valerie looked at her grandfather's face for the first time in seven years. He looked old and tired lying there, in need of the rest he had obtained. She wanted to tell him how much she loved him and how sorry she was for hurting him, but she had said both many times in the letters she had written him, so she guessed he knew.

Tadd was trying to peer inside. "Mom, I can't see," he whispered.

Bending down, Valerie lifted him up. His arm rested on her shoulder, his face close to her own. "That's your great-grandfather." She felt the need to tell him something.

"Oh," Tadd breathed, and turned a questioning look at her. "How come we didn't bury Fred in a box like that?" he asked softly.

A smile played at the edges of her mouth. His nonchalance at death seemed somehow right. She wasn't going to scold him for being unintentionally disrespectful.

"We couldn't find one that small," she answered, and it satisfied him.

As they turned to walk back to where the other mourners were talking, Judd gave her a questioning look, his eyes cool and distant. "Who's Fred?"

"A pet turtle," she admitted, unable to keep from giving him a faint smile.

"I should have guessed," he murmured dryly, shared amusement showing briefly in his look.

More friends of the family arrived. Judd made no

attempt to remain with her as Valerie greeted them. Almost immediately he drifted to one side, although Valerie was aware that he was never very far away from her.

It wasn't long before the novelty of Tadd's surroundings wore off. He became increasingly restless and impatient with the subdued conversations. He fidgeted in the folding chair beside Valerie's and began swinging his feet back and forth to kick at his chair rung. The clatter of his shoes against the metal was loud, like a galloping horse.

"Don't do that, Tadd," Valerie told him quietly, putting a hand on his knee to end the motion.

He flashed her a defiant look that said *I-want-to* and continued swinging his feet without letup.

"Stop it, Tadd," she repeated.

"No!" the boy retorted, but he found himself looking into a pair of cold green eyes that wouldn't put up with brattiness.

"Do as your mother tells you, Tadd," Judd warned, "or you'll find yourself sitting alone in your mother's car. The attendant out there will keep you company."

Tadd pushed his mutinous face close to Judd's. "Good." Olive green eyes glared into a brilliant jade green pair. "I want to sit in the car," Tadd declared. "I don't want to stay here in this dumb old place."

"Okay." Judd straightened, taking one of Tadd's hands and pulling him from the chair.

"No, wait." Valerie rushed out the words. "Tadd is tired and irritable after that long trip," she explained to excuse her son's behavior, and glanced anxiously at Clara. "Maybe you'd better take him back and put him to bed, Clara." She opened her bag and took out the car keys. "Here."

"And how will you get back?" her friend asked in a meaningful tone.

It didn't seem proper to Valerie to leave yet. Mickey Flanners was standing only a few feet away, chatting with a horse trainer.

"Mickey?" When he turned, Valerie asked, "Is it all right if I ride back to the farm with you?"

For an instant she thought Mickey glanced at Judd before answering, but she decided she had been mistaken. "Sure," he agreed immediately.

Judd released Tadd's hand as Clara walked over to take him with her. Tadd glanced at Valerie. "I'll be there soon," she promised.

It was more than an hour later when Mickey asked if she was ready to leave. Valerie agreed. She didn't have to make small talk as Mickey began relating a steady stream of racehorse gossip while they walked out of the funeral home. Only one car was parked in the area that Mickey was heading toward, and Judd was behind the wheel.

"Where are you parked?" Valerie interrupted Mickey with the question.

"I thought you knew." His startled glance was strictly innocent of deception. "I rode in with Judd."

"No, I wasn't aware of that." There was a hint of grimness in her voice, but she didn't protest.

Mickey opened the front door on the passenger side for her. She had barely slid in when he was asking her to move over. She found herself sitting in the middle, pressed close to Judd. For such a small man, Mickey Flanners seemed to take up a lot of room.

Judd seemed indifferent to the way her shoulder kept brushing against his as he reversed the car into the street. It was impossible to avoid the accidental contact with him unless she hunched her shoulders forward and held herself as stiff as an old woman, and she refused to do that.

The scent of expensive men's cologne filled her lungs and interfered with her breathing. Mickey continued his nonstop banter, which was a source of relief to Valerie, for without it she was sure Judd would have been able to hear the erratic pounding of her heart.

When Judd had to swerve to avoid a pothole, Valerie was thrown against him. Her hand clutched at the nearest solid object to regain her balance. It turned out to be his thigh. His muscles contracted into living steel beneath her hand. She heard him sharply inhale a curse and jerked her hand away as if she had suddenly been burned.

She recovered enough of her poise to offer a cool, "I'm sorry." His bland, "That's quite all right," made her wonder if she had only imagined that he had been disturbed by her unintended touch.

Her grandfather's house was a welcome sight when Judd slowed the car to a stop in front of it. Mickey didn't immediately climb out. Instead he leaned forward to take a look at Judd.

"There's some of Eli's good brandy in the house. Will you come in, Judd, and we'll have one last drink to old Eli?" A second after he had issued the invitation he glanced at Valerie. "That is, if you don't mind. After all, it is your grandfather's house and his brandy."

"It's as much your house as it is mine," Valerie insisted. What else could she say? Mickey had worked for her grandfather long before she was born. His years of loyalty far outweighed her less than exemplary relationship with her grandfather, regardless of the blood ties.

"In that case, will you come in for a little while, Judd?" Mickey repeated his invitation.

There was an instant's hesitation from Judd. Valerie felt his gaze skim her profile, but she pretended to be oblivious. She hadn't seconded the invitation because she didn't want to give him the impression that she craved his company. He didn't have to know he still exerted a powerful attraction over her.

"Thank you, Mick, I'd like that," he agreed finally. "But I'll only be able to stay a little while. I've got a sick colt to check on."

"Oh? What's wrong with it?" Mick opened the car door and stepped out.

As Valerie turned to slide out the passenger side, the skirt of her grape-colored dress failed to move with her, exposing a sheer nylon-covered thigh and knee. She reached hastily to pull the skirt down, but Judd's hand was there to do it for her. In the confusion of his touch against her virtually bare leg, Valerie didn't hear his explanation of the colt's problem. She managed to push his hand away, an action that was at odds with her sensual reaction.

The warmth that was in her cheeks when she stepped out of the car wasn't visible in the fading sunset of the summer evening. It was a languid night, heavily scented with the smell of horses and hay and the blooming roses that grew next to the house.

Mickey waited for Judd to continue his discussion of horses and their ailments. Valerie started immediately toward the house, not rushing, although that was what she wanted to do. As a consequence, Judd was there to reach around her and open the porch door.

Hearing them return, Clara appeared from the living room. She had already changed into her nightgown, its hem peeping out from the folds of her quilted robe. A pair of furry slippers covered her feet. At the sight of the two men following Valerie inside, Clara stopped and scowled. Only Valerie, who knew her, was aware it was a self-conscious and defensive expression for being caught in that state of dress.

"What are you staring at?" Clara demanded of Mickey. "Haven't you ever seen a woman in a bathrobe before?"

"Not in a good many years." Mickey recovered from his initial shock, his cheeks dimpling with mischief. "I'd forgotten what a tempting sight it could be."

"As if," Clara snapped, reddening under his sweeping look.

Hiding a grin, Mickey turned aside from the bristling woman. "I'll get some glasses from the kitchen. Why don't you go on into Eli's office, Judd? I'll be along directly."

"Don't hurry on my account," Judd replied.

Valerie felt his glance swing to her when Mickey left the room, but she didn't volunteer to show him to her grandfather's study. Instead she walked into the living room to speak to Clara, silently denying any interest in where he went or when.

"Is Tadd asleep?" she asked Clara.

"Finally, after pitching a fit to see the horses again," was the gruff response.

"I'll go and look in on him." Her sensitive radar knew the instant Judd turned and walked toward the study.

"Leave him be for now," Clara insisted. "You might wake him, and I don't care to hear him whining again about those horses." She shot a look in the direction Judd had taken and whispered angrily, "You could have warned me you'd be inviting them in when you got back. I wouldn't have been traipsing around the place in my robe if I'd known."

"I had no intention of inviting them in," Valerie corrected her. "In fact, Mickey was the one who invited Judd, not me."

"It's neither here nor there now," Clara muttered. "I'm going up to my room where I can have some privacy."

Valerie was about to say that she'd come along with her when Mickey appeared at the living room entrance. Clara scurried toward the staircase under his dancing look.

"I'll be up shortly," she called after Clara, then asked Mickey, "Did you want something?"

"I know you're tired and will be wanting to turn in, but will you have one small drink with us to the old man?" He wore his most beguiling expression as he raised an arm to show her he carried three glasses.

The haunting loneliness in his blue eyes told Valerie that he truly missed her grandfather and wanted to share his sense of loss with someone who had been close to Elias Wentworth. Her glance flickered uncertainly toward the study where Judd waited.

"Sure," she agreed, and wondered whether she was a sentimental fool or a masochist.

Judd's back was to the door, his attention focused on the framed pictures of thoroughbred horses that covered one paneled wall of the study. Valerie tried not to notice the way he pivoted sharply when she and Mickey entered, or the almost physical impact of his gaze on her. She walked to the leather-covered armchair, its dark brown color worn to patches of tan on the seat and arms.

"I've got the glasses," Mickey announced. "All we need is the brandy." He walked to the stained oak desk and opened a bottom drawer. "Up until a few years ago Eli used to keep his liquor locked up."

Valerie's fingers curved into the leather armrest at Mickey's unwitting reminder of her past misdeeds. He obviously didn't know why her grandfather had locked it away in the first place. She still didn't understand why she'd had to have it. She hadn't liked the taste of alcohol and had usually ended up getting sick.

"Eli never touched a drop himself," Mickey went on as he held the bottle up to see how much was in it. "He was an alcoholic when he was younger. He told me once that it wasn't until after his wife died that he gave up drinking for good." He poured a healthy amount of brandy into the first water glass.

"Only a little for me," said Valerie, understanding at last why her grandfather had been so violently opposed to drinking.

"Eli swore he kept liquor in the house purely for medicinal reasons." When he reached the third glass, Mickey poured only enough brandy in to cover the bottom. "Personally, I think he kept it on hand to befuddle the brains of whoever came to buy a horse from him."

Picking up two of the glasses, Mickey carried the one with the smaller portion to Valerie and handed the other to Judd. Judd took a seat on the worn leather-covered sofa that was a match to her chair. Mickey completed the triangle by hoisting himself onto the desk top, his short legs dangling against the side.

"To Eli." Judd lifted his glass in a toast.

"May he rest in peace," Mickey added, and drank from his glass. Valerie sipped her brandy, the fiery liquid burning her tongue and throat, conscious that

Judd's gaze seldom wavered from her. "Yeah, old Eli never smoked or drank," Mickey sighed, and stared at his glass. "They say a reformed hellion is stricter—and he sure was with you, Valerie. I remember the time he caught you with a pack of cigarettes. I thought he was going to beat the livin' daylights out of you."

"I caused him a lot of grief when I was growing up." There was a poignant catch in her voice, but she lifted her shoulders in a dismissing shrug.

"You were a chip off the old block," the ex-jockey insisted with a smile, countering her self-criticism. "Besides, you gave him a lot of pleasure these last years." His comment warmed her. "Remember how Eli was, Judd, whenever he got a letter from her?"

"Yes," Judd answered quietly.

At his affirmative reply, her gaze swung curiously to him. "Did you visit Granddad? I don't remember that you came over when I was still living here."

He rotated his glass in a circle, swirling the brandy inside. He seemed to be pretending an interest in the liquor while choosing how to word his answer.

"Your grandfather had a yearling filly that I liked the looks of a few years ago. Her bloodline wasn't bad, so I offered to buy her," Judd explained with a touch of diffidence. "After a week of haggling back and forth, we finally came to an agreement on the price. It was the first time I really became acquainted with Eli. I like to think that we had a mutual respect for each other."

"After that, Judd began stopping by once or twice a month," Mickey elaborated. "Your granddad would get out his letters from you and tell anybody who would listen how you were."

Apprehension quivered through Valerie that Judd might have seen what she wrote. Of course, she had never told her grandfather the identity of Tadd's father, not even in the letters. Not that she cared whether Judd knew, but she didn't like the idea that he might have read the personal letters intended only for her grandfather. Mickey's next statement put that apprehension to rest.

"He never actually read your letters aloud, but he'd tell what you said. All the time he'd be talking, he'd be holding the envelope with your letter inside it and stroking it like it was one of his horses."

"I wish . . . I could have seen him before he died." But she hadn't thought she would be welcomed. Her fear had become a habit of mind.

"I wanted to call you when he was in the hospital," Mickey told her. "But Eli told me that in your last letter you'd said you and your husband were going to take a Caribbean cruise. I didn't know he was so sick or I would have got in touch with you anyway."

"On a cruise?" Valerie frowned.

"That's what he said," Mickey repeated.

"I didn't go on any cruise." She made the denial before she realized that it was another story her grandfather had made up.

"Maybe he got your letters confused," he suggested. "He kept them all, every one of them. He hoarded them like they were gold. He carried them around with him until they stuck out of the pockets of his old green plaid jacket like straw out of a scarecrow."

"He did?" Valerie was touched by the thought. The idea that he treasured her letters that much made her forgive him for making up those stories about her.

"He sure did. As a matter of fact, they're all still in his jacket." Mickey hopped down from his perch on the desk and walked to the old armoire used as a storage cabinet for the farm records. The green plaid jacket hung on a hook inside the wooden door. "Here it is, letters and all."

As he walked over to her, Mickey began gathering the letters from the various pockets, not stopping until there were several handfuls on her lap. Some of the envelopes had the yellow tinge of age, but all of them were worn from numerous handlings.

Setting her brandy glass down, Valerie picked up one envelope that was postmarked five years ago. She turned it over, curious to read the letter inside, but the flap of the envelope was still sealed. A cold chill raced through her.

"No!" Her cry was a sobbing protest of angry and hurt disbelief. She raced frantically through the rest of the envelopes. All were sealed. None of the letters had ever been read. "No! No! No!" She sobbed bitterly, overwhelmed in an instant by a truth too painful to accept.

"What is it?" Mickey was plainly confused.

"What's wrong?" Judd was standing beside her chair. He reached down and took one of the envelopes.

"Look at it!" Valerie said through her tears.

When he turned it over and saw the sealed flap that showed no sign of ever having been opened, his darkly green, questing gaze sliced back to her. In each of her hands she held envelopes in the same unopened condition. Her fingers curled into them, crumpling them into her palms. In agitation she rose from the chair, letting the letters in her lap fall to the floor. She stared at the ones in her hands.

"It isn't fair!" In a mixture of rage and pain, Valerie cast away the envelopes in her hands. She began shaking uncontrollably, her fingers still curled into fists. "It isn't fair!"

Scalding tears burned hot trails down her cheeks. The highly charged emotions and temper that maturity had taught her to control broke free at last.

"Valerie!" Judd's voice didn't help.

The instant his hands gripped her shoulders and turned her around, she began pummeling his shoulders with her fists. She was wounded, utterly and deeply wounded, and lashing out in hurt.

"He never opened them. He never read any of my letters," she sobbed in frustration and anguish.

Indifferent to the hands on her waist, she pounded Judd's shoulders, hitting out at his solid flesh. Her crying face was buried in his shirtfront, moistening it and the lapel of his jacket.

Somewhere on the edge of her consciousness she was aware of concerned voices, Mickey's and Clara's. Only one penetrated and it came from Judd.

"Let her cry. She needs to. Leave us alone. Please."

After that, there was only silence and the heart-tearing sounds of her own sobbing. When the violent storm in her mind subsided, she cried softly for several minutes more. Her hands stopped beating at the indestructible wall of muscle and clutched Judd's jacket instead. His arms were around her, holding her closely in silent comfort. Gradually she began to regain her senses, but there were still things that needed to come out.

Lifting her head far enough from his chest to see the buttons of his shirt, she sniffed, "He hated me." Her voice was hoarse and broken as she wiped tears from her cheek with a scrubbing motion of her hand.

"I'm sure he didn't," Judd said.

"Yes, he did." Valerie bobbed her head, her rippling

hair falling forward to hide her face. "He couldn't stand the thought of having me as a granddaughter, so he made up a fake one, complete with lies about marriage and vacation cruises. It was all lies!"

His hand raked the hair from one cheek and tilted her face up for him to study. "What are you saying?" he demanded, tight-lipped.

Golden defiance flashed in her eyes, a defiance for convention and her grandfather. "I work for a living. I couldn't afford a trip on a rowboat. I'm not married—I never have been. Tadd is his great-grandchild, but my son's father doesn't know a thing about him."

"Valerie!" His head came down, his mouth roughly brushing across a tear-dampened cheek to reach her lips. "I've been going through hell wondering how I was going to keep my hands off somebody else's wife." He breathed the words into her ear. "And all the time you weren't even married!"

His unexpected kiss claimed her lips, devouring their fullness. Her battered emotions had no defenses against his sudden reaction to her confession and he took advantage of that. She was dragged into the powerful undercurrent of his passion, then swept away by the response of her own senses. Held back for so long, the feelings on both sides ran high and burned hot. This consuming fire fused her melting curves to the iron contours of his body. Not content with tasting her lips, Judd turned his attention to her throat and the sensitive hollows below her ears.

His hand moved slowly down her back, unzipping her dress, but when the room's air touched the exposed skin, it was the cool breath of sanity that she had needed. She pushed out of his arms and took a quick step away, stopping with her back to him. She was trembling from the force of the passion he had so easily aroused. "No . . . no. Not now—"

At the touch of his hand on her hair, Valerie stiffened. Judd brushed the long mane of hair aside. His warm breath caressed her skin as he bent to kiss the ultra-sensitive spot at the back of her neck, and desire quivered through her.

"You're right, Valerie." His fingers teased her spine as he zipped up her dress. "This isn't the time or the place, not with your grandfather's funeral tomorrow."

"As if you give a damn!" Her voice wavered, then echoed the parting phrase she'd thrown at him seven years ago. "Go to hell, Judd Prescott!"

She closed her eyes tightly as she heard his footsteps recede from her. When she opened them they were dry of tears and she was alone. A few minutes later Clara came scuffing into the room in her furry slippers.

"Are you all right now?" she asked.

Thank God that was all Clara wanted to know. Valerie turned, breathing in deeply and nodding. "Yes, I'm fine." The letters were still scattered on the linoleum floor, and she stooped to pick them up. "Granddad never opened them, Clara."

"That doesn't mean anything. He kept them, didn't he? So he must have felt something for you," her friend said quickly, "otherwise he would have burned them."

"Maybe." But Valerie was no longer sure.

"What did Prescott have to say?" Clara bent awkwardly down on her knees to help Valerie collect the scattered envelopes.

"Nothing really. I told him I wasn't married and that Tadd—that Tadd's father knew nothing about him. So now Judd knows Granddad was lying all this time," she replied with almost frightening calm.

"So you didn't tell him he was Tadd's father. Is that why he left in such a freezing silence?"

"No. He never asked. I don't mean anything to him and I never did. I bet he even believes I don't know who the father is," she said, releasing a short bitter laugh. The postmark of one of the envelopes in her hand caught her eye. It was dated two days after Tadd's birth, unopened like the rest of them. "If granddad never opened any of my letters, how did he know about Tadd?"

Clara stood up, making a show of straightening the stack of envelopes she held. "I phoned him a couple hours after Tadd was born. I thought he should know he had a great-grandson."

"What . . . did he say?" Valerie unconsciously held her breath.

Clara hesitated, then looked her in the eye. "He didn't say anything. He just hung up." The flickering light of hope went out of Valerie's eyes. "I was talking to Mickey today," Clara went on. "It wasn't until a year after Tadd was born that he told everybody he had a great-grandchild."

"I suppose so there was a decent interval between the time I supposedly was married and Tadd was born," Valerie concluded acidly. "Damn!" she swore softly and with pain. "Now all of them think Tadd is five years old instead of six."

"I know it hurts." Clara's brisk voice tried to offer comfort. "But in his way, I think your grandfather was trying to keep people from talking bad about you."

"I'm not going to live his lies!" Valerie flashed.

"You don't have to, but I wouldn't suggest going around broadcasting the truth, either," the other woman cautioned. "You might be able to ignore the gossip, even in this day and age, but there's Tadd to consider. Kids hear things and kids pick on other kids."

Valerie released a long breath in silent acknowledgement of her logic. "Where's Mickey?" she asked.

"He went out to the barn, said there was a place for him to sleep there where he could be close to the horses," Clara answered.

"I'm tired, too." Valerie felt emotionally drained, her energy sapped. Exhaustion was stealing through her limbs. She handed the letters to Clara, not caring what her friend did with them, and walked toward the stairs.

Chapter 4

A bee buzzed lazily around the wreath of flowers lying on the coffin and a green canopy shaded the mourners from the glare of the sun. Valerie absently watched the bee's wanderings. Her attention had strayed from the intoning voice of the minister. At his "Amen," she lifted her gaze and encountered Judd's steady regard. Her pulse altered its regular tempo before she glanced away. The graveside service was over and the minister was approaching her. Valerie smiled politely and thanked him, words and gestures that she repeated to several others until she was facing Judd.

"It was good of you to come." She offered him the same stilted phrase.

His carved bronze features were expressionless as he inclined his head in smooth acknowledgement. A dancing breeze combed its fingers through his black hair as he drew her attention to the woman at his side, ushering her forward.

"I don't believe you've met my mother, Valerie," he said. "This is Valerie Wentworth." That born-and-bred Southern courtesy prompted him to make the

introductions, no matter how he was feeling about
her. "My mother, Maureen Prescott."

"Hello, Mrs. Prescott." Valerie shook the white-
gloved hand, her gaze curiously skimming the woman
who'd raised him.

Petite and still pretty, she had black hair with startling wings of silver at the temples. Her eyes were an
unusual shade of turquoise green, not as brilliant as
her son's or as disconcerting. She was attractive, her
face generally unlined. She conveyed warmth and
inner strength where her son revealed cynicism. Valerie decided that Maureen Prescott was a classic steel
magnolia.

"I didn't know your grandfather that well, dear—
Judd was better acquainted with him—but please
accept my sincere sympathies," the woman offered in
a pleasant, gentle voice.

"Thank you." Valerie thawed slightly.

"If there's anything you need, please remember
that we're your neighbors." A smile curved the perfectly shaped lips.

"I will, Mrs. Prescott," she nodded, knowing it was
the last place she would go for assistance.

Others were waiting to speak to her and Judd didn't
attempt to prolong the exchange. As he walked his
mother toward the line of cars parked along the cemetery gates, Valerie's gaze strayed after them, following
their progress.

When the last of those waiting approached her,
Valerie almost sighed aloud. The strain of hearing
the same words and repeating the same phrases in
answer was beginning to wear on her nerves.

She offered the man her hand. "Good of you to
come," she recited.

"I'm Jefferson Burrows," he said, as if the name was

supposed to mean something to her. Valerie looked at him without recognition. He was of medium height, in his early fifties, and carried himself with a certain air of authority. "I was your grandfather's attorney," he explained.

"I'm pleased to meet you, Mr. Burrows." She kept hold of her fraying patience.

"Maybe this isn't the proper time, but I was wondering if I could see you tomorrow," he said.

"I'll probably be fairly busy. You see, I stored many of my personal things at my grandfather's, childhood mementoes, et cetera," she explained coolly. "I planned to sort through them tomorrow and I'll be leaving the day after to return to Cincinnati. Was it important?"

"I do need to go over your grandfather's will with you before you leave." He seemed a little irked at her question.

"There's a provision for me in his will?" Her response was incredulous and skeptical.

"Naturally, as his only living relative, you are one of the beneficiaries of his estate." His tone was reprimanding. "May I call in the morning? Around ten o'clock, perhaps?"

"Yes. Yes, that will be fine." Valerie felt a little dazed.

As she and Mickey drove away from the cemetery a short time later, she saw the attorney standing beside the Prescott car talking to Judd. She'd been convinced that she would be disinherited. Valerie had difficulty adjusting to the fact that her grandfather had left a bequest for her in his will.

It was even more difficult for her to accept the next morning after Jefferson Burrows read her the will. She stared at the paper listing assets and liabilities belonging to her grandfather and the approximate net worth of the estate. All of it, except for a cash amount to Mickey, had been left to her.

"You do understand," the attorney said, "that the values on the breeding stock and the farm are approximate market prices, but I've been conservative in fixing them. Also, this figure doesn't take into account the amount of tax you'll have to pay. Do you have any questions?"

"No." How could she tell him she was overwhelmed just at the thought of inheriting?

"You're fortunate that your grandfather wasn't one to take on a lot of debt. The only sizable one is the mortgage on the farm."

"Yes, I am." Valerie tried to answer with some degree of poise.

"I know this inheritance doesn't represent a large sum of money," he said, and she wondered what he used as a standard of measure. There was money for Tadd's education and enough left over that she wouldn't have to work for a year if she didn't want to. "But I'm sure you'll want to discuss it with your husband before you make any decision about possibly disposing of the property."

"I'm not married, Mr. Burrows." She corrected his misconception immediately.

He raised an eyebrow at that, but made no direct comment. "In that case, perhaps I should go over some of the alternatives with you. Minus taxes and the bequest to Mr. Flanners, there isn't sufficient working capital to keep the farm running. Of course, you could borrow against your assets to obtain the capital, but in doing, so, you would be jeopardizing all of what you inherited."

"Yes, I can see that," Valerie agreed, and she didn't like the idea of risking Tadd's future education.

"I would advise that you auction all the horses to eliminate an immediate drain on your limited resources and to either lease or sell the land." He began going into more detail, discussing the pros and cons of each possibility until Valerie's mind was spinning in confusion. It was a relief when he began shoving the legal papers into his briefcase. "It isn't necessary that you make an immediate decision. In fact, I recommend that you think about it for a week or two before letting me know which course of action you would like to pursue."

"Yes, I'll do that." She would need that much time to sort through all the advice he had given her.

After he had gone, she broke the good news to Clara, but even then it didn't really sink in. It wasn't until after lunch when the dishes were done and she and Tadd and Clara had walked outside that the full meaning of it struck her.

Valerie looked out over the pastures, the grazing mares and colts, the stables and barns, and the house, dazzled by what she saw.

"It's mine, Clara," she murmured. "I inherited all of this. It's really and truly mine."

"Do you mean it's yours like the car is?" Tadd asked, sensing the importance of her statement, but not understanding its implications.

"The car belongs to me and the bank," Valerie corrected him with a bright smile. "I guess the bank has a piece of this, too, but I have a bigger one."

"Does that mean we can live here?" His eyes rounded at the thought.

"We could live here if we wanted to," she agreed without thinking, since it was one of the choices.

"You're forgetting you have a job to go to in Cincinnati," Clara inserted dryly.

"I'm not forgetting." Valerie shook her head, then turned her bright gaze on the older woman. "But don't you see, Clara, I have enough money to quit?"

"La-di-dah. Now you're beginning to sound like a heiress," Clara said tartly.

"I wouldn't be able to quit working forever," Valerie conceded, "but there's enough money here to sock away for Tadd's college education and to support us for a whole year besides."

"Are we really going to live here, Mommy?" Tadd was almost jumping with excitement.

"I don't know yet, honey," she told him.

"I want to. Please, can we live here?" he asked breathlessly.

"We'll talk about it later," Valerie stalled. "You run off and play now. Don't go near the horses, though, unless Mickey is with you," she called as he went dashing off.

"You shouldn't get his hopes up," Clara reprimanded her. "You know you can't live here permanently."

"Maybe not permanently, but we could stay here through the summer." At her friend's scoffing sound, Valerie outlined the idea that had been germinating in her mind. "It would be a vacation, the first time I'd be able to be with Tadd for more than just nights and weekends. And I'd like him to know the freedom of country life."

"What would you do with yourself out here?" Clara wanted to know.

"There's a lot that could be done. First, the horses would all have to be auctioned. And Mr. Burrows suggested that I might get a better price for the farm if I invested some money in painting the buildings and fences. The lawn would need to be cleaned up and maintained. There's something to be gained from staying the summer. Besides, it would take time to sell or lease the place," she reasoned. "What are we talking about anyway? Just two and a half or three months."

"What about your job? You're supposed to be back to work on Friday," Clara reminded her.

"I know," Valerie admitted. "I'll just have to see if Mr. Hanover will give me a leave of absence until the fall."

"And if he won't?"

"Then I'll have to find another job." Valerie refused to regard this point as an obstacle. "This time I'll have enough money to support myself until I find a good one."

"Seems to me you have your mind all made up," Clara sniffed, as if offended that she hadn't been asked for advice.

"The more I think about it, the more I like it," Valerie admitted. "You could stay, too, Clara. The doctor said you'd be doing yourself a favor if you rested for a month. Why not here in the fresh air and sunshine?"

"If you're set on staying here, I might, too." There was something grudging in the reply. "I'm just not sure in my mind that you're doing the right thing."

"Give me one good reason for not staying the summer," Valerie demanded with a challenging smile.

"Judd Prescott." The answer was quick and sure.

The smile was wiped from Valerie's face as if it had never been there. "He has nothing to do with my decision!" she snapped, her eyes flashing.

"Maybe he doesn't, but he's someone you're going to have to contend with," Clara retorted. "And soon."

Her eyes narrowed, gazing in the direction of the pasture beyond Valerie.

Hearing the drum of galloping hooves, Valerie turned to see a big gray hunter approaching the yard. The rider was instantly recognizable as Judd. Alertness splintered through her senses, putting her instantly on guard.

Tossing its head, the gray horse was reined in at the board fence. Judd dismounted and looped the reins around the upright post. He crossed the board fence and walked toward the two women with an ease that said it was a commonplace thing for him to be stopping by. His arrogant assumption that he would be welcomed rankled Valerie.

"What do you want, Mr. Prescott?" She coldly attempted to put him in his place.

His hard mouth curved into a smile that lacked both humor and warmth as he stopped before her. "I have some business that I want to discuss with you."

"What business would that be?" she challenged him, her chin lifting.

His gaze skimmed her once over, taking in the crisp Levi's and the light blue print of her cotton blouse. His look didn't confirm that his purpose was business, not personal.

"I understand Mr. Burrows was here to see you this morning," he replied without answering her question.

"And where did you get that piece of information?" Valerie demanded.

"From Mr. Burrows," Judd answered complacently. His mouth twisted briefly at the flash of indignation in her look. "I asked him to call me after he'd informed you of your inheritance."

"Just what do you know about my inheritance?"

She was practically seething at the attorney's lack of confidentiality.

"That your grandfather left everything to you."

"I suppose Mr. Burrows supplied you with that information, too." Irritation put a razor-sharp edge to her tightly controlled voice.

"No, your grandfather did," Judd smoothly corrected her assumption.

"I see," she said stiffly. "Now that we have that straightened out, what did you want?"

"As I said, I have some business to discuss with you regarding your inheritance." His gaze flicked to Clara. "In private."

"There isn't anything you have to say to me that I would object to having Clara hear," Valerie stated.

"But *I* object," Judd countered. "If you want to discuss my proposal with Clara after I'm gone, that's your business, Valerie. But my business is with you and you alone."

Valerie held her breath and counted to ten. Was it really business he wanted to discuss or was this a trick to get her alone? There was nothing in his expression to tell her the answer.

"Okay," she agreed, somewhat ungraciously. "Let's walk, then. You won't have to worry about anyone eavesdropping on your oh-so-private business conversation."

"By all means, let's walk." Amusement glittered in his eyes at her sarcasm.

Valerie started off in the direction of the pasture fence where the gray hunter was tied. When they had traveled what she considered a sufficient distance, she glanced at him. "Is this far enough?"

He glanced over his shoulder at Clara, a taunting

light in his eyes when their gaze returned to Valerie. "For the time being," he agreed.

"Here we are. What's going on?" Her nerves felt as tight as a drum and the pounding of her heart increased the sensation.

"I don't know if you've had time to decide what you want to do about the farm, whether you're going to keep it or sell it," Judd began without hesitation. "I'm willing to pay whatever the market price is for the farm if you decide to sell."

So it was business, she realized, and was angered by the disappointment she felt. "I see." She couldn't think of anything else to say.

"I offered to buy the place from your grandfather, but he wouldn't sell. It isn't a money-making concern, Valerie," he warned. "Your grandfather has a good stallion in Donnybrook, but his mares are less than desirable. I tried to convince him that he should be more selective in the mares he bred to the stallion, but he needed the stud fees and couldn't afford to buy better-bred mares."

But Valerie's thoughts had strayed to another area. "Why did Granddad tell you he was leaving all this to me?"

His gaze narrowed with wicked suggestion. "Do you mean did he know that you and I were once lovers?"

She hadn't expected him to word her suspicion so bluntly. The uncomfortable rush of color to her cheeks angered her. Turning her back on Judd, she walked to the pasture fence, closing her hands over the edge of the top rail.

"Did he guess?" she demanded, letting him know that she had never told her grandfather.

"No. If he had, he'd probably have chased me off his land with a load of buckshot," he answered.

"I . . . wondered," Valerie offered in a weak explanation for her question. She didn't say anything more for a few moments and neither did he.

He cleared his throat. "Hmm. You look more like the Valerie I remember," he said softly. "Just standing there."

"So?"

"Takes me back. All that shiny hair down over your shoulders and those tight jeans that show off your perfect bottom."

If he had stripped her on the spot, Valerie couldn't have felt more naked. She pivoted around to face him, hiding the part of herself he'd mentioned from his roaming gaze. Leaning against the fence, she hooked the heel of one boot on the lowest rail.

"I think you said it was business you wanted to discuss," she reminded him with a touch of temper.

"Oh yeah." He looked amused. "Sorry. Got distracted. So. Have you given any thought to selling?"

Despite his compliance with her challenge, Valerie didn't feel much safer. "I'm considering it . . . as well as several other possibilities."

"Such as staying on here permanently?" he suggested.

"I don't think that's possible," she said, rejecting that idea with a brief shake of her head. "Like you said, the horses barely pay for themselves, so it would be difficult for me to earn a living from the farm."

"You could always sell the horses and lease all the land except the house." Judd took a step toward the fence, but he was angled away from her, posing no threat.

"I could," Valerie conceded, "but the income from

a lease wouldn't be enough to support us. I'd need a job and there aren't a whole hell of a lot of opportunities around here, especially well-paying ones. It's too far to commute to Baltimore. For that reason leasing practically cancels itself out."

"Don't be too sure that you wouldn't have enough money from a lease," he cautioned. "The right party might be willing to pay what you need."

He began wandering along the fence row, gazing out over the land as if appraising its worth. Valerie watched him, confused by the possibility he had raised. She didn't know whether he was telling her the truth or baiting her to lead her into a trap. Or had there been a hidden suggestion in his words that she hadn't caught?

Before she could puzzle it out, Judd was asking, "Do you mind if we walk on a little farther?" His sideways look held a bemused light. "I'd like to get out from underneath her eagle eye."

"Do you mean Clara?" Valerie was startled but not offended by his mocking reference to her friend. Without being aware of moving she began following him, matching his strolling pace.

"Yes," he admitted. "She's kind of a battle-ax. Reminds me of one of those warrior maidens in a German opera. All she needs are pigtails, a spear and an armored breastplate."

Valerie visualized Clara in that costume and couldn't help smiling at the image and the aptness of his description. "Does she make you nervous?" she asked.

"Not really." Judd stopped, his level gaze swinging to her with a force that rooted her to the ground. "But you—well, you're getting to me, Valerie. Big time."

His hand lifted and his fingers stroked the line of

her jaw before she could elude them. The light touch was destroying. When his fingertips traced the length of the sensitive cord in her neck all the way to the hollow of her throat, her breath was stolen by the traitorous awakening of her senses. She sank her white teeth into the softness of her lower lip, unsure whether she was about to protest or beg him to kiss her.

Taking her silence as acceptance, Judd moved closer. He hooked a finger under the collar of her blouse and followed its line to the lowest point where a button blocked his way, but not for long. A languorous warmth spread over her skin when his hand slid inside her blouse to caress the rosy skin of her breast. He bent his head to kiss the lip her teeth held captive, and they abandoned it to his sensual inspection. Her heart throbbed with aching force under his sweet mastery. Valerie trembled.

Satisfied with her initial response, Judd began nuzzling her cheek, his tongue sending shivers of raw desire through her as it licked her ear. The heady male smell of him stimulated her instinctive response. Her lips nibbled and kissed the strong, smooth line of his jaw.

"I'll lease the place from you, Valerie," Judd muttered against her cheek, "and pay you whatever you need to live on."

His offer stopped her heartbeat. "Would you visit me?" she whispered, wanting to be sure she hadn't misunderstood.

"Regularly." His massaging hand tightened possessively on her breast as he gathered her more fully into his encircling hold. He sought her lips, his warm breath mingling with hers. "Night and day."

With shattering clarity, his true proposition was brought home to her. Leasing the land was only a

means to give her money—money that would oblige
her to be available whenever he felt the urge for her
company. She inwardly reeled from the thought with
pain and bitterness.

Her lips escaped his smothering kiss long enough
to ask chokingly, "Would the lease be . . . long-term
or . . . short?"

"Any terms, I don't care." Impatience edged his
voice. "After seven years, I want to make love to you
very slowly. If that's what you want. You drive me to the
edge of control," he muttered thickly, his mouth
making another foray to her neck.

Sickened by the weakness that made her thrill to
his admission, Valerie lowered her head to escape his
insatiable kisses and strained her hands against his
chest to gain breathing room. Judd didn't object. It
was as if he knew how easily he could subdue any
major show of resistance from her.

"I'll tell you what my terms are, Judd." She lifted her
head slowly, keeping her lashes lowered to conceal the
hard look in her eyes until she was ready for him to
see it. "My terms are"—she paused, taking one last
look at her fingers spread across his powerful chest
before lifting her gaze to his face—"no terms."

As his green eyes began to narrow at her expression, she struck with feline swiftness. Her open palm
lashed across his cheek for a slap that was meant to
sting, but was immediately caught in his viselike grip.

"I won't lease you the land, the buildings, or my
body," she hissed. "You can't use me the way you
think you can!"

She tried twisting her wrist out of his hold, but Judd
wrapped it behind her back. Her other hand met the
same fate. It was as if he knew she wanted to scratch
his eyes out. She was completely trapped in the steel

circle of his arms. Damn him. A long-suppressed part of her actually liked it. A physical confrontation had a way of exciting her. But there was anger in his expression.

"Go ahead. Be a hellcat," he jeered. "You haven't changed that much in seven years. Scratch and slap if you want to, but I have a feeling that you want me to make love to you."

"No!" Valerie rushed the vigorous denial.

"You sure?" He smiled slightly as if he knew how hollow her denial was. "Okay. I won't argue," he said with infuriating complacency, and let her go. "Sooner or later you'll admit it."

Turning away smoothly, he began walking toward his horse, leaving Valerie standing there with a mouthful of angry words.

She ran after him, shaking with rage. "You'll rot in hell before I do," she told him furiously.

He flashed her a lazy, mocking look before he slipped between the rails of the board fence with an ease that belied his six-foot frame and muscled build. The tall gray horse whickered as he approached. Valerie stopped, staying on the opposite side of the fence, her hands doubled into useless fists.

Unhooking the reins from the post, Judd looped them around the horse's neck and swung into the saddle with an expert grace. The big gray bunched its hindquarters, eager to be off at the first command from its rider, but none came. Judd looked down at Valerie from his high vantage point in the saddle.

"I meant it when I said I wanted to buy this place," he said flatly. "If you decide to sell, I want you to know my interest in purchasing it is purely a business one. No other consideration will enter into the negotiations for the price."

"I'm glad to hear it." She struggled to control her temper and sounded cold as a result. "Because any offer from you with strings attached will be rejected out of hand!"

His half smile implied that he believed differently. If there had been anything within reach, Valerie would have thrown it at him. Before she could make a withering comment to his look, her attention was distracted by the sound of someone running through the tall pasture grass.

It was Tadd, racing as fast as his short legs could carry him straight toward Judd. A breathless excitement glowed in his face, the mop of brown hair swept away from his forehead by the breeze that had sprung up.

"Is that your horse?" The shrill pitch of his voice and his headlong flight toward the horse spooked the big gray. It plunged under Judd's rein, but its dancing hooves and big size didn't slow Tadd down. "Can I have a ride?"

"Tadd, look out!" Valerie shouted the warning as the gray horse reared. It looked as if Tadd was going to run right under those slashing hooves.

In the next second he was scooped off the ground and lifted into the saddle, Judd's arms around his waist. Her knees went weak with relief.

"Hasn't your mother taught you that you don't run up to a horse like that?" Judd reprimanded the boy he held, but Valerie noticed the glint of admiration in his look because Tadd hadn't been afraid. "It scares them. You have to let them know you're near and walk up slowly."

"I'll remember," Tadd promised, but with a reckless smile that reminded Valerie of Judd. "Will you give me a ride? I've never been on a horse before."

"You're on one now," Judd pointed out. "What do you think of it?"

Tadd leaned to one side to peer at the ground, his eyes rounded when he straightened back up. "It's kind of a long way down, isn't it?"

"You'll get used to it." Judd lifted his gaze from the dark-haired boy to glance at Valerie. "I'll give him a short ride around the pasture."

"You don't have to," she replied stiffly, and tried to figure out why she resented that Tadd was having his first ride with Judd, his father, and not her. "And it won't get you anywhere with me."

A dangerous glint appeared in his look. "Until this moment that hadn't occurred to me. I have a pack of nieces and nephews who are always begging for rides, and I put your son into their category. Sorry I can't admit to a more devious motive. I bet you're disappointed."

Their exchange went right over Tadd's head. The boy couldn't follow it, but he had caught one of the things Judd had said. "Are you going to really give me a ride?" he asked.

"If your mother gives her permission," Judd told him, issuing a silent challenge to Valerie.

At the beseeching look from her son, she nodded her head curtly. "You have my permission."

"Thank you," Judd said mockingly as he reined the spirited gray away from the fence.

At a walk, they started across the grassy field. Tadd laughed and nearly bounced out of the saddle when the horse went into a trot, but he didn't sound or look the least bit frightened. After making a sweeping arc into the pasture, Judd turned the horse toward the fence and cantered him back to where Valerie was waiting.

With one hand, he swung Tadd to the ground. "Remember what I told you. From now on, you'll *walk* up to a horse." Tadd gave him a solemn nod of agreement. With a last impersonal glance at Valerie, Judd backed his mount away from the small boy before turning it toward its home stables.

"Come on, Tadd," Valerie called to him. "Let's go to the house and have something cold to drink."

He lingered for a minute in the pasture watching Judd ride away, a sight that pulled at Valerie, but she resisted it. Finally he ran toward her and Valerie wondered if he knew any other speed. He ducked under the fence as if he had been doing it all his life. He skipped along beside her, chattering endlessly about the ride.

"Where did you two disappear to?" Clara asked when Valerie reached the house. Her question bordered on an accusation.

"I went for a ride," Tadd sang out his answer, unaware he wasn't the second person Clara had meant.

"We just walked along the fence," Valerie answered, realizing a bushy shade tree had blocked her and Judd from Clara's sight.

"What was his business?" Her tone was skeptical that there had been any.

"He offered to buy the place," Valerie answered, and murmured to herself, "among other things."

Chapter 5

After much discussion and debate, Valerie persuaded Clara that the three of them should spend the summer on what was once her grandfather's farm. She refused to be intimidated by having Judd as a neighbor. This was the only chance she would ever have to show her son what it had been like for her to grow up in this house. And it might be the only time she would have to devote solely to Tadd while he was still a sweet little boy and not a sullen teenager.

Eventually she swayed Clara into going along with her. Once the agreement had been reached, they had to tackle the problem of arranging things in Cincinnati for an absence of possibly three months.

Clara's married sister agreed to box up and send both of them more clothes from the apartments, forward their mail, and see that everything was locked up. Valerie called in her request to her employer for an extended leave of absence and chickened out by saying it on voicemail. Her boss called back in person to tell her she was fired. Not a surprise, as Clara had warned. But all in all, the arrangements were made with minimal complications.

And then there was the decision of what to do about the farm and consultation with Jefferson Burrows, the attorney. At the end of the following week Valerie came to the decision she'd known all along she would have to make. After confiding in Clara, she sought out Mickey at the stables. No matter what, she intended to do right by him.

Valerie got right to the point. "I wanted to let you know, Mick, that I've decided to sell the farm."

Sitting in the shade of the building, cleaning some leather tack, the retired jockey didn't even glance up when she made the announcement. He spat on the leather and polished some more. "Then you'll be selling the horses?" he asked.

She nodded, waiting for the right moment to discuss her provisional plans for him. "Yes, I'll have to."

"Since you're not keeping the place, you'll be better off to sell them soon," Mickey advised. "Were you going to have an auction?"

"Yes. Mr. Burrows, the lawyer, said if I decided to sell the horses, an auction could be scheduled within two weeks," she explained.

"It won't give you much time to do very much advertising," he shrugged, "but word has a way of getting around fast among the horsey set. I'm sure you'll have a good turnout. As soon as you set the date, I'll call some of my friends in the business and start spreading the word."

"Thanks, Mick."

"It's the least I can do. There is one thing, though." He put the halter aside and stood up. "You see that bay mare grazing off by herself?"

Valerie glanced toward the paddock he faced and saw

the bay mare he meant, a sleek, long-legged animal with a chestnut brown coat with black points.

"She's a beauty," Valerie commented in admiration.

"Don't put Ginger in the auction," Mickey said. "She's the best get out of old Donnybrook, but she's barren, no good for breeding at all. Got no speed, but she's a good hack, might even make it as a show jumper. But you'd never get your money's worth out of her in a breeding sale. If I was you, I'd advertise her as a hunter and try to sell her that way."

"Thanks, I'll do that," she promised. His thoughtfulness and ready acceptance of her decision made her feel a little guilty. This farm and these horses were practically like his own. He had lived here and taken care of all the animals here, many of them since the day they were foaled. Now they were being sold and he was out of a job and a place to live, even though she was going to do her utmost to see that neither would happen. Then it occurred to her that the ever-resourceful Mickey might have made plans of his own. "What will you do, Mickey? Where will you go?"

"Don't worry about me, Valerie," he laughed. "I've had a standing offer from Judd for years to come to work for him taking care of his young colts. He claims that I'm the best he's ever seen at handling the young ones."

The mention of Judd's name made her glance toward the paddock again to conceal her expression. "Judd wants to buy this," she said.

"Are you going to sell it to him?" he asked, not surprised by her statement.

"It depends on whether or not I get a better offer than his." Common sense made her insist that it didn't matter who ultimately purchased the property. She wouldn't be here when they took possession.

"If Judd has set his mind on buying it, he'll top any reasonable offer you get," Mickey grinned. "'Cause once he makes up his mind he wants somethin', he seldom lets anything stand in his way till he gets it."

It was a statement that came echoing back a week later. Valerie was walking out of the bank in town just as Judd was coming in. Courtesy demanded that she speak to him, at least briefly.

"Hello, Judd." She nodded with forced pleasantness, and would have walked on by him, but he stopped.

"Hello, Valerie. I saw the auction notice." His tone sounded only conversational.

"For the horses? Yes, in less than two weeks from now," she admitted. He was inspecting her in way that was a little too personal. Valerie had the feeling a strap was showing or something, and her hand moved protectively to the elastic neckline of the peasant-styled knit top. "Is something wrong?" she asked a bit sharply.

"You look different with your hair fixed like that," Judd answered. It was pulled away from her face into a loose chignon at the back of her head.

"It's a very warm day. I feel cooler if my hair is away from my neck," Valerie replied. As if her change of hairstyle required an explanation.

"Kind of severe. It isn't exactly you," he commented in a knowing voice. Without skipping a beat, he continued, "I guess you'll be leaving after all the legal arrangements are completed after the auction, huh?"

"We're staying a little longer." She didn't see the

need to tell him she would be there for the summer. He would discover it soon enough, so there was no point in informing him in advance.

"We?" A jet-dark brow lifted.

"Yes—Tadd, Clara and myself," Valerie admitted.

"So the old battle-ax isn't leaving either." Something about the way he said it was oddly respectful. Then his manner became withdrawn. "I must be keeping you from your errands. Will you be at the auction?"

"Yes." She was puzzled by his behavior and curious as to why he hadn't mentioned anything about buying her land.

"I'll probably see you there," he said.

Valerie had the feeling she was being brushed off. "Probably," she answered with a cool smile, her chin lifted stiffly, then walked away.

Between that brief meeting in town and the auction, she didn't see Judd. She ignored the knotting ache in her stomach and told herself she was glad she had finally convinced him that she wanted nothing to do with him. She was positive Judd had only pursued her at the beginning of her return because he had thought she would be easy. Now he knew differently. She wasn't easy and she wasn't available.

But the way her heart catapulted at the sight of his familiar figure in the auction crowd made a mockery of her silent disclaimers of interest in him. It was difficult to admit, even to herself, that she was still half in love with him.

The stable and house yard was jammed with cars, trucks and horse trailers. There seemed to be an ocean of buyers, lookers and breeders. Around the makeshift auction ring was an encircling cluster of people jostling to get a look at the brood mare up for bids.

Valerie looked for Tadd and saw him firmly holding on to Mickey's hand, as if concerned he might get separated from his friend in the shuffle of people. Another look found Judd working his way through the crowd toward the trailer being used as the auctioneer's office.

A horse neighed behind her, a nervous sound that betrayed its agitation at the unusual commotion going on around it. Valerie turned to watch a groom walking the horse in a slow circle to calm it, crooning softly. All the horses looked sleek and in excellent condition, thanks to Mickey's unstinting efforts.

She glanced back to the auction ring where the auctioneer was making his pitch in a rhythmic, droning voice. She walked in the opposite direction to the relative peace and quiet of the stables. Here the fever pitch of activity was reduced to a low hum. The grooms Mick had handpicked for the day prepared the brood mares and colts for the sale.

The warm air was pungent with the smell of horses. Straw rustled beneath shifting feet. Valerie wandered down the row of stalls, pausing to stroke the velvet nose thrust out toward her. She stopped at the paddock entrance to the barns and gazed out over empty pastures.

"It looks strange, doesn't it, not to see any mares grazing out there with their foals," Judd commented.

Accurate mind-reading. Valerie jumped at the sound of his voice directly behind her. "You startled me," she said accusingly.

"Sorry," he offered, but she doubted that he meant it. "Is the auction going well?"

"So far," she answered with a shrug, and turned to look out the half door to the pasture. "It's bedlam out there," she said to explain her reason for escaping to the barns.

"Lots of buyers send the prices up," Judd reminded her. "And from the sound of the bidding on the number-fourteen mare, Misty's Delight is going to bring top dollar."

"Misty's Delight," Valerie repeated, and released a short, throaty laugh. "When I saw the names on the sale catalogue, I didn't know any of the horses. Granddad called that mare by the name of Maude. As far as I'm concerned, they aren't selling Black Stockings. They're auctioning Rosie, or Sally or Polly."

"Yes, I'm glad your grandfather isn't here. Those mares were his pets, and the stallion, Donnybrook, was the most precious to him of them all," Judd admitted.

"If Granddad were here, there wouldn't be a sale. There wouldn't be any need for one," Valerie sighed, and turned away from the empty paddocks. "But there is. And I'm selling. And I'm not going to have any regrets," she finished on a note of determination.

"Have you listed the farm for sale yet?" he asked, taking it for granted that she was selling it.

Since it was true, she didn't see any point in going into that side issue. "In a way," she answered, and explained that indecisive response. "It won't officially be listed for another couple of weeks."

"Why the delay?" He studied her curiously.

"I had a couple of appraisals from two local real estate agents," Valerie began.

"Yes, I know," Judd interrupted. "I saw them, and I'm prepared to buy it for two thousand more than the highest price they gave you."

She took a deep breath at his handsome offer and nibbled at her lip, but didn't comment on his statement. "They suggested I'd be able to get about five thousand more if I painted all the buildings. So I'm going to take some of the profits from the horse sale and have everything painted."

"I'll match that, and you can forget about the painting," he countered. "I'd just have to do it all over again in the Meadow Farms colors."

Leaning back against a wooden support post, Valerie eyed him warily, unable to trust him. She knew how vulnerable she was; she had only to check her racing pulse to be reminded of that. So she was doubly cautious about becoming involved in any dealings with him.

"Tell me the truth, Judd. Why are you so determined to buy Worth Farms?" she demanded, her mouth thinning into a firm line.

A brow arched at her challenge as he tipped his head to one side, an indefinable glint in his eyes. "Why are you so determined to believe that I have some reason other than business?"

"Don't forget that I know you, Judd Prescott," she countered.

The corners of his mouth deepened. "You know me as intimately as any woman ever has, considerably more so than most." He taunted her with the memory of their affair.

Her cheeks flamed hotly as conflicting emotions churned inside of her. "I meant that I know you as a man—"

"I should hope so," Judd drawled, deliberately misinterpreting her meaning.

"In the general sense," she corrected in anger.

"That's a pity." He rested a hand on the post she was leaning against, but didn't move closer. "Meadow Farms needs your grandfather's acreage, the pastures, the grass, the hay fields. The stables and barns can be used for the weanlings and the yearlings. The house can be living quarters for any of my married help who might need it. If the old battle-ax had inherited it, I would still want to buy it. Got that clear, Valerie?" His level gaze was serious.

"Yes," she nodded, a stiff motion that held a hint of resentment.

"Good." Judd straightened, taking his hand from the post and offering it to her to seal their bargain. "Have we got a deal?"

"Yes." Wary, Valerie hesitated before placing her hand in his and added the qualification, "On a strictly business level."

"Strictly business." He gripped her hand and let it go, a faint taunting smile on his lips. "Let's leave the details to our respective attorneys. We've agreed on the price, so the only thing left is for me to pay you the money for your signature deeding the land to me."

"There's just one thing," Valerie added.

"Oh? What's that?" Judd asked with distant curiosity.

"I'm not giving you possession of the house until the first of September. The barns, the stables, the pastures, everything else you can have when we sign the papers, except the house," she told him.

"And why is that?" He seemed only mildly interested.

"Because that's how long we'll be staying. I want to have this summer with Tadd," Valerie explained with a trace of defensiveness. "With working and all, I haven't been able to spend much time with him up until now. He's been growing up with babysitters. I've decided to devote this summer to him and begin working again this fall when he goes back to school."

"In that case, the house is yours until the first of September," Judd agreed with an indifferent shrug. "Are there any other conditions?"

"No." She shook her head, her long toffee hair swinging freely around her shoulders.

"Then everything is all settled," he concluded.

"I guess it is."

It all worked as smoothly as Judd had said it would. The matter was turned over to their attorneys. There wasn't even a need for Valerie to see Judd. When all the estate, mortgage and legal matters were completed, Jefferson Burrows brought out to the house the papers she needed to sign and gave her a check. The property became Judd's without any further communication between them and the documents gave her possession of the house until the first of September. It really was strictly business.

Something jumped on her bed, but the mattress didn't give much under its weight. "Mom? You'd better get up," Tadd insisted.

Valerie opened one sleepy eye to look at her son and rolled onto her stomach to bury her head under a pillow. "It's early. Go back to sleep, Tadd."

His small hand shook her bare shoulder in determined persistence. "Mom, what's that man doing on a ladder outside your window?" he demanded to know.

"A ladder?" she repeated sleepily, and lifted her head from under the pillow to frown at the pajama-clad boy sitting on her bed. "What are you talking about, Tadd?"

His attention was riveted on her bedroom window. A scraping sound drew her bleary gaze as well. The sleep was banished from her eyes at the sight of a strange man wearing paint-splattered white overalls standing on a ladder next to her window.

"What's he doing there, Mom?" Tadd frowned at her.

There wasn't a shade at the window, nothing to prevent the man from looking in and seeing her. Valerie was angered by the embarrassing situation she was in. She tugged the end of the bedspread from the foot of the bed and pulled it with her. It was white chenille with a pink rose design woven in the center. She sat up on the side of her bed with her back to the window.

She picked up the old-fashioned alarm clock ticking away on the small table. Its hands pointed to seven o'clock. She began wrapping the bedspread sarong-fashion around her, fighting its length as her temper mounted. Pushing her sleep-rumpled hair away from one side of her face and tucking it behind her ear, she rose from the bed.

Tadd followed. "What's he doing there?" he repeated.

"That's what I'm about to find out!" she snapped, flinging a corner of the bedspread over her shoulder in a gesture unconsciously reminiscent of a caped crusader.

She stalked to the staircase and hitched the bedspread up around her ankles to negotiate the steps. Part of the bedspread trailed behind her like a train and she had to keep yanking it along to prevent Tadd from tripping on it.

As she slammed out of the screen door onto the porch, another white-clad stranger was walking by carrying a stepladder. At the sight of Valerie, he stopped and stared.

"Would you mind telling me what's going on here?" she demanded, ignoring his incredulous and slightly ogling look. "And where are you going with that ladder?"

"Don't get mad at me, ma'am." The man backed away, absolving himself of any blame. "I just do what I'm told. The boss said to come here and I'm here."

"Where is your boss? I want to speak to him." Valerie forgot to hitch up the spread before starting down the porch steps, and nearly tripped.

"He . . . he's on the other side of the house," the man stuttered as one side of the spread slipped, revealing the top swell of one breast but not the nipple before Valerie tucked the material back in place.

She had taken one step in the direction the flustered man had indicated when she heard the cantering beat of horse's hooves and looked around to see Judd riding up on the big gray. She stopped and glanced back at the man.

"You can go on about your business now," she snapped.

"Yes, ma'am!" He scurried off as if he had been shot.

Tadd stood on the porch, one bare foot resting on top of the other. He was watching the proceedings with innocent interest, curious and wide-eyed. Like his mother, his attention had become focused on Judd, who was dismounting to walk to the house. Valerie stepped forward to confront him.

"Care to explain what these men are doing here at this hour of the morning?" she demanded, red in the face with annoyance.

"I came by to let you know I'd hired a contractor to paint the place. I think I'm a little late." As he spoke, his gaze was making a leisurely inspection from her tousled mane of honey-dark hair down her bedspread-wrapped length and returning for an overall view of her improvised cover-up.

At the touch of his green-eyed gaze on her bare

shoulder and its lingering interest on the point where
the white material barely covered her breasts, Valerie
tugged the spread more tightly around her. She realized he was very much aware that she was naked beneath it.

"A little late? That's a major understatement," she
fumed. "I woke up this morning to find a man outside my bedroom window on a ladder!"

"If I'd known you slept naked, I would have been
the man on the ladder outside your window," Judd
drawled with soft suggestiveness.

An irritated sound of exasperation came from her
throat. "You're impossible. And you can just quit
smirking. I'll speak to the contractor myself and tell
him to come back at a decent hour!" As she started to
take a step, her leg became tangled in the folds of the
bedspread.

Judd reached out with a steadying hand on her arm.
"I think you'd better go back into the house before you
trip and reveal more of your charms than you'd like."
He lifted her off her feet and into his arms before she
realized his intention. The bedspread swaddled her
into a cocoon that didn't lend itself to movement.

"Put me down!" Valerie raged in fiery embarrassment.

A lazy smile curved his mouth as he looked down
at her. "I hired house painters, not artists. Not that I
wouldn't object to having a private portrait of you."

She caught sight of Tadd staring at them with open-
mouthed amazement. "Stop it," she hissed at Judd,
and he just chuckled, knowing she was at his mercy.

"Will you open the door for me, Tadd?" he requested in an amused voice as he carried Valerie
onto the porch.

Tadd scampered forward in his bare feet to comply,

staring at his mother's reddened face as Judd carried her past him. He followed them inside, letting the screen door close with a resounding bang. In the entry hall Judd stopped.

"Now will you put me down?" Valerie demanded through clenched teeth, burning with mortification and a searing awareness of her predicament.

"Of course," he agreed with mocking compliance.

The arm at the back of her legs relaxed its hold, letting her feet slide to the floor while his other hand retained a light, steadying grip around her waist. Having both feet on the floor didn't give Valerie any feeling of advantage. Without shoes, the top of her head barely reached past his chin. To see his face, she had to tip her head back, a much too vulnerable position. She chose instead to glare upward through the sweep of her lashes.

"I think it would be wise if you put some clothes on," he suggested dryly as his gaze swung downward from her face, "or at least rearrange your sarong so that pink rose adorns a less eye-catching spot."

Checking to see that Tadd wasn't looking, Judd traced the outline of a rosebud design on the chenille bedspread. In doing so, he drew a circle around the hard button of her breast. Heat raced over her skin as Valerie jerked the bedspread higher, pulling the rose design almost to her collarbone. Judd chuckled for the second time, knowing full well what a touch like that did to her.

Spinning away from him, Valerie lifted the folds of the material up around her knees and bolted for the staircase. On the second step she stopped, remembering the predicament that awaited her upstairs. She sent an angry look over her shoulder.

"You go out there and tell that painter to get away

from my window!" she ordered in an emotion-choked voice.

"I'll have him on the ground at once." Judd grinned at her, laughter putting a wicked twinkle in his eyes.

Valerie glanced at the boy standing beside him. "Tadd, you come with me," she commanded. "It's time you were dressed, too."

Reluctantly Tadd moved toward the stairs. As Judd started toward the door, Valerie began climbing the steps to the second floor. Clara met her at the head of the stairs, her nightgown ruffling out from beneath the hem of her quilted robe.

"What's all the commotion about?" Clara ran a frowning look over Valerie's attire. "And what are you doing dressed like that?"

"Mr. Prescott neglected to inform us that he'd hired some painters to come out to the farm," was the short-tempered reply. "I woke up to find one outside my window on a ladder."

Bunching the spread more tightly around her hips, Valerie started toward her bedroom.

"I've told you about going to bed like that," Clara's reproving voice followed her. "I warned you that someday there'd be a fire or something and you'd be caught!"

Valerie stopped abruptly to make a sharp retort and Tadd, who was following close behind her, bumped into her. Her hand gripped his shoulder to steady him and remained there as she sent Clara a look that would have withered the leaves off a mighty oak. But Clara was made of stronger stuff.

Swallowing the remark she had intended to make, Valerie muttered, "You're no help, Clara," and glanced at the small boy. "Come on, Tadd. Let's get you dressed first."

Altering her course, she pushed Tadd ahead of her to her old bedroom that Tadd now occupied. While she went to the dresser to get his clean clothes, Tadd padded to the window and peered out.

"I don't see those men anymore, Mommy. Judd made them go away," he told her.

"Good. Now off with those pajamas and into these clothes," she ordered.

When Tadd was dressed, Valerie sent him downstairs and went to her own room. She made certain there wasn't a painter anywhere near the vicinity of her window before getting dressed herself. When she came downstairs she walked to the kitchen where the aroma of fresh coffee wafted invitingly in the air.

Tadd was sitting at the breakfast table. An elbow was resting on the top and a small hand supported his forehead, pushing his brown hair on end. A petulant scowl marked his expression.

"Mom, Clara says I have to drink some of my milk before I have another pancake." He glared at the stout woman standing at the stove. "Do I have to? Can't I drink it afterward, Mom? Please?"

Valerie glanced at the glass of white liquid that hadn't been touched. "Drink your milk, Tadd."

"Aw, Mom!" he grumbled, and reached for the glass.

"Don't fix any pancakes for me, Clara." Ignoring her son, Valerie walked to the counter and poured a cup of coffee. "I'm not hungry."

"You'd better eat something," the woman insisted.

Before Valerie could argue the point, there was a knock on the back door and a taunting voice asked, "Are you decent in there?"

"Yes!" Valerie shot the one-word reply at the wire mesh where Judd's dark figure was outlined, and carried her cup to the table.

The hinges creaked as the screen door opened and Judd walked in. "Hey, that coffee smells good," he remarked. After one quick look at Valerie's still simmering expression, he addressed his next words to Clara. "Mind if I have a cup?"

"Help yourself," the woman agreed with an indifferent shrug.

As he walked to the counter on which the coffeepot sat, Valerie watched the easy way he moved. His broad shoulders and chest, his narrow male hips, and the muscled columns of his long legs moved in perfect harmony. His body was programmed and conditioned to perform every task well. An ache quivered through her as Valerie remembered how well.

Pausing at the stove, Judd observed, "Pancakes for breakfast. Buckwheat?"

"Yes." Clara expertly flipped one from the griddle.

"Help yourself, Judd," Valerie heard herself offering in a caustic tone born out of a sense of inevitability. In an agitated desire for movement she rose from her chair to add more coffee to her steaming cup. "Orange juice. Bacon. Toast." She looked at her son, who fortunately didn't seem to be listening. "Just help yourself to anything."

"Anything?" The soft, lilting word crossed the room to her. She pivoted and caught her breath as his gaze leisurely roamed over her shape to let her know his choice.

Valerie felt as if her toes were curling from the heat spreading through her. She turned away from his sex-charged look and breathed an emotionally charged, "You know very well what I meant." Adding a little more coffee to her cup, Valerie silently acknowledged that she didn't have many defenses against him left, certainly none when the topic became intimate. She attempted to change it. "Did you straighten those painters out about starting work at such an ungodly hour?" she demanded.

"In a manner of speaking," Judd replied, casually accepting the change in subject. "They started early to avoid working in the heat of the day. Unfortunately, they were under the impression that all the buildings were vacant, including the house. They know better now," he added with a sugar-coated smile.

Aarrgghh.

Valerie didn't need to be reminded of the early-morning episode. He hadn't answered her first question, which prompted her to ask, "You did arrange for them to begin work at a more respectable hour, didn't you?"

"No," he said. "There isn't any reason to change that—"

"No reason?" she began indignantly.

But Judd continued, "However, from now on they'll be working on the barns and stables in the mornings."

"I should hope so," Valerie retorted tightly.

"I drank some of my milk," Tadd piped up, a white mustache above his upper lip. "Can I have another pancake now?" Clara set another one in front of him. As Tadd reached for the syrup, he glanced at Judd. "They're really good. Do you want one?"

"No, thanks. I already had my breakfast." Judd drained the last of the coffee from his cup. "It's time I was leaving. If the painters give you any trouble, Valerie, call me."

"I will," she agreed, but she could have told him that the only one who gave her trouble was himself. He troubled her mentally and emotionally, and there didn't seem to be any relief in sight.

Chapter 6

A restlessness raced through Valerie. She tried to contain it as she had for the last several days, but it wouldn't be suppressed. There had been too much time on her hands lately, she told herself. She was accustomed to working eight hours, coming home and working hours more with meals, housework and laundry. But here the workload of the house was shared with Clara and she had no job except to play with Tadd.

One of the painters had brought along a blaring boombox and the raucous music scraped at her nerves. Of the half dozen men painting the barns and stables, there always seemed to be one walking around, getting paint, moving ladders, doing something, which was more than Valerie could say for herself.

Sighing, she left the porch and entered the house. Clara was in the living room, watching her favorite soap opera. Her gaze was glued to the TV and she didn't even glance up when Valerie entered the room.

"Clara," Valerie began, only to be silenced by an

upraised hand. A couple of minutes later a commercial came on and she was allowed to finish what she had started to say. "I'm going to take Ginger out for a ride. Tadd is upstairs having a nap. Will you keep an eye on him while I'm gone?"

"Sure. Go ahead," her friend agreed readily.

Outside, Valerie dodged the gauntlet of ladders and paint cans to retrieve the bridle and saddle from the tack room. Several people had come to look at the bay mare Mickey Flanners suggested she sell privately, but so far no one had bought her. Valerie didn't mind. One horse wasn't that difficult to take care of and Tadd enjoyed the rides she took him on.

The bay mare trotted eagerly to the pasture fence when she approached. Lonely without her former equine pals, the mare liked human company. There was never any difficulty catching her and she accepted the bit between her teeth as if it were sugar.

Astride the animal, Valerie turned the brown head toward the rolling land of the empty pasture. The mare stepped out quickly, moving into a brisk canter at a slight touch from Valerie's heel. She had no destination in mind. Her only intention was to try to run off the restlessness that plagued her.

The long-legged thoroughbred mare seemed prepared to run forever, clearing pasture fences like the born jumper Mickey had claimed she was. Valerie rode without concentrating on anything but the rhythmic stride of the animal beneath her and the pointed ears of its bobbing head.

When the bay horse slowed to a walk, Valerie wasn't aware that it was responding to her pressure on the reins. They entered a stand of trees and she ducked her head to avoid a low-hanging branch. When she straightened, it was in a clearing. Her fingers tightened on the reins, stopping the bay.

Without thinking she had guided the mare to the place where she and Judd had met. From a long-ago habit, she dismounted and wound the reins around the broken branch of a tree. The mare lowered her head, blew at the grass and began to graze.

Almost in a trance, Valerie looked around her. The place hadn't seemed to change very much. The grass looked taller and thicker, promising a softer bed. She tore her gaze from it and noticed that lightning had taken a large limb from the oak tree some time ago.

Wrapping her arms tightly around her middle, she tried to assuage the hollow ache. She felt a longing for Judd so intense that it seemed to eat away at her insides. She wanted to cry from the joy she had once known here and the heartache that had followed, but no tears came.

It was crazy—it was foolish—it was self-destructive to want him. She was so successful at stimulating his lusty appetite . . . why hadn't she ever been able to arouse his love? That feeling had reawakened. She was so filled with love that she thought she would explode.

The bay mare lifted her head, her ears pricking. Her sides heaved with a long, questioning whicker. Then the soft swish of grass behind her made Valerie turn as a big gray horse stopped at the edge of the clearing and Judd dismounted. He walked toward her with smooth, unhurried strides. Her heart lodged somewhere in the vicinity of her throat. She was unable to speak, half afraid that she'd discover she was dreaming.

But his voice was no dream.

"I knew you'd come here sooner or later, Valerie."

Neither was the smoldering light in his green eyes as he came closer. The instant he touched her, Valerie was convinced it wasn't a dream and she knew she didn't dare stay.

"It was an accident," she insisted, her breath quickening. "I didn't mean to."

She tried to push out of his arms and make her way past him, but a sinewed arm hooked her waist and pulled her against his side. A muscled thigh brushed her legs apart to rub against her, while the hand at the small of her back pressed her close to him. His fingers cupped the side of her face and lifted it for inspection.

"Ever since the day you returned, I knew you would eventually." His gaze roamed possessively over her features. "You can't fight it any more than I can. It's always been that way with us."

"Yes." Her whispered agreement carried the throb of admission.

As his mouth descended on hers, Valerie realized his persistence had finally eroded her resolve. The surroundings, her love, the feel of him were more than she could withstand and she surrendered to the pulsing fire of his embrace.

Her lips parted under the insistence of his. His practiced hands molded her more fully against his length, but this closeness only heightened their mutual dissatisfaction with their upright position.

Burying his face in the curve of her neck, Judd swept her into his arms and carried her the few feet to the grassy nest. Kneeling, he laid her upon it, lifting the heavy mass of tawny hair and fanning it above her head. Her hands were around his neck to pull him down beside her, part of his weight crushing her.

"I've waited a long time to see that honey hair on

that green pillow." His husky voice vibrated with passion. "And to see that look in your eyes."

His mouth kissed the hollow of her throat as his skilled fingers unbuttoned her blouse. His hand wandered over the bareness of her waist and taut stomach. Its leisurely pace sent a languorous feeling floating through her limbs. His mouth trailed a fiery path to intimately explore the rounded softness of her breast. Her nails dug into the rippling muscles of his back and Judd brought his hard lips back to hers. More of his weight moved onto her.

He rubbed his mouth against the outline of her lips. "There were times when I wondered whether I had the control or the patience to wait for you to come here," he admitted. "I knew you'd been hurt and used badly. But I was also positive that I could make you forget the man who got you pregnant and ran off."

"Forget?" Her breathless laugh was painful and bitter, because he had made her forget. With a twist, she rolled from beneath him and staggered to her feet, shakily buttoning her blouse. "How could I forget?" That question was directed to herself. Then she turned her face to him. "You are that man, Judd."

Stunned silence greeted her tautly spoken announcement. Then Valerie heard him rise and a steely hand hooked her elbow to spin her around. His blazing green eyes burned with fury.

"What are you saying?" Judd ground out savagely.

"You're Tadd's father," she informed him with flashing defiance. "I was almost three months pregnant when I left here seven years ago. Granddad threw me out because I wouldn't tell him who the father was. Yes, it was you!"

"If it's true, why didn't you come to me seven years ago and tell me you were pregnant?" Judd demanded.

"*If* it's true?" Valerie repeated with a taunting laugh. "You just answered your own question, Judd. You're the one and only man who has ever made love to me. Not that it meant a whole hell of a lot to you."

"That isn't true!"

"Isn't it?" she mocked. "I wasn't about to endure the humiliation of telling you and watch you try to deny it."

"I would have helped you," Judd replied grimly.

"What would you have done?" Valerie challenged. "Given me money for an abortion? Or told me to stay away? You made me feel small enough without taking money from you."

"I never guessed you felt that way." A muscle in his jaw was flexing.

"I don't think you ever considered the possibility that I had feelings," she retorted. "You didn't exactly pay attention to things like that."

"If I ever—"

She interrupted him again. "Listen to me for once—I mean *really* listen. I'm a human being with feelings and a heart, Judd. I'm not made of stone like you. Look—I even bleed." She scratched her nails across the inside of her arm, tiny drops of red appearing in the welts.

He caught at the hand that had marked her. "Are you crazy?" he growled, and yanked her into his arms. He held her tightly against him, his chin touching the top of her head.

For an instant Valerie let herself enjoy the hard comfort of his arms before she rebelled. "Let me go, Judd!" She strained against his hold. "Haven't you done enough damage?"

He partially released her, keeping one arm firmly around her shoulders as he drew her along with him. "Come on."

"No!" She didn't know where he was taking her. Stopping in front of the bay mare, Judd lifted her into the saddle. "I'm taking you back," he said, and handed her the reins.

"I can find my own way," she retorted. "I always did before."

His hand held the mare's bridle, preventing Valerie from reining her away. "This time I'm going with you," he stated.

"Why?" Valerie watched him with a wary eye when he walked to the big gray.

Judd didn't respond until he had mounted and ridden the high-stepping gray over beside her. "I'd like to have another look at my son."

Her fingers tightened on the reins and the mare tossed her head in protest. "Tadd is mine. You merely fathered him. He's mine, Judd," she warned.

He didn't argue the point and instead gestured for her to lead the way to her grandfather's farm, one that Judd now owned. They cantered in silence, their horses skittish and nervous, picking up the tenseness of their riders.

Tadd had awakened from his nap when they arrived. He didn't rush out to greet Valerie, but remained sitting on the porch step, sulking because she had gone riding without him. Valerie was nervous as she walked to the house with Judd. Tadd was no longer just another little boy to him. He was his son, and Judd's green eyes were studying, inspecting and appraising the small boy.

"Did you have a good nap, Tadd?" Valerie asked with forced brightness.

"Why didn't you wait until I was up and take me for a ride?" he pouted.

"Because I wanted to go by myself," she answered, and promised, "You and I can go later this afternoon."

"Okay," Tadd sighed, accepting the alternative, and glanced at Judd. "Hello. How come you were riding if Mom wanted to be by herself?"

"We happened to meet each other while I was on my way here," Judd explained easily, his attention not wavering from Tadd's face.

"Were you coming over here to tell those men to go away?" Tadd wondered. "There hasn't been any man outside Mommy's window since that other day. But one of them gave me a paintbrush—I'll show you." In a flash, he was on his feet and darting to the far end of the porch.

Judd slid a brief glance in Valerie's direction. "Have you told him anything about . . . his father?" he asked quietly.

"No." She shook her head.

But his voice hadn't been that low for Tadd not to have picked up a little of the conversation. He came back, holding up a worn-out brush that hadn't been used in some time. The bristles were stiff and broken.

As he showed it to Judd, he glanced up. "I don't have a father. Do you?"

Judd's dark head lifted in surprise. Valerie couldn't tell whether it was from Tadd's directness or what. Emotion softened the tone of his voice.

"Yes, I had one, but he died a long time ago," Judd admitted, and tipped his head to one side to study Tadd more closely as he asked, "Did your father die?"

"No. I just don't have a dad," Tadd repeated with childlike patience. "Some kids don't, you know," he informed Judd with blinking innocence. "Three of the kids I go to school with don't have dads. Of course, Cindy Tomkins has two. Her mom married twice." He lost interest in that subject. "It's a pretty cool brush, isn't it?"

"It sure is," Judd agreed.

"I wanted to help them paint, but they said I couldn't. They said I was too little." Tadd's mouth twisted, his expression indicating it was a statement he had heard many times before. "I'll be seven on my next birthday. That isn't too little, is it?"

"I think you have to be ten years old before you can be a painter," Judd told him.

Valerie's nerves were wearing thin. There wasn't much more of this conversation she could tolerate. Judd had seen Tadd again and talked to him. Wasn't that enough?

"Tadd, run into the house and see if there's a carrot in the refrigerator for Ginger. I think she'd like one," she suggested.

"Okay." He started to turn and stopped. "Can I feed it to her?"

"Of course," she nodded, and he was, off, slamming the screen door and tearing through the house to the kitchen.

Feeling the scrutiny of Judd's eyes, her gaze slid from his direction.

"He isn't too familiar with the birds and the bees, is he?" Judd commented dryly. "Some children don't have a father," he repeated Tadd's statement. "Is that what you told him?"

"No, it's a conclusion he's reached all on his own. He has a general idea about where babies come from, but not all the details," Valerie admitted, a shade defensively.

"What are you going to do when he wants to know more?" His level gaze never wavered from her. "What will you tell him when he asks about his father?"

"When he's old enough to ask the question, he'll be old enough to understand the truth," she retorted, knowing it was a day she didn't look forward to.

The sound of racing feet approached the porch in advance of the screen door banging open. "I got the carrot!" Tadd held it up. "Can I give it to Ginger now?"

At the nod from Valerie, Tadd started down the porch steps. As he went past Judd, he was cautioned, "Remember, Tadd, walk up to the horse."

With a carefree, "I will!" Tadd raced full speed halfway across the yard, then stopped to walk the rest of the way to the pasture fence where the bay mare was tied. Valerie watched him slowly feed the gentle mare.

"I feel that I owe you something for these last seven years," Judd said.

"You don't owe me anything." She shrugged away the suggestion. His words stung.

"I mean it, Valerie. I want to take care of you and Tadd," he stated in a firm tone.

The full fury of her sparkling eyes was directed at him. "I wouldn't take your money then, Judd, and I won't take it now."

Instead of being angry, Judd looked almost amused by her fiery display. His gaze ran over her upturned face, alight with temper and pride.

"You're like a tigress," he murmured. "Defending your cub. It's admirable in a way, but all this doesn't change anything."

Unable to hold that look, Valerie glanced away. She

seemed incapable of resisting him, but she tried anyway. "Yes, it does."

"Valerie." His voice commanded her attention. When she didn't obey, his fingers caught her chin and turned her to face him. "It isn't any use fighting it."

"I've made up my mind, Judd," she insisted stiffly. "I won't be your lover. Please! Just leave me alone."

His mouth slanted in a wry smile. "Do you think I haven't tried?" he mocked, and kissed her hard. When he straightened, he murmured, "And tell that battle-ax that it's rude to eavesdrop." With that, he turned and walked across the yard to where the gray hunter was standing next to Valerie's mare.

The screen door opened and Clara stepped out. "Humph!" she snorted. "So it's rude to eavesdrop, is it? What do you suppose they call what he was proposing?"

"You shouldn't have been listening," Valerie said, and continued to watch Judd, who had stopped to say goodbye to Tadd.

"You shouldn't carry on private conversations where people can overhear," Clara retorted. "So you decided to tell him he was Tadd's father, did you?"

"Yes," Valerie admitted.

"What do you suppose he's going to do about it?"

"There isn't anything he can do. Tadd is mine. Judd knows that," Valerie insisted.

"Mark my words, he'll figure out a way to use it to his advantage. Judd Prescott is a tenacious man." There was a hint of admiration in Clara's voice as they both watched him ride away.

Chapter 7

Judd came over twice more that week, ostensibly to check on the progress of the painting crew, but that possessive light was in his eyes whenever his gaze met Valerie's. It held a warning or a promise, depending on her mood at the time. His attitude toward Tadd remained relatively casual, a little more interested and occasionally warmer at different moments.

Valerie was in the kitchen helping Clara wash the breakfast dishes when a car drove into the yard. The painting crew had finished the day before, so she knew it wasn't one of them. As she walked to the front door, she wiped her hands dry on the towel and wondered if the lawyer, Jefferson Burrows, had more papers for her to sign.

Judd's visits had always been made on horseback. It didn't occur to her that the car might be driven by him. Not until she saw him step out. Tadd was outside playing and immediately stopped what he was doing to rush forward to greet Judd.

After glancing toward Valerie standing on the porch, Judd directed his attention to the boy skipping along beside him. His hair gleamed jet black in the sunlight, with Tadd's a lighter hue. "Do you have any-thing planned to do today?" Judd asked him.

"Mom and me are going riding later on," Tadd an-swered after thinking for a minute.

"That's something you could do tomorrow if you have a place to visit today, isn't it?" Judd suggested. Valerie felt a tiny leap of alarm.

"I guess so," Tadd agreed, then frowned. "But we don't have a place to visit." The frown lifted. "How come you drove a car? Are you going to take us some-place?"

"I might," was the smiling response.

"Tadd, come into the house and wash your hands!" Valerie called sharply.

With a gleeful expression, Tadd came bounding to the porch, hopping excitedly from one foot to the other. "Mom, did you hear? Judd said he might take us someplace."

"Yes, I heard what he said." She sent Judd an angry look and attempted to smile at her son. "Go into the house and wash your hands as you were told."

"Find out where we're going!" Tadd called over his shoulder, and hurried into the house.

Descending the porch steps, Valerie walked out to confront Judd. "Why did you tell Tadd we might be going someplace with you?" she demanded angrily. "It isn't fair to get a little boy's hopes up like that."

"Why?" He returned her look with feigned inno-cence. "I came over to ask you and Tadd to spend the day with me. There's a tobacco auction over by Loth-ian, probably one of the last of the season. I thought Tadd might find it interesting."

"I'm sure he would find it very interesting, but we aren't going," she stated flatly. "And you shouldn't have let Tadd think we would."

"How did I know you'd refuse?" He smiled lazily. "I hadn't even asked you yet when I mentioned it to him."

"You knew very well I'd refuse!" she snapped.

"Temper, temper."

"Of course I'm angry," Valerie argued defensively. "You tend to make me the villain as far as Tadd's concerned, do you know that?"

"You could always change your mind and agree to come with me," he reminded her.

"You know I won't."

"Yes, you will." His level gaze became deadly serious. "Otherwise I'll have to have a talk with Tadd and tell him who his father is."

Valerie paled. "You wouldn't do that!" she protested. "He wouldn't understand. He'd be hurt and confused. You wouldn't be that ruthless."

"I'll get my way, Valerie." It wasn't an idle warning. "Will you come or shall I have a talk with Tadd?"

Tears burned the back of her eyes and she bit the inside of her lip to keep it from quivering. She had known he could be hard, and not above using people to get what he wanted, and he'd already made it plain that he wanted her.

"If I agree to come, will you give me your word to say nothing to Tadd about being his father?" she demanded tightly.

"You have my word," Judd agreed, "if you come."

"I . . . I'll need a few minutes to change my clothes," Valerie requested.

His skimming gaze conveyed the usual message that he preferred her without any, but he said, "Take all the time you need. I'll be waiting."

Frustrated, Valerie ground out, "You can wait until

hell freezes over and it still won't do any good."
Turning on her heel, she rushed into the house.

Fifteen minutes later she emerged cool and composed in a yellow-flowered cotton sun dress. Tadd's
face and hands had been scrubbed and inspected by
Clara, his shirt and pants changed to a clean set. Valerie couldn't help thinking that the three of them
probably looked like the ideal American family, leaving on a day's outing to a traditional tobacco auction
in Lothian, Maryland.

She felt a little guilty about the tobacco part, but it
wasn't like Tadd was going to take up smoking in the
sixth grade or something. It hurt to know that they
would never be a family in the legal sense, but Tadd's
steady stream of chatter didn't give Valerie any time
to dwell on that.

The sights, sounds and smells of the tobacco auction proved to be as fascinating to Valerie as they were
to Tadd. Various grades of Maryland tobacco were
sold off in lots. The practiced cadence of the auctioneer's voice rang through the area, the slurring words
punctuated by a clear "Sold!" at the end. The summer
air was aromatically pungent with the smell of stacks
of drying tobacco leaves. Colors varied from dark gold
to brown.

They wandered around the auction area and
strolled through the warehouse. Tadd saw most of the
scene from Judd's shoulders. They had a cold drink
beneath a shade tree.

Later, Judd drove to a park and they picnicked
from a basket his mother had packed. Through it all,
Judd was at his charming best and Valerie found herself succumbing to his spell as if she didn't have
better sense.

She took his hand, accepted the arm that occasionally

encircled her shoulders, smiled into the green eyes that glinted at her, and warmed under the feather kisses Judd would bestow on the inside of her wrist or her hair. In spite of her better judgment, she relaxed and enjoyed his company, flirting with him and feeling carelessly happy all the while.

As they lingered at the picnic area, Judd peeled an orange and began feeding her sections while Tadd played on the swings. Each time a bead of juice formed on her lips, he kissed it away. Then Tadd came over and demanded his share of the attention by handing Judd an orange to peel for him.

When they started back in the early afternoon, Valerie was too content to care that it would soon be over. She closed her eyes and listened to the mostly one-sided conversation between Tadd and Judd. A faint smile tugged at the corners of her mouth.

The miles sped away beneath the swiftly turning tires. Valerie guessed that they were almost home, but she didn't want to open her eyes to see how close they were. A large male hand took hold of one of hers. Her lashes slowly lifted to watch Judd carry it to his mouth, kissing the sensitive palm. His gaze left the road in front of him long enough to send one lazy, sweeping glance at her.

"Did you enjoy yourself today?" he asked softly.

"Yes, very much," she admitted.

Tadd, who couldn't be silent for long, cried, "Look at all the horses, Mommy!"

Dragging her gaze from Judd's compelling profile, she glanced out of the window. The familiar black fences of Meadow Farms were on either side of the car. She sat up straighter, realizing Judd had turned off the road that would have taken them to her grandfather's old farm.

"Where are we going?" she asked. There was only one destination possible at the end of this lane: the headquarters of Meadow Farms.

"Are we going to see the horses?" Tadd asked, leaning over the seat.

"There's someone who wants to see you," Judd answered, glancing in Tadd's direction.

"See me?" His voice almost squeaked in disbelief. "Who?"

"Who?" Valerie echoed the demand, a quiver of uncertainty racing through her.

"Mickey Flanners," Judd answered. "When I mentioned I'd be seeing you today, he asked me to bring you over if we had time."

"I haven't seen Mickey in a long time," Tadd declared in a tone that exaggerated the time span.

"That's what he said," Judd slowed the car as the lane split ahead of them.

In one direction were the stables and barns of the thoroughbred breeding farm; in the other was the main house in which the Prescotts lived. Judd made the turn in the latter direction. Valerie, who had relaxed upon learning it was Mickey Flanners they were going to see, felt her nerves tensing a little.

The lane curled into a circular driveway in front of a large, pillared house, glowing white in the bright afternoon sunlight. To Valerie, it appeared the embodiment of gracious living, a sharp contrast to the simple farmhouse in which she was raised.

"Is *this* where Mickey lives?" Tadd asked in an awed voice.

"No, this is where I live," Judd explained, stopping the car in front of the main entrance to the house. He glanced at Valerie and saw the hesitation in her gold-flecked eyes. "I'll be on my mother's black list if

I don't stop at the house first so she can say hello to you and Tadd."

"Judd, really . . ." Valerie started to protest, but it was too late.

The front door of the house had opened and Judd's mother was coming out to greet them, petite and striking with those angel wings of silver in her dark hair. The white pleated skirt and the blue and white polka-dot top with a matching short-sleeved jacket in blue that Maureen Prescott wore was so casually elegant that Valerie felt self-conscious about her own simple cotton sun dress.

"There she is now." Judd opened his door and stepped out.

It wasn't manners that kept Valerie inside the car. The magnificent house, the beautifully landscaped grounds, the status attached to the Prescott name, and the woman waiting on the portico warned her that she was out of her league.

Her door was opened and Judd stood waiting, a hand extended to help her out of the car. She turned her troubled and uncertain gaze to him. He seemed to study it with a trace of amusement that didn't make her feel any more comfortable.

"What happened to my tigress?" he chided softly. "You look like a shy little kitten. Come on." He reached in and took her hand to draw her out of the car.

Once she was standing beside him, Judd retained his hold of her hand. Valerie absorbed strength from his touch, but the twinges of unease didn't completely go away. It seemed like a very long way from the car up the walk to the steps leading to the columned portico. To cover her nervousness, Valerie straightened, her chin lifted a fraction of an inch higher than normal, her almond gold eyes wide and proud.

Tadd didn't appear to suffer from any of his mother's self-consciousness. He skipped and hopped, turned and looked, and generally let his curiosity take him toward everything there was to see. He wasn't shy at all when a woman he didn't know walked forward to meet them.

"Hello, Valerie. I'm so glad you were able to stop in," Judd's mother greeted her warmly, a smile of welcome curving her mouth.

"Thank you, Mrs. Prescott," Valerie answered, and suddenly wished that Judd would let go of her hand, but he didn't.

"Please call me Maureen," the other woman insisted with such friendliness that Valerie was reminded her reputation as hostess was without equal.

This open acceptance of her only made Valerie more uneasy. "That's very kind of you . . . Maureen." She faltered over the name.

Maureen Prescott either didn't notice or overlooked Valerie's nervousness as she turned to Tadd, bending slightly at the waist. "And you must be Tadd."

The boy nodded and asked, "How did you know me?"

The woman's smile widened. "I've heard a lot about you."

"Who are you?" Tadd wanted to know.

"I'm . . . Judd's mother."

Did Valerie imagine it or had there been a pulse beat of hesitation before Maureen Prescott had explained her relationship? Then Valerie realized she was being ridiculously oversensitive to the situation.

"Say hello to Mrs. Prescott, Tadd," Valerie prompted her son.

Dutifully he extended a hand to the woman facing him and recited politely, "Hello, Mrs. Prescott."

"Mrs. Prescott is quite a mouthful, isn't it?" The teasing smile on Maureen's lips was warm with understanding. "Why don't you call me Reeny, Tadd?" she suggested.

"Reeny is what my nieces and nephews call her," Judd explained quietly to Valerie. "When they were little, they couldn't pronounce her given name so they shortened it."

Valerie was uncomfortably aware that Tadd had been given permission to use the same name that the other grandchildren called their grandmother. She felt a warm flush of embarrassment in her cheeks. Did Maureen Prescott know Tadd was her grandchild? Had Judd told her?

Almost in panic, she searched the woman's face for any indication of hidden knowledge. But the turquoise eyes were clear and tranquil. A tremor of relief quaked through Valerie. She wasn't sure she could have handled the situation if this gentle woman had known the truth.

"Reeny is easy," Tadd said. "I can remember that."

"I'm glad you like it, Tadd." Maureen Prescott straightened and cast an apologetic smile at Judd. "Frank Andrews called and left a message for you to phone him the instant you came back." With a glance at Valerie, she added, "It seems every time a person tries to set aside a day strictly for pleasure, something urgent like this crops up."

Valerie's head moved in a polite nod of understanding before a slight movement from Judd drew her attention. A grim resignation had thinned his mouth and added a glitter of impatience in his eyes.

"I'm sorry, Valerie," he said in apology for the intrusion of business. "But it'll only take a few minutes to phone him."

"That's all right. Go ahead," she insisted, and un-
tangled her fingers from the grip of his to clasp her
hands nervously in front of her.

"While Judd is making his phone call, you and
Tadd can come with me. After that long drive, I'm
sure you're thirsty. I have a big pitcher of lemonade
all made and some cookies," Judd's mother said.

"No, thank you, Mrs. Prescott . . . Maureen," Valerie refused quickly, and reached for Tadd's hand.
"It's very kind of you, but Tadd and I will walk down
to the stables and find Mickey."

"You'll do no such thing, Valerie." Judd's low voice
rumbled through the air. His look held a silent warning not to persist in her refusal of the invitation. "I'll
be through in a few minutes to take you myself. In
the meantime, I'm sure that Tadd"—his gaze flicked
to the boy—"would like to have some cookies and
lemonade. How about it, Tadd?"

"Yes." The response was quick and without hesitation, followed by an uncertain glance at Valerie.
"Please," Tadd added.

"Okay," Valerie agreed, smiling stiffly, and added a
defensive, "If you are sure we're not putting you to
any trouble."

"None at all," Judd's mother assured her, and
turned to walk toward the front door.

Judd's fingers gripped Valerie's arm as he escorted
her up the steps to the portico. At the wide double
entrance to the house, he let her go to open the
door for his mother, then waited for her and Tadd to
precede him inside.

"Excuse me." Almost immediately upon entering,
Judd took his leave from them. "I won't be long." His
look warned Valerie that he expected to find her in
the house when he was finished.

"We'll be on the veranda, Judd," his mother told him.

Valerie watched him walk away, skittishly becoming conscious of the expansive foyer dominated by a grand staircase rising to the second floor. The foyer was actually an enormous, wide hallway splitting the house down the center with rooms branching off from it.

Furniture gleamed with the rich-grained luster of hardwood, adorned with vases of flowers and art objects. Valerie took a tighter grip on Tadd's hand, knowing she couldn't afford to replace anything he might accidentally break. It was a stunning, beautifully decorated home, elegance blended with comfort, like something out of the pages of a magazine.

"We'll go this way." Maureen Prescott started forward to lead the way, the clicking sound of her heels on the white-tiled floor echoing through the massive house.

"You have a lovely home." Valerie felt obliged to make some comment, but her tone made the compliment sound uncertain.

"It's a bit intimidating, isn't it?" the woman laughed in gentle understanding. "I remember the first time Blane, Judd's father, brought me here to meet his parents. It was shortly after we'd become engaged, and the place terrified me. It was much more formal then. When Blane told me that we would live here after we were married, I wanted to break the engagement, but fortunately he talked me out of that."

Maureen Prescott's instinctive knowledge of Valerie's reaction allowed her to relax a little. It was comforting to know that someone else had been awed by this impressive home.

"The house is at its best when it's filled with people, especially children," Maureen continued in an affectionate voice. "It seems to come to life then. When my five were growing up, the house never seemed big enough. Sounds hard to believe, doesn't it?"

"A little," Valerie admitted.

"They seemed to fill every corner of it with their projects and pets and friends. That reminds me—" She glanced down at the brown-haired boy trotting along beside Valerie. "There's something outside that I want to show you."

"What is it?" Tadd asked, his eyes rounding.

"You'll see," Maureen promised mysteriously, and paused to open a set of French doors onto the veranda. As she stepped outside, she called, "Here, Sable!"

A female German shepherd with a coat as black and sleek as its name came loping across the yard, panting a happy grin, tail wagging. Ten roly-poly miniatures of her tumbled over themselves in an effort to catch up with their mother.

"Puppies!" Tadd squealed in delight and followed Maureen Prescott to the edge of the veranda. Sable washed his face with a single lick before greeting her mistress. Tadd's interest was in the ten little puppies bringing up the rear. "Can I play with them?"

"Of course." The instant she gave permission he was racing out to meet the pups. When he kneeled on the ground, he was immediately under siege. Valerie joined in with the older woman's laughter as Tadd began giggling in his attempts to elude ten licking tongues. "Puppies and children are made for each other," Maureen declared in a voice breathless from laughter. "Come on, let's sit down and have that drink I promised you. I don't believe Tadd will be interested in lemonade and cookies for a while."

"I'm sure he's forgotten all about it," Valerie

agreed, and followed the woman to a white wrought-iron table with a glass top.

A pitcher of lemonade sat in the center, condensation beading moisture on the outside. Four glasses filled with ice surrounded it as well as a plate of chocolate drop cookies with frosting on the top. Valerie sat down in one of the white wrought-iron chairs around the table, plump cushions of green softening the hard seats.

"Tadd is really enjoying himself. The apartment where we live in Cincinnati doesn't allow pets, so this is a big treat for him," Valerie explained, taking the glass of lemonade she was handed and thanking her.

"Misty, my second daughter, lives in a complex that doesn't allow animals, either, and her children are at an age when they want to bring home every stray cat and dog they find. She and her husband have had a time keeping them from sneaking one in. I think their love of animals is part of the reason they come home to Meadow Farms so often. There's Sable and her puppies, the horses, and cats at the barns. But I don't mind what their reason is," Maureen insisted. "I just enjoy having them come. Although it's quite a houseful when they're all here at once."

"Are all your children married?" Valerie asked politely.

"Yes, with the exception of Judd, of course," Maureen answered with a smiling sigh. "There have been times when I've wondered if my firstborn was ever going to get married, but I've never said anything to him."

"I'm sure there are any number of women who would like to." Valerie kept her tone casual, careful not to make it sound as if she was one of them.

"That's the problem—there've been too many

women," Maureen Prescott observed with a trace of sad resignation. "The Prescott name, the wealth and his good looks—Judd gets a little too much attention. I'm afraid it's made him feel very cynical about the opposite sex."

"I can imagine," Valerie agreed and sipped at the tart, cold liquid in her glass.

"Yes, I've often teased him that I don't know if he's more particular about matching the bloodlines of his thoroughbreds or finding a compatible bloodline for a wife. He always answers that if he ever finds a woman with breeding, spirit and staying power, he'll marry her. Of course, we're both joking." His mother qualified her statement with a dismissing laugh.

Maybe Maureen was teasing, but Valerie wouldn't be surprised to discover that Judd wasn't. She knew how cold-blooded he could be about some things . . . and how hot-blooded about others.

She wondered whether Judd's mother was subtly trying to warn her that she wasn't good enough for her son. Not that it was needed. Valerie had long been aware of Judd's low opinion of her, an opinion she sometimes forgot, as she had earlier that day. That feeling of unease and a panic to get away came over her again. She had to change the subject, find a way not to discuss Judd.

Her gaze swung over the lawn, and she got a glimpse of a swimming pool behind some concealing shrubbery. "You must enjoy living here, Mrs. Prescott. It's peaceful, yet with all the conveniences."

"Yes, I love it here," Maureen agreed. "But you must call me Maureen. I learned that there were two requirements to enjoy living here the first year I was married. You have to like country life and you have to *love* horses. Fortunately I managed to fulfill both. The only objection I have is at weaning time when the mares and foals are separated. It tears at my heart to hear them calling back and forth from the pastures to each other. I usually arrange to visit my youngest son, Randall, and his family in Baltimore then. Judd insists that it's silly and impractical to be upset by it, but then he isn't a mother."

The veranda door behind Valerie opened. She glanced over her shoulder, her heart skipping madly against her ribs as Judd's gaze slid warmly over her. Why couldn't she stop loving him? She had admitted to herself only a moment ago that it was no good.

Smiling crookedly, he walked to the table. "I told you I wouldn't be long." He glanced to the lawn where Tadd was still playing with the puppies, with Sable lying in the grass and looking on maternally. "Looks like Tadd's having a great time. What have you two been doing?"

"Gossiping about you, of course," his mother replied.

"I didn't realize you gossiped, mother." His comment held a touch of dry mockery.

"I'm human," she said in explanation. "Would you like some lemonade?"

"Sure, I'll have a glass. Thanks." Judd pulled one of the chairs closer to Valerie and sat down. His hand rested on the back of her chair, a finger absently stroking the bare skin of her shoulder. She felt that quivering ache to know the fullness of his caresses and had to move or betray that need.

"Tadd's been so busy playing with the puppies he hasn't had time for lemonade," said Valerie, rising from her chair. "I think I'll see if he wants some now."

Avoiding the intensity of Judd's green eyes, she walked to the edge of the veranda. All but one of the puppies had grown tired and rolled into sleepy balls on the lawn.

"Let the puppies rest for a while, Tadd," she called. "Come and have some lemonade and cookies."

"Okay," he agreed, and stood up, hugging the last puppy in his arms as he started toward the veranda. The mother dog rose, made a counting glance at the sleeping litter, and pricked her ears toward Tadd.

"Leave the puppy there, Tadd," Valerie told him. "Sable wants to keep them all together so they won't accidentally get lost."

Glancing over his shoulder, Tadd saw Sable looking at him and reluctantly put the puppy onto the grass. The puppy didn't seem sure what it was supposed to do, but its mother trotted over, washed its face and nosed it toward the others. Tadd ran to the veranda at his usual warp speed. He stopped when he reached Valerie, his face aglow, happiness beaming in his expressive eyes.

"Did you see the puppy? He likes me, Mom," he informed her with an eager smile.

"I'm sure he does." She tucked his shirt inside his pants and brushed at the bits of grass on his clothes. Finished, she poked a playful finger at his stomach. "How about some cookies and lemonade for that hole in your tummy?"

"Okay." Tadd skipped alongside of her to the table, hopping onto one of the chairs and resting his elbows on the glass-topped table.

Maureen Prescott gave him a glass of lemonade and offered him a cookie. He took one from the plate. "Are all those puppies yours, Reeny?" He used the nickname without hesitation.

"I guess they are," she answered with a smile.

"You're lucky." Tadd took a swallow from the glass

as Valerie sat down in her chair, moving it closer to the table to be out of Judd's reach, a fact he noted with an amused twitch of his mouth. "I wish I could have one puppy," Tadd sighed, and licked at the frosting on the cookie.

"I'm afraid they aren't old enough to leave their mother yet," Maureen Prescott explained.

"Are you going to keep all of them?" His look said that would be greedy.

"No, we'll keep one or two and find good homes for the others," the woman admitted. "But not for another two or three weeks."

"We have a good home, don't we, Mom?" Tadd seized the opportunity.

"No, not exactly, Tadd," Valerie said. "Those puppies are going to grow into big dogs like their mother. They need lots of room. Besides, you know that pets aren't allowed where we live."

"Your mother's right," Judd said as Tadd scowled. "A puppy needs room to run. You really should live in the country to have a dog like Sable, somewhere like your great-grandfather's farm. Maybe then you could take one of the puppies."

Valerie shot him an angry look. She recognized Judd's ploy for what it was and resented his using Tadd's desire for a puppy as a wedge to get what he wanted. Predictably, Tadd latched onto the idea.

"But we already live there." He turned an earnest, beseeching look on Valerie.

"Only until the end of the summer," she reminded him.

"Why can't we stay there forever? Then I could have my puppy," Tadd argued, forgetting the cookie he held.

"Because we don't own the place." She felt the lazy

regard of Judd's green eyes and knew he was enjoying the awkward situation she was in. "Eat your cookie before you make a mess."

"We don't own the apartment in Cincinnati, either," Tadd pointed out. "So why can't we stay here?"

"Because I have to work. I have a job, remember?" Valerie tried to be patient and reasonable with his demands, knowing she shouldn't let him get under her skin.

"No, you don't. You got fired—I heard you tell Clara," he retorted.

"We'll discuss this later, Tadd," she said firmly. "Finish your cookie."

For a minute he opened his mouth to continue his stubborn argument, but the warning look Valerie gave him made him take a bite of the cookie. Tadd was wise enough to know that arousing his mother's temper would accomplish nothing.

"I'm sorry, Valerie," Maureen Prescott sympathized with her dilemma. "It isn't easy to say no to him."

"It isn't," she agreed, and flashed a look at Judd. "But it's a word you learn when you become an adult, sometimes the hard way."

A dark brow flickered upward in a faintly challenging response, but Judd gave no other sign that he had received her veiled message. Tadd washed his cookie down with lemonade and turned to Judd.

"Are we going to see Mickey?" he asked.

"Whenever you're ready," Judd conceded.

Tadd hopped off the chair, not even cookies and lemonade keeping him seated for long. "Maybe we can look at the horses, too," he suggested.

"I think Mickey's planned to show you around and meet the new horses he's looking after." Judd rose from his chair when Valerie did. She avoided the hand that would have taken possession of her arm, and walked to Tadd.

"Thank you for the lemonade and cookies, Mrs . . . Maureen," she said.

"Yes, thank you," Tadd piped his agreement.

"You're very welcome. And please, come any time," the other woman insisted generously.

"Maybe I could play with the puppies again," Tadd suggested, looking up at Valerie.

"We'll see," she responded stiffly and pushed him forward.

"It's shorter to cut across the lawn," said Judd with a gesture of his hand to indicate the direction they would take.

Despite Valerie's efforts to keep Tadd at her side, he skipped into the lead and she was forced to walk with Judd. She was aware of the way he shortened his long strides to match hers. She made no attempt at conversation, unable to avoid his nearness. It wreaked havoc on her senses.

At the barns, they had no trouble finding Mickey. He appeared from one of them as they arrived. He hurried toward them, his bowed legs giving a slight waddle to his walk. Tadd ran forward to meet him.

"Hello, Valerie. How have you been?" Mickey greeted her with his usual face-splitting grin.

"Fine," she responded, a little of her tension easing. "Tadd's missed you."

"I've missed him, too." Mickey glanced down at the boy holding his hand. "Come on, lad. I want you to see some of the finest-looking horseflesh there is in this part of the world. You've got to learn to know a great horse when you see one if you want to work with horses when you grow up."

"I do." Tadd trotted eagerly beside him as Mickey

turned to retrace his path to the stable. "I'm going to have a lot of animals when I grow up—horses and dogs and everything."

Valerie followed them with Judd remaining at her side. She glanced at his rugged profile through the sweep of her gold-tipped lashes. The hard sensuality of his features attracted her despite her anger.

"It wasn't fair of you to tempt Tadd with a puppy," she protested in a low, agitated breath.

Judd's gaze slid lazily down to her face. "All's fair," he countered smoothly.

In the shade of the stable overhang, Valerie stopped. "While we're swapping clichés, the end does not justify the means," she said sharply.

Judd stopped, looking down at her in a way that heated her flesh. "You can justify any means if you want something badly enough—and you know what I want."

The message in his eyes seemed to cut off her breath. She could feel the powerful undertow of desire tugging at her, threatening to drag her under the control of his will. She felt powerless to resist.

Farther down the stable row, Tadd glanced over his shoulder at the couple lagging behind. "Mom, are you coming?" he called.

Her breath came in a rush of self-consciousness. "Yes, Tadd," she answered, and turned to catch up with them.

"You can't run away from it," Judd's low voice mocked her disguised flight. He lingered for an instant, then moved leisurely to follow her.

Chapter 8

The quartet led by Mickey Flanners had made almost a full tour of the brood farm, impressive in its efficiency. Nothing had been overlooked, especially in the foaling barn, a facility that Valerie was sure had no equal.

The tour had paused at a paddock fence where Tadd had climbed to the top rail to watch a pair of galloping yearlings cavorting and kicking up their heels. From the stud barns came the piercing squeal of a stallion answered by the challenging scream of a second. Valerie glanced toward the sound, noticing Judd had done the same.

A frown flickered across his face, followed by a smile of dismissal. "Sounds like Battleground and King's Ruler are at it again. They're always feuding with each other across the way."

Valerie nodded in silent understanding. Stallions were often jealously competitive. The instinct within them to fight to protect their territory was strong, which was why they had to be kept separated by the strongest of fences. With Judd's explanation echoing in her mind, she ignored the angry exchange of whistles that had resumed.

A muffled shout of alarm made Judd turn around. More shouts were followed by a flurry of activity around the stud barn. A grimness claimed his expression. "Back in a sec," he said without glancing at her.

His long, ground-eating strides were already covering the distance to the stallion pens before either Valerie or Mickey thought to move. Tadd followed curiously after them, sensing something different in the air.

When Valerie reached the barrier of the first stud pen, she felt the first sickening jolt of danger. The two stallions were locked in combat, rearing, jaws open and heads snaking for each other's jugular vein. The clang of steel hooves striking against each other vibrated in the air amid the blowing snorts and rumbling neighs. Stablehands were warily trying to separate the pair. The blood drained from her face as she saw Judd wading into the thick of it.

"Stop him, Mickey!" she breathed to the ex-jockey beside her.

"Are you crazy?" he asked in disbelief. "Judd isn't going to stand by and watch his two prize stallions kill each other."

She could hear him snapping orders to coordinate the efforts. Fear for his safety overpowered her and she turned away. "I can't watch." Valerie knew what those murderous hooves could do. They were capable of tearing away hunks of human flesh, exposing the bones. "Tell me what happens, Mickey." She closed her eyes, but she couldn't shut her ears to the sounds. "No, I don't want to know," she groaned, and remembered Tadd.

She reached for him, trying to hide his face from

the sight, but he tore out of her arms. "I want to see, Mommy!" he cried fearlessly, and raced to Mickey's side.

Valerie felt sick with fear. The turmoil within the stud pen seemed to go on without end. Her eyes were tightly closed, her back to the scene as she prayed desperately that Judd would be unharmed. She didn't possess the strength for anything else. Fear had turned her into jelly.

"Hot damn! He did it!" Mickey shouted, and danced a little jig, stopping at the sight of Valerie's ashen face as she collapsed weakly against a fence post. "Hey, Valerie—" His voice was anxious with concern. "It's over."

"Judd . . . ?" was all she could manage as a violent trembling seized her.

"He's fine." Mickey said it as though she shouldn't have thought otherwise. Tipping his head to one side, he looked up at her, smiling in gentle understanding. "You're still in love with him, aren't you?" he commented.

She nodded her head numbly before catching the phrasing of his question. "How . . ." she began, but her choked voice didn't seem to want to work.

"I noticed all those rides you were taking seven years ago and the look that was in your eyes when you came back. I knew the reason why," Mickey explained softly. "And I happened to notice that Judd was taking rides the same time you were. I just put two and two together." At the apprehensive look in her eyes, he answered her unspoken question. "Your grandad didn't know and I didn't see where it was my place to enlighten him. There was enough grief around the place after you left without adding to it."

A sense of gratitude rippled through her and she

smiled weakly. Her stomach had finally begun to stop its nauseous churning, but her legs were still treacherously weak. She gripped the fence tightly for support as Mickey turned away. She didn't guess why until she heard Judd's grim voice speaking as he approached them.

"I've fired the new guy, Rathburn. The stupid fool had to clean King's paddock, so he put the stallion in the one next to Battleground and didn't check the gates," Judd said with ruthless scorn for the guilty man's incompetence. "Battleground has some wicked-looking cuts. The vet is on his way, but you'd better see if you can give Jim a hand, Mick."

"Right away." The ex-jockey moved off at a shuffling trot.

"That was awesome!" Tadd said excitedly.

"Is that right?" Judd's voice sounded weary but amused.

Valerie didn't find anything humorous about the near disaster that could have ultimately crippled horse and man. Glancing over her shoulder, she cast Judd an accusing look. His white shirt was stained with dirt and sweat, and a telltale scattering of horse hairs showed he had put himself in as much danger as his stablehands.

"You could have been killed or maimed!" A thin thread of her previous fear ran through her hoarse voice.

His gaze narrowed on her in sharp concern. "You look like a ghost, Valerie," Judd said. "Tadd, run and get your mother some water. Be quick."

His hand gripped the boy's shoulder and sent him speeding on his way. Then he was walking to her. Valerie turned toward the fence, relieved that he had come away unscathed, frightened by what might have happened, and weak with her love for him. His hands spanned her waist to turn her from the fence and make her face him.

"And you told me to go to hell. More than once. Guess you didn't mean it," Judd said.

"No, I didn't," Valerie protested with pain. "Don't tease me like that!"

"Why? Do you really care what happens to me?" His voice was dry and baiting.

"Yeah. I do." What was the use in denying it? Her downcast gaze noticed the smear of red blood on the sleeve of his shirt. It was horse blood. At the sight of it, her hands spread across his chest to feel the steady beat of his heart. She swayed against him, the side of her cheek brushing against the hair-roughened chest where his shirt was unbuttoned. She wished she had some of his indomitable strength. "I don't want to care, but I do," Valerie admitted in an aching breath.

His arms tightened around her in a crushing circle. The force of it tipped her head back and his mouth brushed her cheekbone.

"You're mine, Valerie," he growled in possession. "You belong to me."

"Yes." It was inevitable. She had to agree.

"There'll be no more talk about you leaving in September," Judd warned.

"No." Valerie surrendered to his demand. "I mean yes."

With that final acquiescence, his mouth sought and found her parted lips. He kissed her deeply, savoring this moment when she had yielded to his will and admitted what she couldn't hide. He stirred her to passion, creating a languorous flame that ravished her. She pressed herself to his length, wanting to fire his blood as he had hers, consoled by the sudden, bruising demand of his mouth that told her he couldn't resist her, either.

"Mommy?" Tadd's anxious voice broke the spell. She tore her lips from the satisfaction of Judd's kiss. Her dazed eyes focused slowly on the small boy running toward them. "Reeny's bringing the water. Mommy, are you all right?"

Judd's body was shielding Valerie from the view of both the boy and the woman hurrying behind him. With some reluctance Judd relaxed his hold and let Valerie's feet rest firmly on the ground, instead of just her toes. His green eyes blazed over her face in promise and possession, letting her see he didn't welcome the interruption before he turned to meet it. A supporting arm remained curved across her back and waist, keeping her body in contact with his side.

"What's happened, Judd?" His mother hurried forward, a glass of water in her hand.

Her gaze flicked from her son to Valerie, and Valerie guessed that Maureen Prescott had recognized that embrace for what it had been. She blushed.

"I heard an uproar down around the stallion barns, then Tadd came running to the house talking about horses fighting and Valerie needing water. I didn't know whether to listen to him or call an ambulance."

Judd explained briefly about the stallion fight, glossing over his part in it, and concluded, "Valerie was a little shook up, so I sent Tadd to the house as an excuse to get him away. I thought she was going to faint and I didn't want that scaring him." He took the glass from his mother's hand and offered it to Valerie. "You might want that drink now, though."

"Thank you." Nervously she took the glass and sipped from it, too self-conscious about the scene his mother had witnessed to draw attention to herself by refusing his suggestion.

"Do you feel all right now, Valerie?" Maureen asked with concern.

"Yes, I'm fine." But her voice sounded breathless and not altogether sure.

"You look a little pale," the other woman observed, frowning anxiously. "You'd better come up to the house and rest for a few minutes."

"No, really I—" Valerie tried to protest.

But Judd interrupted. "Do you want me to carry you?"

"No, I . . . I can walk," she stammered, and flashed an anxious glance at his mother.

Incapable of conversation, Valerie was relieved that no one seemed to expect any from her as they walked to the house. Judd's arm remained around her, his thigh brushing against hers. She kept wondering what his mother was thinking and whether she objected to what was apparently going on. But she guessed that Maureen Prescott was too polite and well-bred to let her feelings show.

As they crossed the lawn to the veranda, Tadd began his own description of the scene at the stud pens. "Mickey and I were watching it all, Reeny. You should have seen Judd when he—"

Judd must have felt the slight tremor that vibrated through her. "I think that's enough about that, Tadd," he said the boy. "We don't want to upset your mom again, do we?"

"No," Tadd agreed, darting an anxious look at Valerie.

"Why don't you play with the puppies, Tadd?" Maureen suggested, and he wandered toward the sleeping pile of black fur, but with some reluctance.

"I'm sorry." Valerie felt obliged to apologize for her behavior after she came under the scrutiny of Judd's mother as well. "I'm not usually a fraidycat about such things."

"No, you're not," Judd agreed with a slight smile, and escorted her to a cushioned lounge chair. "Another kind of feline, maybe," he qualified.

"There's no need to apologize, Valerie," his mother said. "I saw a stallion fight once. It was a vicious thing, so I understand your reaction."

"Comfortable?" Judd asked after seating her in the chair.

"Yes." But she was beginning to feel like a fraud.

"You relax for a little while," he ordered. "I'm going to wash up and change my shirt," he said, glancing down at the dirty front of his. "I won't be long."

When he had disappeared into the house via the veranda doors, his mother suggested, "There's lemonade left if you'd like some."

"No, but thank you," Valerie denied.

Tadd came wandering back onto the veranda, a sleepy puppy in his arms. He stopped at the lounge chair, studying Valerie with a troubled look in his eyes. "Are you really all right, Mommy?"

His appealing concern drew a faint smile. "Yes, Tadd, I'm fine," she assured him.

"Maybe you'd feel better if you held the puppy." He offered her the soft ball of fur and enormous paws.

"Thanks, Tadd, but I think the puppy would like it better if you held it," Valerie refused, her heart warming at his touching gesture.

"It's sleepy anyway," he shrugged, and walked over to the grass to let it go. "Would you want to play a game, Mom?"

"No, thanks."

He came back over to her chair. "What am I going to do while you're resting?"

"Would you like some more cookies and lemonade?" Maureen Prescott suggested.

"No, thank you." He half turned to look at her. "Um, do you have any more animals for me to play with?"

"No, I don't believe so." The woman tried not to smile at the question. "But there's a sandbox over by those trees. If I'm not mistaken, there's a toy truck in that chest over there. You can take the truck and play with it in the sandbox."

"Yay!" Tadd dashed to the toy chest she had indicated, retrieved the truck and headed for the sandbox.

"Tadd isn't used to entertaining himself," Valerie explained. "There are a lot of children his age in the apartment building where we live, so he's used to playing with them."

"It's good that he has children to play with," Maureen commented.

"Yes," Valerie agreed. "I think that's the only thing he's missed this summer. Mickey entertained him at the farm a lot. Now that he's gone, Tadd gets lonely once in a while."

"Ellie, my oldest daughter, is coming this weekend with her husband and their six-year-old daughter. Meg is a real tomboy. Why don't you bring Tadd over Sunday afternoon?" Maureen suggested. "They'll have fun playing together."

"I . . . I don't think so." Valerie hesitated before rejecting the invitation.

"Please try," the woman urged.

"Try what?" Judd appeared, catching the tail end of their conversation.

"I suggested to Valerie that she bring Tadd over on

Sunday to play with Meg, but she doesn't think she'll be able to," his mother explained.

"Oh?" His gaze flicked curiously to Valerie. "Why?"

"I'm not sure it will be possible yet. I'll have to speak to Clara." Valerie couldn't explain the reason for her hesitation. She had the feeling it wouldn't be wise to become too closely involved with any more members of the Prescott family.

"Don't worry, Mother," said Judd. "I can almost guarantee you that Tadd will be here. Valerie and I are having dinner together on Saturday night. I'll persuade her to change her mind."

Dinner together? It was the first she knew about it, but she tried not to let on. Things were happening at such a rapid pace that she couldn't keep up with them. She needed time to take stock of things and understand what was going on.

"I hope you will," his mother said. "Tadd is a wonderful boy. You must be very proud of him, Valerie."

"I am," Valerie admitted, feeling vaguely uncomfortable again.

"He has such a sweet face." Maureen was looking toward the sandbox in which Tadd was playing with the truck. "And those eyes of his are so expressive. There's something about him that makes him so very special, but those children generally are," she concluded.

"Those children?" Valerie stiffened.

A pair of turquoise eyes rounded in dismay as Maureen realized what she had said. She glanced quickly at Judd, an apology in her look. Valerie's questioning eyes were directed at him, as well.

Undaunted by either of them, he replied carefully, "I believe my mother means those children who are born out of wedlock."

"I'm sorry, Valerie," Maureen apologized. "I didn't mean to offend you by that remark—truly I didn't."

"It's quite all right." Valerie hid her embarrassment behind a proud look. "I've never attempted to hide the fact that Tadd's father and I weren't married. And I have heard it said that love children are beautiful. I think Tadd is, but then I'm his mother, so I'm biased."

"I certainly didn't mean to hurt your feelings," Maureen insisted again. "It's just that I've been watching Tadd," she rushed her explanation, "and he's so like Judd in many ways that—oh, dear, I've made it worse!" she exclaimed as she looked at Valerie.

"No, no," Valerie denied with a tight, strained smile. "I understand perfectly."

A lump was rising in her throat as she truly began to understand. Maureen Prescott had known all along that her son was Tadd's father. Judd had obviously told his mother, but hadn't bothered to tell Valerie that he had. She hadn't thought it was possible to feel so humiliated again, but she did.

"I didn't see any reason not to tell her," Judd explained, watching Valerie through narrowed eyes.

"Of course there isn't," she agreed, feeling her poise cracking and struggling inwardly to keep from falling apart.

"I'm relieved." His mother smiled, somewhat nervously. "And I do hope it won't influence your decision about bringing Tadd here on Sunday. I would sincerely enjoy having him come."

"Don't worry about that, Mom," Judd said. "I'm sure Valerie will agree."

"Your son can be very persuasive," Valerie commented, and felt a rising wave of panic. "I don't mean to be rude, Mrs. Prescott"—she rose from the lounge chair—"but I'm really not feeling all that well. Would you mind if Judd took us home now? You've been very gracious to Tadd and me and I want to thank you for that."

"You're very welcome, of course," Maureen returned, hiding her confusion with a smile. "I'll call Tadd for you."

"Thank you." Valerie was aware of Judd standing beside her, examining the pallor in her face.

"What's wrong, Valerie?" he asked quietly.

"A headache—a nervous reaction, I suppose." Her temples were throbbing, so her excuse wasn't totally false.

He seemed to accept her explanation without wanting to delve further. When Tadd came racing to the veranda, Maureen Prescott walked them through the house to the front door and waved goodbye. As they drove away, Tadd's face was pressed to the car window to watch the horses in the pasture.

Valerie sat silently in the front seat. Judd slid her a questioning look. "Does it bother you that my mother knows?" he asked, phrasing it so Tadd wouldn't attach any significance to it.

"No." She leaned her head against the seat rest. "Why should it?" she countered with forced nonchalance.

But it beat at her like a hammer. To realize that her relationship with Judd was out in the open was worse than if it had been a secret, clandestine affair. She had more or less agreed to it—in the stable yard in Judd's arms. There was no doubt about how deeply she loved him.

But she had more to think of than just herself. There was Tadd. Valerie closed her eyes in pain. Maureen Prescott was eager for him to visit on Sunday, but the invitation naturally hadn't included her. Was Tadd going to grow up on the fringes of the Prescott family, invited into the circle on their whim? He would be a Prescott without a right to the name. How would he feel when he discovered the truth? When he was old enough to get what was going on, he would undoubtedly resent his mother not telling him the entire truth about the man who was his father.

Valerie was tormented by the love she felt for Judd and the thought of the life with him that she wasn't likely to ever know. Her heart ached—for herself and for her son.

"Valerie?" Judd's hand touched her shoulder.

She opened her eyes to discover the car was parked in front of the farmhouse. The screen door was already slamming behind Tadd, who was racing into the house to be the first to tell Clara all that had happened that day.

"I . . . I didn't realize we were here already," Valerie began in painful confusion.

"I noticed," he responded dryly. His hand slid under her hair, discovering the tense muscles in her neck and massaging them. "You do know you're having dinner with me on Saturday night. That's tomorrow night," he emphasized.

Like she would forget. "So you told me." She couldn't relax under his touch; if anything, she became stiffer.

"You're going." It was a statement that demanded her agreement.

"Yes." Valerie lied because it was easier.

Judd leaned over and rubbed his mouth against the corner of her lips. She breathed in sharply, filling her lungs with the scent of him. It was like a heady wine. Judd began nibbling the curve of her lip, teasing and tantalizing her with his kiss.

"Please, Judd, don't!" She turned her head away from his tempting mouth because she knew the power of his kiss could make her forget everything.

He hooked a hard finger around her chin and turned her to face him. His sharp gaze inspected her pale face and lowered lashes.

"What is it?" He sensed something was wrong and demanded to know the cause.

"I really do have a headache," Valerie insisted with a nervous smile. "It'll go away, but I need to lie down for a while."

"Alone?" His brow quirked suggestively, then he sighed, "Never mind. Forget I said that. I'll call you later to be sure you're all right."

"Make it this evening," Valerie asked quickly, and hurried to answer the question in his eyes. "By the time I rest for an hour or two, it'll be time to eat. Then the dishes have to be done, and Tadd won't take a bath unless someone is standing over him. So I'll be busy until—"

His fingers touched her lips to silence them. "I'll phone you later this evening," he said. "Or I'll come over if you can think of a way to get Clara out of the house."

It was starting already, she thought in panic. "You'd better call first," she said.

"Okay, I will." He kissed her lightly.

Chapter 9

Valerie paused on the porch to wave to Judd and stayed until he had driven out of sight down the lane. She felt the beginning of a sob in her throat and knew she didn't have time for tears. Lifting her chin, she turned and walked into the house.

"Well, it sure sounds like you've had a full day," Clara commented. "Tadd has been running nonstop for the last five minutes and doesn't give any indication of wearing down. What's all this about horses and puppies? I thought you were going to a tobacco auction. That's what you told me."

"We did go," Valerie admitted, "but that was earlier today. Then we went over to the Prescott place to see Mickey." She glanced down at her son. "Tadd, why don't you go outside and play for a while?"

"Aw, Mom," he protested, "I wanted to tell Clara more about the puppies."

"Later," she insisted. Reluctantly Tadd walked to the door, his feet dragging, and slammed the screen shut. Valerie turned to Clara. "How much gas is in the car?"

"I filled it up the other day when I was in town. Why?" Clara was startled by the question.

Valerie was already hurrying through the living room, picking up the odds and ends of personal items that had managed to get scattered around. She began stuffing them in a paper bag.

"What about the oil? Did you have it checked?" she asked.

"As a matter of fact, I did." A pair of hands moved to rest on broad hips. "Would you mind telling me why you're asking these questions?"

Valerie stopped in the center of the room, pressing a hand against her forehead. "I can't remember—did we put the suitcases in the empty bedroom upstairs or down in the basement?"

"Upstairs. And what do we need the suitcases for?" Clara followed as Valerie headed for the staircase.

"Because we're leaving. What other reason would I have for asking about the car and suitcases?" Valerie retorted sharply.

"Would you like to run that by me once more? Did I hear you say we were leaving?" repeated Clara.

"That's exactly what I said." Valerie opened the door to the empty bedroom, grabbed two of the suitcases in the corner, and walked to Tadd's room.

"I thought we were staying here until summer was over," her friend reminded her.

"I've changed my mind, obviously." Valerie opened drawers, taking out whole stacks of clothes regardless of their order or neatness, and jamming them into the opened suitcase.

"Suppose you give me three guesses as to why." Clara answered her own rhetorical question. "Judd Prescott, Judd Prescott and Judd Prescott. What happened today?"

"I don't have time to go into it right now," Valerie stalled. "Would you mind helping me pack?" she demanded. "I don't want to take all night."

"I'll help," Clara replied, walking to the closet without much haste. "But I doubt if what you're doing could be called packing. What's the big rush anyway? You surely aren't planning to leave tonight?" Shrewd blue eyes swept piercingly to Valerie.

"We're leaving tonight." The first suitcase was filled to the point of overflowing. Valerie had to sit on it to get it latched. "We'll never be able to put everything in these suitcases. Where are the boxes your sister used to send our stuff in? We didn't throw them away, did we?"

But her friend was still concentrating on her first statement. "Tonight? You can't mean that." She frowned. "There's only a few hours of daylight left. The sensible thing is to leave first thing in the morning."

"No, it isn't," Valerie argued. "We're leaving tonight. Now where are the boxes?"

"Forget the boxes. I want to know why we have to leave tonight. And I'm not answering another question or lifting a hand until you tell me." Clara dropped the clothes in her hand on a chair.

"Clara, please. I don't have time for all this." Valerie hurried to the chair and grabbed the clothes to stuff them in the second suitcase. "Judd's going to call later on and I want to be gone before he does."

"So that's your reason?" Her friend sniffed disapprovingly. "Okay, but it seems ridiculous, if you don't mind my saying so."

"Don't you understand?" Valerie whirled to face her. The conflicting emotions and raw pain that she had pushed aside now threatened to surface. Her chin quivered as she fought to hold them back. "If I don't leave tonight, I never will!"

"I think you'd better sit down and tell me what's happened," said Clara in a voice that would stand for no argument.

"No, I won't sit down." Valerie sniffed away a tear and shook back her disheveled hair. "There's too much to do and not enough time." She walked to the chest of drawers and opened the last suitcase to take out the balance of clothes.

"Well, you're still going to tell me what happened," Clara insisted.

Another tear was forming in the corner of her eye and Valerie wiped it quickly away. "Judd's mother, Mrs. Prescott, knows about Tadd—that Judd is his father. She wants Tadd to come over on Sunday to play with another one of her grandchildren. It's all out in the open, and I can't handle it."

"What does Judd think about all this?" Clara gathered up Tadd's few toys and put them in a tote.

"He told his mother he would persuade me to bring Tadd."

"So? Don't let him persuade you," her friend suggested with a shrug.

Valerie's laugh held no humor. "All he has to do is hold me in his arms and I'll agree to anything. I did today. I promised I wouldn't leave here. I'm so in love with him I'm losing my pride and my self-respect."

"It isn't one-sided. Judd is totally crazy about you," Clara said. "I've seen the way he watches you. Like he doesn't want to look away or he'll lose you."

"I know and it doesn't make it any easier. Clara, he wants me to become his—" She broke off the sentence with a hurtful sigh. "I can't even say the word without thinking what it would ultimately do to Tadd."

"Maybe he'll marry you," Clara suggested in an effort to comfort her.

Valerie shook her head, pressing her lips tightly together for an instant. "I'm not good enough for a Prescott to marry. I lack breeding," she said bitterly. "I can't stay, Clara." Her hands absently wadded the bundle of clothes in her hand, her fingers digging into the material. "I can't stay."

There was silence. Then a detergent-roughened hand gently touched her shoulder. "The boxes are in my bedroom closet. I'll get them."

"Thank you, Clara," Valerie muttered in a voice tight and choked with emotion.

When the two suitcases were packed, she set them at the head of the stairs and took two more to her bedroom. With Clara's help, all her personal belongings were packed in either the luggage or the cardboard shipping boxes. As soon as that room was cleared of their possessions, they started on Clara's. No time was wasted on neatness or order.

"Done. All that's left is to lug all this downstairs and out to the car," said Clara, taking a deep breath as she studied the pile of luggage and boxes in front of the staircase.

"And to check downstairs," Valerie added, picking up one case and juggling another under the same arm. "We'd better be sure to get everything because I'm not coming back no matter what we leave behind," she declared grimly, and reached for the third.

Leading the way, Valerie descended the stairs. Clara followed with one of the boxes. Tadd came bounding onto the porch as Valerie approached the door.

"Open the door for me, Tadd," she called through the wire mesh.

"I'm tired of playing, Mom." He held the door open for her and stared curiously at the suitcase she carried. "What are you doing? Are you going somewhere?"

"Yes. Don't let go of the door, Clara is right behind me," Valerie rushed when she saw him take a step to follow her.

"Hurry up, Clara." Tadd waited impatiently for the stout woman to maneuver the box through the opening, then let the door slam and raced to catch up to Valerie. "Is Clara going, too?"

"We're all going," Valerie answered, and set the cases on the ground next to the car. "Where are the keys for the trunk, Clara? Are they in the ignition?"

"I'll bet they're in the house in my handbag," the woman grumbled, and set the box beside the luggage. "I separated the keys for a parking attendant last time I drove. Stay here. I'll go and get them."

"Where are we going, Mom?" Tadd wanted to know, tugging at her skirt to get her attention.

"We're going home," she told him, only Cincinnati didn't seem like home anymore. This place—its paddocks, its fences, its farmhouse and stables—was home.

"Home? To Cincinnati?" Tadd frowned.

"Yes. Back to our apartment," Valerie answered dully.

"But summer's not over." His expression was both puzzled and crestfallen.

She didn't want to look at the sadness in his eyes. "No, not quite," she admitted, and glanced to the house. What was keeping Clara? Valerie could have been bringing out more of the boxes herself instead of standing there.

"But I thought we were going to stay here until summer was over," Tadd reminded her. "That's what you said."

"I changed my mind." *Please,* Valerie thought desperately, *I don't want to argue with you.*

"Why are we leaving?" he asked. "If summer isn't over, why do we have to go back?"

"Because I said we are." She wasn't about to explain the reasons to him. In the first place, he wouldn't understand. And in the second, it would be too painful. The breeze whipped a strand of hair across her cheek and she pushed it away with an impatient gesture.

"But I don't want to go back," Tadd protested, little-boy misery in his voice.

"Yes, you do," Valerie insisted.

"No, I don't." His mouth drew down into a mutinous pout.

"What about all your friends?" Valerie attempted to reason with him. "Don't you want to go back and play with them? It's been a while since you've ridden on Mike's new bike. That was a lot of fun, remember?"

"I don't care about Mike's dumb old bike," Tadd grumbled, the pout growing more pronounced. "It's not as much fun as riding Ginger, anyway. I want to stay here."

"We're not going to stay here. We're leaving. We're going back to Cincinnati." Valerie stressed each sentence with decisive emphasis. "So you might as well get that straight right now."

"I don't want to go," he repeated, his voice raised in rebellious protest. "Judd said if we lived here, maybe I could have a puppy."

"I'm not going to listen to any more talk about puppies!" Valerie retorted, her nerves snapping under the strain of his persistent arguing. "We're leaving, and that's final!"

"Well, I'm not going!" Tadd shouted, backing away and breaking into angry tears.

"Tadd." Valerie immediately regretted her sharpness, but he was already turning away and running toward the pasture. She could hear his sobbing. "Tadd, come back here!"

But he ignored the command, his little legs churning faster. He was running into the lowering sun. Valerie shaded her eyes with her hand to shield out the glaring light. She waited for him to stop at the paddock fence, but instead he scooted under it and kept running.

"Tadd, come back here!" she called anxiously.

"I've got the keys." Clara came out of the house, dangling the car keys in front of her. "I couldn't remember where I had left my handbag. I finally found it underneath the kitchen table. If it were a snake, it would have bit me."

"Go ahead and get all this in the trunk." Valerie motioned to the luggage as she started toward the pasture. "I have to find Tadd."

"Where's he gone?" Frowning, Clara glanced around the yard, missing the small figure racing across the pasture.

"I lost my temper with him because he said he didn't want to go," Valerie explained. "Now he's run off."

"Let him be." Clara didn't seem to think there was anything to worry about and indicated as much with a wave her hand. "He's just going to sulk for a while. He'll be back. Meanwhile, he won't be underfoot."

"I don't know . . ." Valerie answered hesitantly.

"He won't go far," the other woman assured her as

she walked to the car to unlock the trunk and begin arranging the luggage and boxes inside.

"He was very upset." Gazing across, she could see Tadd had stopped running and was leaning against a tree to cry.

"Of course he was upset," Clara agreed in a voice that disdainfully dismissed any other thought. "All kids get upset when they don't get their way. You go right ahead and handle the situation any way you want. I don't want to be telling you how you should raise him."

Valerie got her friend's subtle message that she was making a mountain out of a molehill and sighed, "You may be right."

"If you're not going after him, you could give me a hand with some of this stuff. You're the one who was in such an all-fired hurry to leave," came the gruff reminder. Then Clara muttered to herself, "I get the feeling we're making our getaway after robbing a bank."

When another glance at the pasture showed that Tadd was in the same place, Valerie hesitated an instant longer, then turned to help Clara with the luggage. A second trip into the house and they'd brought everything down from upstairs.

A search of the ground floor added a box of belongings. Valerie carried it to the car. Her gaze swung automatically to the paddock, but this time there was no sign of Tadd. She walked to the fence and called him. The bay mare lifted its head in answer, then went back to grazing.

What had been merely concern changed to worry as Valerie hesitantly retraced her steps to the house. The sounds coming from the kitchen located Clara for her. She walked quickly to that room.

"You haven't seen Tadd, have you?" she asked hopefully. "He isn't in the pasture anymore and I thought he might have slipped into the house."

"I haven't seen hide or hair of him." Clara shook her wiry, graying hair. "Would you look at all this food? Seems like a shame to leave it."

"We don't have much choice. It would spoil if we tried to take all of it with us." Valerie's response was automatic. "Where do you suppose Tadd is?"

"Probably somewhere around the barns." The dismissing lift of Clara's broad shoulders indicated that she still believed he wasn't far away. "Since we haven't had any supper, I'll fix some sandwiches and snacks to take along with us. That way we'll get to use up some of this food and not leave so much behind."

"I'm going to check the barns to see if Tadd is there," Valerie said with an uneasy feeling growing inside her.

A walk through the barns proved fruitless and her calls went unanswered. She hurried back to the house to tell Clara.

"He wasn't there," she said with a trace of breathless panic.

"Hell." Clara wiped her hands on a towel. "He's probably off hiding somewhere."

"We can't leave without him," Valerie said irrationally, as if Clara had somehow implied that they would. "I'm going out to the pasture where I saw him last."

"I'll check through the house to make sure he didn't sneak in here when we weren't looking." Clara put aside the food she was preparing for the trip and started toward the other rooms.

While Clara began a search of the house, Valerie hurried to the paddock. She ducked between the fence rails and walked swiftly through the tall grass to the tree on the far side of the pasture where she had last seen Tadd.

"Tadd!" She stopped when she reached the tree and used it as a pivot point to make a sweeping survey of the surrounding countryside. "Tadd, where are you?" A bird twittered loudly . . . the only response she received. "Tadd, answer me!" Her voice rose on a desperate note.

Angling away from the tree was a faint trail—she could just make out where the tall, thick grass had been pushed down by running feet. The trail seemed to be heading in the opposite direction from the house. It was the only clue Valerie had and she followed it.

It led her to the boundary fence with Meadow Farms and beyond. Halfway across the adjoining pasture, the grass thinned. Grazing horses had cropped the blades too close to the ground. She lost the trail that had taken her this far, and stopped, looking around for any hint that would tell her which direction Tadd had gone.

"Tadd, where are you?" she muttered, wishing she could connect with her lost son's mind and discover his intention.

Did he know he had crossed onto the Prescott land? It didn't seem likely. Despite the time they had spent there, Tadd wasn't familiar with the area beyond the farm and its immediate pastures. Yet it was possible that he knew the general direction of Meadow Farms' main quarters.

But why would he go there? To see Judd and enlist his support to persuade her to stay? No, Valerie dismissed that idea. Tadd was too young to think like that. The idea of finding Judd wouldn't lead him to the Prescott house, but the puppies might.

Hoping that she was reading his mind, she set off in the general direction of the Meadow Farms buildings. Her pace quickened with her growing desire to find Tadd before he reached his destination. The last thing she wanted was a confrontation with Judd. She had to find Tadd before he found the puppies and Judd.

As she crossed the meadow, Valerie caught herself biting her lip. She fought a painful constriction in her chest, her breath coming in half sobs. It did no good to try to calm her shattering nerves.

The ground rumbled with the pounding of galloping hooves and she glanced up to see Judd on the gray hunter riding toward her. She looked around for somewhere to hide, but it was too late. He had already seen her. Besides, she had to know if he had found Tadd, regardless of whether Judd had learned of her intention to leave. At the moment, finding Tadd was more important.

Judd didn't slow his horse until he was almost up to her. He dismounted before it came to a full stop. Then his long strides carried him swiftly toward her, holding the reins in his hand and leading the horse to her.

"Have you seen Tadd?" Her worried gaze searched his set face. "He ran off and I can't find him."

"I know," said Judd, and explained tersely, "I called the house a few minutes ago to find out how you were feeling and Clara told me Tadd was missing." His large hand took hold of her arm and started to pull her toward the horse. "Come on."

"No!" Valerie struggled in panic. "You don't understand. I have to find Tadd," she protested frantically.

If Judd hadn't seen Tadd, it meant her son was still out there somewhere, and really lost. The gathering shadows of sunset were already long. Soon it would be dusk. She had to find him before darkness came, and there was a lot of ground to cover. That knowledge made her resist Judd's attempt to take her with him all the more wildly.

"Valerie, stop it! You're coming with me," Judd said with savage insistence. Her arms were captured in the iron grip of his hands.

"No, I won't!" she protested violently. "I won't!"

A hard shake jarred her into silence. "Will you listen to me?" His face was close to hers, his eyes looking into hers intently so she couldn't freak out. "I have a feeling," he said tightly. "I think I know where Tadd is. Now, will you come with me or do I have to throw you over my shoulder and take you with me?"

Frightened tears had begun to scorch her eyes. She blinked them back and nodded her head mutely. But Judd didn't alter his hold. He seemed determined to hear her say yes before he believed her.

"I-I'll come with y-you." She managed to force out a shaky agreement.

His hands shifted their grip from her arms to her waist. He lifted her up to sit sideways on the front of the saddle. Then he swung up behind her, his arms circling her to hold the reins and guide the gray.

The horse lunged into a canter, throwing Valerie against Judd's chest. The arm around her waist tightened to offer support. The solidness of his chest offered comfort and strength. Valerie let herself relax against it. She hadn't realized how heavy the weight of concern for Tadd's whereabouts had been until Judd took on half of the burden.

Through the cotton skirt of her sundress she could feel the hard muscles of his thighs. Her gaze swept up to study his face through the curl of her gold-tipped lashes. The jutting angle of his jaw and the line of his mouth were set with grim purpose. He slowed the horse as they entered a copse of trees and wound their way through them.

As if feeling her look, he glanced down and the light in his green eyes became softly mocking. "When you were spitting at me in all your fury, did you really believe I was going to try to keep you from finding our son?"

"I didn't know," Valerie answered, uncertain now as to what she'd thought or believed his intention was.

"I guess I have given you cause not to trust me," Judd admitted. "In the past, anyway."

"Sometimes," she agreed, but she didn't want to argue about it now.

His gaze was drawn beyond her and he reined in the gray. "Look," he instructed quietly.

Valerie turned and saw a familiar grassy clearing. They had stopped on the edge of it. In the middle of it, a small figure lay on his stomach. Tadd had cried himself to sleep.

Her gaze lifted in stunned wonderment to Judd's face. "How?" she whispered.

"I can't begin to explain it." He shook his head with a similar expression of awed confusion mixed with quiet acceptance of the fact. His gaze wandered gently back to hers. "Any more than I can explain how I knew Tadd would be here."

Valerie remembered stories of lost animals finding their way to home and safety and wondered if Tadd had relied upon that same mysterious instinct when he ended up here. The thought filled her with a glowing warmth.

Judd swung off the horse and reached up to lift her down. His look, as their eyes met, mirrored her marvelous feeling. When her feet were on the ground, her hands remained on his shoulders as she stood close to him, unmoving.

"It's right, isn't it?" Judd murmured. "It proves that what we shared here was something special."

"Yes," Valerie agreed, a throb of profound emotion in her answer.

His mouth came down on hers to seal the wonder of their blessing. The closeness they shared was marked by a spiritual union rather than mere physical contact. The beauty of it filled Valerie with a serene sense of joy, something she had always hoped to experience in his arms. They had known passion together . . . but never peace. Not until this moment. It was nearly as awe-inspiring as the miracle they had witnessed.

When they separated, she didn't want to talk. Judd let her turn from his arms and followed silently as she made her way across the clearing to the place where their son lay. She kneeled beside him, staring for a moment at his sleeping, tear-streaked face.

"Tadd . . . wake up, angel." Her voice sounded husky and unbelievably loving. "It's Mommy. I'm here."

He struggled awake, blinking at her with the misty eyes of a child who'd suffered a bad dream and still wasn't sure it was over. She smoothed the rumpled mop of brown hair on his forehead and wiped his damp cheek with her thumb.

"Mommy?" His voice wavered.

"I'm really here," she assured him.

"I didn't mean to run away." His lips quivered. "I was going to come back after I got a puppy. But I couldn't find Judd's house, and I . . . I couldn't find you."

"It doesn't matter." Valerie only wanted to love away the remnants of his fear. "We found you."

She gathered him into her arms, letting his arms wind around her neck in a strangling hold as he began to cry again. Judd crouched down beside them, his hand reaching out to hold Tadd's shoulder.

"It's all right, son," he offered in comfort. "We're here. There's nothing to be frightened about anymore."

Tadd lifted his head to stare at Judd, sniffling back his tears. Almost immediately he turned away and buried his face against Valerie. Hurt flickered briefly in Judd's eyes at the rejection in Tadd's action.

"I think he's embarrassed to have you see him cry." Valerie whispered the explanation.

The stiffness went out of Judd's smile. "Everyone cries, Tadd, no matter how old he is," he assured the small boy, and was rewarded with a peeping look. Valerie had difficulty in imagining that Judd had ever cried in his life, but his quiet words of assurance had eased the damage to a small boy's pride. "Come on," said Judd, rising to his feet, "it's almost dark. It's time we were getting you home."

Tadd's arms remained firmly entwined around her neck. At Judd's questioning look, Valerie responded, "I can carry him," and lifted her clinging son as she rose.

Judd mounted the gray horse and reached down for Valerie to hand him Tadd. When Tadd was positioned astride the gray behind him, Judd slipped his foot from the left stirrup and helped Valerie into the saddle in front of him. The gray pranced beneath the extra weight.

"Hang on, Tadd," Judd instructed, and a pair of small arms obediently tightened around his waist. Judd turned the gray horse toward the farmhouse.

Chapter 10

Twilight was purpling the sky as they approached the house. Judd reined the gray horse toward the paddock gate and leaned sideways to unlatch it, swinging it open and riding the horse through. Stopping in front of the porch, he reached behind him and swung Tadd to the ground, then dismounted to lift Valerie down.

"Thank God you found him!" Clara came bustling onto the porch as if she had been standing at the window watching for them.

"A little frightened, but safe and sound," said Judd, his hand resting lightly on Valerie's waist. He glanced down at her, smiling gently at the experience they had shared.

Tadd went racing onto the porch. "I was going to Judd's house to see the puppies and I got lost," he told Clara. Now that he was safely back, the episode had become an adventure to be recounted.

Clara's knees made a cracking sound as she bent to take hold of his shoulders and scold him. "You should be spanked for the way you made us all worry!" But already she was pulling him into her arms to hug him tightly. Tadd squirmed in embarrassment when Clara kissed his cheek, and rubbed his hand over the spot when she straightened. "If you hadn't come back before dark, I was going to call the sheriff and have them send out a search party."

"I think we're all glad it wasn't necessary," Judd said, and started toward the porch with Valerie at his side.

"Isn't that the truth!" Clara agreed emphatically.

"If it hadn't been for Judd, I wouldn't have found him." Valerie had to give credit where credit was due.

"Someone else had more to do with it than I did." Judd gave the responsibility to someone higher up.

As he took the first step onto the porch, Valerie felt his gaze slide past her to the car. The moment she had been dreading ever since the house had come into sight was there. The trunk of the car was open and all of the suitcases and boxes stuffed inside were in plain sight. Judd stiffened to a halt. As his arm dropped from her waist, Valerie continued up the porch steps, a tightness gripping her throat.

"What's going on here? Is someone leaving?" His low question was initially met with pulsing silence.

She turned to face him. Leaving after what they had just shared was going to be a hundred times more difficult, but Valerie knew it was a decision she had to stand behind. The words of response were a long time in coming.

Finally it was Tadd who answered him. "We're going back to Cincinnati. That's why I ran away—'cause I wanted to stay here and have a puppy and Mom said I couldn't."

At the cold fury gathering in Judd's gaze, Valerie half turned her head, her eyes never leaving Judd's face. "Clara, will you take Tadd in the house? He hasn't had any supper. He's probably hungry."

"Of course," her friend agreed in a subdued voice. "Come with me, Tadd." Clara ushered him toward the door and into the house.

When the screen door closed behind them, Judd slowly mounted the steps to stand before Valerie. "Is it true what Tadd said? Are you leaving?" His voice rumbled out the questions from somewhere deep inside, like distant thunder.

She swallowed and forced out a calm answer. "Yes, it's true."

"You promised you'd stay," Judd reminded her, his emotions barely controlled.

"No, I promised there'd be no more talk about my leaving." It took a lot of effort for her not to sob out the words.

"So you were going to leave without talking about it," he said accusingly. "You knew I was going to call. You knew I wanted to see you tonight."

"And I wanted to be gone before you did," Valerie admitted. He grabbed her shoulders. "Don't touch me, Judd. Please don't touch me," she demanded in a voice that broke under the strain. If he held her, she knew she would give in, whether or not it was right or wrong.

He released her as abruptly as he had taken her. Turning away, he swung a fist at an upright post. The force of the blow shook the dust from the porch rafters.

"Why?" he demanded in a tortured voice and spun around to face her. "Dammit to hell, Valerie! I've got a right to know why!"

For a choked moment she couldn't answer him. Welling tears had turned his eyes into iridescent pools of anguish. She wanted to reach up and touch the sparkling drops to see if they were real. Judd was too tough to cry. The sight of them held her spell-bound.

"When I discovered your mother knew about us—and Tadd—I realized I couldn't stay no matter how much I wanted to," she explained hesitantly. "Maybe if I hadn't learned that she knew, or maybe if I'd never met her, it would have been easier to stay. Now, it's impossible."

"Why is my mother to blame for your leaving?" Confusion and anger burned in his look as he searched her expression, trying to follow her logic.

"I don't really blame her." Valerie was having difficulty finding the right words. "I'm sure it's only natural that she wants to become acquainted with your son."

"You'd better explain to me what you're talking about, because you aren't making any sense," Judd warned. "In one breath you say you want to stay and in the next you're saying you can't because of my mother. Either you want to stay or you don't!"

"I can't," she stated. Her chin quivered with the pain she felt inside. "Don't you see, Judd? What will Tadd think when he learns about us? Eventually he will. We can't keep it from him forever. I can't just be your girlfriend or your mistress—God, that sounds old-fashioned but I can't think of a nicer word."

"Oh, Valerie—"

"No matter what, I can't put my wants above Tadd's needs."

"Then you do love me?" His hands recaptured her arms. "Valerie, I have to know," he demanded roughly.

"Yes, I love you," she choked out, and averted her gaze. "But it doesn't change anything. Nothing at all, Judd." Relief trembled through her when he let her go. She closed her eyes and fought the attraction that made her want to go back into his arms.

"I wanted to see you tonight to give you this." A soft snap made her open her eyes. Judd was holding a small box. In a bed of green velvet was an engagement ring, set with an emerald flanked by diamonds. Valerie gasped at the sight of it. "And to ask you to marry me."

Her gaze flew to his as she took a step backward. "Don't joke about this," she pleaded.

"It isn't a joke," Judd assured her. "As a matter of fact, I bought the ring the day after you told me about Tadd. But I didn't give it to you before now because I didn't want you marrying me because of him."

"I don't understand," she murmured, afraid that Judd didn't mean what he was implying.

"I didn't want you marrying me in order to have a father for your child—our child," he corrected himself. "I didn't want you marrying me for the Prescott name or wealth. I wanted your reason to be that you loved me and wanted me as much as I love and want you."

A piercing joy flashed through her. She stared into the warm green fires of his eyes, repeating in her mind the words he had just spoken. She was afraid to say anything in case she was dreaming.

"Until today I wasn't sure how much you really cared about me," Judd continued. "But when I saw the terror in your eyes when you thought I might have been hurt by the stallions, I knew what you felt for me was real. My family name and position meant nothing to you compared to that. And it's a fact that I'm the father of your son. I can see myself in him."

"I know," she whispered. "I do too. It meant—it meant that you and I were never really apart."

"And that you and I were meant to be together."

Without waiting for an acceptance of his proposal, Judd took her left hand and slipped the ring on her finger. Valerie watched, slightly dazed, as he lifted her hand to his mouth and kissed the emerald stone that was the same vivid color as his eyes.

"You can't really want to marry me," she heard herself murmur. "I'm not good enough for you."

Anger flashed in his eyes. "Don't ever say that again!"

Valerie glowed at his instant dismissal of her statement, but he went on.

"You raised our boy all by yourself," he said. There was a heartbreaking catch in his voice. "And you did a fantastic job. He's a great kid. But if you let me do what's right—and be a father to him from now on—" He broke off and rubbed his hand across his eyes. "You don't have to go it alone. I'm here. For both of you. And I love you, Valerie. Don't you know that by now?"

Her self-doubt kept her from believing it with all her heart. "Your mother told me you wanted your wife to have classy breeding, spirit and staying power. My family isn't anything. I'm nothing special."

Judd's mouth tightened. "You come from fine stock. And you're a fighter. That untamed streak in you proves your spirit. And as for staying power, after seven years I believe that question's been answered."

"Judd . . ." she began.

"No more discussion," he interrupted. "You're going to marry me and that's the end of it."

"Yes!" She breathed the answer against his lips an instant before he claimed hers.

An involuntary moan escaped her throat at the completeness of her love. His kiss was thorough, his masterful technique without fault. Beneath her hands she could feel the thudding of his heart, racing as madly as her own.

"I thought I loved you seven years ago, Judd," she murmured as he trailed kisses down to her neck, "but it's nothing compared to what I feel for you now."

"And I thought you were too young to know what love was," he muttered against her skin. "But I couldn't get enough of you—couldn't stay away. Forgive me, angel."

"It doesn't matter that you didn't love me then," she told him softly. "It's enough that you love me now."

"Is that really what you think? Christ, I was obsessed with you seven years ago," Judd confessed, lifting his head to let his fingers stroke her cheek and trace the outline of her lips.

"I was just someone you made love to." Valerie still couldn't quite believe she had been special to him. But even so, the past was behind them. It couldn't be rewritten—couldn't be relived. The way he felt toward her at this moment was all that counted.

"For every time I made love to you, there were a hundred times that I wanted to," Judd replied. "Drove me crazy that a fiery little kitten could sink her claws into me that way. All you had to do seven years ago was crook your little finger at me and I came running. Do you have any idea what it did to my stupid masculine pride to realize that I had no control where you were concerned?"

"No, I didn't know." She looked at him in surprise.

His green eyes were dark and smoldering. There was no mistake that he meant every word he was saying. His caressing thumb parted her lips and probed at the white barrier of her teeth. Wantonly

Valerie nibbled at its end, the tip of her tongue tasting the saltiness of his skin.

"God, you're beautiful, Valerie." He said it as reverently as a prayer. "More than ever." He moved to let his mouth take the place of his thumb, which he let slide to her chin.

He fired her soul with his burning need for her. Valerie arched closer to him, pliantly molding herself to his hard length. His hands were crushing and caressing, fanning the flames that were threatening to burn out of control. Just in time, he pulled back, shuddering against her with the force of his emotion and rubbing his forehead against hers. He breathed in deeply to regain his sanity.

"Do you see what I mean?" he asked after several seconds. The rawness in his teasing voice vibrated in the air. "I never intended to make love to you that first time, but your kisses were addictive. After a while, they weren't enough. I needed a whole hell of a lot more. Even if you hadn't been willing, I would have taken you that first time. It isn't something I'm very proud to admit."

"But I did want you to make love to me, Judd," Valerie assured him, hearing the shakiness in her voice. "I thought it was the only way to hold you. Also, I wasn't satisfied anymore, either. I wanted to be yours completely and I thought that was the way."

"If you hadn't, there are times when I think I might have crawled all the way to your grandfather to beg his permission to marry you. That's how completely you had me under your spell," Judd told her, and rubbed his mouth against her temple. "But it's something we'll never know for sure."

"No," Valerie agreed. "And I wouldn't want to turn back the clock to find out. Not now."

He couldn't seem to stop slowly trailing kisses over her face. His gentle adoration was almost worshipful, while Valerie felt like a supplicant begging for his caresses. This freedom to touch each other with no more self-imposed restraints was a heady elixir to both of them.

"When I made love to you that first time and realized no other man had ever touched you, I was filled with so much self-contempt and loathing that I swore I'd never come near you again," Judd murmured. "I felt like the lowest animal on earth. Then you confronted me—said I'd just used you for my pleasure and dropped you, and I was lost."

"I thought you were avoiding me because I was so inexperienced," Valerie remembered, her fingertips reaching up to explore his jaw and curl into his hair. "Because I hadn't satisfied you."

"It was never that," Judd denied. "You were a wonder to me. I wanted you to know the same feeling of fulfillment that you gave me."

"Judd, there's something I want to ask." Valerie hesitated, hating to ask the question, yet after his revelation it troubled her.

"Ask away," he insisted, lightly kissing her cheekbone.

Her hands slid down to his chest, her fingers spreading over the hard, pulsing flesh. Eluding his caressing mouth, she lifted her head to see his face. The contentment mixed with desire that she saw in his eyes almost made her dismiss the question as unimportant, even trivial.

"Why didn't you ever take me anywhere, ask me out on a date?" she finally asked the question, her look soft and curious.

Judd winced slightly, then smiled. "You were my

private treasure," he explained. "I wanted to keep you all to myself. I wanted to be the only one who knew about you. I guess I was afraid if I took you somewhere someone might steal you from me. So I kept trying to hide you, but I ended up losing you anyway."

"Only for a time," she reminded him and sighed. "I thought it was because I was just Elias Wentworth's granddaughter, not worthy enough to be seen in the company of a Prescott."

"I figured. Or at least, I realized it that last time we met," he qualified his statement. "Made me angry, too. But I was more worried that some guy at the party you were so anxious to attend might take you from me. And yeah, I listened to the devil on my shoulder and told myself that maybe you were just a social climber, looking for somebody better. I'm ashamed to say it even now. And I got all worked up at the thought that you might be using me."

"Judd, you didn't!" Valerie protested incredulously, frowning.

"It was a weird way of being jealous," he admitted. "I wouldn't admit it, not even to myself."

"You don't need to be jealous. Not now and not then," she told him, her heart aching from the love she felt. "There's never been anyone else but you. Oh, I've dated a few times these last seven years," she admitted in an offhand manner that said those dates had meant nothing. "But if I couldn't have you, I didn't want to settle for second best."

Judd kissed her hard, as if grateful for the reassurance and sorry that he had needed it. "The week after we argued and you stormed away, I practically haunted our place. Then I went into town and overheard someone mention that you'd gone away. For a while I told myself I was glad you'd left because I could finally be in control of my own life again. When I found myself missing you, I tried to make believe it was only because you'd been so much fun to fool around with."

"And it wasn't that?" she whispered hopefully. Her hands felt the lifting of his chest as Judd took a deep breath before shaking his dark head.

"No, it wasn't that," he agreed. "After six months, I finally accepted the fact that good old lust wouldn't last that long. That's when I rode over to your grandfather's to find out where you were. Remember that filly I told you I bought from him?"

"Yes," Valerie said.

"That's the excuse I used." There was a rueful twist of his mouth. "It took me a week of visits to get the subject around to you. When he finally did mention you, it was to tell me you'd eloped with some man."

"But—"

"I know." Judd staved off her words. "It wasn't true, but at the time I didn't know it. I almost went out of my mind. Half the time I was calling myself every name in the book for letting you go. Or else I was congratulating myself on being rid of a woman who could forget me in six months. But mostly I was insane with jealousy for the man who now had you for himself."

"And I was trying so desperately to hate you all that time." Her voice cracked and she bit at her lip to hold back a sob. "Seven years." So much time had been wasted, unnecessarily.

"Everybody pays for mistakes, Valerie," he reminded her. "Not trusting each other was wrong and we both had to pay. My price was seven years of visiting your grandfather and listening to him talk about your happy family and his grandchild and all the places your husband was taking you to see. I had seven years of endless torture picturing you in another man's arms. While you had to bear my child alone and face the world alone with him."

"But in Tadd"—she hesitated for a fraction of a second—"I had a part of you. I loved him even more because of that." Valerie hugged him tightly to share the pain they had both known.

"When your grandfather died and Mickey told me you were coming for the funeral, I vowed I wouldn't come near you. I didn't think I could stand seeing you with your husband and child. But I couldn't stay away from the house."

His voice was partially muffled by the thickness of her tawny hair as his mouth moved over it, his chin rubbing her head in an absent caress. "I think I was trying to rid myself of your ghost. I was almost hoping that having a child had worn you out and being married had turned you into a nagging shrew—anything to rid me of your memory. Hell, did I get that wrong. You grew up into a stunningly beautiful woman."

"When you walked out of that door, I nearly ran into your arms," Valerie admitted. "It was as if those seven years we were apart didn't exist."

"If I hadn't believed you had a husband somewhere, that's exactly what would have happened," he said, and she felt his mouth curve into a smile against her hair. "It wasn't until that night that I found out you weren't married. I felt so damn lucky. All I wanted to do was get you to surrender."

"Before I came back, I thought I'd got over you. All it took was seeing you again to realize I hadn't," she confessed. "I fought it because I knew how much you'd hurt me the last time and I didn't think I could stand it if that happened again. And I . . . thought all you wanted was to have me back as your lover."

"My lover, my wife, my friend, my everything," Judd said fiercely. "It was after the funeral that I told my mother about our affair seven years ago and that this time I was going to marry you no matter how I had to make you agree. But first I had to try to convince you to stay."

"I thought you were trying to set me up as your mistress when you offered to lease the farm," Valerie remembered.

"Okay, it was an option," he admitted. "Maybe you didn't want to marry me or marry anybody. But I knew you still felt a spark of desire for me."

"A spark?" she laughed. "It was a forest fire!"

"I didn't know that," Judd reminded her. "I was desperate to try anything that would bring back what we once had. Later I could persuade you to marry me."

"But when you found out about Tadd . . ." Valerie began.

"Yes, I had the weapon," he nodded. "I knew that for his sake I could persuade you to marry me. But somewhere in there I realized that if you married me without loving me, the hell of the last seven years would be nothing compared to what the future would hold. I had to find out first whether you felt more than sexual attraction for me."

"Convinced yet?" She gazed into his face, her eyes brimming with boundless love.

"I'm getting there." His mouth dented at the corners. "I'll be totally convinced when you stand in front of a minister with me and say, 'I do.' And if I can arrange it, that day will come tomorrow."

"The sooner the better," Valerie agreed, and couldn't

resist murmuring, "Mrs. Judd Prescott . . . Valerie Prescott. It sounds beautiful, but I'm not sure it's me."

"Get used to it," he warned. "Because it's going to be your name for the rest of your life."

"Are you very sure that's what you want?" Just for an instant, she let herself doubt it.

"Yes." Judd kissed her hard in punishment. "As sure as I am that you and I are going to make another beautiful baby. For us. For Tadd. We're going to be a family—"

He was interrupted by Clara ordering, "Tadd! Come back here this minute!" from inside the house.

A pair of stampeding feet raced to the screen door and pushed it open as Tadd came rushing out, staring wide-eyed at the embracing pair. "Clara said maybe we're not leaving!" he declared. "Mom, is that true? Are we going to stay?"

"Yes," Valerie admitted, making no effort to move out of Judd's arms, not that he would have permitted it.

"Until summer's over?" he badgered her.

"No, you're going to live here," Judd answered him this time.

Clara came hustling to the door, scolding, "Tadd, I thought I told you not to come out here until I said you could." Her shrewd blue eyes glanced apologetically at Valerie. "He bolted out of the kitchen before I could stop him."

"It's all right," Valerie assured her, smiling.

"Does that mean I can have a puppy?" Tadd breathed in excited anticipation.

"You not only can have a puppy, you're also going to have a father," Judd told him. "I'm going to marry your mother. Is that all right with you?"

"Sure." Tadd gave his permission and switched the

subject back to the more important question. "When can I have my puppy?"

"In another couple of weeks," Judd promised. "As soon as it's old enough to leave its mother."

"That long?" Tadd made a disappointed face.

"It's better than seven years," Judd murmured to Valerie as his arm curved more tightly around her waist.

"It will go by fast, Tadd," Valerie told him. "In the meantime, you can choose the one you want and play with it so it will get to know you."

"Can I go over now? I know which one I want," he said eagerly.

A wicked light began to dance in Judd's green eyes. "Clara might be persuaded to take you," he suggested. "While you're playing with the puppies, she could be helping my mother make arrangements for the wedding reception tomorrow."

"And leave you here alone with Valerie?" Clara spoke impulsively, forgetting that a little kid was listening. "Judd Prescott, there'd be a baby born eight months and twenty-nine days after the wedding! Oops—Tadd, don't you repeat that."

Judd chuckled and Valerie felt her cheeks grow warm at the thought. He glanced down at her, his gaze soft and loving.

"She's right," he said. "After seven years, I can wait one more night. Because it's the last night we're ever going to be apart. I promise you that, Valerie." Unmindful of the small boy and the older woman looking on, his dark head bent to meet the toffee gold of Valerie's.

AFTER THE STORM

Chapter 1

Outside the sky was pale blue, as if it had been bleached by the searing sun. The trees that lined the street were thickly covered with rich green leaves. Wide, deep lawns with manicured grass and immaculately trimmed shrubs contrasted sharply with the gleaming oyster shell coloring of pavements and driveways. Inside the imposing brick and wood homes of this neighborhood of Denver, Colorado, lived families with money, a lot of money.

Lainie MacLeod stared through the gauze of white sheer curtains, her arms crossed and her hands rubbing her elbows in a gesture of nervousness. A bright yellow dandelion sprang up in solitary isolation on the front lawn. She noticed the intruder and sighed.

What they really needed, she thought dejectedly, was a part-time gardener, but she knew there was no way to stretch the budget to include one. Somehow she would just have to find time to get around to it herself, just as she had done with so many other things.

There was really no need to keep up any pretense that their annual income was even close to equaling that of others on the block. Lainie was sure their neighbors were fully aware of the precarious financial position they were in. No matter how discreet she'd tried to be, word got out. All it took was one nosy person to notice an auctioneer's or antique dealer's van in the driveway, someone who'd dawdle long enough to watch a valuable object or painting being taken from the house, and all of a sudden the whispers started. But Lainie had been reared in this house and she was too proud to allow its outward appearance of her home to deteriorate. They didn't have to shout out the true state of their affairs.

A shiny convertible sports car turned into their driveway, its driver stopping the car and running her hands through her silky brown hair before hopping out. Lainie smiled as she moved to the front door, glancing up the open staircase toward her mother's bedroom. The last thing she wanted was for the front doorbell to ring and rouse her mother, who had just drifted off to sleep. It would mean endless explanations as to the reason for Ann Driscoll's visit, and Lainie wasn't ready to explain.

Her mother had never approved of her friendship with Ann, insisting that Ann lacked breeding and culture, qualities that had been instilled in Lainie since her early childhood. It was immaterial that Ann's parents were affluent, or that Ann had married well. Mrs. Simmons considered Ann not quite good enough and wanted to keep her at a distance. But Lainie's own determination had kept their friendship intact.

Lainie thought of Ann as a true-blue friend, the only one who had stood by her in every crisis. So when she greeted her at the door, her welcome was genuinely warm. Ann's greeting was just as fervent as always. Her emotions were mirrored in her eloquent blue eyes which never failed to reflect her feelings whether they were happy, sad, flirtatious or angry. Yet for all her elation at meeting her best friend, Lainie still remained subdued, her eyes straying to the door at the top of the stairs.

As the pair retreated to the kitchen at the rear of the house, Ann studied Lainie with concern. To a stranger, Lainie would have seemed pretty enough, but somehow . . . to Ann, who had known her for over ten years, the telltale signs of strain were very clear. The dark circles under Lainie's eyes, which heightened the incredibly thick lashes and the hazel green of her eyes, revealed nights of interrupted sleep. The tan and white checked skirt hung loosely around her waist, and the white linen blouse with its scooped neck accented the prominence of her collarbones.

Both indicated the weight loss that was robbing Lainie of her energy. Even her dark hair, which had once been so well cared for that it gleamed with a satiny sheen, was now dull. Now that Lainie had so little time to care for it, she had drawn it away from her face and caught it at the back of her neck with a gold clasp. The severe style further emphasized her always prominent cheekbones, but in an unflattering way.

Ann knew that any expression of her concern would be wasted, so she blinked away her anxiety and smiled as she accepted the tall glass of punch Lainie offered her.

"How's your mother? Did the doctor stop in this morning?"

Ann watched a fleeting frown pass across Lainie's smooth forehead before she replied with deliberate lightness. "Yes. Thank God someone still makes house calls. He seemed very pleased with her, which really irritated her." Lainie sighed heavily as she seated herself at the round table. "She complains so often about her aches and pains that it's difficult to know how serious her condition is at times. And poor Dr. Henderson swears she reads my father's medical books just to come up with new symptoms for him to diagnose."

"But everything is all set for tonight?"

"I mentioned it to him." Lainie met Ann's questioning glance, indecision in her own eyes. "He felt as long as there was someone competent staying with my mother, it would be all right."

Ann shrugged. "Who could be more competent than a registered nurse?"

"I just don't feel right about it." Lainie tapped the edge of her glass nervously. "Obviously you're right about the nurse, but Mom is so uncomfortable with strangers around. I think it would be best if we postponed it until another time."

"Listen, we've done nothing but talk about this concert for a month now. It's all settled. Adam bought the tickets and everything. You can't back out now!"

Ann flashed her a look of annoyance as Lainie hedged at meeting her gaze. She chose instead to lean an elbow on the table and rub her forehead.

"I've been looking forward to the concert," Lainie admitted, "but I just can't help worrying about my mother."

"You ought to start worrying about yourself for a change," Ann retorted sharply. "The worst mistake you ever made was coming back here to Denver when your mother became ill. You should have found a social worker specializing in geriatrics to help you find care instead of knocking your brains out trying to do it all yourself. In the seven months you've been back, how many times have you been out of this house? Trips to the pharmacy or grocery store don't count."

"I don't know. A few times," Lainie replied reluctantly.

"I'll tell you exactly. Three times! Once to have dinner with us, once to go shopping with me, and once to go to the movies." Ann leaned forward to plead, "Lainie, if you don't make some time for yourself you're going to have a breakdown."

"Don't be melodramatic."

"I'm not. You'd just better look in the mirror and tell yourself that you can't do it all and you're not indispensable. Someone else can look after your mother just as adequately as you."

"Oh, Ann!" Lainie's generous mouth curved into a smile. "I know you have a point and I really am listening—I just don't know what to do. If only I didn't feel so guilty."

"It's your mother who's making you feel guilty. She's running your life. Your three years in Colorado Springs forced her to change her tactics and use emotional blackmail to retie the umbilical cord."

"I had no choice," Lainie replied, her pride stiffening her chin. "There was no money left from my dad's estate and Mom had allowed her health insurance to lapse. She may not be the kind of mother that . . . that I would like her to be, but I would never humiliate her by forcing her to accept charity."

"She's almost old enough to qualify for Medicare," Ann pointed out.

"Almost. Not there yet. She was young when I was born."

"Which does not entitle her to turn *you* into her parent. De facto."

"It's not that bad, Ann," Lainie protested.

Ann studied her for a long moment before switching to an even more uncomfortable subject. "Have you ever considered that you might be depressed, Lainie? As in clinically depressed?"

"No."

"You might need help too."

"I don't."

"I'm not so sure about that," Ann said quietly.

"You don't understand," Lainie said. "I mean, it's true that's nothing the same since Rad and I—well, never mind."

Ann sighed but didn't say anything.

"Helping my mother helps me feel less sad about all that."

"But—"

"We get by."

"There's more to life than getting by," Ann pointed out. "A lot more."

"For me, right now, there isn't," Lainie argued. "So I do what I can."

"And you feel obligated to do it all by yourself?" Ann shook her head.

"Yeah. I do."

"And how long will your money last?" Ann asked quietly.

"It doesn't matter." Lainie couldn't bring herself to tell her friend that her money had run out over a month ago and the bills were still coming in. The little income her mother received combined with

Lainie's monthly check from Rad were what kept food on the table and a roof over their heads.

"All right, it doesn't matter and it's basically none of my business." Ann's cupid's-bow lips pressed into a tight line. She leaned over the table toward Lainie, frustrated urgency visible in her expression. "But you have to come to the concert tonight. The chances of Curt Voight returning to Denver in the near future are, like, zero. I won't let you miss it if I have to drag you there!"

Voight was a world-class musician and an incredibly gifted pianist, someone Lainie had admired for several years. She knew she would be nuts to turn down an opportunity to see him perform in person, especially in the face of Ann's opposition. In the last several years there had been few occasions when she had been able to attend such exclusive events, not since Rad . . .

She gave an almost imperceptible shake of her head at the unwanted memory.

"I'm going," Lainie said quietly, while Ann wondered what had caused the flicker of pain in the hazel green eyes.

The nurse, Mrs. Forsythe, arrived at six that evening, in time to assist Lainie with her mother's dinner and allow Mrs. Simmons to adjust to the fact of her daughter's absence that evening. Lainie had refrained from informing her mother earlier because she knew she would not be in favor of the idea. She was aware of her mother's manipulativeness—it was just that she couldn't control it. Or her own response to it.

As it turned out, she was absolutely correct.

"Lainie honey, please don't leave me." Her mother clutched her hand tightly as Lainie seated herself on the bed. Her dainty feminine features were drawn in petulant lines.

"You're going to be just fine, Mom," Lainie soothed her, glancing over at the sympathetic face of the nurse. "Mrs. Forsythe is very competent. She's been trained to take care of people in your condition."

"But you're my daughter." Her mother's chin trembled fretfully. "What if something should happen to me? I had a premonition—"

"Now, now," Lainie said. Her mother found ESP very useful for getting her way.

"I dreamed I was going to die, Lainie! I want you to be here with me."

"Nothing is going to happen to you," Mrs. Forsythe said in a comforting voice. "And with as much spunk as you're displaying, I think it's highly unlikely that you'll die tonight."

Mrs. Simmons immediately reversed her tactics and sunk weakly against her pillow. Her lashes fluttered toward Lainie to show how little strength she had.

"Mrs. Forsythe knows exactly how to get in touch with me, Mom. I can be home in minutes if necessary, but either way I promise you I'll come straight home after the concert."

"You won't stay out late with that Ann girl, will you?"

"No, I'll come straight home."

Her mother's eyelids closed slowly as if to show Lainie that she was making a supreme sacrifice by allowing her daughter to leave her when death might be imminent. Not even the aging wrinkles on her face could take away the remnants of Mrs. Simmons's youthful beauty, nor her ability to portray the helpless female. Lainie knew this sudden show of emotion was supposed to make her feel guilty at leaving. The awful thing was that it pretty much worked.

But it didn't change her mind.

A hand touched her shoulder and Lainie turned.

"Might be best if you left her with me," the nurse whispered.

Lainie nodded and retreated quietly. Her mother feigned sleep, but Lainie wasn't deceived. It was merely another ruse to force her daughter to return to her bedroom before she left for the concert and thus allow Mrs. Simmons another chance to persuade her not to go.

Lainie fought the pointless guilt that assaulted her, refusing to give in to the blackmail her mother was so expert at. Trouble was, Lainie's weapon was self-pity, which didn't do much to bolster her weakening desire to attend the concert, even though she'd been looking forward to it for ages. Now she doubted if she'd even enjoy it.

Ann was right, Lainie thought. She was depressed. And passive. And stuck. She could come up with a long list of things to dislike about herself, and not one reason to change anything.

Which was a textbook definition of depression. Her lips twisted bitterly at the realization. What a thing for her to admit at twenty-six, she thought. In high school and college, she'd been really popular. Crazy happy. And then Rad had come into her life and she'd fallen madly in love.

And assumed it would last forever. Hah. Now she was trapped by—by everything. Of course, no one else was going to care for her mother in the years to come.

She remembered Ann's advice on finding help. But you won't let anyone help, she scolded herself.

All the same, what if her mother was seriously ill? The medical tests so far showed nothing much wrong, but there was another round of examinations coming up: EKGs and EEGs and repeats of blood work and brain scans, and, just in case, additional tests of her mother's thyroid and liver and pancreatic function— it was never-ending.

How selfish and cynical that sounded, as if she were totally unmindful of the potential seriousness of her mother's condition. Yet she did care, Lainie decided sadly. She didn't object to nursing her mother. It wasn't that at all that made her so depressed at times. It was the knowledge that she would never know the happiness of love again.

Once Lainie had blamed her mother for that; now she shouldered the blame herself. Her own ignorance and inexperience had persuaded her to listen to her mother, and that hadn't changed much, even though she was no longer the naïve, nervous girl who'd listened to her in the past. Lainie gazed indifferently at her reflection in the mirror while brushing her long, thick hair. She remembered the summer of her seventeenth year when her mother began a series of makeovers on her only daughter.

The words drifted back as clearly as if they had been spoken yesterday.

"Too bad you didn't inherit my looks." Mrs. Simmons studied her daughter with faint disapproval. "Beauty is what's going to move you ahead in this world, Lainie. So don't ever be afraid to use it to get what you want. Character doesn't count as much as you might think."

Lainie had stared at her petite, dainty mother, every short inch of her displaying confidence and dominance.

"But I'll never be as beautiful as you," Lainie had sighed wistfully, looking at her own face and tall frame. She was . . . interesting-looking. Or so one of her high school friends had said, a cheerleader type who was perky in a scary way.

"Yes, you will," her mother had replied. "But it's going to take work. I'm happy to help. First of all, there's your hair—it's a nice, rich color. Sable brown."

"Hair is not that big a deal."

"It's your most important asset. You'll wear it long," her mother had ordered, "and we'll pull it back and away from your face. Your cheekbones are much too prominent to hide, so we'll emphasize them . . ."

And so on, her mother taking each feature and instructing Lainie on the way to show them to the best advantage. Her lips were generous, so they must always be shiny and inviting. The almond shape of her eyes was to be emphasized to make them different from the round, innocent eyes of her friends. The green in her hazel eyes was to be accented to make it more noticeable. Lainie's wardrobe should consist of only the simplest tailored dresses, nothing that would detract from her face.

Her mother hadn't been totally wrong. The result was that Lainie was the most strikingly beautiful girl in her group. She had been popular beyond her wildest dreams, the envy of other girls who didn't make a point of being friends with someone who provided them with so much competition. All except Ann, who simply admired Lainie's looks and didn't see her as a threat to her own future happiness.

Lainie knew of only two people who had ever liked her for herself. Ann was one. Her fingers trailed over the frame of the picture on her dresser as she studied the fun-loving blue eyes that beamed out at her. And her father had been the other, with his smiling eyes and iron gray hair as thick and full as her own. He had been a highly skilled, sought-after surgeon who'd lost his life in a plane crash nearly two years ago. He had only wanted happiness for her and he had no idea how insecure her mother had made her feel.

Lainie had been the quiet type, more inclined to accept things as they were than complain or challenge people. That was still true, she thought miserably.

She'd begun to change when Rad—oh, it didn't matter now. Her father had commented on the change in her, though, and he'd liked Rad so much. Her dad had been really upset with Lainie when . . . she frowned, refusing again to allow those memories back.

Instead she hurried to the bathroom off her bedroom, forcing her mind to concentrate on the evening to come. But the past kept returning with incredible persistence. Although Lainie still had plenty of clothes, everything seemed to hang on her, at least a size too large because of her recent weight loss. She knew of only one dress that would not reveal her thinness, and it was pushed to the rear of the closet. Her hands trembled as she withdrew the black lace gown. It had always been Rad's favorite. She had promised herself numerous times that she would give it away or burn it, but it had remained tucked away, out of sight but never out of mind. For one brief moment she almost thrust it back before she chided herself for letting such an association prevent her from wearing the only gown that fit her.

By the time Ann and her husband had picked Lainie up, driven to the concert hall and parked, it was nearly time for the performance to start. It was impossible for Lainie not to remember the times she had been in the hall before. The memories brought the familiar hollow feeling inside as the trio were escorted to their seats. Not until Voight was on stage and well into his second piece was Lainie able to push aside her recollections and give herself up to the sheer pleasure of hearing a genius play live.

The intermission came all too quickly. Classical music always uplifted Lainie's spirits. Her face was more animated than Ann had seen it in several years. Her footsteps were eager and her smile generous as she joined Ann and Adam in the exodus to the lobby. Lainie nodded easily when Ann excused herself to phone home to check on her four-year-old daughter, Cherry. The perfection of her contentment was so complete that when someone jostled her roughly, Lainie wasn't startled, just turned around to pardon the culprit. A man looked down at her inquiringly as a slow smile spread across his handsome face.

"Lainie," he breathed softly. "It is you!"

"Lee!" she echoed in the same stunned voice he had used, allowing him to take her hand in a gentle grasp. "Wow, it's been ages!"

"You're more beautiful than I remembered." His light blue eyes traveled admiringly over her face. "Where have you been hiding? The last time I heard, you were in Colorado Springs."

"Well, now I'm back in Denver. I wasn't gone all that long." Lainie smiled as she studied Lee's strong, thoughtful face. She couldn't help wondering who else from her old crowd was here.

"You've changed."

She waited for him to say why without speaking.

"Quieter than you used to be, for one thing."

"Am I?"

"What happened to your sassiness, Lainie?"

"That? I was faking it."

"Really?"

"Lee, I just grew up, like everyone else." Lainie laughed as she withdrew her hand from his. "Catch me up on the news—how is everyone?"

"Got an hour?"

Lainie thought of her mother and shook her head. "I saw on Facebook that MaryBeth was married."

"Yeah, the pictures were fun. All five thousand of them."

"MaryBeth was never shy."

"There's someone who'll never grow up. Like most of them," Lee Walters answered her first question. "As for MaryBeth, she's married, but she hasn't changed."

Lainie wasn't really interested in what he was saying. She was busy gathering together her impressions of him. He was still hot in his nice-guy way. Well, almost hot. He hadn't really changed through the years. His kind expression lulled you into feeling safe and secure. His smile, slow and sincere, still had the irresistible charm as before. But there was nothing staid and dull about him. Lee had always been as ready for a good time as the rest of their group, yet in a different way.

Since she wasn't listening closely to his words, it wasn't until he raised his hand and motioned an invitation that Lainie realized he intended for someone to join them.

"My sister Carrie was just talking about you the other day. She'll be pleased to see you." Lee smiled at her. He started to speak again, but the words faded away as he concentrated on the people behind Lainie.

Curiosity at his sudden silence turned her around

just as his sister called out, "Look who I've found, Lee!"

Lainie was barely aware of the hush that fell over their small group or of the uncomfortable glances exchanged between Lee, his sister, and her escort. Only the fifth person claimed her attention, the tall, dark-haired man who stared back at her, a mixture of boldness and reserve in his eyes. The blood faded away from her face and was pounding loudly in her ears. Her legs shook as she wished hopelessly that the floor would open up and swallow her. No one seemed capable of speech. No one except the man whose gaze moved over Lainie.

The years haven't been good to me, she thought, aware that he had to see the shadows under her eyes and the pallor in her cheeks.

"You're looking good."

He couldn't possibly be telling the truth. Arrogant bastard. And she would have to add the word judgmental to her low opinion of him too. For a fraction of a second it occurred to her that he just might mean exactly what he said—and that she was hard on herself in a way no one else was. Then she swiftly dismissed the foolish thought.

Her face flamed with anger she couldn't hold back. "You haven't changed, Rad. You're the same old you. "

His dark brown eyes seemed veiled, his emotions hidden. That didn't stop her from reading the worst into his behavior. She heard someone she didn't know make a low-voiced remark about her sharp tone but she ignored it, as did Rad. He didn't look away. Neither did she. Lainie studied him, not trying to hide it. He didn't have a handsome face, because the features looked as if they had been carved with a blunt chisel. The line of his mouth wasn't soft and the set of his jaw and chin was uncompromising. His expression was unchanging.

A mutual friend of theirs had once described him as being carved in stone. He radiated masculinity and, worse, a powerful virility. She would have to admit that Rad was compellingly attractive.

"Was that supposed to hurt?" he asked, seeming amused. The bland tone of his voice made his gibe hurt more, but Lainie didn't get an opportunity to comment. "What are you doing here?"

She drew herself up so that all five foot eight inches of her in heels stood rigidly in front of him. "I wasn't aware this was a private concert for your benefit only." There was a certain satisfaction in seeing his nostrils flare in anger at her sarcastic retort.

"You know very well I didn't mean that." His voice was oddly soft.

"My parents"—Lainie halted and corrected herself— "my mother lives in Denver, or had you forgotten?"

"I . . . I heard about your father's death." She heard no sympathy in Rad's voice and she didn't like the twist of his mouth. "My father died recently, too."

That was news to Lainie. She had always liked Rad's father. "I'm sorry, I didn't know." Her sincere words of condolence were well-meant, but he immediately made her regret it.

"Too bad they both had hoped for grandchildren." Rad's eyes were unreadable. "You and I didn't last that long. Kind of a shame. But it happens."

The remark took her breath away for several excruciating seconds. "You're unbelievably obnoxious." Lainie couldn't stop her voice from trembling violently. "Bringing that up here—when people are listening—"

"They've all gone back to the bar. No one's listening," Rad said.

Lainie turned away and saw that what he said was true—there was a line and everyone who'd been near them was in it, waiting their turn for an over-priced drink. She wouldn't have minded one. A double.

Then Carrie Walters caught her eye and moved toward her, reaching out with her hand to touch Lainie's arm.

"I didn't know you were with Lee," she said softly.

Lainie smiled and nodded, still feeling Rad's censorious eyes on her back. "I'm not, really, but it's all right," she said after she had found her voice. "The people I came with are around here somewhere. They'll be looking for me. I'd better get back."

"I heard your mother was ill," said Carrie. "How's she doing? I hope she's better."

"Pretty well, actually."

"What's the matter with her? If you don't mind my asking."

"The doctors don't really know yet. She's been through test after test—you know how it is."

Carrie nodded.

"And I'd have to say that she can be a awful hypochondriac," Lainie went on, "But even so—"

"Hey, hypochondriacs do get sick once in a while," Carrie said with an understanding smile. "But I really hope it's nothing serious."

"I'll let you know. We're doing okay."

"That's great. It's good to see you again, Lainie. Oh—hello again, Lee."

Both women glanced up at the blond-haired man in front of them, his gaze silently reassuring Lainie.

But before Lainie could say something similar and

excuse herself from them, someone took her arm and she was looking again into Rad's face.

"So . . . I guess you've taken a vow of silence where I'm concerned."

"I wish I could," she said vehemently.

"But you say everything's okay."

"More or less." Lainie glared at him. Like her life was any of his business.

"Hmm. I've heard differently. But . . . well, let me know if you need advice on your investments or whatever else I can—"

The know-it-all look on his face made something snap in Lainie. She raised her hand and, with all the force she possessed, slapped his face. "It'll be a cold day in hell when that happens! Don't do me any favors, Rad MacLeod!"

The fury in his eyes was clear but he controlled himself, thrusting his hands into his pockets and gazing at her calmly. That didn't stop Lee, who did the knight-in-shining-armor thing and came up to interfere.

Fear coursed through her as Lainie realized just how successful she had been at riling Rad. This was not the first time she had glimpsed that look in his eyes, but she still hated it.

"Hey, you two." Lee's tone was cool and almost patronizing. "Enough glaring, okay? Play nice."

Lainie watched Rad's jaw clench as he slowly regained control of his anger. His chest rose and fell as his dark eyes returned to their impassive blankness. He stepped back to straighten his tie and adjust the lapels of his black evening suit. Her heart was still beating erratically as Rad moved away. His gaze passed over the milling people, alighting on the ones he knew as if daring them to comment, before moving with unruffled composure out of sight.

He hadn't done anything. Lainie didn't care. She still couldn't stand him. From the corner of her eye Lainie saw Lee turning toward her, his expression plainly that of one about to champion her cause.

She was too upset to hear it, feeling or imagining that there were expressions of pity in the eyes of the spectators. The tears that were never far away these days welled in her eyes. Her flight to the powder room went unchecked. The few who might have chosen to follow her were halted by the announcement that the intermission was over and the performance was to begin again.

Alone in the powder room, except for the attendant, who was polishing the marble counter, she looked at herself in the mirror.

Maybe Ann was right. Maybe she was clinically depressed. Maybe she stayed inside day after day because the world was just too damn much for her right now.

Too overwhelming. Too filled with people who seemed to be expecting things from her that she just couldn't give. Above all, she was confused and sad.

She splashed cold water on her face, not caring if her makeup was ruined. Her mind reiterated her exchange of words with Rad, and she wondered if she had overreacted, even made a fool of herself. The attendant left the powder room and Lainie gave in to wrenching sobs that seemed to come from some deep, unknown place. She wasn't even aware of Ann entering the room and cradling her in her arms. Not until the spasms of pain were reduced to choking sobs did Ann attempt to find out what had happened.

"Rad. He's here." Lainie turned her red eyes to

the face of her anxious friend. "During the intermission . . . oh, God . . ." Fresh sobs broke out while
Ann patted her arm comfortingly. "He just got to
me."

"What did he say?"

"I—I don't know exactly—it's just that seeing him
was so upsetting. Ann, I . . . I can't stay here. I've got
to go home."

Her fingers clutched Ann tightly. She was ashamed
of her childish outburst, but the heartbreaking bewilderment of the last minutes had robbed her of the
little pride she had left.

"I'll call a taxi."

Lainie straightened up, wiping the tears from her
eyes and attempting to get control of her emotions,
"You and Adam don't have to leave."

"Don't be ridiculous." Ann smiled. "Adam can get
the car and will meet us outside in five minutes. The
concert wasn't that good anyway."

"Ann . . ." Lainie sought for words to express her
gratitude.

"Oh, hush. I'll be back."

Ann must have explained the situation to Adam as
best she could. When she returned to accompany
Lainie to the car, her husband shrugged off Lainie's
apologies with an understanding glance. And Lainie
smiled back at the man with curly hair and twinkling
blue eyes.

"I don't know what I did to deserve friends like
you," Lainie sighed, leaning back exhaustedly in the
front seat between Ann and Adam.

"Probably because you married a man like Rad
MacLeod," Adam replied, his now stern gaze watching
the glaring headlights of the traffic ahead of them.

"I thought after being separated from him for five

years that I would have forgotten how incredibly insecure he makes me feel. Like I'm just not good enough. Never was. Never will be. Like he has all the answers and I'm just . . . nobody." Pain dug deep furrows into her forehead. "We couldn't even make small talk. Maybe it's me—I don't know."

"It's not just you," Ann insisted. She put a hand to her mouth and inhaled sharply. "Oh, I just thought of something."

"What?"

"Ann," her husband said warningly.

"You don't know what I'm about to say," Ann said.

"Maybe not. All right, spit it out."

"Just that I imagine Sondra viewed the whole scene with her typical satisfaction," Ann commented.

"Sondra?" A vivid picture of Rad's titian-haired secretary leaped in focus in her mind's eye. Lainie stiffened, trying to study her friend in the dim interior of the car. "Was . . . was she there?"

"I saw her in the lobby when I was calling home." Lainie could tell that Ann was having second thoughts about pointing out that Sondra had been at the concert, especially since it was so obvious that Lainie hadn't known it. "I guessed that Rad must have been there and I could only hope you wouldn't see them."

"Poor Rad." Lainie laughed with a bitterness even she could hear, which surprised her a little. Objectivity hadn't been her strong point lately. "He deserves her."

A heavy silence weighed uncomfortably on the trio as the full impact of the evening settled over them. It seemed right to Lainie that they rode safely in the dark interior of the car with the impersonal world of streetlights and neon signs outside. It was a struggle to emerge from her cocoon of darkness when Adam finally halted the car in front of her house.

"I'm sure the nurse wouldn't mind staying overnight," Ann suggested gently, "if . . . if you don't feel up to dealing with your mom tonight."

"No." Lainie knew her mother would be sleeping anyway. "It won't be necessary."

"Would you like Ann to stay too?" Adam offered with the generosity so characteristic of them both.

"I'd rather be alone." She shook her head and thanked them again for their kindness and understanding before hurrying into the house to let the nurse know her friends were waiting outside to take her home.

The prescribed pill had done the trick and her mother was sleeping peacefully when Lainie settled in the chaise in her mother's bedroom. It wasn't necessary for her to sit with her, but Lainie knew the bed in the adjoining room had looked too lonely to occupy. At least in the comfortable chaise she wouldn't have to make a pretense of trying to sleep. Lainie gazed up at the ceiling, letting memories drift back that she had been trying to forget.

It was six years ago that she had first met Rad MacLeod at an impromptu after-theater gathering. Rad had arrived at her friend's house to discuss business with her parents. Lainie remembered whirling out of the room wearing a long flowing gown and stopping abruptly as she saw him standing in the entry hall. There had been something breathtaking about the way he had eyed her, his look appreciative and frankly sensual. Minutes later she had cornered Andrea, the daughter of the people Rad had come to see, managed to discover exactly who he was and that his firm was constructing a large industrial plant for Andrea's parents in Oklahoma, and had persuaded Andrea to invite him to their gathering, all in one breath.

Still, Lainie had been slightly surprised when he joined them later. It was obvious from the beginning that he didn't fit in with the boisterous group that was horsing around and getting loud. He possessed so much self-assurance that she felt kind of frivolous and silly. The young guys in the group that Lainie had been dating suddenly seemed like little boys beside this confident specimen of male virility. Lainie had been startled to discover that his eyes were openly mocking her attempts to flirt with him, as if she were playing an immature game.

"Noisy party," Rad said, surveying his competition with distaste. "And it's going to get noisier."

"So?" The light question definitely made her sound immature, Lainie had thought.

"Okay if you leave? I mean, with me. Will your friends mind?"

"I don't think so."

"Good. Then let's go," Rad had said, his gaze moving over her face and figure with enjoyable thoroughness. "I want to be with you and you want to be with me."

An exhilarating shiver of fear had raced through her as Lainie had briefly considered her sports car parked in the driveway before she had thrown caution to the wind and agreed to accompany him.

A week of swanky dinners, flirty calls and text messages, and nightclubbing had followed. And Rad quickly shattered Lainie's notion that she knew how to kiss. She smiled ruefully remembering the girlish metaphor she'd come up with at the time: her bones turned to marshmallows and Rad's fiery touch roasted her clear through.

Common sense and patience got the heave-ho. Not to put too fine a point on it, she became his to command. Lainie was all too willing to surrender, swept away with the idea of passion—okay, with him passion was a reality. Their lovemaking in the first four weeks was a revelation. Rad, she'd decided, was the only man for her. Forever and ever. Her love for him was completely irrevocable and without boundaries.

When she was apart from him, all she could do was think about him. The second they were together, she'd been ashamed at the abandonment with which she responded to being in his arms again.

And she could never forget that rapturous night when he had finally proposed to her. They were sitting in the car in front of her house, and Lainie was trying to get control of herself—Rad, for reasons he wouldn't explain, was keeping her at arm's length. She hated the feeling of sensual frustration and she'd looked at him pleadingly. To her chagrin he seemed completely unmoved, except for that one betraying muscle on the side of his mouth that twitched. She loved that little bit of him. It was a dead giveaway. The man had iron self-control. But just by running a finger along it she knew whether he desired her, too. No matter what he said.

"What am I going to do with you?"

"Well," she began, but he held up his hand before she could share some really interesting ideas on that subject.

"I might have to marry you sooner rather than later, Lainie." His dark eyes had gleamed at her.

"Huh?" Oh, brilliant, she'd thought disgustedly at the time. Was it possible to sound any more clueless than that?

"You and I really have something."

"We do?"

"Yes. But how am I going to turn a girl into the mother of my children?"

"The usual way, I guess."

He'd laughed and covered her mouth for a passionate kiss that went on and on.

At the time, it hadn't bothered her that Rad didn't say he loved her, and she'd responded with all the enthusiasm and relief that had been bottled up for weeks.

And said yes to whatever he wanted.

Looking back, Lainie knew he almost appeared amused at her excitement, but her parents' reactions had been divided. Her father had taken one look at the blissfully happy look in her eyes and given his blessing. Although her mother didn't object to the engagement, she did express her doubts.

"Lainie, honey," she'd said, exhibiting a degree of parental concern that was a lot more evident back then, "you've just turned twenty. Rad MacLeod's eleven years older than you. That isn't a huge difference, I know, but he's so much more experienced than you."

"Oh, Mom, what can that possibly matter?" Lainie had laughed. "It's a good thing. He's ambitious. Driven, almost."

"And you're headstrong."

Lainie shook her head in the darkness and stretched out on the chaise. She wasn't like that any more. She couldn't begin to think of what she ought to do with her life these days, except take care of her mother. Her twenty-something eagerness had been swallowed up by a sadness that permeated every aspect of her life.

If only she had some of Rad's take-charge attitude. Well, she thought, she'd kept him at bay tonight. Maybe she wasn't completely hopeless.

Her mother had expressed what Lainie now saw as fear for her. Years ago she'd just thought of it as interference . . . mingled with jealousy. Another conversation on that subject came back to her.

"Lainie, think twice about what you're getting into. Rad is accustomed to giving orders, to controlling the lives of the people who work for his company. Dominating others is second nature to him."

"Yeah," she'd said happily. What an idiot.

"He's already pushing you to fit in with his plans. Whoever heard of a wedding only two weeks after the engagement? It just isn't done."

"Mom, is that what's bothering you? That it's all happening too fast?" Lainie had hugged the resisting woman around the shoulders. "But you know I don't care about a big society wedding. All I want is Rad."

"And he knows it," Mrs. Simmons had retorted grimly. "Already you've allowed him to have the upper hand."

"Sorry, Mom. I can't be your little girl forever."

"No," her mother snapped. "In a matter of months, you'll be pregnant.

"Why not? Rad and I both want children." There had been a shy blush in Lainie's cheeks. But it was the thought of motherhood that'd made her feel awkward, not what led up to it.

"I can see that nothing I say means anything to you. You're too full of your own emotions to listen to reason. Rad MacLeod is a little too possessive, in my opinion."

Unlike you, right? Lainie hadn't made the retort but she sure as hell had thought exactly that.

"And you're not grown up enough to handle him."

"How can you say that?" Lainie had been appalled by her mother's doubts about the man she wanted so much. "He loves me and wants to marry me. His family's wealthy. Isn't he what you'd call a good catch?"

"As you say, he loves you," her mother had agreed, but with a dry note of cynicism that had frightened Lainie. "But there's more to marriage than that, as you're about to find out. However, I won't stand in your way even though I don't approve of him."

Lainie had assumed that her mother was simply reluctant to let anyone else boss her around, reserving that privilege for herself. Rad had seemed like salvation, in a way.

Out of the frying pan, into the fire. Letting a man do the thinking for you was an effective way to not grow up, a little voice in her mind said.

"Lainie, before you bring children into this world," her mother had intoned in a final warning Lainie had brushed off, "wait until you know for sure what kind of man you've married."

As much as she had tried to push her mother's warnings to the back of her mind, they'd kept creeping back. When at first she would have accepted a statement from Rad with the faith of her love, Lainie found herself examining his words and picking fights. She could see now how torn she'd been between the two of them—and that she'd been unable to think things through.

The day of the wedding had arrived swiftly, bringing with it all the culmination of her dreams. It was followed by an idyllic fortnight at Rad's cabin in the Rocky Mountains. He had been as tender and gentle and loving as any bride wanted her groom to be. Yet he had managed to fan the sparks of desire between them into a full, burning fire.

Those days of exploring love's enchantment had

ended too soon and they returned to Denver, where Lainie discovered how empty the days were when Rad was at his office and she was home alone. She had tried to content herself with taking care of their new home, but with a maid to do the cooking, and a housekeeper to do the cleaning, and a gardener to take care of the lawns and gardens, she had been an ornament, pretty but not very useful.

It was then that she first felt the stirrings of a pervasive unhappiness that was impossible to shake. Decorating the place, getting out to exercise, seeing her friends—it all felt like too much. She'd told herself that she ought to be happy; she hadn't been. For a time, the evenings with Rad had made up for the loneliness of the days. Then Lainie forced herself to renew her friendships with her college crowd, spending an afternoon shopping with one, or playing tennis with another. Rad hadn't seemed to mind at all.

Of course, it was during that time that Lainie had met Sondra, her husband's beautiful red-haired assistant. Blindsided by heartbreaking jealousy of a woman who spent more hours with her husband than Lainie did, she'd begun to fall apart inside. Little arguments grew bigger and highly charged with emotion.

Looking back, Lainie could see that it was her own immaturity that had undermined their marriage. She'd begun to resent the demands of his business, to nag him relentlessly to spend more time with her, to spend major money on clothes to entice him to her side; but Rad had only regarded her with amusement, chiding her occasionally to grow up.

Four months after the wedding had come the first business trip, their first separation. Lainie had accompanied Rad to the airport, only to find Sondra already there.

"Okay," Sondra had said to her boss, "we're checked in and our baggage is heading down the X-ray chute. I sure hope they don't find my—um, never mind. Hello, Lainie." Sondra's green eyes had looked wide with surprise. Lainie had taken it for guilt.

"Is she going with you?" Lainie had burst out in anger. Sondra's suggestive comment, broken off, wasn't likely to be clarified for the benefit of Lainie, the not-so-new bride.

She hadn't been prepared for Rad's reaction. With the same lithe swiftness that had already surprised her for such a muscular guy, he'd taken her arm and propelled her to a secluded corner. The annoyance in his tone had made her even more furious.

"Chill. She's talking about a pair of scissors, okay? She had to take it out of her carry-on and check it through. It's not what you think."

"God, it's hard to say 'it's not what you think' and sound convincing."

Rad's face was set and calm. She almost hated his self-control. "I'm not going to tolerate childish displays of jealousy in public." The tight hold on his temper was revealed by the muscle ticking in his jaw. The very same one that she'd gauged his desire for her with.

"I don't trust her," Lainie had retorted, refusing to allow him to browbeat her.

"I don't believe you trust me."

"Maybe I don't." Her chin had quivered tremulously before she tossed her head back with disdain. "I'm sure you'll enjoy the trip. No doubt Sondra will see to that. You've told me more than once that she's indispensable. And incredibly competent. Now I'm beginning to see why!"

She'd stalked away, half-expecting Rad to come running after her. But he hadn't. That night Lainie had removed his belongings from their bedroom and put them in the guest bedroom.

Big mistake. One that she would never have made if she had known her husband better. Rad seemed remote when he'd eventually returned. Even her heartfelt apology a few days later didn't work. The change in their relationship had hurt and confused Lainie. More and more she sunk into brooding for hours, or the opposite of that, whooping it up with her old friends and excluding him.

She got an entry-level job she hated in marketing and immersed herself in that. Pretty soon it was Rad who was returning home from work before Lainie.

There were fights. And more fights.

The winter that year had brought more than snow. It had brought icy indifference into their house each time Rad walked in the door. The terrible arguments were over, but Lainie found a hellish sense of emotional isolation in the coldness that had taken their place. Then came the evening when they'd both been invited to a very important dinner party by one of Lainie's friends. Rad had arrived home late. Almost too late to get there on time.

"Did you forget we were invited out tonight?" Lainie had demanded as she met him in the foyer.

"Nice to see you too. You always know how to make me feel welcome in my own home," Rad had sneered, walking past her into the den where he tossed a couple of ice cubes into a short glass and poured himself a stiff whisky.

"That would be *our* home."

He swallowed the drink in two gulps. "Ours, huh? I didn't know you knew what that word meant. So this is *our* home. How about that." His tone was flat. "Could've fooled me."

"Skip the self-pity. We're supposed to be there in ten minutes."

The way he regarded her so calmly had irritated Lainie beyond endurance. "Call them up and tell them we aren't coming." He had turned his back on her.

"I can't do that!"

"I've had a rough day. That damned party isn't important."

"No, my friends are giving it, so of course it isn't important to you," Lainie had retorted sarcastically.

"Your constant bitching is getting on my nerves." Rad's jaw had been tightly clenched and Lainie's tense stomach churned. She'd wanted to cry despite of her air of defiance. She said nothing, just watched him. "I am not going to that party tonight, and that's final."

"Well, I am!"

"I'd think about it if I were you," Rad had said coldly as Lainie turned to leave the room.

"Is that some kind of threat?" She'd spun around sharply.

"You can't put yourself and your needs first every damn time, Lainie. Maybe I am asking you to choose between me and your friends. And maybe just once it would be a good idea you chose me."

"Is that your solution to saving our marriage?"

He poured himself a second drink. "I wasn't aware it was on the rocks."

"It is. Just like that whisky you're swilling."

"Oh, here it comes. Rad is a drunk. Rad is mean. Rad is bad. Poor little Lainie."

Furious, she put her hands on her hips and glared at him. "I'm sick of this."

He sipped at the second whisky, a little more thoughtful. "What do you want, Lainie? Just tell me."

"Not this." She waved her hand at the beautifully decorated house. "Not anything you have to give."

"Not even kids?"

Lainie snorted. "What a time to ask that question. I can hear the patter of little feet. Ready or not, here they come."

"You're not ready."

"Why the hell do I have to answer that now?"

Rad only shook his head. "I would have been better off keeping you as a girlfriend. You're not even ready to be a wife, let alone a mother."

The complete lack of emotion in Rad's voice had taken Lainie's breath away. There was no further doubt in her mind at that moment that the love he had felt for her was gone. She'd left the room, shaky legs carrying her farther away from him.

Chapter 2

Ann dropped in the following afternoon and looked at Lainie's sleep-deprived face with concern.

"You should have let me stay with you last night," she scolded, not unkindly.

"We would have talked half the night anyway," Lainie smiled faintly, "and I still wouldn't have had enough sleep."

"Well, at least I could've shared the nightmare."

"Ann, don't," Lainie whispered.

Ann studied her for several long moments. "You still haven't forgotten Rad, have you?"

"I used to love him. A lot," Lainie replied quietly. "You can't block out the happy memories altogether."

"Now that you've seen him again, you don't still love him, do you?"

"No." It was a breathy protest and there was a tiny gleam of uncertainty in Lainie's eyes. Last night Rad had taken her by surprise. That was why her heart had beat so wildly.

"Was there never any talk of you two getting together again? When you first broke up, I mean?"

Ann asked. "You told me that Rad stalled about giving you a divorce—that he filed one court motion after another, anything to gain time."

"Yes, he did."

"He's a control freak."

"Not exactly. He's in charge. There is a difference."

Ann shrugged. "Explain it to me some other time."

Lainie's throat closed. Something that was half a sigh and half a sob came from her. "Oh, Ann . . . when we were first married, I loved him so much I let my heart rule my head." Lainie turned her unseeing gaze to the gold-flocked paper on her bedroom wall. "I was jealous of every minute he spent away from me. I resented his work, his associates, anything that deprived me of him. I behaved like a brat, spending money to draw attention to myself, deliberately going to parties without him, trying to make him jealous—"

"But—"

"Sometimes I wonder if I'd been just a little more grownup and a lot more understanding if we wouldn't still be married today. Maybe I was just blissfully ignorant of what a hollow shell our marriage was from the beginning."

"What are you talking about?" Never in the few times that Lainie had discussed her marriage with Ann had she ever made such a statement.

Lainie stared down at her slender fingers, interlocking her hands. "Rad never loved me." A shimmering veil of tears covered the hazel green eyes that met Ann's startled glance with quiet dignity. "He told me so. Okay, he did think I was totally hot. And socially I was acceptable, so I was the prime candidate when he decided to take a wife."

"To take a wife? That's so cute. And old-fashioned.

Not in a good way." She groaned aloud. "Of all the cold-blooded—" Ann subsided before turning puzzled eyes on Lainie. "Then why aren't you two divorced yet?"

"He stalled and kept stallig, and so did I. Two can play that game."

"For five years? It's tough on both of you, Lainie. I care much more about you, but geez—"

"He muttered something once during a meeting between us and our lawyers. Off the record. Something about how he'd paid dearly to marry me and he wasn't going to pay to get rid of me." She tried to make her voice light and uncaring, but the pain of that memory went too deep. "I began shouting at him, telling him I didn't want his money, that I just wanted to be free of him, and if he didn't give me a divorce, I'd do something drastic."

Lainie twisted her head to the side as she remembered the one final humiliation. She bit her lip to keep control of its quivering while Ann waited silently for her to continue.

She got it together at last. "I met him once for lunch. Big mistake. He kept talking about this case he'd read about online, some guy who'd asked a friend to swear he'd slept with his wife, just to get the upper hand. He said the dirty tricks some people were capable of made him sick."

"Was that a veiled threat?"

"I really don't know," Lainie said. "We were both so upset. But he had an iron grip on his emotions. I can still remember how cold and calculating he sounded."

Ann drew in a sharp breath.

"Anyway, Rad laughed after the waiter came over and left, and told me he was going to play fair."

"What'd you say?"

"Nothing. I stood up and threw my drink in his face."

"Good for you."

"And the very next week I got hit with another court motion that said I was unstable."

Ann frowned. "What happened?"

"The judge threw it out in a preliminary hearing. Told us that we were both acting like children, and we would do well to pull up our little white socks and behave."

"Huh. You're an inspiration, Lainie, you know that?"

"As if. What do you mean?"

"I'm going to work on my marriage and stay married and—well, I just don't ever want to hear a judge tell me something like that."

"It wasn't fun. But he—the judge, I mean—was right."

"Why didn't you ever tell me this before, Lainie? It explains a lot of things." Ann smiled compassionately at her friend.

"I just didn't. I was so miserable, it seemed wrong to burden anyone else with the dreary details."

"I'm your friend."

"My best friend," Lainie said softly.

"When you two first split up, Lainie, I was astonished by the change in you. You seemed to lose all your self-confidence. I thought you were headed for a total nervous breakdown."

"If it hadn't been for my dad, I probably would have," Lainie admitted. "I remember one evening he came into my room and found me crying. He took me in his arms as if I were still a child and began wiping away my tears. He was the quiet type but philosophical. I'll never forget what he told me. 'The rainbow comes after the storm, so first you must endure the storm.'" She glanced briefly at Ann. "That's why I left Denver, to start my life over and wait for the storm to pass. I thought it had."

"Until you saw Rad again."

"Yes. Last night I was tossed right back into the heart of it."

The tinkling of a bell broke into the sudden silence, followed by a plaintive call from the occupant of the adjoining room.

"I thought your mother was sleeping," Ann whispered as Lainie jumped to her feet.

"She was." Lainie's forehead was knitted in a frown. She motioned for Ann to remain where she was as she walked swiftly to the connecting door, which she left ajar.

Dainty pink flowers were splashed everywhere with complementing pink satin curtains at the windows, complete with ruffles. The marble-topped dressing table at the far side of the room was hidden by delicate Dresden figurines and fragile glass ornaments. From the pink-canopied bed came Mrs. Simmons's repeated summons for Lainie. Her light gray hair went with the pastel room, as did her pale complexion.

"What is it, Mom?" Lainie patted the slender hand that reached out for her.

"I heard you talking in the other room." Long eyelashes fluttered questioningly at Lainie. "You were talking about Rad. Lainie, you aren't seeing him again, are you?"

"No, of course not. I merely ran into him at the concert last night," Lainie assured her.

"You didn't . . . you didn't tell him about our difficulties? You didn't mention how poor we've become?" The plaintive cry of pride in her mother's voice tugged at Lainie's heart. "I couldn't bear it if he knew."

Lainie nibbled at her lower lip before smiling with determined assurance. "I didn't ask him for a thing, Mom," she answered truthfully.

"Good," Mrs. Simmons sighed, and her hand moved weakly away from Lainie's to rest on the pink satin quilt keeping her warm. "I can rest now."

It was a dismissal, with all the affected regal air that was typical of her mother. Lainie often wondered how much of her mother's weakness was an act and how much was real. It was next to impossible to tell, but at least some of her ailments had to be genuine. The tests to come would undoubtedly turn up something.

Two days later Lainie finally found time to do the weeding of the front lawn. Her mother had taken her sedative an hour before and had fallen asleep immediately. It was a blessing to be out in the sunlight, feeling its warmth penetrating her light cotton blouse and cream-colored baggies. Summer was nearing its end. Lainie knew these days of sunshine would soon be blotted out by the cold blast of winter's breath sweeping down out of the Rocky Mountains.

The sweat on her forehead trickled down her face, but the physical exertion was relaxing. Digging and tugging to remove the stubborn weeds demanded a certain amount of concentration. Her mind had been working overtime these last few days, worrying over their financial woes while fighting off the recurring memories of Rad. Lainie had been sure that she had driven him from her thoughts, but after their unexpected meeting the other night she found the bitterness and misery had returned.

Nothing had been resolved. Not the divorce, not the conflict which had estranged them in the first place, not the everlasting standoff punctuated by ominous legal communications from both sides. Which was contributing to her sense of being, now and forever, hopelessly stuck in Unhappy Land.

To hell with it. To hell with him.

Firm steps sounded behind her, swishing through the grass. Lainie turned slightly from her kneeling position, shading her eyes from the sun's glare to identify the person approaching her.

"Lee, what a surprise!" She rose to her feet, removed the cotton glove from her hand and extended it warmly to him.

"I didn't know gardeners could look so cute." Lee smiled, his blue eyes lighting up at the pleased expression on Lainie's face.

"Hey, come up to the house." She flushed under the intensity of his gaze. "But I'm not really dressed for company. Give me a minute to scrub up."

"You look beautiful. Love the glow on your cheeks." He turned her toward the house and firmly tucked her hand through his arm. "I haven't been able to get you out of my mind, so I decided to stop by."

"More flattery, please. I love it!" Lainie laughed, glancing up at the strong face beneath the blond-brown hair.

"No, it's not flattery," Lee replied. The sincerity in his eyes caused Lainie to falter a little. "I haven't been able to get you out of my mind for several years. Before, I waited too long to let you know how I felt about you. Now that I've found you again, I'm going to stake a claim before anyone else has a chance."

"You don't give a girl an opportunity to think."

Lainie's footsteps halted as she stared in astonishment at Lee.

"Neither did Rad MacLeod," Lee replied quietly, watching Lainie's face. "And you married him."

"I'm not as impulsive as I used to be. I won't make the same mistake again." She firmly withdrew her hand from his.

"I'm glad." He smiled that quiet, serene smile. Lee could make her feel secure without even trying. "Because I would want you to be very sure of yourself before you married me."

"You're going way too fast!" She shook her head as if to free herself from the web that was being spun around her. "We haven't seen each other for five years. You can't begin to know me. And I don't really know you at all."

"Let's get acquainted again. Have dinner with me this evening?"

"Lee, my mother is bedridden. She can't be left alone. It's out of the question for me to consider dating anyone," Lainie explained, lifting her chin proudly as she met his steady gaze.

"Would you object if I came over here, visited with you in your home? Because I won't be put off."

"What can I say?" Her shoulders lifted in bewilderment. "We've known each other a long time. I've always considered you a friend, and now all of a sudden you're trying to change that. You're confusing me."

"Okay. As a friend, may I come over some evenings, then?"

"My friends are always welcome," Lainie replied.

"How about offering this friend something cold to drink?"

As quickly as Lee had become serious, he became lighthearted. He followed Lainie, unperturbed, into the kitchen and relaxed at the table, discussing nothing more serious than the whereabouts of various acquaintances they had in common. Lainie was left with the feeling that the previous conversation had never taken place. Except that she knew it had. An uneasiness gripped her, which made it difficult for her to react naturally to the situation.

She found herself examining her own feelings. After her disastrous marriage to Rad, she didn't know if she wanted to become involved with anyone else to that extent again. But there was no doubt that Lee was pleasant company, and a dependable guy. The whole situation struck her as being humorlessly academic anyway and she mocked herself for being so concerned about it. After all, she was still legally married to Rad.

Now that Lee had declared his intentions, to use a phrase her mother would love, the smartest thing for her to do was to sit back and wait to see what happened. Although she'd been unwilling to admit it to herself before, Lainie had been desperately lonely with only her invalid mother for company and an occasional visit from Ann. As long as Lee kept it light, what was the harm in letting him visit her a couple of times a week?

The following evening Ann called her and Lainie mentioned Lee's visit and his intention to come over that Friday. She wasn't exactly attempting to get Ann's advice, but she was curious to see what her friend's reaction would be to the situation. Ann endorsed it.

"Lee is exactly what you need," she said firmly. "Someone who's solid and dependable and won't bounce you around like a yo-yo."

"You make him sound really dull!" Lainie chuckled. "I don't think he'd appreciate that. He's really a good-looking guy, always has been."

"Yes, and he's got it together, which is exactly what you need right now." There was obvious determination in Ann's voice. It startled Lainie.

"Why do you say that?"

"It's just a feeling I have." Lainie could almost visualize Ann shrugging her shoulders. "What I really called for was to invite you to lunch with me tomorrow. My mom came over today and mentioned she'd been wanting to call on your mother but she wasn't sure whether she should or not. So I volunteered her to visit tomorrow noon."

"I'd love to go—"

"No 'buts,' please. My mother used to be a nurse," Ann said. "She isn't likely to panic if your mother takes a bad turn. Once a nurse, always a nurse. Besides, with my mother there to talk her ear off, she won't even miss you."

"I do have a prescription for Mom that needs to be filled," Lainie admitted hesitantly. "I suppose I could do that while I'm out."

"See? If you really want an excuse, there's always one available." Ann laughed. "We'll be over tomorrow about eleven-thirty."

"I'll have the chef's salad," Lainie ordered, glancing over the menu briefly before smiling up at the waiter, "with the house's blue cheese dressing. Coffee later."

As Lainie expected, Ann had brought her to one of the more plush restaurants in town. Elegant chandeliers hung in clusters from the ceilings with all the abundance of evergreen garlands at Christmas time.

The muted voices of the room's occupants mingled with the tinkling of crystal and the ring of silver. White linen tablecloths stretched over the endless reaches of tables graced by chairs covered with gold velvet. Lainie draped her napkin over the gentle olive shade of her skirt, unbuttoning the matching jacket to reveal the ivory shell beneath.

"Do you suppose they're still discussing your mother's illness, or have they progressed to our childhood maladies?" Ann grinned at her conspiratorially after the waiter had left.

"My mother has many symptoms. They should be through about half of them," Lainie replied, her eyes twinkling with amusement while she took a sip of the ice-laden water in her goblet. "How is it that Adam didn't snap you up for lunch today?"

"There was a directors' meeting at his firm this morning and he was sure it would carry over through lunch. So I polished his briefcase and made sure he wasn't wearing trousers with a shiny seat before sending my young executive husband off to the lion's den." Ann's mercurial manner changed abruptly from suppressed giggles to intense interest. "Now tell me more about Lee."

Lainie recounted Lee's visit yesterday and suffered through Ann's matchmaking tendencies and her freeform wit. It always seemed that when her sense of humor had vanished, Ann would pop over and tease it to the surface again. There were times when her friend refused to take any situation seriously and Lainie was given no choice but to do the same. Yet laughter kept all her other woes in their proper place. With Ann around, they never had the opportunity to take control.

The time passed swiftly. No sooner, it seemed, had

they sat down at the table than their meal was finished and they were lingering over their coffee. Ann
made another audaciously funny comment about
Lee's prospects as a future lover and sent Lainie into
peals of laughter.

"You make me feel like I'm back in high school
again." Lainie brushed her long hair away from her
face, still smiling. "Giggling over my latest conquest."

"That's the idea," Ann said brightly. As her gaze
strayed over Lainie's shoulder her eyes suddenly glinted
with the fire of battle. "Oh no," she whispered, "why
does he have to be here?"

Lainie glanced over her shoulder to see who'd
drawn such an angry reaction from Ann. She found
herself staring into Rad's dark eyes. There was a mes-
merizing quality about his gaze that held her own even
when she wanted to look away. If it hadn't been for the
sardonic lines on his face, Lainie could have believed
there was a glint of pleasure in his eyes. But that was
ridiculous. Rad couldn't possibly be pleased to see her.
He was nearly at their table before Lainie noticed the
rest of the people in his party. Especially the red-haired
girl preceding him who didn't attempt to hide the hos-
tility in her green eyes.

"Mrs. MacLeod!" Sondra exclaimed with a tinge of
sarcasm in her husky voice. "What a surprise to see
you!"

"Yes, isn't it?" Lainie could barely stop herself from
bristling with old jealousy, but she felt it seethe as she
watched Rad's hand, the one wearing the gold wedding band she had given him, touch Sondra's arm.

"Why don't you go on over to our table and tell
Bob and Harry I'll be right there?" Rad suggested
to Sondra. The private look that passed between
them set Lainie's teeth on edge. After Sondra walked

off, accompanied by two other men in business suits, Lainie felt Rad's eyes return to her, causing a tide of warmth to flood through her.

"Was there something you wanted to speak to me about?" She struggled to remain calm, fingering the stem of her water goblet to give her nervous hands something to do.

"I thought there was something you wanted to talk to me about." His mocking tone unwillingly lifted her gaze to where he stood towering above her. "After five years, I've now seen you twice in one week."

"You should mark it in your calendar," Lainie retorted bitterly, "and hope we can make it another five years."

"Nice of you to say so." The harsh lines around his mouth twisted with cynicism. "I've got all the time in the world."

"Good for you. But I've already told you there's nothing I want from you," Lainie hissed, "so why don't you just leave me alone?"

Her insides were tied into knots. She didn't know how much more she could take without revealing the torment Rad was putting her through. She could hardly look at his perfectly tailored gray suit without remembering the broad chest beneath, or look at his dark hair without recalling its softness when she had run her fingers through it.

"Check, please," Ann signaled the waiter with barely disguised impatience.

"Don't let me run you off," Rad jeered. "I'd hate to think I spoiled your luncheon."

"I just bet you wouldn't," Ann retorted, placing her neatly folded napkin on the table and fixing her smoldering eyes on Rad.

"It's time I was getting back to my mother," Lainie

said, knowing that her friend wasn't the kind to hold back her temper. The last thing Lainie wanted was an embarrassing scene in the restaurant.

"Your mother must be feeling better, since her dutiful daughter has left her side to enjoy a casual lunch." Rad didn't keep the edge out of his voice or the contemptuous gleam out of his gaze.

"Yes, she is better." Lainie breathed in deeply to keep from answering in kind.

"That's not true at all. " Ann rose from her chair in rigid anger. She spared Lainie a brief apologetic glance before turning on Rad with a vengeance. "Her mother is really ill and might not ever recover. Listen, Rad, I despise your condescending attitude toward Lainie. She isn't like you. She stands by the people she loves. She gave up her job and everything else to come back here to try to make her mother more comfortable."

Rad looked at her levelly but he didn't say anything.

"So," Anne went on, "I won't stand for you abusing her this way. Like she doesn't have enough worries with hospital bills and nursing and all the regular household chores. You don't have to come back into her life to upset it again!"

"I'm deeply moved by your defense of Lainie." But Rad was obviously completely unmoved by Ann's outburst. "How did you manage to inspire such loyalty?" he asked Lainie.

"I don't know. I never had it when I was with you, did I, Rad?" Lainie answered with cold quietness.

"I get it. Hey if I was ever unfaithful, and you didn't know one way or the other, it could have only been because my home life was—"

"Oh, please. Give it a rest, will you?"

"You seem to be saying that the cause of our separation was my lack of, uh, loyalty." He lifted one eyebrow arrogantly as he regarded her with amusement. "After five years, you can come up with something more original than that."

"Five years, six months and fourteen days ago," Lainie corrected in frustration and could have immediately bitten her tongue off at his accompanying laughter. "I remember every happy moment."

"You've kept track!" Rad's triumphant expression was even more irritating.

"People always remember exactly how long it's been since they've been free. Maybe tyrants don't!" Her jab at him was rewarded by the hardening of his jaw.

"I'm glad you have pleasant memories of something." Anger laced every word as Rad nodded abruptly toward Ann, then back at Lainie. "I won't keep you any longer. It's obvious you're anxious to be gone."

Lainie watched him striding away with a mixture of relief and sorrow. Their harsh arguments had always left her shaking, and this time had been no different. And, as before, she wanted to run after him, touch his broad shoulders, his arm, and have him stop so that her eyes and lips could beg her forgiveness and feel once again the magic of his caress. But the time when she could do that had passed. So instead she rose to her feet and joined Ann.

"Well, that really blew our lunch," Ann sighed. "You aren't going to want to come out with me anymore if he keeps turning up."

"There was no way either of us could know he'd be here." Lainie scowled. "Besides, I've run away from him long enough and I'm too tired to try again."

"So do you still love him?" Ann's voice was filled with quiet compassion.

Lainie breathed in deeply, bracing herself to deny it, but as she met her friend's open gaze she sighed, "I'm not sure. I'm not sure about anything."

"Rad is a hard man to forget."

Lainie silently agreed with her, praying that someday she would be able to forget him and the emotion she had once felt for him.

The next day, knowing that Lee would be coming over that night, Lainie responded to a sudden compulsion to clean house, getting into the corners and the crannies with a rag and a spray bottle. She tried to convince herself that it was because of Lee and not wanting to fill her time with work instead of thoughts of Rad MacLeod.

Unfortunately her mother was unusually restless, constantly ringing the little silver bell at her bedside, making progress in the housework difficult and nearly impossible. Lainie lost count of the number of times that she'd set down a duster or turned the vacuum cleaner off to race up the stairs. It was already the middle of the afternoon and she hadn't completed the downstairs yet. At this rate, she thought grimly, she would be lucky to have time to shower and change before Lee arrived.

A bell jingled demandingly for her. She was halfway up the stairs before she realized it was the phone and not her mother's bell that was ringing. With a disgusted sigh she turned around and hurried toward the den.

"Hello," she answered.

"Mrs. MacLeod, please," a male voice replied.

"Speaking." An apprehensive chill raced through her as Lainie tried to place the voice and failed.

"Mrs. MacLeod, this is Greg Thomas. I'm a lawyer representing your husband." Lainie sucked in a gasp. A new lawyer. Was Rad finally filing for a divorce? The idea filled her with a feeling of dread.

"Mr. MacLeod would like me to get together with you so that you and I could discuss some changes he would like to make."

"What kind of changes, Mr. Thomas?" Lainie asked quietly. The black telephone receiver in her hand seemed to be made of lead. She had difficulty keeping it to her ear.

"Changes regarding the support payments you're receiving from your husband each month."

A sickening nausea attacked Lainie's stomach. She knew she had been pretty damn rude to Rad, lashing out with spiteful, bitter statements. But she never dreamed she had angered him to the point where he would attempt to stop the small sum he had been sending her each month, agreed upon in their temporary settlement.

It was maintenance, if you could call it that. Since he was living in their, cough cough, gracious home and not her. That tiny check was insignificant by itself, but coupled with her mother's pension, it enabled them to survive.

"My mother is quite ill right now. It's nearly impossible for me to get away." Her voice trembled in spite of her attempt to sound calm and controlled.

"Yes, Mr. MacLeod explained that to me. I believe it was your mother's illness that prompted him to increase the amount of the monthly maintenance." There was a condescending note in the lawyer's voice.

"Increase?" Lainie echoed weakly.

"Yes. Your husband is aware that your financial circumstances have deteriorated since your separation, and that you must be having difficulties making ends meet now that you're forced to care for your mother. I think it's a magnanimous gesture on his part."

Mr. Thomas then named a figure so much larger than the pittance she was receiving that Lainie was stunned. She had been expecting the opposite, prepared to fight for the little she was supposed to get from their interim agreement. The lawyer was speaking again. Lainie had to mentally shake her head to concentrate on what he was saying.

". . . illness, you'll have doctor's bills and hospital bills, as well as other expenditures such as medication. No doubt these have piled up on you. Mr. MacLeod has suggested that this increase be retroactive, which would enable you to take care of some of your larger debts."

"Why is he doing this?"

"I've just explained, Mrs. MacLeod," the man replied patiently. "He's learned of your mother's illness and is aware of the strain it must have placed on your resources. He didn't mention any other motive. Now if we could just make an appointment for you to come into my office, there are a few papers for you to sign."

"Motive?" The word struck a sour note. "As in ulterior?"

"No."

"There must be something I don't know. I'll have to talk to my lawyer." Lainie's voice rang sharply, made stronger by her nameless fear.

Would her lawyer even return her call? He'd billed every penny of his retainer and she hadn't been able to give him more. Yet another reason her so-called divorce seemed like something that would never happen.

"Of course. You can do that at any time, Mrs. MacLeod, but I'm sure you'd like to have this increase initiated as soon as possible."

"Both of us and our lawyers signed off on our previous arrangement," she retorted. "But not you. This news would be welcome if I knew more about the possible long-term consequences. But my husband isn't exactly the most moral guy."

"Mrs. MacLeod." The obvious dismay in the lawyer's voice filled her with amused satisfaction.

"I've managed for five years without the benefit of his pity or charity, if that's what you could call it. If my quote-unquote circumstances cause him too much humiliation, then he ought to get this divorce underway and stop stalling. He's not responsible for my happiness or my mother's health." She made sure her words were laced liberally with sarcasm. "You pass that message on to Mr. MacLeod."

She replaced the receiver with all the finality of a person cutting her own throat. Heaven knew, she needed the money.

Chapter 3

"Who was that on the phone this afternoon?" her mother asked as Lainie walked into the room carrying her dinner tray.

"This afternoon?" Lainie replied. "Oh, just someone soliciting for magazine subscriptions."

"Are you sure?" Blue eyes blinked appealingly up at her. "It wasn't some bill collector you're trying to shield me from?"

"Oh, Mom, of course not." Lainie smiled widely. For one precarious moment she had been afraid that her mother, with her all-knowing perceptive instincts, figured out who'd called. "We may be in a difficult position moneywise, but our creditors aren't calling at all hours and camping on our doorstep."

"How can you treat it so lightly?" Mrs. Simmons queried, her fingers fumbling with the coverlet.

"Because you're being so melodramatic about it." Lainie was determinedly light and teasing, having discovered that was the only way she could avoid the tear-jerking sessions where, for hours, her mother bemoaned the fate that had deprived them of the lifestyle they had once known. "Now, I've fixed you some really good broth and a salad. You stop worrying about the bills and eat."

She shook the Irish linen napkin free and placed it over her mother's lap before adding an extra pillow behind her back.

"I really don't feel much like eating. The pain is so much worse today," her mother said fretfully.

"Eat as much as you can," Lainie soothed. "I have to shower and change, but I'll be back in a mo to see how you've done."

"Is someone coming over?"

"Lee Walters. For a little while, this evening."

"We can't really afford to entertain, can we?"

"Will you stop worrying about money?" Lainie raised her eyebrows meaningfully before leaning over to place a light kiss on her mother's cheek. "I've got fondue ready for a light snack. I found the old set in the attic, teeny forks and all. Cheese is cheap and stale bread is cheaper."

"Lee Walters," her mother mused, her mind already sidetracking itself. "Isn't he the son of Damian Walters?"

"Yes."

"With fair hair and blue eyes. I remember him now. I always thought he was fond of you." Mrs. Simmons smiled wistfully up at her daughter. "But I never encouraged him to come around. His father is filthy rich, but he has this peculiar idea that his children should make it on their own. I believe his son is works as a broker in his real estate firm, doesn't he?"

"I really don't know, Mom."

"You'd think Damien would at least have given him an administrative position. I remember Mrs. Walters telling me that all their children received was a limited allowance and a car and they had to live on what they made. Why, their children don't even have a trust fund set up for them! I wouldn't be surprised if Damian Walters left all his money to some charity when he dies." Mrs. Simmons leaned her head back onto her pillow as if the brief spate of indignation had weakened her. "Which was the very reason I wasn't too anxious for you to become involved with his son, even though his family is prominent." She sighed. "But considering our present position, it doesn't really matter anymore. I'm almost grateful that Lee's coming. It makes me feel we're not really social outcasts."

"I'm glad you don't mind." Lainie squeezed her mother's hand. "It's time I was getting ready. You can do me another favor by finishing your dinner while I'm changing."

"I will."

Lainie blew the fragile figure a kiss as she walked through the door adjoining her own bedroom. Money, she thought angrily, why did every conversation always seem to revolve around money? Or was she just being sensitive because of the phone call this afternoon? If only she hadn't allowed her feelings to intervene. Pride. Paranoia. She had reason for both.

She adjusted the water temperature before turning the shower on full force in her black and gold bathroom. In minutes she was undressed and standing under the needle-sharp spray of water, turning so that it could pelt every inch of her and drive out this angry depression that held her.

With the taps turned off, Lainie stepped out of the shower stall and swaddled herself in a large white terry towel, slipping her feet into white mules. Feeling refreshed, her skin tingling from the force of the spray of water, Lainie stopped in front of the mirror. She pushed a stray lock of her hair back with the rest piled on top of her head, secured with an oversized bob-bypin, before reaching for the jar of moisturizing cream for her face.

The doorbell sounded downstairs, causing Lainie to glance at her gold watch lying on the dressing table. It was too early for it to be Lee, unless he'd decided to be early. Impatiently she stepped into her lounging robe, tying the sash with a hard tug. She was starting to let her hair down when the bell sounded again.

If only he'd given her another fifteen minutes, she thought uselessly as she sped from her room and down the open staircase, she would have been ready. The words were already forming in her mind to excuse herself for a few more minutes as she flung open the front door.

Her mouth remained open, but no words came out as she stared into the granite-hard face of Rad. The unmistakable fire of challenge in his eyes caused her to step aside, allowing him entry into her home.

"Surely you aren't surprised to see me," he drawled, his eyes raking the thin fabric of her gown with sardonic amusement. "Mr. Thomas passed on your message."

Lainie's hand reached up to clutch the high neckline tighter together, knowing full well that the material was clinging to her still damp skin and emphasizing her curves. She turned away as if giving in to the desire to flee from him before pivoting back to face him. She did glance hesitantly up the stairs toward her mother's door.

"If you received my message, then I don't see why you're here." Lainie kept her voice low, not wishing her mother to overhear their voices and recognize

Rad's. "I thought I made myself clear. There isn't anything more to discuss."

"That's where you're wrong." His clipped statement revealed the tight hold he had on his temper. As usual. Ann was right about him being a control freak.

Lainie swallowed as her eyes roamed nervously over his impeccably tailored blue suit and the gleaming white shirt that contrasted with the golden tan of his skin. Rad still could make her feel vulnerable and inadequate. His air of authority always made her arguments seem so futile.

"Then say whatever it is that you've come to say and leave." But her words were choked, betraying his ability to upset her.

"Here?" Rad's eyebrow lifted in questioning mockery. "Wouldn't it be better to go into the living room? Our voices won't carry upstairs."

"Not the living room," Lainie said, the words coming in a rush, "the . . . the den would be better."

"I prefer the living room." Rad eased past her before she could think of a solid excuse to prevent him.

She stopped just inside the doorway, watching him as he glanced around the room. At first glance the room was done in unfussy but authentic Victorian style, with fancy rose-covered chairs and matching sofa, but a discerning eye could pick up rectangular patches on the wall where the paint was brighter. Where valuable artwork used to be. Lainie lifted her chin with defiant pride as Rad turned toward her.

"I seem to recall some Impressionist paintings on that wall. Minor masters, but good paintings all the same." To anyone else, Rad's comment would have sounded idly curious, but Lainie knew better.

"We're having them reframed."

"And the sculpture that was on the mantel?"

"It's been packed away. We got tired of it."

"I see." Mockery curled the corner of his mouth. "Did you get tired of that antique Chinese vase your mother was so proud of, the one your father gave her?" Then he smiled. "I suppose it got broken."

"Yes," Lainie retorted sharply.

"It would be interesting to take an inventory and find out how many valuable objects have either been packed away, are being reframed, or were broken." He studied her thoughtfully. "I suppose the jewelry was the first to be sold, wasn't it?"

High color filled her cheeks as she wrapped her arms around herself and turned away from him. "Yes," she hissed. "Can we not talk about this?"

"Do you know how much you owe? Have you any idea how deeply in debt you are?" Rad stepped closer to her.

She attempted to shrug his question aside, but he wouldn't allow her to. Then he enumerated their every creditor and the amounts owed with frightening correctness. Tears burned the back of her eyes, making them incredibly bright when she turned them on him.

"Did you have fun rooting out all our debts?" Her temper flared readily even though she trembled with humiliation. "Yes, we're poor. Does that make you happy?"

"Damn you, Lainie! I'm trying to make things easier for you!" Rad's voice raised to match hers.

"How?" she demanded. "Turning me and Mom into charity cases? Shaming us more?"

"What do you expect me to do?" He glared at her, exasperation in his expression. "Should I wait until you're forced to declare bankruptcy? How about when your mother and you are driven into foreclosure? Am I supposed to treat you like strangers and turn away?"

"How noble you are!" Lainie spat out. "Thank you, oh gracious benefactor. What am I supposed to do to repay you?"

"Nothing! I don't expect any repayment from you," Rad growled through tightly clenched teeth. "You need the money and I'm prepared to see that you get it. It's as simple as that!"

"With you, nothing is simple." Her hands were doubled into fists held rigidly at her side. "I can't deny that we need it, but I won't take a cent of your money. Do you hear me? I don't want your money!"

"So I should stand by and see you humiliated and embarrassed in front of all your friends. You want me to watch you lose your pride and self-respect, is that it?" He studied her contemptuously.

"Are you afraid they'll blame you?" Lainie challenged him. "Do you think they'll condemn you for not stepping forward to help me? Well, don't worry. I'll be sure to tell them of your generosity."

"You do that!" Rad grasped her shoulders and shook her, dislodging the tears that had remained precariously on her lashes. "Do you think I care what people say? It doesn't matter to me. It's you I'm worried about."

The bobbypin holding her hair on top of her head came out, sending her dark curls cascading around her face in abundant disarray. The shaking stopped, but her shoulders remained in his grip while her hands rested on the muscular hardness of his chest. A stillness permeated the air between them as Rad studied the tears trickling down her cheeks. Her lips were parted to protest, but Lainie found it impossible to speak. The harshness of his gaze silenced her. Inside, her senses were vibrating from his closeness.

"Why, Lainie?" he asked in a husky voice. "You've taken my name. You've taken me into your bed. Why can't you take my money?"

"Rad, please let me go," she whispered. Her eyes pleaded with him to release her.

She watched the scowl lift from his forehead and the look in his eyes change from demand to mockery. And her frightened heart raced at a frantic pace. He gave a slight negative movement of his head before he drew her closer to him. One hand gripped the back of her neck with compelling strength while the other slid to the small of her back and forced her body to mold to the hardness of his. Lainie struggled ineffectually against him, but her heart wasn't in it.

"Do you want me to go farther?" Rad asked in a low voice. "I think you do. It's there in your eyes. It was always like this between us. We fought as hard as we made love."

"No!" Her protest was a breathless murmur even as her pulse leaped in anticipation of his kiss.

Rad didn't disappoint her. His mouth descended on hers with sensual authority, possessing her lips, until he at last evoked the response from her that he had been seeking. When his hands firmly moved her away from him, it took only one glance at the satisfied glint in his eyes for Lainie to bow her head in humiliation, her heart aching that she hadn't had the strength to resist him.

"There hasn't been anyone else since me, has there?" Rad's rhetorical question brought her chin up so her eyes, glittering with shame and hurt, could gaze accusingly at him.

Lainie had no comeback at the ready and no lie came to her mind. But the need to reply was scotched by the tinkling of her mother's bell. Rad made no effort to hold her as she moved away, but she heard his light footsteps behind her as she made her way into the foyer and to the staircase. She paused once halfway up the steps to glance down at him. His enigmatic dark eyes stared back and Lainie raced the rest of the way to the top.

"Did you want something, Mom?" Lainie left the door open as she entered the bedroom.

"Was that Lee Walters at the door? I thought perhaps he could come talk to me. Lainie, you're not dressed!" Her voice rang out with amazing clarity.

"No, not yet." Lainie had difficulty smiling and her hands shook as she removed the tray of dishes from her mother's bed. "Lee hasn't arrived, but when he does, I'll see if he can come up for a few minutes." She didn't want to prolong the conversation and moved swiftly toward the door.

"Then who rang the doorbell?"

Lainie paused in the doorway to glance down to the bottom of the stairs where Rad stood casually staring into space, but obviously hearing every word.

"Just some harmless old guy who got lost," she lied. "He's partly deaf. Doesn't listen." She hoped he heard that too.

"Well, draw him a map. Make yourself perfectly clear."

"I'll do that." Lainie closed the door behind her.

She made her way slowly down the steps, deliberately avoiding meeting Rad's gaze. At the bottom of the steps she brushed past him, turning down the hallway toward the kitchen with Rad following. Once in the kitchen, she set the tray on the counter and began clattering the dishes into the sink, fighting the urge to hurl one of them at him. Rad leaned nonchalantly against the counter a few feet away.

"So Lee Walters is still hanging around?"

There was a razor-sharp edge to his voice that caused Lainie to glance up. "He isn't 'hanging around,'" she retorted. "This is the first time I've seen him in years. Not that it's any of your business.

"You are still legally my wife."

"By whose choice?" She spun angrily around. "Not mine, believe me. And don't tell me that crazy story again, the one about the guy who tried to make a false charge of adultery stick. It wouldn't work. Our judge isn't that stupid."

"*Our* judge," he mocked. "Sweet. I'm so glad we still have something that is ours."

"Shut up, Rad. Just shut the eff up."

A cold shaft of fear pierced her as she watched Rad move toward her. Even fighting the way they had once, she'd never cursed him. He halted inches away. Lainie saw him clench his jaw. He successfully controlled his temper.

"I'm glad you know what our judge would think, Lainie. I wouldn't venture a guess. Divorce cases can have unpredictable outcomes." Rad was now icy cool and contemptuous.

She understood the bitter truth of his statement. They would both suffer—that was how the legal system worked in contested cases. They should have opted for a mediated settlement and gotten the whole miserable business over with in a few months. But Rad had refused to do that. The utter futility of the situation washed over her.

"Why don't you just leave, Rad? We have nothing more to say to each other." Lainie suddenly felt bone tired. Speaking was an effort. "I've refused your offer. Even though I'm probably being ridiculously noble, at least let me keep some of my pride."

"Go ahead." A muscle twitched near his mouth. "I don't know if it'll put food on the table or pay for the care that your mother is going to need. I didn't make you an open-ended offer. But if I do it again, you can be sure the conditions will be different." His gaze roamed over her tear-brightened eyes and belligerent expression with analytical indifference. "Don't walk me to the door. I'll find my own way out."

Chapter 4

Removing the savory chunks of leftover ham from the oven, Lainie placed them in a warmed serving dish. The fondue sauce of tomato, cheese and onions had already been reheated, giving off a tantalizing aroma from its earthenware dish. She placed the chafing dish containing the sauce on the little burner and carried the whole thing into the living room, where crunchy cubes of bread were waiting with the serving plates and wooden-handled forks.

Wow. It just didn't get any more fabulously Seventies than this. Ashton Kutcher could walk through the door any minute and mooch a meal, then a kiss. Returning to the kitchen, she untied the apron that had protected her clothes and adjusted the multicolored sash around her waist.

She had just left the kitchen carrying the dish of ham when the front doorbell rang. This time it had to be Lee, Lainie thought. Her sanity couldn't take another visit from Rad. She opened the door, saw the smiling face of Lee Walters, and said a silent thank-you.

"I thought I was supposed to be the one bearing

gifts," he joked, sniffing appreciatively at the steam coming from the dish in her hand.

"I made fondue," Lainie explained. "I was just taking these ham chunks into the living room when the door-bell rang."

"Do you suppose rosé goes with fondue?" Lee asked. He waggled his eyebrows as he held out the bottle of wine that had been behind his back.

"My mother always told me you could never go wrong with rosé. Thanks. Take it on into the living room while I go get the glasses." Lainie laughed, then handed him the dish she had been carrying. "Here, take this, too."

Lee accepted it obligingly. The small talk relaxed Lainie's nerves, still jangled from Rad's visit. Not that anything was going to help her forget that he had come. That would be like asking for the moon. As she took out the wineglasses from their nook in the kitchen cupboard, she felt a sense of relief that Lee was going to keep her company this evening. The revelation of her own still vitally alive emotions where Rad was concerned had had a traumatic effect. It was frightening that he still had the ability to make her respond so wantonly. Lainie was hesitant to mull over the reasons. The idea that she still might be in love with him was a thought that she didn't want to face.

That was the reason she allowed herself to be drawn into Lee's good mood. When she re-entered the living room she found Lee already sampling the savory ham chunks, dipping one in the fondue sauce. He had such a funny expression of guilt on his face, like a little boy caught tasting the icing on a cake. She wished she could go back to the time when doing something like that was her worst sin.

"Got me!" Lee reached out for the wineglasses and the corkscrew.

"I take it as a compliment. You couldn't resist my cooking," Lainie laughed, watching as he expertly opened the bottle of wine.

"Too true," Lee agreed. He poured equal portions of rosé into the stemmed glasses, handing one to Lainie and keeping one for himself. Then he raised his toward her in a toast. "To this delicious fondue, and this bottle of wine, and—and to many more evenings with you."

It was difficult meeting his gaze. Lainie raised her glass in acknowledgment of the toast, knowing Lee had given it sincerely, yet not knowing how true she wanted it to be. Lee seemed to sense this, and immediately tried to change the slightly serious tone. In minutes they were both attacking the retro repast, dipping crunchy cubes of bread into the fondue sauce. Later, replete, they relaxed against the back of the sofa, Lee patting his stomach in satisfaction. "So. Thanks for that. What now?"

"Small talk."

"Okay. What's new in your life?"

"Nothing much." She blushed to the roots of her hair. If he had been able to read her mind, he would have seen Rad MacLeod standing at the bottom of the stairs not all that long ago, looking way too sexy for someone she hated.

Patting back imaginary strands, Lainie fought to control her rising tension. It seemed silly to conceal the fact that Rad had been there. But it wasn't necessary to tell Lee of his visit. For five years she'd tried to shut Rad out of her thoughts and her life, and hadn't succeeded. Perhaps the best course would be to treat the subject casualty.

"Oh, I saw Rad today." She got busy collecting the serving plates and forks, feeling Lee's gaze upon her, yet not ready to meet it. "He hasn't changed. Just as take-charge as ever."

She tried to make that sound only natural, but Lee had been at the concert and he knew better. His hand reached out for hers. She watched the struggle in his face as he tried to find comforting words. She smiled at him reassuringly, letting him know that she had escaped the confrontation nearly unscathed and that she would spare him the details.

"I think that calls for a change of subject." Lee exhaled slowly. "I'm sure it would be in bad taste to express my blatant dislike of the man you were once married to. So what do you say? How about I help you with the dishes?"

"That won't be necessary. I planned to stack them in the sink and leave them till morning."

"It's hardly a romantic way to spend an evening," Lee admitted, rising from the couch and extending a hand to Lainie. "But we can always put on some music to do the dishes by and liven it up."

Lainie hesitated before giving in to his captivating smile. "You pick a CD while I run upstairs to check on my mother."

"What, no iPod dock?"

"Can't afford one."

Rad's name wasn't mentioned again. Lee set out to be amusing and succeeded, drawing bubbly laughter from Lainie. It had been so long since she'd had a good time with a guy that she was sorry to see the evening end. He didn't make her feel nervous, accepting without a word her need to check on her mother at different times in the evening, yet not bringing up her mother's condition or expecting

Lainie to recount the details of her illness. So if her goodnight kiss seemed overwarm and she lingered in his arms, it was out of gratitude. It was only later in her room alone that she wondered whether gratitude could turn into love.

The sunlight hours shortened and the wind shifted out of the northwest and the Rocky Mountains. Summer had drawn to a close.

Lainie was curled up on a kitchen chair with an old magazine of her mother's. Old as in older than she was. She was reading a sentimental introduction to the change of seasons and nibbling on gingersnaps.

The quaking aspens are turning to a golden shade so like the precious metal that came from the mountains. Mother Nature is having her one last fling, painting the countryside with rampant splashes of scarlet reds, golden yellows, and rusty orange, before Old Man Winter sets in. The days become brisk and the invigorating air from the upper reaches of the mountains is turning noses and cheeks a healthy shade of pink.

It is a time of harvesting, of preparing for the winter ahead. The cut logs that lay forgotten the summer long are being brought into homes to be used as fuel for bright, cheery fires.

Children dream of hobgoblins and witches and ghosts. Pumpkins become jack-o'-lanterns while luscious red apples are covered with caramel and stuck on a stick.

Our lightweight synthetics and cotton are stored away and sweaters, tweeds, and woolens reappear. Tennis and swimming are replaced with football, hunting, and—get out the shovels!—snow.

Awww. The corny article was kind of soothing.

Lainie put the magazine back in the basket. The white-topped higher regions of the Rockies had already received a fresh cover of snow. Winter itself was a cold breath away.

For Lainie, the autumn hadn't been a time for jubilant celebration. There was no time for making merry in anticipation of the cold months ahead. There had been hours enlivened with the presence of Lee or Ann, but for the most part her worries had increased. So gradually that even Lainie herself hadn't noticed it immediately, her mother's condition had worsened. The doctor's visits had become more frequent and his face had grown longer. New treatments were tried and there was no improvement. Lainie was beginning to feel that the only thing that increased were their debts. She could no longer make their monthly income match their monthly expenses. Her mind turned repeatedly to Rad's offer and her pride kept shutting the door. Although she had thought he might contact her again, he never did. She tried to be glad about that, but she wasn't.

Footsteps on the stairs interrupted her vigil in the kitchen. As she reached the door to the hallway, she was met by the portly figure of Dr. Henderson. His smile was practiced and his eyes were sympathetic. In a fatherly gesture he put his hand on Lainie's shoulder and turned her back toward the kitchen.

"Would you make me a cup of coffee, Lainie? Two sugars." The doctor settled his stout frame on one of the chairs at the table while Lainie saw to his request. "My allotted treat for the day." He sighed. "Old age is no fun."

She refilled her own stoneware cup and carried both to the table. Her friendship with Dr. Henderson preceded her mother's illness, going back to the time when her father was alive, so it was more than intuition that told her that the news he had was unpleasant. She watched his spoon make a couple more trips to the sugar bowl.

"Strong and sweet," he smiled, sipping his coffee and smacking his lips in satisfaction. He glanced thoughtfully at her. "Like you, little Lainie, but of course you're not little anymore. Like my German grandmother used to say, 'We grow too soon old and too late smart.' But I'm getting off the track," he said when he set down the cup. "Your mother has deteriorated rapidly in the last couple of months. You only have two choices in front of you. Both of them will probably require hospitalization or, at the very least, round-the-clock nursing here at home."

"What do you mean by two choices?" Lainie asked. Her hands firmly circled the cup, needing the warmth to ward off the sudden chill.

"We've known for a while now—you and I and your mother—that her condition is terminal. As a doctor's daughter, you know what that means in terms of family commitment. Your mother is entering the last phase of life." Dr. Henderson looked her squarely in the eye. "There's a chance—it's just a chance, mind you—that if she accepts hospitalization, a new treatment may prolong her life for a few months and possibly reduce some of the pain she's suffering."

"And the other choice?" Lainie prompted.

"We can let the illness take its course. Her pain will increase and sedatives will no longer give her relief. And the results will be the same. She'll die."

His blunt words made Lainie turn her head down and away. It was a cruel choice. Either door opened into yawning blackness.

"I couldn't bear to watch if the pain gets worse than it is now," Lainie murmured. "I don't know where I'll get the money to pay for it, but I want her to have this new treatment."

Henderson's hands reached out to cover Lainie's. "I wish you weren't so alone," he sighed, squeezing her hands before he rose from the table. "I'll make arrangements for her to enter the hospital the day after tomorrow. She told me she wants to go."

Chapter 5

The hospital corridor was bustling with nurses, technicians and aides. The tweed suit that Lainie wore, perfectly tailored but from a resale shop, suggested a wealth that she didn't possess as she walked beside her mother being wheeled down the corridor. The hopelessness of the situation had struck her forcibly after Dr. Henderson had left. The desire to flee from the responsibility her decision would bring was strong. But it had been a passing fear, one she could overcome. Looking down on her mother's wan face, Lainie knew her compassionate decision to agree had been correct. Her mother was fading away; Lainie had to be stronger than ever.

They arrived at her mother's room. One of the aides held the door open. Lainie followed, glancing around uneasily at the other occupants of the room. One of the women smiled back at Lainie in welcome. Another, older, woman was sleeping. The two aides carefully shifted her mother from the gurney to the hospital bed. The movement seemed to bring her mother out of the state of lethargy she had been in, and Lainie watched her dull blue eyes take in her surroundings. Then her frightened and questioning gaze was turned on the two aides.

"This isn't my room," her mother insisted with a weak but imperious air. "You've taken me to the wrong room."

"I'm sorry, ma'am. This is where we were told to take you."

"It's a mistake." Mrs. Simmons's head moved fretfully against the pillow. "Somebody's made a mistake. Lainie, you have to check on it at once."

"Yes, Mom, I will." Lainie moved forward to caress her mother's nervous fingers picking at the bed's coverlet.

"You know I always have a private room." It was a plaintive, protesting cry.

"We could pull the dividing curtains," one of the aides suggested gently.

"Would you, please?" Lainie replied, smiling at the thoughtful and considerate offer.

The beige curtains were pulled, but they did little to alleviate her mother's distraught fussing. The younger aide smiled sympathetically at Lainie before the two of them wheeled the gurney out of the room.

Lainie had known her mother would be upset when she discovered she would have to share a room with other patients. But the admissions clerk was adamant when Lainie had requested a private room. The bills from her mother's previous hospitalizations were still on the books, although Lainie had made monthly payments toward them. The clerk had told her that the hospital didn't feel it would be fair to Lainie or to themselves to add the extremely high cost of a private room.

Logical enough. She couldn't really argue against it. She'd hoped to persuade her mother to become reconciled to other patients in the room, but the furtive glances that her mother was casting toward the unseen people beyond the curtain led her to believe that was hopeless.

"I can't stand to have those people watching me," her mother whispered.

"But they can't see you," Lainie replied calmly.

"They're right on the other side. I have no idea who they are. They're complete strangers." She clutched Lainie's hand tightly. "You must do something."

Before Lainie could reply, the curtains were parted and a nurse in a white uniform and starched cap walked in. With an instinct born of long association with overwrought patients, the nurse immediately sensed the tension. She glanced briefly at Lainie before turning a bright, cheery smile toward the frail woman in the hospital bed.

"I'm Nurse Harris." The friendly voice was meant to put the patient at ease. "I see you've established your own private nook."

"There's been a mistake, nurse. I'm supposed to have a private room." The urgent, almost sobbing statement got Lainie a startled glance from the nurse. Lainie gave a brief, negative shake of her head.

"Let's see, you're Dr. Henderson's patient." The nurse consulted the chart at the end of the bed. "You should discuss this error with him. He should be making his rounds soon. I'm sure he'll take care of everything."

This seemed to mollify Lainie's mother a little. "It's just that you never know who's in the room with you." The snobbish ring in Mrs. Simmons's voice made the nurse's smile stiffen, while the color rose in Lainie's cheeks.

"They're all human beings in need of care," the

nurse replied a little sharply. "Now if you'll excuse me, I have other duties. The doctor will be with you shortly."

"Oh, I wish Lawrence would come," her mother whimpered, referring to Dr. Henderson, after the nurse had left the room.

Lainie seated herself in the chair alongside the bed. But it was nearly a quarter of an hour later before the doctor arrived. He was accompanied by a tall, slender, balding man with glasses, introduced as Dr. Gordon, a specialist in the field of her mother's illness. The pair had barely begun their examination when Mrs. Simmons began complaining about being in the room with other patients. Dr. Henderson attempted to laugh off her fears, but it only served to make her increasingly nervous.

Leaving his colleague to continue the examination, Henderson motioned for Lainie to step out of the room with him. She quietly explained the hospital's position and he nodded understandingly but ruefully. Minutes later they were joined by Dr. Gordon.

"What seems to be the problem? Surely this hospital has a private room available?" he asked.

"It does," Henderson agreed. "But perhaps we could convince Mrs. Simmons to the contrary." Then he went on to explain the situation.

The specialist's reaction to the news was unfavorable. "I can appreciate your problem," Dr. Gordon said to Lainie. "But unfortunately, if your mother's agitation persists, it may negate any progress these treatments might make."

The morning moved to noon; the noon moved to afternoon and the afternoon moved to evening. Despite Doctor Henderson's assertion that there were no private rooms available, Mrs. Simmons only became more distressed. He was forced to put her under heavy sedation before her nerves drove her to a progressively worse state of relapse. Lainie realized the only solution to the problem was money but there was nothing left at home to sell. Nothing would make a dent in the hospital bill. If she had only accepted Rad's offer . . . But she tried to banish that thought from her mind.

A magazine lay closed in her lap as she tried to think herself out of the situation. The lobby of the hospital floor was nearly empty. But Lainie wasn't interested in the other occupants, or the potted plants that were supposed to add a touch of nature to the clinical atmosphere, or the antiseptically clean, vinyl-covered sofas. She was so wrapped up in her dilemma that she didn't notice Ann or her husband Adam walk into the room followed by Lee Walters. She jumped half out of her skin when Ann's hand touched her shoulder.

"How's your mother?" Ann asked as she settled in a seat beside Lainie.

"Not very good. She's sleeping, but they had to give her a sedative." Lee brushed her cheek with a light kiss that Lainie barely noticed.

"Then it's a good thing that we came tonight," Ann decreed, "you need help too."

"Why? I'm okay. Considering I've just about been living in this hospital."

"Seriously, Lainie, there must be something we can do." The look in Lee's eyes mirrored the concern felt by all three over Lainie's situation.

"I don't think so," Lainie sighed. "Being in a room with strangers makes my mother freak out and our finances won't stretch to cover a private room. The specialist is afraid it might be detrimental to the treatments." A humorless laugh escaped her lips. "I guess I was hoping I would win the lottery."

Concerned glances passed between Ann and her husband. Lainie felt chagrined that she had introduced a subject that not only was depressing, but also, so far, unsolvable. It wasn't fair to burden her friends with her problems.

"Before anything else happens"—Lainie smiled brightly, if a little falsely—"I need caffeine. Let's all go down to the coffee shop."

"I think that's an excellent idea," said Lee, offering his arm to Lainie.

For almost an hour they sat around a table in the coffee shop, but their laughter and lighthearted attempts at conversation were stilted. The atmosphere around them wasn't exactly convivial. The periods of tense silence grew more frequent as Lainie's face grew more drawn, her nagging worries at the forefront of her mind. After one prolonged silence, Lee's hand reached under the table and found hers. It was a comfort to know that he was there if she needed him.

"You're a lawyer, Adam!" Ann burst out suddenly. "Why couldn't Lainie sell the house?" She glanced apprehensively at Lainie, fearing her impulsive remark might have given offense. "I mean, after all, it's a big, rambling old place. It must be so expensive to keep it running, what with the cost of heating and all. It's in a good neighborhood, so it shouldn't be too difficult to sell. Well, maybe not in this market. Housing's down. It's probably a lousy suggestion," she ended lamely.

"No, it's not." The words were hesitant as Lainie

spun the thought around in her mind, gradually warming to it. "I have suggested it to Mom once or twice. She could never bear to part with it before, but now . . ." Lainie couldn't bring herself to give voice to the fact that her mother would never leave the hospital. "Is it possible, Adam?"

"Theoretically, yes," he said. "The house is solely in your mother's name?"

Lainie nodded.

"Off the cuff," he continued, "I know that you'd either have to get your mother's permission or have to have a doctor certify she's physically and mentally incapable of handling her own affairs. In that case, the courts would probably allow you to act in her behalf."

"Then it could be done," Ann said. Her eloquent blue eyes gave Lainie a warm look. "Lucky thing that we have a lawyer and a real estate broker here. How fast would you be able to sell the house?" She turned eagerly toward Lee.

Lainie could feel renewed hope building inside her. It was as if the first star had been revealed in the dark evening sky. This could be the answer to her problem. She turned toward Lee hopefully, waiting anxiously for his opinion. But Adam wasn't finished.

"You understand it'll take time." His cautious words were unwelcome and earned him a glaring look from his wife. "Not months, but certainly a few days."

Time was a factor, Lainie acknowledged inwardly. She didn't want to delay any longer than was necessary in finding a solution. Without being told, she knew it was essential to have her mother moved to a private room as soon as possible. She turned back toward Lee, looking for encouragement.

"I'd like to tell you I could sell the house tomorrow."

His gaze was filled with compassion. "But I can't. It's a case of supply and demand, and right now, the supply outweighs the demand."

"Back to Plan B," Ann said, suddenly dejected at the idea that it might not happen.

"There's nothing wrong with Plan A. The issue is time. No getting around it."

Lainie's evening star turned into a shooting star that faded out of sight. Still, her gaze stayed on Lee's apologetic face, trying by force of will to make him relight her dream.

"It wouldn't be right to tell you differently," Lee continued. "It could take a day, a week, a month, or more. There's just no way to predict."

"That pretty well squashes that," Adam said with finality.

"I refuse to give up!" There was a suggestion of a frown around Ann's mouth. Her hand tugged at her husband's sleeve. "We can talk to our parents, persuade them to buy the house as an investment."

"No!" Lainie forcefully rejected such a plan. "I can't let you or your parents do that. It's too risky. I'll find some other way to raise the money."

"But there isn't any other way," Ann protested. "What kind of risk would they be taking? After all, it's a great house in a great area."

"The area is good," Lainie conceded. "But the house could turn into a white elephant. It has for me."

Her decision was final. Further protests, mostly from Ann, couldn't change her from what Lainie knew to be right. The little etchings of relief around Adam's eyes when they finally caved made her glad that she hadn't given in to her friend's generosity. Rather than inflict any more gloom on the gathering, Lainie made the first move to leave, picking up her leather bag and rising from the table. The other three had no choice but to follow.

"Oh, stop looking at me as if I were a lost kitten tossed out in a blizzard," she teased as a very dejected Ann stared mournfully at her.

"But what are you going to do?"

Lainie couldn't meet her friend's beseeching gaze. Another idea had been forming in her mind, but it still wasn't likely to withstand Ann's disapproval. Lainie's pride had stopped her once before, but under different circumstances. Now the situation was critical. And the question was whether she could afford to let her pride stand in her way again. The answer was one only she herself could give.

"I want to go check on my mother again." Lainie reached out for her friend's hand. "I can't thank you all enough for what you tried to do."

"You make it sound as if we were successful." Ann studied the solemn expression on Lainie's face. "But we weren't."

"If you women are going to get emotional, I'm going home," Adam announced.

"Men!" Ann sighed in exasperation, rolling her eyes significantly at Lainie. "Heartless beasts."

Lee's arm encircled Lainie's waist as she exchanged a chorus of good-byes with Ann and Adam. After they had left, her head rested just for a second on his shoulder, enjoying the comfort of his arms. When she glanced up at his gentle blue eyes, his adoration was there for her to see. She wished briefly that he would bestow one of those tender, warm kisses on her lips, but she knew his sense of propriety wouldn't allow him to in a public place.

"How are you getting home?" he asked.

"I have the car," Lainie replied.

"Would you like me to follow you?"

"No, I don't know how long I'll be."

By unspoken agreement they left the coffee shop and headed toward the elevator that would take her to her mother's floor. He pushed the button and almost simultaneously the door to the elevator opened. Lainie stepped inside, then turned to face Lee. His hand reached out and captured a brown curl, and lingered on her cheek.

"If you need me . . ." he said softly.

Lainie smiled and nodded. His hand moved away and the elevator doors closed.

She walked down the corridor alone, her footsteps echoing. As if a fog in her mind had dissolved in an instant, some things suddenly seemed very clear. Above all that she, Lainie, had wasted too much time—five years—waiting for life to happen to her instead of making it happen for her. That she'd hidden herself away, first in shock as a reaction to her separation from Rad and then in numb depression. Five years was a very long time but it was at an end.

No matter what happened with her mother, Lainie vowed to get on with her own life as she stood there. Go back to college. Find work that challenged her, work that would enable her to do more than just survive. And look for love again.

But you love Rad.

Lainie brushed the thought and the tears it triggered away.

She noticed the number of her mother's room and went in. The curtains were still drawn, wrapping her mother in an insecure cocoon, but Lainie knew that the drug-induced sleep could hardly be called restful. She stood for many silent moments at the foot of her mother's bed, staring at the still feminine form and the lines of pain on the once perfect features.

There wasn't anything she could do.

Walking slowly out of the room, Lainie paused at the nurses' station, making sure that they had her cellphone and home phone numbers in case she was needed during the night. Leaden feet carried her down and out to the parking lot where her car was parked. The person who climbed behind the wheel was an automaton of herself, mechanically making the correct turns that would take her home, while her conscious mind remained with her mother.

As she inserted her key in the front door lock, Lainie knew she was still far from free. The issue of her mother's care wasn't going to go away. Never mind her good intentions for the future. She had to deal with what was going on in her life right here and right now.

And that meant dealing with Rad.

Once inside, she leaned against the heavy oak door without bothering to switch on the light in the foyer. She made her way through the half darkness to the door of the den, opened it, stepped inside, and switched on the light.

Her eyes focused on the phone on the desk as she removed her coat and placed it with her bag on the leather sofa. She walked around and seated herself behind the walnut desk. Her heart kept saying tomorrow and her mind kept saying now. Her hand reached out slowly, then almost snatched the black receiver from its cradle. She was shaking all over and the blood was hammering in her ears, but she willed her trembling fingers to dial Rad's number. Her hard-won courage nearly deserted her when Sondra answered the phone. Somehow she gathered the nerve to ask for Rad.

"Who should I say is calling?" The cold distaste in Sondra's voice grated on Lainie.

"It's personal," Lainie replied with the same amount of coldness.

She sensed the hesitancy on the opposite end of the line and realized there must have been just the right air of authority in her own voice to make Sondra unsure.

"I'll see if Mr. MacLeod is available." The line went silent except for a distant mumble of voices. Rattled, Sondra must have forgotten to put the call on hold. The seconds seemed to be minutes and again Lainie fought the desire to replace the receiver on the hook.

"MacLeod here." Her heart lodged in her throat at the sound of the masculine voice. "Hello?" Rad repeated when Lainie failed to reply.

For a moment she was afraid she wasn't able to speak. Then finally she breathed, "It's Lainie."

This time there was silence on his end of the line. She thought he might have broken off the connection.

"Yes?" His voice was coolly impersonal.

"I . . . I wanted to discuss something with you," Lainie said hesitantly.

There was another pause. "I'll be free in half an hour. I'll send a car for you."

"No!" Her cry was instantaneous. She was suddenly afraid to face him. She wanted time to think before she met him again. "I mean, it's not that important. It can wait until tomorrow."

"In half an hour," Rad repeated firmly. He had hung up. For ten minutes she thought about calling him back. Bad move. Rad knew her too well, and therefore he wasn't going to give her the opportunity to back out once she had made the initial move. She could imagine the smug smile on his face when she identified herself. It was probably giving him a lot of satisfaction that she was the one who was running to him, after she had previously thrown his offer back in his face. Lainie glanced down at her tailored suit. Too businesslike for begging in, she told herself bitterly. She would use a woman's weapons. Clothes, makeup—whatever it took to undermine his practical side and work on his emotions. He did have them. Underneath it all, Rad was a passionate man.

The thought brought a wry smile to her lips. How clueless she'd been when she and Rad had first been together. Her naïveté was almost incomprehensible to her now.

Girlishly, she'd thought of him as the handsomest, nicest guy in Denver, and the only man she could ever truly love. He wasn't good enough for her, in her mother's opinion, which had only added to Lainie's confusion at the time, but she could forgive that now. With her mother nearing the end, it was time to forgive everything. Her mom had wanted only the best for her daughter.

She needed Rad's help to make her mother comfortable, that was all there was to it. The emotions that had been stirred up by their unexpected encounter at the concert and his visit had to be controlled.

For better or for worse, Rad was back in her life. The recent call from his new lawyer notwithstanding, what they had to say to each other face to face was still going to be painful. So if the opposite side of love was hate . . . maybe that meant that the love was still there. Just not in sight. Now that they were both a little older and a whole lot wiser, was it possible that someday—no, she told herself. Stick with being wise. Do what needs to be done. Your mother still comes first.

It was time to get over Rad once and for all and put her broken hopes aside.

And speaking of time, there wasn't much left before the car was due to arrive. Knowing Rad, it would be there promptly. Her mind was already picking out the dress she would wear as she hurried up the stairs to her room. It was a deep ocher knit with long sleeves and a cowl neckline. It molded the angles brought on by her loss of weight and changed them into curves. With it she would wear her best coat with the black fur collar and hem, Lainie decided, removing it from her closet along with the dress.

With lightning speed she changed her clothes and redid her makeup. She was just debating whether to put her hair up when the doorbell rang downstairs. She had no choice; she had to leave it down. It suited her better that way. Slipping the black coat over her shoulders, she dashed down the stairs.

She took a deep breath to calm her racing pulse before opening the door. She expected to see Rad standing in the doorway, but he wasn't.

"Mrs. MacLeod?" the stranger in the blue uniform inquired.

"Yes," Lainie answered a trifle breathlessly.

The man extended his identification to her, which verified that he was Ralph Mason, employed by Mac-Leod Incorporated. "Mr. MacLeod told me to take you to him," he explained, moving to the side of the door so that Lainie could walk ahead of him to the black limousine parked in the driveway.

The chill that whispered over her skin had nothing to do with the brisk night air. It was caused solely by her very mixed feelings about Rad MacLeod. But she wished Rad had met her instead of sending someone in his place.

She slipped into the back seat, nodding politely at the man before he closed the door behind her. The world outside the car windows seemed like an alien place with intermittent beams of streetlights, blinding flashes of oncoming car headlights, and blinking neon signs. Occasionally people would be seen on the pavements, their mouths moving as they exchanged conversation, but no sound penetrated the luxury car. Lainie huddled deeper in the corner, pulling the coat around her face so that the silky fine fur brushed her cheeks.

She questioned her decision mentally, over and over. Why was she going to see Rad? Hadn't he told her that the offer might not remain open? Lainie would rather have discussed things over the phone, which was probably the reason he'd cut her off.

Ratcheted up to high by fatigue and worry, her paranoia kicked in: maybe Rad was getting off on having her make this tension-filled journey across town so that he could refuse to help her when she arrived. Another chill of apprehension swept over her as she remembered something else he'd said: the conditions might not be the same.

What could he have meant by that? If it was security or collateral he wanted, Lainie decided she could always put up the house. The car made a sharp turn, jerking her thoughts back to the present.

"Where are we going?" She glanced around, not recognizing the route they were taking. "This isn't the way to the house."

"House?" The man's glance in the rearview mirror was curious. "Mr. MacLeod doesn't live in a house. He lives in an apartment. It's just a few more blocks, ma'am."

"I see." Lainie felt herself blush. "Has he lived there long?" She was startled by the news that Rad no longer lived in their house on the outskirts of Denver in the foothills of the Rocky Mountains.

"Since before I came," the chauffeur replied, "which is nearly three years ago." There was a smile playing at the corner of the man's mouth, as if he were secretly amused that she didn't even know where her husband lived. But it was more upsetting to know that Rad hadn't bothered to tell her that he had moved. It would have saved her from making a fool of herself.

True to his word, minutes later the chauffeur halted the car under the canopied entrance of a tall building. Leaving the motor running, he got out of the car, walked around to Lainie's side and opened the door for her. The barest gleam of amusement was in his eyes as he motioned toward the large glass doors.

"The elevator is to your right, ma'am," he said. "Press the button for the penthouse. The passcode has been entered. You're expected. And don't worry. Security's there even though you might not see it."

How very James Bond. But Rad was a rich man and he had to take precautions. Lainie clamped her lips together tightly and nodded. The chauffeur touched his cap, walked back around the car and drove away. She moved slowly toward the doors, pushed them open and turned to the right toward the elevator. There she hesitated, knowing she could turn around and go home if she chose. But that wasn't the reason she had come.

Once she had stepped inside the elevator and the doors had closed behind her, she stared unblinkingly at the top button that would take her to Rad's apartment. She pushed it quickly, hating the way her hand shook and hating her nervous tension even more. Silently she was zoomed upward and brought gently to a stop at the top floor. The elevator doors stretched open and she stepped through into a richly paneled foyer accented by double doors of carved black walnut. Lainie felt as if she was going through an obstacle course. Her knees trembled as she ordered them to take her to the door.

She pushed the button on the brass doorbell and heard the answering buzz sound inside the apartment. If Sondra was still there, Lainie thought rebelliously, she would turn around and walk out.

There was a click and then the doors swung open. There was another stranger standing in front of Lainie. She nearly sighed in exasperation. She identified herself to the man in the black suit and he immediately stepped aside and allowed her to enter. At least Rad was not going to leave her standing in the foyer. The black walnut doors were closed behind her and she heard the click of a lock. She cast a startled glance at the man who had greeted her.

"We keep the doors locked at all times, ma'am," he explained. "We set the passcode for you, but just in case . . . Wouldn't want anyone to get into the elevator and come to the top floor, and gain entrance to the apartment without us knowing it."

Lainie knew she should have realized the logic in that, but it seemed as if her avenue of escape had been blocked. She didn't have time to dwell on the discovery, as the man was already walking ahead of her and indicating that she should follow. He paused at an open archway.

"Mr. MacLeod will join you shortly," he said.

So she was destined to wait again. Lainie sighed, stepping through the archway. Her suede heels made almost no sound as they sank into the plush white carpeting. Her gaze roamed over the room, taking in the unusual, subdued color combination. Yet there was nothing too modern about the furnishings, only its hues: white, gray, and black.

The walls were creamy white interspersed with beams of black walnut, with crossbeams of black walnut on the ceiling. In the center of the opposite wall, flanked by floor-to-ceiling white draperies, was an enormous fireplace of polished gray stone. Two plumply cushioned sofas covered in matching gray velvet with large throw pillows of black and gray faced each other in front of the fireplace. Between them was a large rectangular coffee table, again of black walnut. Other cushioned side chairs were in a deeper shade of gray, also accompanied by tables of black walnut.

Scattered around the room were statues, a blend of contemporary and ancient design, but all of metal. Indirect lighting was concealed in the ceiling beams, adding to the sense of cozy luxury and elegance. The daring décor fascinated Lainie as she reveled in the spaciousness afforded by the light colors and the opulence of the lush materials. Yet it was essentially a very masculine space. There was a quicksilver feeling of seductiveness and virility to it that made her apprehensive.

The back of her neck began tingling. Although she hadn't heard a sound, Lainie knew that Rad had entered the room.

She steeled herself to remain calm as she turned to look at him. As she met his dark gaze, her determination dissolved. He was so compelling just standing there inside the archway, wearing charcoal-colored pants that fitted tautly over his thighs. But it was the gray linen shirt with its impeccable Italian tailoring that did the most for his dark handsomeness and made him look like a rogue. A rogue with a lot of money who didn't need to advertise that fact.

His sudden presence made the understated room come alive, pervaded by his vitality. Lainie turned back toward the fireplace as one side of Rad's mouth curved with a humorless smile. She knew the color had left her cheeks, just as she knew that he had disturbed her more than she wanted to admit. She had to get control of herself, or flee.

Lainie was conscious again of Rad's movement. Without looking, she knew it was not in her direction. She grasped at these moments of reprieve, hearing ice cubes thunked in glasses and the sound of pouring liquid. In her mind's eye she remembered the alcove as she had stepped through the archway and the carved black walnut bar in its recesses. Then there was silence. Lainie cursed the carpeting that so completely muffled the sound of footsteps so that she had no way of knowing exactly where Rad was unless she looked.

But she did hear the tinkling of ice in a glass just a few feet behind her, which warned her he was approaching. Now that she knew she had to fight her awareness of him, she was able to turn toward the sound.

"You look like you need a drink." Rad extended a simple glass of clear liquid brightened by a twist of lime.

Probably vodka. Lainie took the glass hesitantly, careful to avoid touching his hand. The gleam in his eyes revealed his amusement at her self-protective gesture. She moved away, sipping quickly at the drink and letting the potency of the vodka return the color to her face.

"Well? How do you like the place?"

"Interesting décor." Lainie knew that wasn't the response he wanted, but it was all she could say. She wasn't quite ready to tell him the reason for her visit, even though she knew he was aware of it. "So . . . neutral."

"Yeah." Rad was laughing at her. "You and I do best on neutral territory."

Her nervous steps had taken her to the fireplace, where she was forced to turn around. Rad was sitting on the sofa, an arm stretched out across the back as he studied her with amusement. He was in command of the situation and totally at ease, and that knowledge made Lainie even more uncomfortable. The room seemed suddenly too warm, and Lainie realized she was still wearing her coat. With an attempt at a poise she didn't feel, she unbuttoned her coat and shrugged it back across her shoulders.

"Mr. Dickerson!" Rad called out. Almost instantly the man who had greeted Lainie appeared in the doorway. "Would you take Mrs. MacLeod's coat?"

With a tight smile of discomfort, Lainie removed her coat and handed it to the man. Did nothing escape Rad's attention, she wondered in irritation. As the man walked out of the room carrying her coat, she wished for it back. It had given her a fragile sense of security and provided another barrier from Rad's penetrating gaze.

"That'll be all for tonight, Dickerson," said Rad as

the man reappeared in the archway. She glanced nervously at Rad. Why had he dismissed the man when she was still here?

"I didn't think you wanted servants listening in on our conversation." Rad answered her unspoken question with his usual perception.

The silence stretched out, allowing her tension to mount. Unwillingly she seated herself on the sofa opposite Rad. He was obviously waiting for her to explain, and she had no idea where to begin. Now she rolled the half-empty glass of vodka nervously between her hands.

"Mom was admitted to the hospital today," Lainie began hesitantly. "Dr. Henderson is looking into the efficacy of some new treatments—okay, in plain English, he thinks he can help her. He's called in a specialist."

She stopped and stared at the unreadable expression on Rad's face. His lack of cooperation angered her. A smile of understanding or a sympathetic glance would make it so much easier for her, but that was not his intention. Liquor splashed out of the glass as she shoved it onto the black walnut table.

"Isn't that enough? You're good at reading between the lines," she cried out. Her temper flared quickly to the surface. "And you know why I'm here, too."

His raised eyebrow got her quickly to her feet. She walked hurriedly to the fireplace and paused in front of the blackened hearth as if to gather warmth from the dead ashes. Tears burned the back of her eyes and her breath came in quick gasps. Misery, humiliation, and pride warred with the sensible, logical side of her mind that kept reminding her of the need for Rad's help.

She felt a sensation of warmth beside her. Lainie turned her hurt gaze toward the man who emanated it.

"So you've come to see if my offer is still open," Rad said calmly.

"I don't want your money!" The words were hurled out in a burst of pride. "It's not for me!"

"Ah, but your mother needs it," Rad replied smoothly. "Otherwise you wouldn't be here."

"You are so arrogant," she breathed. "I hope someday you find out what it means to be weak and to really need someone's help—"

"And you're so sure I don't know that."

She made no reply to his flat statement. She couldn't think.

"Anyway, that isn't exactly the attitude to take when you're trying to get money from a man."

"What should I do?" Lainie asked sarcastically. "Grovel at your feet or kiss your hand?"

"It would be a novel experience," Rad replied with the same degree of composure as before, unmoved by her spitfire attack.

"Well, I won't do it. I won't!" Lainie turned away, despair taking the conviction out of her voice. "All I want from you is a simple yes or no. Either you'll help me or you won't."

"But that's not all I want from you," Rad murmured. All of a sudden his soft voice was so lacking in the arrogance she'd accused him of that she had to turn around and look at him. There was something in his eyes—something deeply emotional. It held her mesmerized. His hand reached out and twined a lock of her hair in his fingers.

"If . . . if it's collateral," Lainie's voice was a husky whisper, "I could arrange to sign over the house to you."

A mirthless chuckle escaped Rad's lips. "That

wouldn't begin to cover your debts. No, I'll help you, Lainie . . ."

The sentence hung unfinished in the air.

Lainie allowed herself to breathe deeply. Maybe, just maybe, he really would. No strings attached. But—

The possessive way he was looking at her made her whole body tighten and her nipples tingle. His gaze was drawing her into its unfathomable depths. She had to lower her eyes to escape it, although his magnetism drew her closer. Black curling hairs on his chest were revealed by the open collar of his shirt, evoking a desire in Lainie to slip her hands under the finely tailored linen and feel the warmth of his skin and the hardness of his muscles as she had done so long ago. It was a heady thought, one that sent her reeling backward, away from him. The distance was still only inches.

"What do you want from me, then?" The question was really a plea to be released from her heightened awareness of him.

"I want what's always been mine. Or at least I liked to think you were mine. Am I wrong?" His words were clipped and harsh. Yet when Lainie glanced up, he was looking at her in that strangely emotional way again. "I want you, Lainie. Come back to me. For real. Not because you need something from me."

She stepped backward. "That's never going to happen," she breathed, blinking up at him with rounded eyes. Her statement seemed to amuse him.

"You're still legally my wife," Rad pointed out. "If it matters to you. Does it?"

Wherever he was coming from, Lainie didn't want to go there. She ought to grab her coat back and run out into the night. Why was she hesitating? Why didn't she speak up? Why didn't she say it was over and had been over for five long years?

"Let's leave that up to the lawyers. Just stay on topic. You know why we need financial help and—" Was that really her voice speaking so calmly?

"I'll pay your debts and any future costs relating to your mother's illness." He watched the conflicting emotions flit across Lainie's face.

The knowledge that Rad had all the cards, as usual, made her feel more powerless than ever. If life was a game, he would always win. But for her to still be so needy, so dependent on him, after she'd had five years to get it together was her own fault and ultimately her own responsibility. Asking him for more money, dire as the need was, put her right back in a place she'd just decided never to be in again. But she had no choice. Nothing changed the hard fact that bills had to be paid if her mother was to be helped. Tears overflowed her eyes.

"I don't believe you!" Her voice was choked but clear.

"What's going on with you?" Rad reached out, grasping her wrist and pulling her toward him so that her hands were resting against his chest. "You're shaking. You don't have anything to be afraid of. Not from me."

She was far from sure that was true or ever would be. She felt incredibly vulnerable. "I'm not yours, Rad."

"But you could be."

"Yeah, right. Don't tell me you're lonely. Rich guys don't sleep by themselves. Are you tired of Sondra or did she give up? Is that it?" Lainie lashed out with the only weapon she had left, a spiteful tongue.

Her angry words got to him. Even Rad wasn't bulletproof. His dark eyes flashed but he spoke calmly. "Sondra has always given her all—in every respect."

Lainie wanted to smack him. "Then why do you want me?" she hissed, feeling a surge of strong jealousy pulse through her.

"Isn't it obvious?" A muscle at the corner of his mouth twitched involuntarily. "I still think you're unbelievably sexy."

"Hey, Rad," she murmured, looking him straight in the eye. "You can hate me but you don't have to use me."

"We never did straighten out exactly who was using whom," he jeered. He tightened his hold when she would have pulled away. He did have a point. She had run up their credit cards, had taken him for granted, had done a lot of things she regretted—but none of that could be undone.

"We couldn't stop fighting," she whispered, hanging her head.

"I know. I want another chance. I can't let go. Not until I'm absolutely sure that you—"

"No!" Her whispered protest was accompanied by the realization that she wanted what he wanted—but the thought of making the same mistakes a second time was terrifying.

There was no way she could think through what he was saying, not with her mother in the hospital and . . . Lainie's unlocked emotions threatened to engulf her.

He brought her against his chest and held her tightly. Too tightly. The blood pounded in her head as she fought to control the urge to put her hands around his neck and bury her face in chest.

Her longing to yield to him was intense; she tensed her body to make it go away. Brief seconds flitted past while his gaze studied her frightened face, then he released her swiftly and stepped away.

"Whatever. I'm not going to renege on my offer to help you and your mother. I can see how much it hurt you just to come here." His back was to her as he spoke. He didn't glance around to see her reaction. Instead he picked up his empty glass and walked to the bar.

Lainie watched him as he refilled his glass and gulped it down. Her mind decreed that she was glad he had walked away, but her traitorous heart was crying. She was torn in two; one part of her wanted to rush out the door and never come back, and the other part wanted nothing more than to be in his arms.

Starting over. Trying to trust. Why were both so hard?

It just is. You and Rad don't know how to do anything but hurt each other. She should have anticipated the disaster her life had become. If she'd accepted his previous offer, she wouldn't have had to come here. Being alone with him was dangerous, and it was her neediness that made it so.

Her initial refusal had been dictated by her pride. Now need had replaced pride. Maybe she'd been secretly hoping that he'd sweep her off her feet and she wouldn't have to think. But what frightened Lainie now was that this need for Rad had nothing to do with her mother. It seemed entirely possible that she still loved him underneath all the craziness. And she was beginning to wonder if she had ever stopped.

"You're right about it hurting me. But I've toughened up a lot." From out of her chaotic thoughts came the calmly worded reply.

Rad turned to lean against the bar, and regarded

her cynically, the glass in his hand. There was a raking thoroughness in his gaze that seemed to strip away all her carefully erected barriers.

"Have you?"

"Yes."

"So what are you saying?"

"We could . . . you know, see each other. I mean, try again. Worth a shot."

Rad nodded. "And how long do you think that would last?"

She wanted no time limit, no set day when she would be forced to make a final decision. She'd spent five years going exactly nowhere. Learning to think for herself and figure out what she really did want in life—whether or not that life would include Rad—wasn't something she could decide on the spot.

Judging by the frown gathering on his forehead, her lack of an answer to his question was posing a problem to him.

"Okay, Lainie. Let's keep it simple. When we get tired of each other, we quit."

"When will that be? A day, a week, a month, a year?" Pain etched bitter edges to her words.

"Who knows? But we seem to understand each other."

"I guess we do."

"Let's get back to why you came here."

"It's as good a place to start as any," she said defensively.

"First things first. The bills. Maybe when that's done, you'll be able to think more clearly."

"Maybe so."

"When you've calculated everything down to the last damn nickel and I've handed over the money,"

Rad said quietly, "then you can think about whether you want me or need me or what. I don't know what's really going on with you and I suspect you don't either."

Lainie flinched. "That's unfair!"

"Is it? Hey, no pressure. I'll keep the width of a room between us while you make up your mind." Lainie turned away under his contemptuous glance. "A minute ago, all I had to do was kiss you a few times, murmur the right things in your ear, and you would have resisted me just long enough to make the sex really hot."

"Who do you think you are?" she said furiously, fighting the urge to smack him again.

He only smiled. Rad's measured gaze held Lainie's for a long moment. Then he spoke. "So what's it going to be? Want to stay or should I have the driver take you home?"

Lainie had to admit, if only to herself, that his instincts were excellent. A few minutes ago, if he had begun making love to her she would have agreed to anything—and she never would have known for sure if the decision had been her own.

So. What did she want? The answer was simple. Him. Giving her what she'd gone without for far too long. Nothing more. If they kept their renewed connection purely physical, her heart was probably safe enough.

"I'll stay." She made a small half turn away from him, lifting her blurred eyes toward the unseen heavens.

"Not coerced. Not pressured. You actually agree." Rad's voice came from only a few feet away.

"God help me, yes!" There was a choked sob in her voice as she wondered what in hell she was getting herself into.

The touch of his hand upon her shoulders was light but firm as he gently turned her around toward him. She refused to lift her gaze and see the triumphant glitter in his eyes. Yet when his hand cupped her chin and forced her to look up into his face, she found herself staring into two dark pools of still water that were suffused with tenderness.

"You always made loving you so damn difficult, Lainie. I don't know why," he said quietly. "You're the only woman I ever wanted as my wife and you deserve all the honor and respect I can give you."

He slowly folded her into his arms, his hand entangling itself in the thickness of her dark hair. Lainie wished he had spoken more of love as if it was something he felt for her now, not something that was in the past. She would have to be satisfied with his handing her back a little of her dignity.

Rad held her tightly against him until some of her rigidity faded away and the warmth of his body melted the coldness that surrounded her heart. Lainie didn't resist when his mouth moved down over her hair, her closed eyes, to settle on her lips.

Her hands even managed to encircle his neck and cling to him with bittersweet urgency as he lifted her off her feet and carried her into his bedroom.

There was a fleeting glimpse of dark draperies contrasting with the white carpet before Rad paused beside the bed, still holding her in his arms, his expression as he gazed at her unreadable in the dim light. He set her gently on a soft bedspread. She touched it hesitantly.

Fur? Maybe. Or the next best thing to it. Suitable for getting wild. She began to unfasten her dress. It wasn't long before she'd slid her naked body under all that sensual warmth, between satin sheets.

Waiting.

Suddenly unafraid, lying there in the dark after he switched off the light, she heard him murmur her name before he joined her.

The satin sheets felt smooth to her skin and Lainie snuggled deeply into the unaccustomed luxury. Then the faint aroma of a man's cologne drifted past her nose. She blinked herself awake and the knowledge of where she was came back to her. Her eyes immediately went to the empty space beside her and the hollow place on the next pillow where Rad's head had lain.

She reached out and touched the smooth sheet beside her, remembering the incredible sensuality of last night. She felt . . . fulfilled. Almost whole again. An aching loneliness had been assuaged, even if the method was purely physical.

Lainie rolled over on her back, stretching her arms above her head, and studied the room, feeling as if it belonged to her and her husband alone. Her toes curled at the thought.

Again the walls were white, as was the carpeting, but this time she saw vivid splashes of color that added life to the room. Energizing her.

Why had she waited so long for this? Unsure, withdrawn, drowning in her own troubles, she'd allowed no other man to get near her, let alone love her.

Love. Did she dare use that word to define her reawakened feelings for Rad? Maybe not. In the abstract, loving someone could make anyone feel like a brand new life was just about to happen.

She took a mental inventory then and there. Her

senses were heightened, freed of the apathy and anger that had kept her down for so long. Her mind seemed alive to new possibilities . . . whatever came next, she would embrace it. Life was simply too precious not to cherish.

The man who'd made her feel this way was nowhere to be seen, but he couldn't be far away. Despite the events of the last several days, her heart was hopeful. Even happy. What an incredible feeling. It might not last, but she would take what she'd been given.

The clock on the dresser indicated 8:30 and beeped. Lainie wondered if Rad had set it for her and also wondered where he was, hoping he hadn't left for his office. His lovemaking last night had told her he was rocked by their reunion too.

If they both did their damnedest—and worked with a marriage counselor to get past entrenched patterns of behavior and win back each other's trust, they might be able to win at love. Because when all was said and done, love wasn't a game.

A knock on the door interrupted her musings. Assuming it was Rad, she quickly rearranged her pillow, leaning against the back of the bed and pulling the covers closer around her chest. Her voice was eager as she told the person to enter. But the door was opened by a woman in her late forties in a crisply starched green dress. What the—?

She regarded Lainie with a briskly intimidating expression on her face as she marched on into the room, carrying a tray.

"Mr. MacLeod thought you'd like breakfast." The words were snappish, plainly indicating that the woman was on the offensive. "It's not normally part of my duties to see that breakfasts are served in bed."

"I don't normally eat breakfast in bed." Lainie

soothed the housekeeper's ruffled feathers. "But it was thoughtful of Rad to suggest it. Would you put the tray over on the table by the window?"

The housekeeper sniffed, which brought a secret smile to Lainie's lips. This household wasn't accustomed to having a woman around, she realized. The servants—hoo hah, Rad actually had a staff—weren't likely to instantly take to a woman who appeared out of the blue, declaring herself to be Mrs. MacLeod. She would have to tread lightly at first.

"I don't know your name," she said as the housekeeper was about to leave the room.

"I'm Mrs. Dudley," the woman replied.

"It's nice to meet you." Lainie smiled. The woman nodded and reached for the doorknob. "Has my— has Rad left for the office?"

"No, ma'am." Mrs. Dudley's eyes glinted at her brightly. "Ms. Gilbert arrived a little before eight. He's in the den with her now."

That put a definite damper on Lainie's sunny mood. The housekeeper left. Lainie felt a cloud gathering over her head.

A light blue robe lay on a nearby chair. Judging by the size, it belonged to Rad. Lainie reached out from beneath the covers and drew it toward her. She slipped into it quickly, rolling up the sleeves that tried to cover her hands. She walked around the bed to the table where the breakfast tray sat. Brushing her long hair behind her ears, she poured herself a cup of coffee, ignoring the eggs, bacon and muffins on the gold-rimmed china plate. She lifted the cup to her mouth while holding back the knobby linen curtain of blue and looking out at the city below.

The moment of elation had passed. Lainie was,

using a very old-fashioned definition, Rad's wife again, but the old obstacles were still there, including Sondra Gilbert. The break in her heart that she thought had been mended by Rad's passionate love-making seemed to have broken open again. Nothing was simple. And nothing was going to get easier.

She swore under her breath. Running home to Mother and keeping herself in an emotional limbo for so long . . . Lainie sighed. It had done her more harm than she'd ever realized. Denver with all its tall buildings and concrete roads seemed like someplace she'd never seen. But it had been there all along. It held plenty of opportunities for work, for education, but she hadn't been willing to risk doing anything new. The businesslike, impersonal angles of the growing city reminded her of harsh realities she'd dodged for years—above all, the need to form new relationships with other men who weren't Rad . . .

"Hey. Mrs. Dudley told me you were up."

Lainie looked over her shoulder as Rad entered the room. Not more than ten minutes ago she would have run to greet him. Now, as she stared at the man in the dark business suit, she feared rejection. He hadn't shut himself off from the world the way she had. He'd succeeded, made a fortune, moved on.

"Sleep well?" he was asking her.

She took a few seconds to reply. More than anything else, she feared her own weakness where he was concerned. The image of her mother, helpless and alone and near the end, besieged Lainie. Just another reason to play it cool and not give her heart away.

"Uh-huh," she murmured. "Comfortable bed." Her bland response brought a questioning look to his dark eyes. Lainie turned back to the window, sipping her coffee to keep from inadvertently revealing her emotions. Rad walked around the bed and paused in front of the table where Lainie's breakfast tray sat.

"Your food's getting cold."

"I don't really have much of an appetite this morning." Her stilted words betrayed her uncertainty about their new relationship. This was getting her nowhere. They were making polite conversation like two strangers. Lainie let the curtain fall back, shutting out the city.

"Rad, why did you want me back?" The question that had been uppermost in her mind was blurted out without conscious effort.

"Why do you think?" His voice held a rough edge.

"I don't know." Lainie's eyes blurred as she stared at the coffee cup in her hand. "Maybe you wanted revenge. I know I hurt and disappointed you all those years ago. I also know that physically you still want me." Her voice trembled and she tried to steel herself to remain composed. "And I'm not totally immune to you, either."

She wished she hadn't turned and looked at Rad's face. It possessed the unfeeling coldness of stone.

"Okay, let me take it from there," Rad said sharply. "Rhetorically speaking, there's no better revenge than to take you back as my wife and subject you to the humiliation of being in my debt. Not true, but if you want to believe it—what have you been doing for five years, watching soap operas nonstop? Give me a break, Lainie."

"I'm trying to." Her gaze begged him to take her seriously.

"You're very smart, Lainie, to figure it out all by

yourself." There was no mistaking the sarcasm in his voice. "What other reason could there have been? I suppose I could have been so desperately in love with you that I wanted you back under any circumstances."

"But you never were in love with me," Lainie said unwillingly.

"No, I never was, was I?" His cold agreement lacerated her heart. "Now that we've cleared the air, shall we get down to business?"

"Business?" Lainie echoed, cocking her head to one side in bewilderment.

"Yes," Rad snapped. "Sondra came over this morning so I could give her a list of the creditors who were to receive payment. Here it is." He passed a sheet of paper to her. "See if we've missed anyone."

Lainie accepted the paper with a dazed look on her face.

"Sondra's next stop will be the hospital. Always easier to get results in person instead of being put on hold forever, don't you agree?"

"Yes."

"I think the biggest issue was whether or not your mother could afford a private room."

With a trembling hand Lainie handed him back the paper. She wished she had never brought up the subject of why she was back with him. For a few ridiculous moments she'd thought it was for a reason other than the one he had stated. But Rad had pretty much let her know that love hadn't been a part of his decision. She felt his eyes stray over the blue robe she wore. Her pale cheeks pinked up as his gaze lingered on the low V neckline where the cleavage of her breasts was visible.

"That robe's too big for you."

"Yeah, I know. It's yours."

"Sorry. I'm not running a hotel and there is no smaller size."

Despite everything, she was secretly glad to hear it.

"The next thing on the agenda," he went on, "is to take you home so you can pick up some of your things."

Any thought that she might have looked seductive in her attire was quickly doused.

"If you don't intend to eat your breakfast, I suggest you get dressed so we can leave."

"Don't you have to go into the office today?" Lainie asked, surprised by his implication that he would be accompanying her.

"One of the few benefits of owning your own company is that you can take days off and delegate."

"Right."

"You'll probably want to stop at the hospital, so I'll tell Mrs. Dudley we won't be in for lunch."

"Why are you taking me?" She couldn't stop herself from asking.

"To be perfectly honest, Lainie"—Rad stopped in front of the doorway—"and this seems to be a morning for honesty—I think you're getting cold feet. Let's just say I want to keep you near me. For sentimental reasons. Unless you mind."

"I told you last night I would stay." Her chin lifted with pride.

"Then we agree. Just see what it's like to be my wife again. Give me half a chance."

"I'll keep my word."

"Sometimes the light of day changes people's minds. I recall another promise you once made till death do us part."

"You made the same vow, Rad, along with 'to love

and cherish,'" Lainie flared out quickly, her words ending in a choked sob.

"You were the one to walk out. That decision was entirely your own."

The door closed with a bang behind him.

Chapter 6

Lainie wanted to hurl herself onto the bed and give way to the storm of tears welling up inside her. There seemed to be no way to reach Rad. It was unbelievable that she once had been deeply in love with him. Not a second time, she vowed. Play wifey, make sure he made good on his promise to help her mom, and get out. That was as far as she was going to go.

Where is the rainbow, Daddy? the child in her cried out. *Where is the end of the storm?*

A cold, wet towel did wonders to brighten her eyes and bring color to her cheeks. A single lipstick was the only makeup in her purse, but the scrubbed look suited her mood. Lainie fluffed the ends of her hair, grateful for the natural body that kept its bounce.

Satisfied with her appearance, she stepped out of the bedroom wearing the knit dress from the evening before. She paused in the living room, half expecting to see Rad there. There was no indecision in her movements; her steps revealed a self-control she didn't know she had. She realized that Rad was probably still in his den and she had no intention of opening doors trying to find him. Nor did she intend to wait like a patient dog until her master came for her.

Lainie walked determinedly through the archway to the small foyer that led to the black walnut doors and the elevators. Almost immediately the man who had greeted her the night before appeared.

"Dickerson, right?" Her tone was authoritative. Not too bad for the new mistress of the household. "Would you get my coat and tell Mr. MacLeod that I'm ready to leave?"

Minutes later Dickerson returned, carrying her black, fur-trimmed coat. "Mr. MacLeod will be here directly."

Her smile was coolly polite as she accepted Dickerson's assistance in donning her coat. Her composure was firmly in place and she couldn't afford the slightest warmth to put a nick in it. But the man didn't seem to expect it as he silently withdrew down the hallway.

There was only the smallest wait before Rad joined her. His politeness grated on her already raw nerves as he opened the door for her and allowed her to precede him into the elevator. Lainie refused to allow him to occupy even a corner of her side vision. She didn't even spare him a glance when, once they were outside, he opened the door of his Mercedes-Benz for her. Only when he had slid into the car did she break the self-imposed silence.

"I'd like to see my mother first," she said calmly.

Rad shrugged indifferently. "Whatever you say."

She sat back, clasping her hands primly in her lap. They were missing a prop for this scene. A wedding band. Her fourth finger, left hand, felt strangely naked.

"There are a few forms that still need to be filled

out," Rad told her after they had arrived at the hospital and were in the lobby. "So I'll be in the administration office for a while."

Lainie only nodded.

"You should check at the reception desk to get your mother's new room number. I imagine she's been moved by now."

Rad was right. Her mother was safely installed in a private room on another floor, and the change in her attitude was almost miraculous. Her smile was bright and cheery and there were no more fearful glances over her shoulder for Lainie's benefit. Dr. Henderson had already been there on his morning rounds.

The improvement in her mother's overall well-being was so noticeable that Lainie didn't even want to contemplate discussing the change in her relationship with Rad. A glossed-over explanation that there were things to be done at home seemed to satisfy her mother. Lainie was able to leave before Rad was able to come up. The time for explanations would come later.

Although her heels clicked loudly in the hospital corridor, Lainie was not all that conscious of her surroundings. In her mind she was caught in a maze and no matter which way she turned she couldn't get out.

She never even noticed the man and woman standing at the nurses' office door when she walked past. The voice that called out for her to stop might as well have come from another planet. She kept on walking—until she was taken by the shoulders and spun around.

"Lainie! Where have you been?" Lee Walters's blue

eyes raced over her face and her upper body as if making sure she was unharmed. "I was worried sick about you!"

Lainie stared at his hair, incredibly tousled as if he had been running his fingers through it. There was no mistaking the concerned expression on his face, even though relief was replacing it. He glanced around him, suddenly becoming conscious of the public display he was making, and quickly led her to the secluded waiting area. It was then that Lainie noticed that Ann was there too.

"What are you doing here? What's happened?" Lainie asked, noting Ann's concerned expression.

"Trying to find you," snapped Ann.

"This is just crazy," said Lee. The shaky edge in his voice confirmed that.

"I don't understand," Lainie said, looking from one to the other in confusion. "Why were you looking for me?"

"I called you last night, to make sure you'd arrived home safely," Lee started to explain, "but nobody answered your phone."

The awful realization began to dawn on Lainie. "Oh. Right." She didn't want to explain.

"At first because I thought you'd stayed at the hospital a while longer, but I kept calling and there was still no answer. Then I checked with the hospital, thinking you'd decided to stay all night with your mother, and they told me you'd left earlier."

"And of course he couldn't get hold of us because we have an unlisted number," Ann put in.

"I thought maybe you'd gone over to her house to spend the night rather than stay in your house alone," Lee explained.

"So Lee was camped at our doorstep at eight

o'clock this morning." There was a nervous laugh as Ann tried to make light of the situation. "That's when he really got worried and me, too, as far as that goes. But Adam made a few phone calls to make sure you hadn't been involved in some accident, and then we came here to the hospital."

"I'm so sorry I've put you through all this," Lainie said sincerely.

"As long as you're all right—" Ann smiled at her warmly. "It doesn't matter. How did you manage to get your mother a private room, by the way? We were so shocked when we got here and found she'd been moved."

"Where were you last night?" Lee persisted in the previous line of questioning.

Lainie glanced from one to the other with a slightly panicked expression on her face. Explanations were being demanded and she wasn't ready to make them yet. Lee was still holding her arm.

She moved uncomfortably out of his possessive grasp. Lee's gaze quickly picked up the flush in her cheeks.

"Where were you, Lainie?" He repeated, but more grimly this time.

"When . . . when I got home last night—" The mounting heat in her face gave away her embarrassment. "I called Rad."

The expressions on both their faces told of their astonishment, except that Lee's was tinged with outrage. He moved toward her, then stopped. Lainie faltered, trying to find a way to break the news to both of them. She doubted if either one of them would understand, any more than she did.

"I thought he would help me. I couldn't think of anyone else to turn to."

"MacLeod!" Lee snorted. "How could you bring yourself to go to him?"

"Rad had offered to help me once before," Lainie told him, her head tilted back defensively. "At the time I was too proud to accept it, but now I needed it."

"Judging by the fact that your mother now has a private room," Ann said with a measure of composure, "I guess we can assume he agreed to help you."

"Yes, he did," Lainie answered. Now was the time to tell them both that she had gone back to him, but the words wouldn't come out.

"If you called him and talked to him, then why weren't you there when I called?" Lee wouldn't give up.

"I called him, yes, but I had to go over to his apartment to talk to him about it."

"You did what?" Lee stared at her.

"Lee!" Ann placed a restraining hand on his arm. He immediately released Lainie, running a hand through his tousled hair.

"Well, you could have waited until the morning," he growled. His agitation carried him a few steps away from Lainie. "You didn't have to go over in the middle of the night."

"It wasn't the middle of the night," Lainie said quickly. "It was early evening."

"Then where were you the rest of the night? How long did you stay, anyway?"

His nosiness was beginning to rankle Lainie. "That's none of your business," she retorted.

An odd sound—applause—shattered the tension in the room. They all turned to see who was clapping. Rad was standing in the doorway, his amused gaze taking in their startled glances.

"I was wondering how you were going to dodge

that question, Lainie," he laughed, moving forward to join them.

"What are you doing here, MacLeod?" Lee almost shouted.

Rad frowned at Lee's loss of control, but ignored the question. "You might be interested to know that it was after nine o'clock this morning before Lainie left my apartment."

Lee's face was mottled with ill-concealed emotion as he turned his accusing glance on Lainie. "Is that true?"

Lainie was only able to nod her head that it was.

Lee was obviously upset, and Lainie was nonplussed. He'd always seemed so calm. His hand continually massaged the back of his neck as he fought to control his temper.

"If you'd only told me how desperate you were—if I'd only known that you—" His hands lifted toward her in a hopeless gesture. "My God, Lainie, I wanted to be with you. I was even thinking I'd marry you if—"

"Whoa. Slight problem with that. She's never been divorced from me," Rad said bluntly, drawing a dark look from Lee.

"I guess there's no need to ask if that's true." Lee's blue eyes were cold crystals of ice as they turned on Lainie. "How did I get the idea that you hated this guy? Were you lying about that?"

Lainie froze. She couldn't think of a word to say that wouldn't get her in worse trouble.

"And you two were still married? Am I missing any other vital information?"

"If you want to leave this room standing up, you'd better apologize to my wife." Rad snapped savagely. Lainie wasn't the only one to glance in surprise at the man bristling by her side.

"You don't know how sorry I am. But not because

of any threat from you, MacLeod." There was a softening in Lee's eyes as he turned toward Lainie. "I should have kept my mouth shut. Basically, this is about your loyalty and concern for your mother."

"Yes."

"Then you didn't deserve that kind of attack."

"I understand," Lainie murmured, recognizing the pain that Lee was going through.

"I hope you do. Because if you ever need me"— Lee's gaze carried a hostile challenge to Rad—"I'll be there, Lainie."

Lee turned and left the waiting room. A sideways glance at Rad as he stared after the retreating figure revealed the fury that still seethed inside him. Ann stepped forward hesitantly, her rounded eyes taking in the strained look on Lainie's face and the grim one on Rad's.

Lainie wanted to smile, but she was afraid it would crack her control.

"Listen, I'd better go." Ann's voice was uncertain and apologetic. "Call me in a few days."

"I will," Lainie promised.

Then she and Rad were left alone.

"So. Life goes on. How's your mother?" Rad asked.

She refused to meet his eyes. "Fine. Considering."

"How did she react when you told her we were back together again?"

"I didn't tell her."

"And just when do you intend to?" Rad asked.

It wasn't an unreasonable question. "Soon." Lainie sighed. She cast him a sideways glance.

"Are you ready to leave?" he asked.

She nodded. "Just let me say goodbye to Mom."

* * *

When they arrived at her house about an hour
later, Lainie was glad to escape the confinement of
the white Mercedes-Benz. The deafening silence between them had been intolerable, but not any more
so than her awareness of how near he was. She'd
wished he would stop the car, gather her into his
arms, and hold her tightly against his lean hard body.
But his fingers had only gripped the wheel and his attention was on the traffic. For all the attention he
paid her, the seat beside him could have been empty.

When Lainie extracted the key to the front door
from her purse, Rad took it from her, inserted it in
the lock, opened the door and replaced the key in
his own pocket.

"I can unlock my own door, you know. Give it
back."

"Here." He preceded her into the house, shrugging off his dark overcoat and tossing it over the
stairwell railing. Rad knew she would follow him into
the house and close the door behind them.

She guessed the encounter with Lee was bugging
him. Typical male competitiveness. It wasn't like she
was trying to pit one guy against the other, they'd just
happened to meet. Lainie studied his wide shoulders, wondering why and how she had fallen in love
with this complicated man. Pretending to be his wife
when she wasn't, in spirit, was just plain weird.

"Will you be long?" Rad turned toward her suddenly.

"No, not really," she answered, moving quickly
away from his gaze and toward the stairs.

"I have some calls to make. I'll be in the den."

"Make yourself at home," she said wryly.

The first thing that Lainie did upon reaching her
room was to change from the dress into pants and

sweater. From a drawer she took an multi-hued scarf and folded it into a wide band to secure the hair away from her face, tying it at the back of her neck and letting the long tails of silk mingle with her own hair. The tips of her lashes she touched with mascara, then brushed a peach pink blush onto her cheeks. Then she removed her suitcases from the cupboard and began the task of packing her clothes.

She didn't allow her mind to dwell on anything other than the mechanics of her task, precisely folding each garment and laying it neatly in the opened cases.

Rad appeared in the doorway, briefly lounging against its frame before walking into the room. Lainie paused, glancing up into his stony features as if thinking she could find a reason for his presence, but the only thing she could see was a hint of impatience. Rad walked restlessly around the room, stopping occasionally to lift back a curtain and gaze out the window, or to look at a framed photo. His tension transmitted itself to Lainie.

"You don't have to worry about packing everything." Rad stopped in front of her dressing table, checking out the things on top of it. "I've opened charge accounts at various stores in town in your name. Shop 'til you drop. On me."

"That wasn't necessary," Lainie murmured.

"Humor me, okay? I think you need to have some fun."

As ordinary as he was trying to make it sound, there was thoughtful consideration for her in his request. He was too intelligent not to have seen that her clothes weren't exactly the latest in fashion, even if he was a man.

He'd sounded like a real husband. One who just

wanted to make his real wife happy. For a moment there it felt like . . . old times. Good times.

They'd had those, often. The thought evoked memories that she preferred to keep from him for now.

"As my wife, you get to attend social functions with me. So you might as well doll up a little."

"I'll do my best to see that I don't embarrass you." Lainie glanced at her piles of clothes, spotting a loose thread here and a stain there. Somewhere along the way, she'd stopped noticing how old a lot of them were. In fact, she'd stopped caring about being a woman.

"Okay. That's a start."

Lainie nodded. If only she knew where this playacting would end.

"By the way, you might as well wear this again." Taking a few strides, Rad was at her side, taking her left hand and sliding her wedding ring on her fourth finger. Lainie's eyes flew to the open jewelry box on her dresser, where he had been standing. Her gaze was caught and held by his, as captive as her hand.

"I was afraid you might have sold it." His smile was sad.

"I meant to send it back to you," she said.

"I'm glad you didn't."

"Why?"

"It saves me from having to buy you another one."

She was fairly sure he didn't mean to sound so cynical, but damn it, she wasn't going to ask what he really meant.

"Can't we stop baiting each other this way?" With an effort Lainie broke free from his gaze and his hold, shutting the filled suitcase in front of her and locking it securely.

"Is that everything?"

"Just about. I have—"

"I'll send someone around to get the rest," Rad interrupted her. "I booked a table for one o'clock lunch. Let's get going."

The restaurant where they lunched was a relatively new one that Lainie had never been to before. Yet it resembled most establishments that catered to executives with lavish expense accounts. Its decor was tasteful enough. Lots of wood. Live foliage, either potted trees and ferns or climbing vines. Secluded tables cordoned off with deeply carved posts.

Rad did the ordering—she wasn't familiar with neo-Asian fusion cuisine or exotic ingredients like *nam pla*. When he finished explaining that it was fermented fish sauce, she'd given up and let him pick. The food when it arrived was excellent, although the non-existent conversation at the table did little to stimulate her appetite.

Lainie was glad when Rad signaled the waiter to bring their coffee, knowing it meant an end to the rather awkward meal. She studied the drinks menu— more exotic ingredients, breathtakingly high prices— realizing she couldn't bear another ten minutes of silence without occupying her hands with something.

"Guess you've seen a lot of Lee Walters in these last few months." Rad's statement brought Lainie's head up, not so much because the silence ended but because of the quiet in his voice.

"Yes, I have." Lainie set the menu on its end, using it as a little paper wall between them. She could see him just fine and he could see her, though.

"Did you know how he felt about you?"

"Sort of. Not really." She guessed the purpose of this cross-examination.

"And what are your feelings toward him?"

The small menu fell onto the table and there was no longer even a symbolic barrier between them.

"Does it really matter?" she asked tentatively.

His expression became unreadable. The words were already forming on her lips to deny that Lee meant anything more than a friend. Then she remembered how macho Rad had been last night; how sure that after a few minutes in his arms she would capitulate to anything he requested. He wasn't far from wrong.

"I like Lee. We had a date or two."

"Going to spare me the details, huh?"

"I haven't asked you for any."

"Point taken."

She marveled at the way she was able to meet his eyes so easily. "There really isn't much more to say about him." A bittersweet smile played at the corner of her mouth. "I felt safe with him."

"I'm not so sure you like being safe, Lainie. You used to be really wild. I loved that about you."

She shook her head. "Not any more. I changed."

"Why?"

"The world got scary. My mother got sick."

"That's no reason to just shut down."

Lainie let out a sigh. "Let me know what you do when something bad happens to you, okay? Until then, don't judge me."

"Fair enough."

"What I'm looking for now . . ." She sighed again, letting her mind drift a little. Then she spoke. "A quiet, comfortable love, with the warmth of a fire in a hearth."

"Sounds nice."

"Doesn't it? Like something you could snuggle up

to. A haven, dependable, always there when you need it."

"Not impossible, even in this scary old world."

"Yeah, well . . . I hope not. I want someone I can count on. Call me old-fashioned, but my guy has to protect me too and stand up for me."

The glint in his eye reminded her that it had been Rad who had come to her defense during the scene at the hospital. Lee hadn't exactly been on her side.

"And you don't believe I would protect you?" His question was flat.

For no particular reason—she couldn't blame her boldness on vodka, she'd only had green tea—Lainie said what was on her mind.

"With you, I always have the feeling I'm hanging by my fingernails at the edge of a cliff."

"I see. And how often do you have these unusual dreams, Mrs. MacLeod?"

"Don't make fun of me. What I'm saying is that the cavalry isn't coming and no one is there to rescue me." Lainie refused to let his amusement daunt her. "Although you are capable of protecting me from everything but yourself."

"Really. And after last night, do you still want to be protected from me?" He gave her a lusty look that really rubbed her the wrong way.

"Shut up, Rad. You don't understand. You never did." Lainie rose from the table, feeling like she'd revealed a silly, way too girlish side of herself. She grabbed her brown leather coat on the way out and dashed out of the restaurant, knowing that Rad would be delayed from following her by taking care of their bill. She hated the knowing look she'd seen in his eyes, but not nearly as much as she hated herself for giving him a glimpse into her thoughts.

Outside she glanced frantically around for a taxi, but there was none in sight. She had taken two steps toward the bus stop when she heard Rad call her name.

She said something unspeakable, loudly, about his bad manners.

He nodded to two shocked older ladies. "She's right, you know."

"Really?" They turned to stare curiously at Lainie, and then back to him, but he'd already reached Lainie.

"The car's over here."

"Screw you and your fancy car."

"Beats walking. Come on. I'll take you wherever you want to go. Sorry if I acted like a frat boy."

"You're not forgiven." But she let him guide her to his car.

"Yet."

"Don't get your hopes up."

They got in with synchronized door slams. Rad didn't start the motor immediately. He stared instead at Lainie, who looked unblinkingly straight ahead. A peculiar numbness possessed her as she waited for more obnoxious comments to start.

"At least we're talking to each other," was all he said.

Not what she expected him to say. Not at all. Lainie wondered if she was being overly sensitive. Considering what she was going through, that was understandable.

"Yeah," she said cautiously. "It's a start."

He didn't respond to her wary comment right away. His hand reached out and turned her chin toward him. The touch of his hand on her skin brought her senses to life, chasing away the numbness. Lainie moved backward to escape his touch before she did something dumb like let herself melt into his arms.

"I believe you meant that," he said quietly.

"It's true, Rad."

"God, I want it to be." He sighed when she stayed pressed back against the seat. He evidently got the message. "I just hope I don't have to compete with Lee Walters."

"Could we not talk about him?"

"Okay. Sorry. You seem pretty emotional."

"The word is raw. Like someone dragged me out of a nice, thick shell."

"That's accurate. But I think you came out of it yourself."

She gave a tiny shrug. "Maybe. It feels weird. I was so stuck and now—now everything's happening so fast. I have a lot on my mind."

"I don't doubt it. Let me help."

"Do you really want to, Rad?" Her voice quivered uncontrollably. "Why?"

"You came back into my life. It's the right thing to do."

"You could have just given me the money and let me alone."

"I could have," he agreed calmly. There was a scorching intensity in the way he studied her. "I probably would have if—"

"If what?" Lainie persisted.

Rad took her hand and slowly pulled her toward him, until she was nearly in his arms. Then he placed her hand underneath his overcoat against his blue-striped shirt. The swift beat of his heart beneath her hand contradicted his calmness.

"Feel that? You still rev me up," he said. "What the hell. Keeps me from thinking."

She pulled away from him. And Rad didn't make any attempt to hold her. He seemed to accept the fact that their conversation was at an end. Lainie was hurt, confused and ashamed by the confirmation that it really was going to be just physical and probably nothing more.

Maybe loving him—she'd thought so—was a reflex left over from the happy days of their brief marriage. And just this morning she'd entertained the thought that their mutual desire for each other might be a way to jumpstart something good.

But not if the glorious mushy stuff like affection and love was all one-sided. She wanted that. Romance was important. Lainie glanced out the window of the car as it went weaving in and out of traffic. She was reminded of her journey across town less than twenty-four hours before.

"Why aren't you living at our house anymore?" The question that had been unasked the night before came to the forefront.

"It was too big and inconvenient," he replied. "I sold it about a year after you left."

"You *sold* it?"

"Did you think I'd keep it for sentimental reasons? There were very few good things that happened in that house." He glanced at her cynically.

Lainie agreed, but she did so silently. What happiness they had known had been at the cabin in the mountains where they had gone for their honeymoon. Love must have clouded her eyes, because then her husband had appeared to be a very tender and loving guy, nothing like the man beside her.

They arrived at the apartment building a few

minutes later. Rad unloaded her suitcases and placed them on the pavement. She waited expectantly by the glass doors for him to accompany her inside, but he walked back instead to the car.

"I have a couple of meetings to attend this afternoon," he tossed over his shoulder. "I'll be back in time for dinner. Send Dickerson down for the luggage."

Chapter 7

It was a long and uneventful afternoon. Lainie filled most of it with unpacking, arranging her clothes in the drawers allotted her by Mrs. Dudley. She called the hospital, discovered that Rad had already given them her change of address and phone number, and talked with her mother. Again she didn't mention that she was back with Rad, unable to explain it in a way that wouldn't be upsettting. Then she treated herself to a long, relaxing bath, filling the tub with mounds of bubbles before finally dressing for dinner, spending nearly another hour in front of the mirror trying to decide how to style her hair. Her indecision stemmed from the desire to avoid meeting Rad again.

When she finally entered the living room, Lainie had chosen to sweep her hair on top of her head in a bun, a severe style that didn't really flatter her angular features. The evening paper was lying neatly folded on the coffee table—courtesy, no doubt, of Dickerson, Lainie thought. He was everywhere, even when she didn't see him.

She picked it up and leafed through it with desultory interest. Dickerson appeared almost instantly, offering her a glass of sherry, which she accepted. He informed her that dinner would be ready as soon as Mr. MacLeod arrived.

Rad came in a few minutes later. He said no to the sherry that Dickerson offered and walked immediately to the bar, where he mixed himself a martini. Lainie continued leafing through the newspaper, refusing to show undue interest in his arrival, even though her heart began to race when he walked in the door.

"Have you settled in?" His voice came from behind the sofa where Lainie sat.

"Yes, thank you. How did your meetings go?" She refused to be drawn in by his show of interest and kept her voice deliberately light.

"Well enough, if you really care. Doesn't sound like you do."

"Did you really care whether I'd settled in or not?" Lainie snapped back.

"Yes."

"Why? Didn't want to spend the evening alone?"

Lainie hated the tension inside of her that was causing her to be so sarcastic, but it seemed the only safe reaction to his presence.

"When I'm alone, it's because I want to be."

"Convenient all around."

"Yes, it is," Rad replied calmly. "I understand our dinner is ready. Are you ready to eat?"

He waited at the archway near the hall, plainly indicating that if Lainie didn't join him, he would go alone. She rose from the couch slowly and walked toward him, ignoring the impatient and demanding gaze in his eyes that ordered her to hurry.

"Arguing is bad for the digestion, so I tell you

what—let's not talk at all. Safer, don't you think?" he
drawled just before they entered the dining room.

"Great idea." Lainie tried to sound as cool as
he did.

But the silence to her was uncomfortable, although it didn't seem to upset Rad at all. The throbbing ache in her chest left little room for food.

If she'd been able to play wifey as she'd intended,
she would have been witty and charming, impressing
Rad with her lighthearted conversation. Instead,
from the minute he had walked in the door that
evening, she'd been bitchy and sarcastic. Why did
they continually have to poke and prod at each
other? There was a constant crackling of electricity
between them, sparks generating more sparks.

Lainie knew she had two options. One was to
maintain the silence that Rad had decreed and she
had agreed to, which would set a precedent for their
future evenings together. Or she could break the silence with small talk and hope to lessen the antagonism and animosity that were just below the surface
almost every time they talked. She chose the latter.

"I thought I would go to the hospital tomorrow
morning," she said. "I'd like to speak to Dr. Henderson when he makes his morning rounds. And my
mother will expect me to spend time with her."

Rad lifted his eyebrow at the break in the silence.
Lainie lowered her gaze to her plate, bracing herself
for the sarcasm that would undoubtedly follow.

"You'll need a car," he said. "The keys for the Mercedes are on the hall table."

"I thought that was your car."

"Of course it is. How else could I give it to you?"
He smiled at her with genuine amusement.

"That's not what I meant." She actually liked the way his eyes had caressed her softly.

"I have another car if you're concerned with my getting back and forth to the office."

"Actually, I was thinking about that." She smiled hesitantly.

"Well, you'll be needing transportation anyway. I believe Ann wanted to get together with you this week, too."

"You don't object?" Lainie immediately wished she hadn't said that. For a minute she saw the shutters start to close.

"You're not a prisoner here." Rad glanced down at his plate thoughtfully before looking up at her. "Or anywhere else, for that matter."

What did he mean by that? Oh—Lainie could guess. She had shut herself away from the world for a long time.

"But I would appreciate it if you wouldn't, uh, go out on dates."

"No, of course not," Lainie murmured in quick agreement, getting his underlying meaning. No Lee. Well, it would be weird if she saw *him*. Beyond weird, in fact.

The meal was suddenly pleasant. The expertly pre-pared dishes had a better flavor. The chocolate mousse was delicately light and delicious. The whole mood seemed to have changed and Lainie basked in its warm glow. Later, in the living room, she was able to lean against the back of the sofa and relax in con-tentment as Rad put an iPod into a dock and set it on shuffle.

He had eclectic taste in music, definitely on the mellow side. She could use some mellowness in her life. The change in mood seemed to have affected him as well. The peacefulness between them encouraged intimate silence, enhanced by melodious strains of violins in the background. A smile of happiness curved Lainie's mouth at the frown on Rad's face when he saw Dickerson appear in the archway, interrupting their privacy.

"What is it?" Rad asked sharply.

"Ms. Gilbert is here to see you. She mentioned paperwork."

"At this hour?" Lainie exclaimed. Her smile was replaced with a frown and she received a quelling look from Rad.

"I won't be long."

There was more than a spark of irritation in her eyes as she watched Rad walk out of the room. Not if Sondra had anything to say about it, she thought ungenerously.

The digital clock showed 9:33. Then 10:12. Lainie was aware of each dragging minute. Rad still hadn't returned.

An inner compulsion got her up and through the archway and on into the hallway, but Lainie was not in the mood to stop herself. Not until she heard voices coming from behind a closed door did she realize how far she had come from the living room. Even as she listened intently to what was being said, a strong feeling of guilt knotted her stomach.

"It won't be long. A few months, no more." Rad's well-modulated voice came to Lainie clearly.

"It seems like such a long time, though." The feminine voice left Lainie in no doubt that Sondra was still there.

"Does it bother you?" Rad asked.

"Of course. Did you think it wouldn't?"

Rad made no reply to Sondra's question. Seconds ticked past and there was no further sound. Then Rad's voice broke the silence again, but it was too low for Lainie to pick out the words. She reached for the doorknob. What did she hope to find in there? The image of Sondra's red head nestled under Rad's chin burned in her imagination.

Damn him.

Lainie didn't want to subject herself to the final humiliation of finding another woman in Rad's arms.

Her hand never reached the doorknob. She turned and walked swiftly back to the living room. This time she was thankful for the carpet that muffled her movements. Her fingers were twined tightly together as she tried to fight the terrible pain in her heart. She paused in front of the fireplace, half-turning to let the harmony of the room soothe her restless spirit.

Didn't work. The masculine magic was gone. The white, gray and black colors looked like nothing more than a perfect backdrop for Sondra with her titian hair. Lainie fled into the bedroom. Jealousy, so bitter she could taste it, consumed the last vestiges of her hope. She stared at the bed, wondering if she could stand to have Rad make love to her again. He was getting up close and personal with his assistant right now. Double damn him.

Slowly, mechanically, she began changing into her nightclothes. Over the long nightgown of green cotton she slipped on a velvet robe of olive green. Taking the natural-bristle brush from the dressing table, she sat on the bed and began brushing her hair. The ritual of counting each stroke acted as a drug that numbed the pain.

When Rad walked into the room a few minutes later, Lainie was able to glance up at him with an aloofness she wouldn't have been capable of earlier. His tie had been removed and was sticking out of his pocket. There was a drawn tiredness about his face that made Lainie wonder with malicious satisfaction if he'd had trouble reconciling Sondra to her return.

"I didn't think it would take so long," Rad said as he walked to his dresser and began emptying his pockets.

Her hairbrush swept through her hair with the one-hundredth stroke. Lainie rose from the bed, walking over to her own dressing table to place it with the rest of her vanity set. She didn't bother to comment on Rad's statement, her remoteness serving as a shield.

"What's the matter with you?" Rad stood, blocking her way to the bed.

"Nothing." She gazed up at him calmly, feeling like a mannequin devoid of any emotion, insulated from the sensual electricity in his gaze.

"There were some difficulties I had to get ironed out with Sondra." A light flickered in Lainie's eyes at his statement. "It was business," he added darkly.

"You don't have to explain yourself to me, Rad."

"Don't I?"

"You know, we never did talk about fidelity. Just vague things. I remember words like 'maybe' and 'if' getting thrown around a lot," she replied smoothly, sidestepping him and walking to the bed. "So you have an automatic out. Do what you want to do. I can't stop you."

If she had been in a more sensitive state of mind she would have recognized the telltale warning signals from Rad. Instead of actually liking the way he

slammed doors and drawers and hoping he'd catch
a finger in one, she would have been frightened.
Slipping out of her robe, she slid under the bed-
clothes, blind to the anger she had caused.

"Good night, Rad," she murmured as the light was
switched off and the room was enveloped in darkness.

"Like hell!"

The sheets and blankets were stripped away from
her. Lainie glanced up with a startled gasp, her hands
moving up to push at the naked chest above her. She
would have screamed, but her mouth was covered by
a devastatingly sensual and tender kiss. Rad had something to prove.

Lainie pushed herself into an upright position,
glancing around to try to identify the sound that had
awakened her. Then she realized it was not a sound
that had wakened her, but the cessation of a sound.
Someone had turned off the shower in the adjoining
bathroom. It had been an amazing night. Lainie
reached out for her robe to cover her nakedness.

As she slipped her arms into the sleeves of her
robe and folded it around her, Lainie remembered
how she had struggled to evade Rad last night. She
was incredibly angry with him and not about to talk
it over.

Which didn't bother him. Rad had pinned her to
the bed, not content until she had responded to his
lovemaking.

Mmmm. Maybe she shouldn't have. Her night-
dress lay on the floor beside the bed. Lainie reached
down and picked it up. It smelled like him and like
her, all mixed up together. She could hear Rad's

husky voice as he nuzzled her ear, demanding, "Love me." It was an unnecessary order, since she had to admit she already loved him more than she had ever thought possible. At least that was how she felt in his arms. In his bed.

But they were a long way from trusting each other all the same.

"I didn't mean to wake you."

Rad stood in the doorway, a blue towel wrapped around his waist. Lainie dropped the nightgown and turned quickly away from him, her blurred vision blocking out the way the sun shone when he looked at her.

"You didn't. Or at least, it was the shower. I'm not used to sleeping late in the morning anyway." The words rushed out to hide her inadvertent glance at his powerful, barely clad body. He was hot. He was dangerous to her peace of mind. "If you're through, I think I'll take a shower."

Lainie attempted to scurry past him, but his hand shot out and got her arm.

"Let go!"

"What's the matter? You're acting like I'm going to hurt you. You know I would never—"

The front of her robe fell open and her bare body was revealed.

"Wow."

"Leave me alone. This—this isn't easy for me."

Rad sighed and pulled her lapels together. "Okay. Whatever you say. Cover up and I'll try to keep my hands off you."

Lainie kept her lowered head turned away, knowing how hungrily her love-starved eyes would devour his face if she looked at him.

"Was it something I said or did? I don't understand why you're so upset," he growled.

Lainie clutched the robe tightly around her neck, feeling a terrible coldness settling over her. "Remember I told you about feeling like I'd been pulled out of my shell?"

"Yeah."

"Well, I'm going back in."

"Shoot." He looked at her with hope. "When are you coming out?"

"I don't know. Don't push it," she begged softly. She loved him so desperately.

"Mind if I just hold you? Maybe we had sex too soon."

"All right," she whispered.

His fingers curled around her neck and his thumbs pushed her chin up so he could see her face. Her lashes were meshed together in tear-wet spikes that remained lowered over her hazel eyes.

"You said yesterday that I couldn't protect you from myself, but I will." His fingers tightened momentarily around her neck and just as quickly let her go. He turned briskly away from her. "No repeats of last night."

"Rad, please—" She did want to make love with him, it was just too much. The intimacy was overwhelming. Her cry to him was torn from her heart. Lainie didn't want to be denied those rapturous moments in his arms, the only times that she was the center of his world. It didn't matter what his reasons were for having her there.

"I'm not letting you go," Rad said softly, misunderstanding her meaning.

"I don't want you to," Lainie moaned helplessly. "I wish I knew what I did want . . ."

"That makes two of us," he laughed a little bitterly.

The sound echoed in her ears as she fled to the adjoining bathroom and let hot tears wash down her cheeks.

Something was breaking up inside of her—she couldn't stop it. She couldn't even define it. But Rad had a power over her that no other man did.

She didn't know why she was fighting him so hard.

Chapter 8

"Honey, I've been expecting you." Her mother's lips brushed Lainie's cheek in greeting. "You just missed Lawrence. He was here a minute ago."

"No, I didn't. I ran into Dr. Henderson in the hall." Lainie smiled. "So he's Lawrence now? Are you sweet on him?"

Her mother blithely ignored the pointed question. "I slept through the night without a minute of pain." Mrs. Simmons beamed cheerfully. "A good night's rest does wonders."

"You're certainly looking better," Lainie said, a feeling of awkwardness taking hold of her.

"The nurse said the same thing, Lainie." Her mother's laughter was like the clear, tinkling sound of a bell that was pleasing to the ear.

"Well, we're all delighted that you do," Lainie said.

"Speaking of being sweet on people, you really caused quite a stir around the hospital yesterday morning," her mother teased.

Uh-oh. Hospitals were hotbeds of gossip. An apprehensive look clouded Lainie's face.

"I overheard the nurses talking about this incredibly

handsome man who was running himself ragged trying to find you."

"Blond?"

"Yes."

"That was Lee. He was here yesterday." Her mother's clear blue eyes still had the ability to make Lainie feel like a child, only telling half the story so she could get away with something.

"You had the nurses green with envy, especially when Lee went away and you left with a dark-haired man. Now I believe *he* was described as being devastatingly attractive by one nurse and totally hot, quote unquote, by another."

Lainie breathed in deeply, preparing to blurt out the entire story.

"I notice you're wearing your wedding ring again," her mother commented.

Here it comes, Lainie thought, lightly touching the gold Florentine band as if it were a talisman.

"Which would mean that man was Rad."

"Yes, it was." Her hair was flung back over her shoulder with a quick toss of her head as Lainie braced herself to meet her mother's eyes squarely.

"You've seen him several times in the last few months, haven't you?"

"Yes."

"I thought something was bothering you, but I was too concerned with myself to care." There was a faint smile on her mother's lips. "But then I've spent most of my life with selfish thoughts."

"Do you mean that you don't object?"

Lainie had expected a storm of protests and recriminations from her mother at her actions. This calm acceptance was something of a surprise.

"No," her mother sighed, for the first time taking her gaze away from Lainie's face. "I think I'm glad."

"But I thought you never liked him."

"I don't think I did. Rad MacLeod isn't the type to stand for an interfering mother-in-law." Her mother leaned back against the pillow, contemplating the ceiling. "When you were first married, you were so happy—just radiant. Your husband was the center of your world."

"Yeah, he was," Lainie said softly.

Her mother coughed. "Suddenly I didn't seem to matter anymore and I hated him for that. I remember your father used to take my hand and recite that old verse: 'A son is a son until he takes a wife, but a daughter's a daughter the rest of her life.'"

"Mom, you knew I was still your daughter. Nothing's ever changed that."

"Well, your dad consoled me by saying that Rad would soon have our house filled with grandchildren." Her eyes turned apologetically toward Lainie. "But when things began to go wrong with you and Rad, I—I tried a little too hard to keep you close to me. I wasn't ready to lose you, Lainie."

Lainie lowered her head, not wanting to admit to her mother how much damage had been done.

"When you finally left him, I was glad. I thought I would have my baby girl back, but you ran off to Colorado Springs instead."

"So I did."

"Was I the reason?"

"It's a lot more complicated than that."

"You never did confide in me much."

Lainie waited several seconds before replying. "I didn't really trust anyone after a while. Ann kept telling me that I was depressed, but I kept denying it."

"I should have been a better mother. Made sure you had the help you needed."

"All we can do is go on from here, Mom," Lainie answered truthfully.

Her difficulties with intimacy had a lot of causes and no one person was to blame. It was best to just keep on going.

"You have to get help," her mother insisted. "Haven't you ever heard of caregiver burnout? I saw Oprah's show on it. I put a huge burden on you."

"Nothing I couldn't handle." Lainie blinked at the tears gathering in her eyes. "I wish we could have talked like this before."

"So do I. But I was never a very good listener. I'm not a very good one now, because . . . Lainie, you didn't go back to him because of all the money we owe?"

Lainie gave a huge sigh. "I might have made the right decision for the wrong reasons and that's all I'm going to say about it."

"Do you still love him?"

"Yes, I love him very much." Her voice was choked by the pain in her heart that knew how uncertain love could be and how much trouble it could cause. Lainie didn't resist as her mother reached out to hold her.

Safe in her mother's arms, she cried a river. Maybe two.

Wearing her high, fur-trimmed boots, Lainie picked her way through the slush near the edge of the pavement. White flakes of snow swirled down like petals onto the concrete pavement, while the leaden gray sky promised more than just a flurry. She clutched the white-hooded parka around her neck as the cold, blowing wind bit into her cheeks. Already shop windows were filled with Christmas decorations.

For Lainie, there was irony in the gratitude she felt in this holiday celebration. Her mother's improvement had astonished the doctors, leading them to suggest that the treatments might have temporarily arrested the disease. Yet much of her mother's happiness was based on the belief that her daughter had at last found happiness. Her mother had believed she'd been the cause of their first breakup. Their reconciliation was the greatest gift Lainie could have given her. But knowing that, there was no way that Lainie could allow her mother to discover that her relationship with Rad was anything but perfect.

Rad kept his word and left Lainie strictly alone. Mrs. Dudley was instructed to take his clothes to the guest bedroom, which did little to improve the strained relationship between Lainie and the housekeeper. Rad and Lainie still had their evening meals together, and there were no more late-night visits from Sondra, but there was a definite distance between them. At least there weren't any more arrows flying back and forth. Rad was almost too polite and she followed his lead.

The now-and-then Mrs. MacLeod was expected to attend a lot of cocktail parties and business dinners, as Rad had told her, most of them on the weekends. Like everything else, those were a mixed blessing. They took up time and allowed Lainie to be near Rad, but never alone with him.

Tonight was the occasion for another party, and Lainie had bought a dress she had intended to wear that evening. There were some alterations to be done and it was supposed to be ready this afternoon, which was the reason she had come into town.

A familiar voice came through the din of bustling traffic. Lainie glanced around and saw Lee Walters saying good-bye to some guy she didn't know. She hesitated, debating whether to hurry by as if she hadn't seen him, but she lost that opportunity when Lee spotted her.

He walked toward her slowly, each of them murmuring a quiet greeting as he took her hands and drew her toward the sheltered opening of a shop front.

"I've missed you," he said simply. "I probably thought about calling you a thousand times. Then I remembered I had no right."

"You probably wouldn't have reached me. Between visiting my mother and going out with Rad, I haven't been home much." Under the warmth of his boyish smile and with snowflakes leaving white stars on his fair hair, Lainie realized how easy it was to be drawn into Lee's undemanding affection. It was a situation she had to avoid, for his sake and her own.

"Are you happy with Rad?"

"Life doesn't allow you to be happy all of the time. But most of the time I'm content, yes," Lainie answered truthfully.

She was with Rad—no, she was his wife, in the letter of the law—and that was all she could handle right now. "And you? How are things going with you?"

"My old man is slowly admitting that I do know something about business." He wasn't complaining, only amused by what he couldn't change.

"You never have objected to working your way up, have you?"

"Occasionally. After all, I am human," Lee replied, smiling. "But I appreciate the lessons I've learned, too. Where are you going now? Could I buy you a drink, or a cup of coffee or something?"

Lainie pushed back her coat sleeve and glanced at the dainty watch on her wrist. "I'm afraid I don't have time. I have a dress to pick up that's being altered, then I have to dash home and get ready for another party at the Fredricksons' tonight."

"The Fredricksons?" Lee's face broke into a big smile. "I've been invited, too. That means I'll be seeing you again tonight."

"Great. We will be there." Lainie's deliberately placed emphasis on the "we" didn't cause the adoration in Lee's eyes to flicker.

He leaned down and brushed her cheek with a kiss, an expression of shy delight lighting his face. Lainie lifted her hand in a goodbye wave as he walked away, then turned to retrace her steps to the department store.

But as she turned she looked into a pair of green eyes glittering with smug triumph. Sondra was standing only a few feet away and had witnessed and heard Lainie's meeting with Lee. The girl stepped forward, her mouth opening to speak, as Lainie hurried past her.

Lainie carefully slipped the apricot-colored dress over her head. The dress was an excellent choice, its simply cut lines making the most of her slender figure while the bright color enriched the highlights in her thick hair. As she smoothed the skirt over her thighs, she took pleasure in her own reflection. The high V neckline in the front made the dress more or less modest, but the plunging V at the back was a lot more daring. She put her hands behind her to zip up the back, only to feel the material catch in the zipper.

With a brief exclamation of disgust, she attempted

to free it. The material was firmly caught and no amount of wriggling was going to help. Sighing heavily, she stepped out of the bedroom, calling for the housekeeper to come to her aid.

"She's busy just now. What was it you wanted?" Rad's sharp voice halted her footsteps.

"I didn't know you were home. You're early." He'd caught her off guard and her surprise was evident in her expression.

"What did you want with Mrs. Dudley?"

"My dress—the zipper is stuck."

"I believe husbands can take care of minor details like that." The mockery in his voice was accompanied by a quirk of his eyebrow.

There was no way Lainie could refuse his help. Her heart pounded in her ears and the blood rushed with surging warmth to her face. The fiery touch of his fingers against her bare back as he expertly worked the material free of the zipper turned her into quivering jelly. She yearned for him to put his arms around her waist and draw her back against the muscular hardness of his body. But as soon as the zipper was free, he zipped it to the top and secured the clasp. Then Rad moved away from her to the fireplace mantel where his drink awaited him.

"That dress looks great on you. Is it new?" he asked.

"Yes," Lainie murmured, secretly pleased by his compliment.

"Is that what you planned to wear to the Fredricksons' tonight?"

Lainie's head lifted at his extra emphasis on the word *planned*.

"Yes."

"Did you buy it just for this party?"

Was she under attack? Lainie couldn't quite tell. His voice was almost too indifferent.

"Do I need a reason to buy a pretty dress? Isn't it right for tonight?"

"Yes, it's fine. Too bad good old Lee Walters won't be able to see you wearing it." This time the fire in his eyes showed clearly. So much for cool indifference.

"Do you mean we're not going to the party tonight?" Her feeling of weakness left her, chased away by anger at his insinuations. Someone had been talking. Guess who.

"Does that disappoint you?" Rad asked. "I wouldn't want to interfere with your plans to meet Lee or anything. You two have been probably been texting each other like crazy. The quiet way to cheat, right?"

"What lies has Sondra been telling you?"

He only shrugged.

"Well, if you really want to know, I accidentally met Lee in town this afternoon. I was going to pick up this dress from the dressmaker. I mentioned to him that we were going to the party at the Fredricksons' and he said he would see me there. I have no control over what Sondra read into that or said about it. Besides, you told me yourself this morning that we were going."

"News flash—change of plans," Rad said.

"Nice of you to let me know," Lainie retorted.

"I didn't have a chance. You've been gone all day." He cut off her indignant response. "I decided this morning that we would spend the weekend in Vail."

"Vail? Skiing?"

"Yup. I mean, I planned on getting some skiing in while we were there, but I have a construction project there that I want to check on too. We'll leave first thing in the morning."

Lainie hated it when he used that domineering

tone on her. She didn't really care about the party or
the dress but his attitude irked her.

"That doesn't explain why we aren't going to the
party tonight."

The corner of Rad's mouth twitched involuntarily—
Lainie couldn't tell whether it was in mockery or
anger. "I assumed you'd need time to pack. And since
you'll be away on vacation, I thought you might want
to contact your mother."

She still couldn't quite read him. It was clear enough,
though, that Rad was jealous of Lee. Which confirmed
her opinion that Rad was just too good at hiding emotions. If he had any. She was so irritated with him at the
moment, she would have sworn he didn't.

"If this is a business trip, then why are you taking
me?" Childishly Lainie attempted to strike back.

"Part of my nefarious plan to treat you right and
change your life." Rad's smile held cynical amusement. "You can go or stay, whichever you want. It
really won't make any difference to me."

A defeated feeling got the better of her. Lainie
knew she shouldn't have expected an avowal from
Rad that he wanted her with him.

"Where will we be staying?" she asked.

"Why?"

"I just wondered . . . I thought . . ." Her eyes took on
a pleading look. "Isn't the cabin somewhere near Vail?"

"What cabin?"

The question effectively shut the door on further
conversation. Lainie shrugged uselessly and retreated to her bedroom.

Chapter 9

With the rising of the sun, the snow had ended. All around was the evidence of its fall. Everything was covered with a fresh blanket, pure and white and glistening under the brilliant rays. Here and there puffs of wind danced teasingly over the powdery crystals, sending them swirling in the air only to drift back to the ground. Branches of quaking aspen, barren of leaves, were dressed in a wintry glaze of hoary white while heavy garlands of snow made evergreen branches droop.

A sign poked its head out of a snowdrift made larger by the deposits of a snowplow. A cap of white snow dipped down, attempting to conceal the words Loveland Pass. Ahead was the flashing caution light of a snowplow patrolling the cleared road. The white Mercedes edged into the next lane, giving the yellow monster a wide berth as it passed. For a moment they were enshrouded by its steamy breath and the whirl and flurry of snow before bursting through. The concrete path of the four-lane divided highway stretched out in front of them, briefly revealing its route.

As they began their descent, snow-covered

outcroppings rose above them, snow clinging tena-
ciously to the boulders, falling away in places to
reveal almost perpendicular rock faces. Ten miles or
so farther on was the engineering feat called the
Eisenhower Memorial Tunnel, its entrance leading
to the other side of the mountain.

The chilly atmosphere in the car had nothing to
do with the freezing temperature outside. Lainie
wished that the serenity and peace of the wintry
landscape before them would somehow transfer
itself to her and Rad. When they had first left Denver,
she had attempted to make conversation, but his
terse replies gave her the impression that Rad regretted inviting her to accompany him. She couldn't
keep her gaze from straying to his dark profile, its
bleak coldness intensified by the winter scene outside the windows.

She jumped a little when he actually took the ini-
tiative and talked to her. "Tomorrow I'll be tied up in
a meeting with the engineers. Thought you'd like to
maybe meet his wife—she lives in Vail. Unless you'd
rather spend the day by yourself?" Rad spared her a
sideways look.

"No," Lainie sighed. Did she get to choose who
he fobbed her off on? Evidently not. She couldn't
help adding bitterly, "Thanks for arranging for a
babysitter, though. What are my marching orders for
today?"

He sighed. "I thought I'd exhaust you on the ski
slopes this afternoon. Tiredness might dull the sharp
edge of your tongue."

"I only hope it improves your disposition," Lainie
snapped back.

His hand wearily brushed the dark hair from his
forehead. "What do you expect me to do? Play the

adoring lover? Even you know that would be pushing things too far."

"I should think it would come naturally to you, considering all the business trips you've taken with Sondra." Low blow, but he deserved it.

"Okay, get it all out of your system." Rad glared at her coldly.

He leaned back against the bucket seat, inhaling deeply and flexing his fingers, which had been clutching the steering wheel. Lainie was stunned by the genuine weariness in his face and eyes.

"For the past month," Rad went on more quietly, "it's been a round of business and parties and a few snatched hours of sleep. I guess you're miffed about being dragged away from Lee Walters, but since you're here, at least pretend to enjoy yourself. For a few days let's forget the past, the future and everything else."

She felt his eyes rest on her thoughtfully, but she didn't glance over to meet them.

"Is it a deal?"

The coaxing tone of his voice brought a whispered agreement from Lainie.

Rad's ski condo didn't begin to compare with the luxury and elegance of his Denver apartment. Yet the decor was in keeping with the rugged surroundings of the Rocky Mountains. The walls were paneled in oak and the shaggy carpet was a warm shade of persimmon. A weathered brick fireplace dominated the small living room, faced by overstuffed sofas and chairs in warm reds and yellows, a startling contrast to the blinding white snowscape outside the picture windows. Here there was no staff to keep things running smoothly—not that the one bedroom and smaller guest bedroom, or the living room and compact kitchen with its adjoining breakfast nook, would require one.

Rad didn't give Lainie much of an opportunity to explore her temporary quarters. He carried her luggage to the larger bedroom and his to the guest bedroom, declining her offer to unpack his things. His calmly worded request that she unpack, change and be ready to leave for the ski slopes in an hour had only the barest ring of command in it. Not much later, Lainie joined him in the living room dressed in her ski suit of honey gold with slashes and stripes of chocolate brown. Rad, in a suit of black and white, seemed unappreciative of her promptness, nodding briskly at her when she entered and immediately escorting her to the door. His impatience was marked. He seemed in a hurry to escape the confines of civilization and pit his skill and strength against the mountains and snow. After his declaration that this was to be a weekend of relaxation, Lainie had thought his air of aloofness would disappear, but all the while his gaze was fixed on the distant slopes.

Later, as they rode the chair lift to the top of the mountain, Lainie realized that she'd been hoping, wistfully, that they would recapture the magic of their honeymoon spent here in these rugged mountains. It was a ridiculous wish, one that required the effort of two people to fulfill. And Rad didn't care.

It was in this state of apathy that Lainie followed Rad on his run down the mountain. At first her eyes studied the black figure in front of her, enjoying the litheness and skill in his movements. Then the mountain demanded the use of her own muscles, dormant for too long, and her own skill automatically returned.

The cold mountain air blew over her face and tugged at her long hair, caught in a clip at the back of her neck. The yellow goggles she wore gave everything a golden hue. Her lethargy gave way to the exhilaration of the moment. She dug her poles into the snow beneath her as she listened to the swishing sound of her own skis. She saw Rad at the bottom of the slope watching her finish her run, and instinctively she kicked a ski out, jumped, turned, and came to a stop at a right angle to the slope.

As she slipped the goggles on top of her head, her eyes were shining brightly. There was a cherry glow to her cheeks and to the tip of her nose. Her inhibitions were wiped away. She gave a laughing smile as she looked at Rad. No more clouds were in his face, either, chased away by the intoxicating mountain air and the invigorating sun.

"Want to catch your breath before going back up?" he asked.

"I'll rest on the chair lift," Lainie puffed, wondering how much of her breathlessness was due to the exertion and how much to the warmth of his smile.

Their second run was slower than the first. Rad no longer was in the lead, content to slow his pace to Lainie's. Halfway down the mountain Rad stopped, took her hand when she did the same, and together they sidestepped up a rise. It was a small ridge that gave them a view, somewhat obstructed by trees, of both sides of the valley. On one side was the cleared run of the slopes, and on the other a forest of trees, fallen logs, a tangle of growth, and beautiful virgin snow. At the bottom of the valley a tiny mountain stream fought vainly to keep from being covered by snow, here and there disappearing altogether only to break free farther on.

"Talk about a Rocky Mountain high," Lainie breathed, and immediately felt embarrassed at saying something so corny. She glanced at Rad hesitantly.

But he was looking at the scenery. "Yes," he agreed quietly. "And a lot more effective than booze or drugs." He smiled down at her. "Are you ready to go again?"

She nodded and followed him as he made the traverse from the ridge back to the slope. They maintained a slow, steady pace with Lainie going first. She knew the cause of her lightheartedness was the sudden opening of the door of communication between them. Maybe there was still something to be salvaged from their relationship.

She was standing upright on her skis, coasting down the slight grade. She turned to ask Rad if they were going up again when her skis hit an uneven patch of snow and slid out from underneath her, and with unbelievable force she landed on her rump in the snow. For a moment she could only sit there, her arms keeping her propped upright trying to figure out what had happened. Then Rad was kneeling beside her, trying to stay serious, looking into her face.

"Are you all right?"

Lainie had to give him credit for keeping the laughter out of his voice. She winced as she tried to shift her position.

"Who would ever believe that snow could be so hard!" She very tenderly rubbed the injured portion of her body.

"Which is injured, your dignity or your derriere?" he teased.

"The first is shattered and the second is bruised."
Lainie shook her head ruefully, his bantering tone
bringing color to her cheeks.

Rad's arm was around her waist to support her after
she had scrambled ungracefully to her feet. She felt
awkward and gauche as she attempted to right her skis
and finish the short distance to the bottom.

"We'll take it slow and easy, okay?"

It didn't matter that he babied her as long as she
remained enveloped by his warm concern. Lainie
was almost sorry when they reached the bottom, although she was beginning to feel the soreness set in.
Rad glanced at her inquiringly.

"I think I'll sit out for a while," she said.

"You don't mind if I take another run, do you?

"No, of course not," she said quickly. "I'll wait for
you at the snack bar and indulge in a big mug of hot
cocoa."

"All right then. I'll see you later.

He gave her a snappy salute and headed toward
the chair lift. It was just as well she'd been brought
back to earth with such a bang, Lainie decided. She
needed a level head to keep from revealing to Rad
how much he meant to her. Although there was no
doubt about it—a little bit of his charm was a heady
thing.

Lainie couldn't stop her heart from jumping when
nearly an hour later she saw Rad threading his way
through the crowd of skiers toward her. The glances
from interested women made her just a little bit
more proud as his hand rested possessively on her
elbow and led her away from the throng. There was
the contentment of a conqueror in his expression, as
if he'd just battled the mountain and won. Lainie

liked the way his eyes lingered on her and only on her. For the moment it was enough.

She wasn't really thinking about where he was taking her. Not until she was led from the brightness outside into the darkness of a building did she take notice of where they were, and her eyes lifted in silent question to his face.

"Now that we've blown the cobwebs away," Rad smiled, "I thought we'd have a drink."

His smile, free of all traces of sarcasm and cynicism, gave sincerity to his words. Once Lainie's eyes had adjusted to the change of light, she found the lounge wasn't as dark as she had first thought. It was almost a picture postcard scene from a ski resort, complete with a blazing fire in the fireplace and laughing people dressed in the latest ski togs.

"How are you feeling?" Rad asked as she gingerly lowered herself onto a chair.

"Fine," she said, shifting her weight so she wouldn't be resting right on her bruised rear end.

Rad ordered hot buttered rum for each of them. The drinks arrived with swizzle sticks of cinnamon, and they sipped them appreciatively. The crowd in the lounge was too noisy to carry on a normal conversation. After they finished their drinks Rad immediately suggested that they leave.

Twilight cast its crimson glow on the snow-covered mountains. By the time they stopped and ate at a locally renowned restaurant and left, a blanket of stars covered the skies, accented by a shimmering pale half moon.

"Tired?"

Lainie's long, drawn-out sigh as Rad stopped the car in front of the apartment prompted his question.

"No, satisfied." Lainie smiled at him serenely.

Almost satisfied, her mind added silently, knowing that to complete the fulfillment of the day Rad would have to take her in his arms.

A nervous silence threatened to take over them as they entered the apartment, and she wanted to avoid that at any cost. "Is there coffee in the kitchen?" She rushed in.

"Instant, I imagine," Rad shrugged.

"I'll make a pot. Why don't you start a fire in the fireplace?" Lainie was a little surprised by Rad's agreement to her suggestion. But then he was in an amiable mood. Several minutes later they were both sitting in front of the fireplace sipping at the hot black coffee. Yellow flames licked hungrily over the logs in the fireplace, snapping and crackling as if smacking their lips over their woody morsels. Rad hadn't bothered to turn on any other lights in the room and the atmosphere was one of quiet intimacy.

"Tell me about this couple we're meeting tomorrow." Lainie forced her eyes away from the hypnotic flames.

"The Hansons?" Although Rad responded, he continued to stare into the fire. "Steve Hanson and I went to college together. I was the best man at his wedding after he graduated. He took a job with our firm, which at the time was my father's and his partner's. And since I did the same, we naturally saw a lot of each other."

"I don't recall you ever mentioning him."

"When you and I were first married, Steve was in Louisiana handling the construction of a large refinery." She didn't catch a trace of bitterness when he referred to their own marriage. "Their third child was born in Louisiana."

"How many do they have?"

"Four. Three girls and one boy, the boy being the youngest. He's my godchild." He glanced over at Lainie and smiled.

"Really?"

"Sean is four, and more of a live wire you'll never find. When he was two, I invariably came out of any meetings with teeth marks. At three, he was always kicking my shins. Linda tells me—that's Steve's wife—that he's on a cowboy and Indian kick now. That probably means I'll be scalped this time."

Lainie laughed and was delighted by this side of Rad that she had never seen.

"Do you know, that's a first?" Rad stared at her, searching her face with a thoroughness that left her breathless. "Ignoring those polite sounds you made at various parties, this is the first time I've heard genuine laughter from you in all these weeks."

Lainie didn't know how to reply because she knew that what he said was true. He stood up and offered her his hand. She joined him, letting her hand remain in his for as long as he wanted.

"It's getting late," he said. "You must be worn out. Why don't you go on to bed?"

"Rad." His name was an aching sound that came from her heart. She swayed closer to him. He released her hand and shook his head negatively.

A little smile of regret lifted the corners of his mouth as he bent forward and brushed her lips lightly with a kiss. "Go on to bed this time."

Lainie did as she was told, basking in the warm glow of his half promise.

Chapter 10

Steve Hanson was about the same height as Rad, only more stockily built. His hair was fine, straight, and the color of corn silk, falling across his tanned forehead. His wife, Linda, was much shorter with ash blond hair that had a tendency to curl.

After Rad had made the introductions, he and Steve lingered at the Hansons' apartment, which gave Lainie a chance to talk to Linda before she was deserted by Rad. She was anxious to become friends with this couple who were so obviously close to her husband. Although Linda was a quiet person, she was not shy. In just a few minutes the conversation lost the strain of strangeness and came easily to both of them. At that point Rad and Steve took their leave, Rad promising Linda that he would have her husband back to her that afternoon.

The Hansons' two older girls were off at a skiing party and their seven-year-old was staying at a friend's house, which only left Sean, Rad's godchild, at home. He spent most of the morning dashing in and out of the apartment keeping his mother up-to-date on the progress of his snowman. His hair was fine and straight, the color of his father's. The cold had brought healthy color to his cheeks and button nose, yet there was nothing cherubic about his face or his bright eyes. Heavy winter clothing hid the wiriness of his little body.

Linda kept Lainie laughing all morning with anecdotes about her son's mischievousness. Shortly after lunch, Linda was able to convince him to take a short nap while she and Lainie relaxed over a cup of coffee. The quietness of the apartment seemed to call for more serious conversation and Linda was the one to begin it.

"Well, tell me all about you and Rad."

The request flustered Lainie. She didn't feel secure enough in the budding friendship to confide the exact status of their marriage. "There really isn't much to tell."

"How long have you two known each other, then?" Linda wasn't a bit put off by Lainie's ambiguous answer.

"I met him six years ago," Lainie admitted.

"You must have known his first wife!" Linda exclaimed. "Steve and I were in Louisiana, so we never got to meet her."

Lainie was so stunned by this statement that for a moment she couldn't speak. She remembered then that Rad had only introduced her as "Lainie." He had made no mention that she was his wife.

"Yes, I know her," she answered, not meeting Linda's eyes.

"She always sounded like a spoiled socialite to me. And too young for him," Linda sighed. "Of course, Rad picked a rotten time to marry anyway."

"What do you mean?"

"Well, his father was just buying out his partner's interest in the business when he met the future Mrs. MacLeod. He knew his father's takeover would mean extra work and responsibility for himself, so he opted for a quick marriage. In a way, I kind of felt sorry for the girl," Linda went on. "Here Rad rushed her off her feet, spent every available hour with her before they were married, and then after they were married he had to practically desert her and go make money. Rad's not like Steve, who brings work home with him. It must have been a difficult adjustment for his wife."

"Yes, I'm sure it was," Lainie agreed, discovering for the first time the cause of Rad's obsession with his business after they were married.

"Of course, when his marriage broke up he really changed. It was like nothing mattered to him anymore. Today, with you, was the first time I recall seeing any softness in his face, except where the children are concerned. He adores Sean."

"What about his assistant?" Lainie couldn't resist the question. Sondra had always been the cause of most of her jealousy.

"Sondra the siren? I used to tease him something terrible about her." Linda laughed. Her blue eyes gave Lainie a sideways glance. "I don't think you have any reason to be jealous of her. If she was anything more than just an assistant, I'm sure Rad would have told Steve, and you can bet I would have wormed it out of Steve. I'm not saying Sondra wouldn't like it to be more."

Lainie took a deep breath, wondering how much difference it would have made if she had only known Linda years ago. "Do you think"—she swallowed to take the huskiness out of her voice—"that Rad loved his wife?"

"I don't know. He still won't talk about her or what

happened. I can't imagine him marrying anybody he didn't care about a lot, but I wouldn't worry about that if I were you." Linda smiled at her reassuringly. "It's over with. Besides, Rad isn't the type to make the same mistake twice with the same person. Whoever she was, I can't see Rad taking her back again."

That statement only made Lainie more curious. He *had* taken her back. Revenge couldn't have been his motive. Deftly Lainie maneuvered the conversation to other topics, wondering all the while.

It was nearly three o'clock before Sean, who had only promised to close his eyes, finally woke up from his nap. After recharging his supply of energy with a tall glass of milk and four cookies, he was ready to return to his task of completing his snowman. Linda was preparing a roast for the evening meal, so Lainie volunteered to help Sean bundle himself up in his winter coat.

"How many children do you have?" Sean asked boldly as Lainie tucked his muffler inside his parka.

"I don't have any. But I hope to someday." Lainie smiled at him.

"How many do you want?"

"Three sounds like a good number to me."

"All boys," Sean announced firmly.

"Actually I thought two boys and a girl would be nice," Lainie replied solemnly, and heard Linda's slight chuckle behind her.

"Yeah, that would be okay, I guess." Sean had hesitated slightly before agreeing. Then his bright eyes looked beyond her and his face broke into a beaming smile. "Uncle Rad!" he cried, hurtling himself past Lainie.

Lainie turned with a start. Rad was standing in the doorway, looking down at her with more than just amusement in his eyes. Color rushed to her cheeks and she was glad when the demanding Sean captured Rad's attention. She took the opportunity to escape to the kitchen where she immediately offered her help to Linda, who handed her a bunch of carrots and a peeler. Lainie was briskly shaving off the outer skin in long orange strips when Rad's hands took hold of her upper arms.

"Are you glad to see me?" he whispered in her hair.

Lainie was saved from replying by Steve's voice calling, "Rad, phone call for you. Long distance. Sound quality, not great."

Rad sighed, squeezed Lainie's shoulders and walked into the living room. By the time he returned, the roast, complete with carrots, potatoes, and onions, had already been placed in the oven. Lainie smiled at him hesitantly when he walked into the room, but his expression stayed serious.

"I'm sorry, Linda, but Lainie and I are going to have to beg off our dinner date. Something's come up and we'll have to leave," he said tersely.

"What's wrong?" Linda asked, speaking the words that were uppermost in Lainie's mind.

His answer was directed to Lainie. "That was the hospital. They've been trying to get hold of us. Your mother's had a relapse and they want us to come as quickly as we can."

Lainie knew she must have paled. He reached out immediately, supporting her waist when she moved toward him and faltered. She nodded at the words of sympathy expressed by Linda and Steve, but she was guided by Rad, who was quickly maneuvering her toward the door and on to the car, as Linda gathered up their things in a hurry.

The drive back to Denver was a nightmare. But Lainie didn't allow herself to lose control. The occasional reassuring glances from Rad really helped. As they mounted the hospital steps, Lainie was amazed to see a familiar figure rushing toward her.

"I called Ann before we left," Rad said, "I thought you would like to have her here."

So it was with Ann that Lainie arrived at her mother's room. Rad was off to consult the doctors. It was so strange, Lainie thought, staring down at her mother. At one time she would have believed that her mother had deliberately brought on the attack in a desire to have Lainie at her side. But the new understanding and closeness that had joined them together in the recent weeks no longer made a given.

"The nurse told me earlier," Ann whispered, "that she was showing signs of improvement."

Lainie could only nod at that statement and pray that it was true. "How long has she been unconscious?"

"She's not really unconscious," Ann explained. "The nurse told me it was more like a drugged sleep."

As if on cue, Mrs. Simmons's eyes fluttered open. Lainie walked around the bed and sat next to her mother, taking her hand. The dull blue eyes focused on her. "Lainie?"

"Yes, Mom, I'm here. Everything's going to be all right."

"I told them not to call you back." Her speech was slurred and weak. "I wanted you to have the time with Rad."

"Sssh. Don't try to talk. Just rest and get better."

"Yes, I will." Her eyelids fluttered shut again, only

to pop open. "I'm not going to die this time, so don't you be worrying about me."

"I won't." There was a suggestion of a smile on her mother's lips as she again closed her eyes, and in seconds she was asleep. Lainie felt Ann's hand touch her shoulder. She breathed in deeply and turned to smile at her friend.

"She was reassuring me," Lainie explained.

"Why don't we go to the waiting room down the corridor?" Ann suggested. "I'm sure you could use some coffee and I know the nurses could spare us a cup of theirs. Besides, Rad should be coming anytime now to give us some idea of what the doctors said. I'm sure they'll want to talk to you too."

Lainie nodded and accepted her friend's guiding hand. Walking down the corridor toward them was Lee Walters. They saw each other about the same moment.

"I called your apartment." Lee looked sympathetically into her face. "The housekeeper told me your mother wasn't well. I came just to let you know I was here if you needed me."

"That was kind of you." Lainie meant what she said, but she discovered that she wished Lee hadn't come. "Actually she's not doing too badly. I think she's better."

"I'm glad."

Lee would have gone on, but Lainie interrupted him briskly, "If you would excuse me, Lee, Ann and I were just going to meet my husband. He's been talking with the doctors."

Lee stiffened and stepped aside. Lainie felt Ann's bemused eyes studying her. She probably had been too matter-of-fact with Lee, but the truth was she wanted to see Rad and not just because of her mother, either. Lainie saw him standing by the nurses' office. He turned at their approach, his expression hard. Lainie couldn't help feeling a flash of hurt. She wanted to see the softness and concern that had been there earlier.

She searched his face, trying to find the warmth behind the coldness. If there was any, she couldn't find it. Weird . . . but she had other things to worry about. Getting to the point, Rad confirmed Lainie's previous optimistic statement that her mother was better. Lainie managed an appropriate murmur of gratitude. Rad said he was going to make some phone calls, and Lainie reached out and placed a hand on his arm, but the suggestion that he join them never got made. He looked down at her restraining hand and his meaning was clear.

Don't.

Startled, she withdrew her hand quickly, and just as quickly turned away toward the waiting room where Ann was.

Silence descended on the waiting room. Not even the hot coffee could thaw its chilly oppressiveness. For a time Ann respected Lainie's obvious reluctance to talk, but it didn't last. She walked over, removed the empty cup from Lainie's hand and sat down beside her.

"What's wrong?" she asked.

At first Lainie just shook her head, attempting to brush off the question. But Ann was having none of that.

"You might as well tell me. I'll get it out of you anyway," she insisted.

"Did you see the way he looked at me?" Lainie murmured, tears springing to her eyes. "It's never going to work. One minute he's lovey-dovey, the

next . . . not. It doesn't make sense. It never will. I
don't know why I ever thought it could."

Ann exhaled. "Do you think it was because he saw
you talking to Lee?"

Lainie nodded. "Probably."

"But that couldn't have been more innocent!"

"Rad sees what he wants to see and thinks what he
wants to think."

"He's crazy, Lainie. That's all there is to it."

"I think I was the crazy one, Ann," Lainie said wistfully, "for thinking it would work. But if one little
thing can set him off like that—"

"End it now. Forget him."

"That's not so easy."

"Lainie. I just wish you hadn't run into him the
night of the concert."

"It was all inevitable, I think. Fate." Lainie's voice
was choked with emotion as she studied the hands
clenched tightly in her lap. "Should I forget about
love, too? I don't think I'm cut out for it."

"Does he know you love him? Have you told him?"
Ann's blue eyes shone with compassion for her friend.

"No. What good would it do? My life would just
become more miserable if I was that open with him.
I doubt he'd even listen—"

A slight sound came from the doorway and Lainie
glanced up to look into Rad's face. There was such
an odd look in his eyes that she gasped at the sight.
So now he knew. He had heard her admit that she
loved him and this was his reaction. She half expected to hear him laugh. At her.

"I want to talk to you alone." His words were
clipped and commanding.

Lainie's lips quivered as she steadfastly met his gaze.
Without a word Ann slipped from the room, knowing

that no matter how much she wanted to stay, the confrontation to come was none of her business. Lainie tensed herself, waiting for the barrage of scornful words that would do away with the last vestige of her hopes, but Rad continued to study her face.

"So talk. Or go. The suspense is killing me," she said flatly.

At last he strode impatiently into the room. There was the faintest look of uncertainty in his expression. It confused Lainie. The Rad she knew was never uncertain about anything.

"Consider our bargain fulfilled," he said. "I'll cover the cost of your mother's medical bills until . . . until it's no longer necessary. But you're free to go."

"Free?" Lainie repeated, baffled.

"Yeah. Whoopee. We no longer owe each other anything. Let's get that divorce."

"Have you lost your mind?"

"No. I think I just came to my senses. Seeing is believing."

"What the hell are you talking about, Rad? What's gotten into you?"

"Careful what you wish for, Lainie. In this case, you just got it. After a long wait," he added sarcastically. "But I would appreciate it if you would change your name back to Simmons. I don't want to be reminded that there's an ex-Mrs. MacLeod walking around."

Lainie closed her eyes. Oh God. So it was Lee. He'd seen them chatting and assumed the absolute worst, just as she'd thought. She wasn't going to put up with it. Just when you thought you could trust the man you loved again . . . hell, you found out he didn't trust you. Life had a way of falling apart no matter what.

"I'll get your stuff back to you," he went on when she failed to speak.

"You're a prince." Lainie's voice managed to squeeze itself out through the tight lump in her throat. "You can keep the ballgown and the glass slippers."

"What—oh, I get it. Yeah, you're right, Lainie. There isn't going to be a fairytale ending. But whose fault is that?"

"I don't know."

Rad stared at her unblinkingly for several minutes. The coldness in his eyes froze the tears in hers. Then he turned his back to her and ran his fingers through his dark hair in a gesture of tiredness.

"My lawyers will contact you," he said. His inexplicable behavior and harsh words wrenched at her heart.

He was walking toward the door and Lainie hoped he was walking out of her life forever. She tasted blood in her mouth where her teeth had bitten her lip. Unwillingly she called his name and saw him turn slowly back toward her. She rose hesitantly to her feet, forcing herself to look into the carved features.

"I wanted to thank you." Her voice was only a whisper.

"For what?" he asked. "Lainie, you really had me going, but—" His eyes raked her face.

Her reply was simple enough. "For bringing me back here today when my mom was so ill."

He exhaled slowly, his shoulders sagging. Lainie sensed the unrest her words had caused.

"Oh God. I hope that I—" He didn't finish whatever it was he was going to say. "I'm glad she's better."

Lainie only nodded. When she lifted her head Rad was gone.

Chapter 11

Two days passed before Lainie summoned up the nerve to return to the apartment. Luckily Rad had left the suitcase she'd packed for their stay in Vail, so that she had a change of clothes ready to go. Returning to the house she'd shared with her mother would have plunged her right back into depression. A worse one. Ann had insisted that she stay with them, and Lainie hadn't objected.

The scene in the hospital wasn't worth puzzling over. So he'd seen her talking to Lee and overreacted. That was a very mild word for extreme behavior. She'd snapped a twig and a whole tree had fallen down. On her. If she stayed with him, he'd just do it again. Sure, he was pleasant a lot of the time and always passionate—but he was not, for all his controlling behavior, a man she could ever rely on.

It was time to face the music and dance . . . alone. The knowledge that their whirlwind reunion had come to nothing weighed on her. She wouldn't even know where to begin to analyze what had happened. It all seemed so sudden and so crazy, although that described most whirlwinds, come to think of it. Including their whirlwind marriage. But the last time they had been separated, five years ago, she hadn't known how deeply she loved him.

She had to get over that.

Lainie slipped the key to the apartment into the lock, glad that she hadn't returned it to Rad that afternoon at the hospital. She had phoned Mrs. Dudley only an hour before to make sure that he wouldn't be home during the lunch hour and to notify the housekeeper that she would be arriving to pack her things. Lainie had been quick to refuse the woman's barely civil offer to help, asserting that she was capable of handling it by herself. But as her shaky legs carried her into the living room, she wondered whether she could.

She stared at the fireplace, remembering again the first time she had been there. She hated the room with sudden violence because it was here that she had realized that she still loved Rad. Pressing her lips tightly together so they wouldn't let her sobs escape, she glanced at the envelope in her hand. Before her resolve could weaken she slipped the apartment key inside, hearing the metal clink against her wedding ring, which was already inside.

Also inside was the terse note she had agonized over writing, trying to keep her emotions from creeping into those few short words. After several attempts at writing it she had finally settled on two noncommittal sentences, knowing that any statements of her love for him would be read with amusement. *Here's your key and my wedding ring. I don't need them anymore.*

It seemed wrong that two short sentences could contain so much unspoken pain. Quickly Lainie placed the envelope on the mantelshelf, staring at Rad's name written on the front. She wiped the tears away from her eyes and scurried into the bedroom. The quicker she finished packing, the sooner she would be able to leave.

She'd underestimated how many clothes she had, and how long it would take to pack them all. She didn't allow herself to admit that she was dawdling because she was remembering the two glorious nights she'd spent in this room in Rad's arms.

Crying openly, she closed the last suitcase and set it on the floor. She spared one last look around the room, wondering if Rad would be able to walk in and not see the bare dressing table that had once held her belongings. Those thoughts only brought more pain, so she quickly picked up two suitcases and her handbag, and walked to the door, then into the living room. As before, her footsteps were muffled by the carpeting.

Her hazel eyes blinked at the dark form sitting on the gray velvet sofa. The mist cleared, enabling her to focus on Rad. The pain of seeing him again seared through her, but she couldn't tear her gaze away from the man she loved.

In his left hand Lainie saw the terse note she had written him. He was gripping the white paper so hard that it was nearly crumpled in his hands. His dark head was bent and his shoulders hunched over the object in his other hand. He curled his hand around it and put it in his pocket.

He didn't look at her. But he spoke to her. "I blew it, Lainie. Big time. I saw you with Lee and I—"

"You acted like a jealous jerk."

He nodded, staring at the floor. "A jerk who really does love you. No matter what, Lainie."

"Yeah, well, love isn't everything. Why did you do it,

Rad?" She bumped and banged the suitcases past him and stood by the door.

"It was the look in your eyes," he began.

"I don't love Lee Walters! I never did! Whatever you saw, you imagined!"

Rad rose, shaking his head. "It wasn't love. It was trust."

"Aha. Well, I do trust Lee. He's a nice guy. It's not a crime to be nice—try it sometimes."

He reached out his hands. "There wasn't anything I wouldn't do for you, Lainie. Then—and now, when you needed me, I came running. I felt like I'd put everything I had on the line this time but you . . ." He trailed off.

"What did I do?"

"Nothing. But you'll trust a nobody like Lee Walters before you'll ever trust me. That hurts."

"Okay. Let's talk about hurt."

He swore savagely. "Seems to be a surprise to you that I actually have emotions."

"Oh, you do. You're a passionate man, Rad—"

Despite his misery, he looked almost proud for a second. "You didn't complain that first night—or the second—"

"Don't change the subject!"

He held out his hands in a peacemaking gesture. "Okay, okay! But there's got to be more than that to a marriage. You know it and so do I. We both want something more." He took a deep breath. "Starting with love. And ending with trust. And passion, uh, goes somewhere in between. Hell, Lainie—I want something that's going to last a lifetime. Don't you?"

"Yes!"

"Can't you forgive me? Give me another chance. Third time counts for all."

She hesitated. Lainie hadn't known how persuasive he could be.

"I don't know which one of us is crazier, Lainie, but it's going to be fun to figure out."

She wanted to laugh. She wanted to cry. Most of all, she wanted to love him and be loved by him. Forever. "You are, Rad. Without a doubt."

He stared deeply into her face, drinking in the love light that shone out of her eyes.

"Do you mean that? Not what you're saying—what I see in your eyes. Is that for me?"

His hands reached up and gripped her shoulders with the fierceness of a man holding on to a lifeline. Lainie could still see the shadows of doubt in his dark eyes and in the tense disbelief on his face. "It's you I love, you lunatic. I always have, Rad," she insisted.

He continued to stare at her, his gaze gradually softening as he read the affirmation in her face. A smile spread across his face.

"It is true," he whispered. "You do love me." He drew her into his arms. He held her so tightly that Lainie could hardly breathe, but she didn't care a bit. She felt him shudder against her and knew he was thinking the same thing that she was.

"Oh, baby," he whispered into her hair. "We nearly ruined our whole lives."

"But we didn't, Rad." Her hands reached up to his face, her fingers touching the remnants of tears on his cheeks. "We have the rest of it."

His mouth covered her lips in a kiss that was unbelievably tender. And though Lainie's eyes were closed, a rainbow seemed to be shining in the heavens, piercing the thunderclouds.

Keep reading for a special preview of
Christmas on My Mind
from
New York Times *Bestselling Author*
Janet Dailey.

FIRST TIME IN PRINT!

The future looks merry and bright . . .

The little town of Branding Iron, Texas, keeps an
annual tradition that makes the holidays especially
festive—the Cowboys' Christmas Ball. But Sheriff
Ben Marsden, busy with work, joint custody of his
son, and caring for his aging mother, has no plans
to attend. Not until a pretty newcomer to his small
town gets involved in the planning. Suddenly Ben
finds himself wanting to keep a close eye on Jessica
Ramsey, and not just because her relatives seem to
be in jail more than out. He can tell the mysterious
redhead has secrets in her past, but now that she's
bought a little fixer-upper with her mom to start a
bed and breakfast, the whole family's turning over
a new leaf. With the prospect of dancing and
celebrating ahead, surely there's time for everyone
to unwind. Because this year, more than ever,
Ben's got Christmas—and loving—on his mind.

"A delightful annual tradition."
—RT Book Reviews

Branding Iron, Texas
Friday, November 26

Jessica Ramsey mouthed an unladylike curse as her aging Pontiac coughed, sputtered and stopped dead on the deserted two-lane road. Hoping for luck, she cranked the starter—again, then again. Nothing happened.

What now? She couldn't be out of gas. The gauge hadn't worked in months, but she'd filled up two hours ago in Amarillo. Maybe it was the fuel pump. Or worse, something like a blown head gasket, whatever that was.

She cranked the starter one last time. The engine didn't even try to turn over. Fighting tears, she slumped over the steering wheel. She'd trusted the old car to make it all the way from Kansas City to Branding Iron, Texas. It had come close, but not close enough. The green highway sign she'd just passed told her she had fourteen miles to go. It was too far to walk with her suitcase—let alone all her possessions stuffed in the trunk—and she had more sense than to hitchhike. She was stranded.

Glancing in the rearview mirror, she saw a battered-looking red pickup approaching. It was coming fast; and her stalled car, she realized with a lurch of panic, was right in its path. She punched the hazard light, praying it would work. But the truck didn't even slow down. The horn blared. Tires squealed as the pickup swung around her, missing the rear bumper by inches. Jess glimpsed two male teenagers in the front seat. Both of them gave her the finger before the truck roared on down the road. So much for chivalry.

Jess released the brake, shifted into neutral and wrenched the steering wheel hard to the right. She had to get the Pontiac off the road before another vehicle came along and crashed right into her. Since the car wouldn't start, her only option was to push it.

After glancing up and down the road, she opened the door, climbed out and walked back to the rear of the car. The sky was overcast. Empty fields of yellow-brown stubble spread on both sides of the road. The flat horizon was broken only by a distant barn and a silo. Jess was a city girl. It was as if she'd set foot on some alien planet, peopled only by distant farms and rude boys in pickups.

The cold November breeze whipped tendrils of her russet hair around her face. She clutched her light denim jacket around her ribs. The sooner she got the car off the road, the sooner she could get back inside. Without the engine to run the heater, the car wouldn't stay warm long, but at least she'd be out of the wind.

Bracing her arms above the rear bumper, she planted her sneaker-clad feet on the asphalt. At five-three and 119 pounds, Jess was no Wonder Woman. Determination—or more likely desperation—would have to make up for her lack of muscle power.

The road's narrow, graveled shoulder sloped down to a grassy barrow pit. If she could push as much as one front wheel onto the incline, the car's momentum should do the rest. How hard could it be?

Steeling her resolve, she threw her whole weight against the car. Her jaw clenched. Her muscles strained. Nothing moved.

Spent for the moment, she straightened to catch her breath. Maybe she was doing this wrong. It might work better to brace her back against the car and push with her legs. At least it was worth a try.

Jess turned around. Only then did she see the big, tan SUV that had pulled up a dozen yards behind her, the lights atop its cab flashing red and blue.

And only then did she see the big, tan person climbing out of it. He strode toward her, a take-charge expression on his face. Wearing a khaki uniform topped by a leather jacket with a sheepskin collar, along with a pistol holstered at one lean hip, he looked capable of lifting her car with one hand. He was also flat-out gorgeous, with dark brown hair, a square-jawed face and stern coppery eyes.

But she wasn't looking for gorgeous here, Jess reminded herself. In her roller-coaster life, the hot men she'd known had turned out to be nothing but bad news. Besides, there was no way a male as spectacular as this long, tall lawman wouldn't have some woman's brand on him.

"Having trouble, miss?" His drawl was pure Texas honey.

Jess willed herself not to sound like a helpless whiner. "My car broke down. I was about to push it off the road, so nobody would hit it."

A faint smile deepened the dimple in his left

cheek. "Could you use some help, or should I just leave you to it?"

"As long as you're here, I guess you might as well give me a hand." Jess spoke through chattering teeth.

"Here." He stripped off his leather jacket and laid it around her shoulders. It was toasty warm. Man warm. Now that he'd taken it off, she could see the badge on his khaki shirt and the name tag below it.

Sheriff Ben Marsden.

"What seems to be the trouble with the car?" he asked.

"I don't know. It just stopped dead, and now it won't start. It can't be out of gas. I filled the tank a couple of hours ago."

"Well, let's get it off the road. Then I'll take a quick look under the hood. Maybe it'll be an easy fix."

Ben Marsden was definitely a breed apart from the brusque city cops Jess had encountered. Following his directions, she climbed back into the driver's seat to steer while he pushed. The car rolled forward as if Superman were behind that bumper. No surprise there.

"That's far enough." She heard his voice through the open window. "Now pull the handbrake and pop the hood release."

By the time Jess climbed out of the car he had the hood up and was peering into the Pontiac's dim interior with the aid of a pocket flashlight. After a minute or two, he closed the hood and switched off the light. "I can't see anything wrong," he said. "But it smells like you might have a fuel leak—maybe a broken line. Nothing I can do here, but it shouldn't be too expensive to fix. There's a good, honest mechanic in town. Want me to call him for a tow?"

Jess thought a moment, then reluctantly nodded. She'd promised herself she wouldn't break into the fifty thousand dollars she'd inherited from her adoptive father—money she'd set aside for a new start. But the cash she'd saved from her waitressing job was almost gone, and she had to have a working car. For now, she'd put the tow and repair on her credit card and hope for the best.

The sheriff made a quick call on his cell phone, then turned back to her. "Silas is busy right now, but he says he can pick up the car in a couple of hours."

Jess suppressed a sigh. "I suppose I can wait here that long."

He gave her a scowl. "That's not a good idea. Get what you need out of the car and leave the keys under the floor mat. I'll drive you into town. At least we can find you a warm place to wait."

"Thanks." Jess retrieved her purse from the front seat and her suitcase from the trunk. All the way from Kansas City, she'd imagined driving into Branding Iron and carrying out her plan—a plan so audacious that, on the way here, she'd almost lost heart and turned back.

Now she was here. But getting around would have to wait until her car was fixed. She'd need a place to stay. But even a small town like this one should have a cheap motel or some sort of rooming house where she could crash until she found a job and an apartment—or left town, if things didn't turn out as she'd hoped.

Meanwhile it would be smart to get her hormones under control and stop ogling the hot Texas lawman who'd come to her rescue. The man was off-limits—for more reasons than she even wanted to think about—starting with *hot* and *lawman*.

He opened the door of his SUV and took her suitcase while she climbed in and fastened her seat belt. The custom dashboard, complete with a police radio, a GPS, a dash cam and a computer, was impressive. The last time Jess had ridden in a police vehicle, she'd been handcuffed in the backseat. But those days were long behind her. After a few rough patches, she was starting a new life—and part of that new life, she hoped, was waiting right here in Branding Iron.

The engine purred as he pulled back onto the highway. "I don't suppose I should worry about anybody stealing my car," she said.

He chuckled, his dimple deepening. "No, I don't suppose you should."

"I'm not hearing much on your radio. Is it always this quiet around here?"

"Pretty much. We get an occasional drug bust, a few bar fights, some domestics and a runaway kid now and again. That's about it. It's a pretty easy place to be sheriff—most of the time." He glanced at her. His eyes reminded her of homemade root beer, just poured, with the bubbles still sparkling. "I don't believe I caught your name," he said.

"It's Jessica. Jessica Ramsey. But everybody calls me Jess."

"Well, welcome to Branding Iron, Texas, Miss Jess Ramsey. Where do you hail from?"

Here, Jess thought. But was she ready to tell him that? "I drove here from Kansas City," she said. "I was hoping my old beater would make it all the way, but no such luck."

"Were you planning a stopover in town, or just

passing through when your car decided to take a vacation?"

Jess gazed out the window a moment. They were passing more fields, some dotted with black Angus cattle and framed by barbed-wire fences. Here and there, a windmill towered above the landscape, its vanes turning in the breeze. The clouds in the vast Texas sky were darkening.

"This isn't just a stopover," she said. "Branding Iron is where I was headed."

"Here?" His laugh was incredulous. "Nobody comes to Branding Iron—unless, maybe, they've got family here."

"Maybe that's what I have." Given that perfect lead-in, Jess decided to tell him her story—at least the important part. As sheriff, he probably knew the townspeople as well as anybody. Maybe he could help her.

"I was born right here in Branding Iron, at the old clinic," she said. "My mother put me up for adoption—I don't know her circumstances, but I'm guessing she was unmarried and in trouble. My adoptive parents were far from perfect. They divorced when I was nine. He disappeared, and she died when I was sixteen. It's been a long, rough road, but a few months ago I decided it was time for a new start." Jess took a breath before getting to the bottom line. "The first thing I wanted to do was find my birth mother."

The sheriff took his time, as if weighing what he'd heard. "That's quite a story," he said. "Did you find her?"

"I think so. I haven't met her, but I'm hoping that's about to change. The private investigator I hired found my mother's name and her address. She's still here in Branding Iron."

"Have you contacted her?" he asked. "Does she know you're coming?"

Jess's hands tightened on her beat-up leather purse. "I was afraid she wouldn't want to see me. That's why I decided to just show up and surprise her."

"Is that wise?"

"Maybe not. But that way, if she slams the door in my face, at least I'll get a look at her. It's important. She's the only real family I've got."

"What if she's married, with children? Maybe she won't want them to know about you."

"I've thought of that," Jess said. "And I wouldn't want to cause her any trouble. But she's still using her maiden name. That could mean she's single or divorced." She turned toward him, straining against the seat belt. "I'm only telling you this because you might know her. If you do, maybe you can tell me what her situation is and how to approach her—or even arrange a meeting if you think that would be best."

Saying nothing, he guided the SUV around a road-killed rabbit. Two ravens feeding on the carcass flapped skyward against the darkening clouds.

He was quiet for what seemed like a long time. Maybe he suspected Jess of being some kind of con artist, out to win the poor woman over and fleece her of her savings. "I can't promise," he said. "But I'll try to do what's best for both of you. What's your mother's name?"

"Francine. Francine McFadden."

The SUV lurched slightly, crunching gravel on the shoulder of the road before he regained control of the steering wheel. Something about the name had clearly startled him.

"Do you know her?" Jess asked. "You do, don't you?"

"Yup."

"Then you must know where she lives. Can you at least drive me by her house?"

"No need for that. I know for a fact she isn't there."

"Well, where is she?" Jess demanded. "Is she out of town?"

"Nope." He shot her a narrow-eyed glance. "Francine is doing time in the county jail."

GREAT BOOKS,
GREAT SAVINGS!

When You Visit Our Website:
www.kensingtonbooks.com
You Can Save Money Off The Retail Price
Of Any Book You Purchase!

- All Your Favorite Kensington Authors
- New Releases & Timeless Classics
- Overnight Shipping Available
- eBooks Available For Many Titles
- All Major Credit Cards Accepted

Visit Us Today To Start Saving!
www.kensingtonbooks.com

More from Bestselling Author
JANET DAILEY

Books by Bestselling Author
Fern Michaels

More by Bestselling Author
Hannah Howell

__Highland Angel	978-1-4201-0864-4	$6.99US/$8.99CAN
__If He's Sinful	978-1-4201-0461-5	$6.99US/$8.99CAN
__Wild Conquest	978-1-4201-0464-6	$6.99US/$8.99CAN
__If He's Wicked	978-1-4201-0460-8	$6.99US/$8.49CAN
__My Lady Captor	978-0-8217-7430-4	$6.99US/$8.49CAN
__Highland Sinner	978-0-8217-8001-5	$6.99US/$8.49CAN
__Highland Captive	978-0-8217-8003-9	$6.99US/$8.49CAN
__Nature of the Beast	978-1-4201-0435-6	$6.99US/$8.49CAN
__Highland Fire	978-0-8217-7429-8	$6.99US/$8.49CAN
__Silver Flame	978-1-4201-0107-2	$6.99US/$8.49CAN
__Highland Wolf	978-0-8217-8000-8	$6.99US/$9.99CAN
__Highland Wedding	978-0-8217-8002-2	$4.99US/$6.99CAN
__Highland Destiny	978-1-4201-0259-8	$4.99US/$6.99CAN
__Only for You	978-0-8217-8151-7	$6.99US/$8.99CAN
__Highland Promise	978-1-4201-0261-1	$4.99US/$6.99CAN
__Highland Vow	978-1-4201-0260-4	$4.99US/$6.99CAN
__Highland Savage	978-0-8217-7999-6	$6.99US/$9.99CAN
__Beauty and the Beast	978-0-8217-8004-6	$4.99US/$6.99CAN
__Unconquered	978-0-8217-8088-6	$4.99US/$6.99CAN
__Highland Barbarian	978-0-8217-7998-9	$6.99US/$9.99CAN
__Highland Conqueror	978-0-8217-8148-7	$6.99US/$9.99CAN
__Conqueror's Kiss	978-0-8217-8005-3	$4.99US/$6.99CAN
__A Stockingful of Joy	978-1-4201-0018-1	$4.99US/$6.99CAN
__Highland Bride	978-0-8217-7995-8	$4.99US/$6.99CAN
__Highland Lover	978-0-8217-7759-6	$6.99US/$9.99CAN

Available Wherever Books Are Sold!

Check out our website at
http://www.kensingtonbooks.com